GOODBYE CUBA

JJ HARRIGAN

Eden Prairie, MN

GOODBYE CUBA

Published by:

Bronzewood Books

14920 Ironwood Ct.

Eden Prairie, MN 55346

Cover Design: Brad Knefelkamp

Interior Design: Bronzewood Books

Edited by: Susan Stradiotto

Paperback ISBN-13: 978-1-949357-51-6

eBook ISBN-13: 978-1-949357-36-3

Publication history: A prior version of this book was independently published by John J. Harrigan in 2016 under the title *Crosshairs on Castro*.

HISTORICAL NOTE

IN WEAVING THIS TALE AROUND the Cuban Missile Crisis, I try to be faithful to the historical record. All thoughts and speech attributed to the historical figures are fictional, but are based on writings by participants or reputable historians. The fictional characters placed in these historical settings are the products of my imagination, and any resemblance of them to any persons living or dead is purely coincidental. Unless the specific date of an event is called for, the events are identified as happening in the week of.

ACKNOWLEDGEMENTS

THANKS TO MEMBERS OF THE Minneapolis Writers Guild and the Bonita Springs Writers Group who scoured repeated chapters with meticulous detail: Don Alston, Kate Bitters, Michelle Caffrey, Patricia Carlberg, John Rogers, Arianna Eddington, Bob Erickson, Brian Keller, Pam Klocek, Miranda Kopp-Filek, Karl Jorgenson, Tim Mahoney, John Paulson, John Rhodes, Glenn Miller, Brendon Moran, Doug Williams.

Thanks to Carrington Ashton, and Barbara Younoszai for help with my Spanish; Stuart Goldbarg for helping flesh out Meyer Lansky among other things; Gary Prevost for sharing his prodigious knowledge of Cuba, Walt Zimmerman for teaching me to fly a Piper Cub, Alexis Stine-Sevey for copyediting the manuscript, and Kathy Huffman who proofed the final copy. A special thanks to Susan Stradiotto, my editor, at Bronzewood Books. And A very special thanks to my wife, Sandy, who put up with my obsession over this project and became an indispensable sounding board.

1

July 26, 1962

HAVANA, CUBA

F IT HADN'T BEEN FOR his sixth sense, Major Oscar Escalante would have been home eating breakfast. Instead, he prowled the lobby of Hotel Habana Libre, poking his head into restrooms, checking names in the registration book, and looking for anything suspicious. But now, that sixth sense, which had served him so well in the past, was not leading him to anything helpful.

He clenched and unclenched his fists as he pondered his task of protecting el comandante, Fidel Castro. This day, July 26, was ripe for trouble, because it marked the ninth anniversary of Castro's assault on the Moncada barracks. Within the hour, Fidel would step from the elevator and head toward L Street to begin the Revolution Day celebration, with complete disdain for any gunman who might lurk nearby.

Escalante draped his arm over the shoulder of the hotel manager standing at the registration desk. "Let's have a coffee so you can bring me up to date on anything that happened overnight."

The manager looked up at the major, then led him into the

hotel restaurant. Escalante gestured for a corporal standing nearby to follow. The three of them ambled through the restaurant to the kitchen.

"Buenos dias, Major Escalante," boomed the chef when the major stepped into his domain. "¿Usted quiere un café?"

"I would love one," replied the major in Spanish, as he eased his heavy frame onto a stool by a table near the chef, his muscular forearms resting on the steel table's edge. He lit a cigarette and took a deep puff. The chef put a café con leche in front of him, along with a pastelito of pastry with a cherry filling, a rare delicacy on the island, due to food shortages.

"What brings you out so early?" asked the chef.

"I want to watch out for el comandante when he comes downstairs." The major gave a disbelieving shake of his head as he thought about the chances the leader took with his own safety. He had been with Fidel since the earliest days and bore a scar on his cheek where he had been wounded at the peak of the insurrection in 1958. Lifting the pastelito, he took a small bite, savoring the sweet taste of the cherry filling. "I need to make sure the way is clear for him to leave." The major heaved a sigh. "What is he having for breakfast? That bread and peanut butter crap he usually eats?"

"I think he ordered a poached egg. Let me ask."

The chef turned to a busboy who had just brought a tray of dishes back to the kitchen. "Find that girl who brought Fidel's breakfast up to him. The major wants to know what he had to eat."

"She's not here," said the busboy. "She got sick and went home. She paid Consuelo two pesos to carry it up to el líder máximo."

The major's eyes bugged. He flicked his cigarette butt on the floor, then screamed at the hotel manager. "Call Fidel and tell him not to touch a thing!" He turned to the corporal. "Have the soldiers out front block the doors so no one can leave. Then call my office and get Sergeant Ramos over here. ¡Inmediatamente!"

He pointed at the manager. "Don't let that one out of your sight and bring him upstairs as soon as he finishes his call. Room 2324."

Then he turned on his heel, pushed through the doors into the dining room, and sped toward the elevators, bumping into a waitress caught in his path. The elevator edged slowly upward, and he banged on the door in desperation for it to speed up. He fingered through a set of keys until he found the one to Fidel's suite. The elevator was so hot and muggy that dark stains of sweat showed up on his shirt by the time the doors opened. With his heart pounding, Escalante rushed down the hall to Suite 2324. He hammered on the door with his fist as he slipped his key into the slot.

"Don't touch that!" he shouted at el comandante who was pouring a coffee for his mistress. The woman wore nothing but a half-opened pink robe that she pulled tight when Escalante had burst into the musky, humid room. Her hair was disheveled from her night with Castro. He, by contrast, looked fresh and awake. Dressed in his green fatigues and holding a cigar in his right hand, he was ready to start the day's activities. They apparently had not yet received a warning call from the hotel manager.

Escalante lifted the coffee pot to his nose. "It doesn't smell right, but we can't be certain until we test it. I will have the chef send up a new breakfast for you."

He was interrupted by the phone ringing. The mistress picked it up. "They said not to eat anything. It might be poison." She stared wide-eyed at the cup of coffee she had been about to drink, and her hand shook as she set the phone back in its cradle. Castro, for whatever emotion he felt, looked calm.

"What happened?" he asked, in a composed voice.

"We're not sure yet. The girl preparing your breakfast disappeared and bribed someone else to bring it up to you."

"Find her," barked Castro as he stood up. At six feet three, he towered over everyone in the room. The mistress stepped back as Castro shouted.

"We will," said the major. "We'll talk to everyone in the kitchen and everybody where she lives, as well."

"Where is she from?"

Escalante glared at the manager who had just been escorted into the room by Escalante's corporal.

In a faint voice, the manager replied, "Santa Clara."

"¡Lógicamente!" exclaimed Castro sarcastically.

Santa Clara was nestled on the edge of the Escambray Mountains, which were a center for opposition to the revolution.

"How long has this girl worked here?" asked the major.

"A month."

"A month!" screamed Castro, waving his cigar in the air, oblivious to the ashes that dropped on the carpet. He stepped toward the manager and towered over him as he stared the man in the eye. "You let a girl who has only been here a month serve my meals?"

"We will check this out, Comandante," said the major attempting to sooth Castro.

Castro paused for a moment before responding in a softer voice to the major. "Gracias, comrade, for being so alert. I am indebted to you. If the Olympics had an event for surviving CIA assassination attempts, I would win the gold medal. Mostly thanks to you." He rested his hand on the major's shoulder and shot a final hostile glance at the manager.

The major turned to his corporal. "Help me escort this manager downstairs and bring that tray of food with you."

"What about her?" asked the corporal, nodding his head toward Castro's mistress.

Escalante glanced at the woman, whose hands still shook from having handled the poisoned coffee. He looked over to Fidel, who gave a slight sideways shake of his head.

"Leave her be," said the major.

As he led the manager out of the room, Escalante started to plan his next steps. He needed to locate the girl, find out who had put her up to this trick, and break up whatever organization was behind it. He would start with the hotel manager who now stood in front of the elevator, fidgeting nervously with his hands. Escalante glared down at him. Why had it taken him so long to phone the warning message up to Castro's room? How did the manager happen to know on the spur of the moment that this girl came from Santa Clara? Who had pushed him to hire that particular girl? And would Escalante be able to extract that information in time to prevent the girl's handlers from smuggling her to Miami?

Reaching the bottom floor, Escalante led the manager back to the hotel office where his aide, Sergeant Ramos, had just arrived. "Interrogate everyone in the kitchen and send that tray of food to a lab for analysis. I want photos of the busboy and the girl, as well as their personal data. Don't let anyone leave this building until you question them and find out where they live."

He breathed in deeply and exhaled in an effort to slow down his racing pulse then scrutinized the manager who cringed in a corner of the office. Escalante said nothing until the long moment of silence prodded the manager to peek up into the major's accusing eyes.

"We need to talk, señor," said Escalante as he led the man by the elbow to the door.

"Let's go to my headquarters where we can have some privacy."

2

Week of August 1, 1962

ARLINGTON HALL STATION, ARLINGTON, VIRGINIA

FIRST LIEUTENANT CHARLES PARNELL LEANED back in his chair with his feet propped up on a desk. A Cuban newspaper from July 1962 rested on his lap as he fantasized about his girlfriend and their plans for that evening.

A sergeant from headquarters stepped through the door and Charlie looked over. "Delroy, my man. What's up?"

"The colonel wants you," he said.

"What is it this time?"

"He didn't tell me."

"My leadership style? My little side business? My haircut?"

"I don't know, but he's in a bad mood. If I were you, I'd get my ass over there ASAP." He paused and added, "Sir."

Charlie swung his feet to the floor, pushed himself out of the chair, and put on his field cap "Thanks for the heads-up, Delroy," he said.

The field cap teetered on his head of shaggy, unmilitary, brown hair as he stepped from the building into the muggy August air of Northern Virginia. And his tall, thin form moved with a pronounced limp in the left leg.

The colonel's battalion headquarters were housed in what had been an exclusive girls' school before the government bought it and renamed it Arlington Hall Station. It was now home to the Army Security Agency and its electronic eavesdroppers, including Lieutenant Charles Parnell. His sweat-soaked shirt clung to his back as he entered the colonel's air-conditioned outer office. He had no sooner removed his field cap and folded it over his belt than the colonel himself stepped forward. He looked the younger man up and down.

"What are you up to now, Parnell? I've got two CIA spooks in my office asking for you. Why, they won't say. What's going on?"

"I have no idea, Colonel. Two spooks?"

"I ask the questions, Lieutenant, not you." The colonel paused. "Is there something you're not telling me about those Cuban refugees you interrogate?"

"No, sir."

The commander stepped closer to Charlie, stopping inches from his face, staring up into the taller man's pale, blue eyes. "When the commander at Brigade tells me to let a couple of civilians use my office to see one of my men in private, I cooperate. But I also get suspicious." He scowled. "When you finish in there, I want a written report of everything that's said—immediately. Understood?" He rapped his knuckles on the receptionist's desk.

"Understood, sir."

Just before stepping aside so that Charlie could pass into the room, the colonel shook his head. "Parnell, you're an embarrassment to the army, what with that gimpy walk and scruffy hair. If it weren't for those golden nuggets of intelligence you sometimes come up with, I would have shipped you out long ago. Make sure your hair is cut the next time I see you."

Charlie stepped through the door onto a colorful Persian rug that graced the hardwood floor. A shiny blue and white Oriental vase sat on a polished oak credenza behind the colonel's desk. By the outside wall stood an old-fashioned steam radiator that would hiss and clank once the heat was turned on in the fall.

"Welcome, Lieutenant." A square-jawed man in his thirties stepped in front of the colonel's desk. He wore a dark blue suit, a white shirt, and a narrow, striped tie. Thick, horn-rimmed glasses magnified his eyes. Shorter than Charlie, he had broader, more muscular shoulders. He sat down at a table in the middle of the room and gestured for the officer to sit as well. A second man, somewhat older, took a seat near the radiator by the outside wall. The man sitting across from Charlie drummed his fingers on the tabletop. Then he opened a file folder, sifted through the papers, and read aloud without lifting his eyes.

"Charles Stuart Parnell, First Lieutenant in the U.S. Army, currently assigned to Army Security Agency headquarters here at Arlington Hall Station. An avid guitar player; you're fluent in Spanish; and you gather intelligence on Cuba. Interesting job."

"It sounds more interesting than it is." Charlie furrowed his eyebrows. "I read Havana newspapers and listen to Cuban radio messages that my brilliant technicians pull off the airwaves. I also debrief Cuban refugees, either up here or down in Miami. Mostly, it's drudge work. But every now and then I pick up a little piece of intelligence that helps my commander in his bid for promotion to bird colonel."

"Very impressive, Charles. And how did you get this plum of a job?"

"Charlie, sir. I go by Charlie. It goes back to my college days. I joined ROTC to pay for school, and they sent me to the Army's language program in Monterey for a summer. With Fidel Castro and all, they needed Spanish speakers. But then, if that's my personnel file in front of you, you already know that." He pointed at the folder in the man's hand.

The other man looked up for the first time, as if annoyed by

Charlie's bluntness.

"There are some things of interest that go beyond your personnel file."

"It would be easier to talk about these things if I knew your names," said Charlie.

"I'm Walter Bishop, and over by the wall is Tom McGillivray." He swept his hand toward McGillivray. "We are with the Directorate of Planning at the CIA."

Charlie curled his lips. "And what would our nation's spies want from me?"

"We need a serviceman for a very important assignment. We need a bright person who is fluent in Spanish, resourceful, and capable of getting around in other cultures. The last part is especially important, and because of your experiences, we think you would be perfect for the role."

"My experiences?"

"You once had a Black girlfriend, so you must have learned how to navigate in her culture. Your current girlfriend, who has wrangled herself an internship at the White House, is Hispanic, so you acclimated to that culture as well."

Charlie bristled. How the hell did they find that out? And why the condescending tone of voice when he said Black and Hispanic?

"They're not from other cultures, Mr. Bishop. They are both American citizens. My Hispanic friend, as you called her, has an Argentine father and an American mother. She came here as a child, and I have no idea how she wrangled her internship."

"We're pretty sure what got it for her. However, that's beside the point. Would you accept a detachment that helps us out?"

"If I knew what you wanted, I might accept it. As I said, what I'm doing now can be a drudge. But what did you mean that you know how she wrangled the internship?"

"She's your girlfriend, not mine. Ask her, not me. Will you help us?"

"What is it you want?"

Bishop pulled off his horn-rimmed glasses and twirled them in his hand. "Before we get to that, you have to understand that everything we say from this point on is classified. You cannot discuss it with anyone. In fact, the Agency has a nondisclosure agreement you need to sign before we proceed."

He slid a pen across the table along with two copies of a short document. Typed in at the top was the key sentence. "I agree, under penalty of prosecution, that I will never disclose to any unauthorized person the contents of my association with Walter Bishop or to violate any of the provisions listed below."

"I can't sign that, Mr. Bishop." He slid the document back across the table and nodded toward the door. "Just now, my commander instructed me to write him a memo summarizing our conversation."

"Don't worry about him. We've had you reassigned to a special detachment at our headquarters in Langley." Bishop pulled a document from his briefcase and passed it across the table. "Unless you turn down our offer, you're out from under his thumb."

The reassignment orders seemed authentic to Charlie. "And if I do turn down this assignment?"

"We'll rescind these orders and return you to the colonel, who doesn't seem to appreciate your talents, despite the golden nuggets of intelligence he says you find for him."

Bishop paused before adding, "He'll appreciate you even less when he learns how you're making money on the side."

Charlie clenched his jaw. "I worked out a contract with a local broker to sell mutual funds. The colonel already knows about that."

"However, he doesn't know you're selling them to enlisted men, which violates the Army's nonfraternization rules. And he doesn't know about your weekly poker games."

"So I provide guys a chance to relax on Thursday nights. There's nothing in Army regs against that."

"There is when you're an officer, and you've got NCOs in the game losing money to you. Not to mention the occasional civilians who show up to make connections with soldiers who can help them pilfer Army equipment."

Charlie's stomach tightened. "I don't know they do that," he said slowly, drawing out the words. "And neither do you."

"True, I don't have proof. However, we infiltrated a couple of your games, and a good detective with the power to subpoena your bank records would find something."

Neither man spoke for a moment, until Bishop went on, "Lieutenant, you not only host the game, you provide free snacks and free booze. You take a percentage of the pot. And you do this on a regular basis. To any aggressive prosecutor, your apartment will be viewed as an illegal gambling den. A den that facilitates the theft of Army equipment."

"Now that you've made me aware of how the game could be perceived, I'll shut it down. I certainly don't want to do anything on the edge of the law."

Bishop laughed.

"What's so funny?"

"You worrying about the edge of the law. That's what's so funny. Lieutenant, you're an operator. It's in your blood. Today it's an illegal gambling den. As a teenager, it was conning your friends into doing things they shouldn't have. And when you finally get that job on Wall Street you dream about, you'll be an operator there as well."

Despite his bravado, Charlie shuffled his feet on the floor. He forced them to stop as he stared into the other man's stern eyes behind the thick glasses. What gave Bishop the clout to engineer a transfer of this sort? How had he acquired so much information about Charlie, his friends, and his dream of landing a Wall Street job? And what else had he dug up?

"The last I heard, Wall Street is perfectly legal. I'm good at investments, and I want to run a mutual fund portfolio. What's wrong with that?"

"There's nothing wrong with it, Lieutenant. At least, not on the surface. It's consistent with some other things we found out about you." He frowned.

Inside, Charlie bristled with annoyance, but he refused to comment.

"We talked to a lot of people: your broker friend, members of your poker game, soldiers in your platoon, even old teenage acquaintances. They all say the same thing. You finesse them and you charm them. They all think you'll wind up with that dream job you talk about so much. You're an operator, and apparently you're good at it."

Then Bishop's stern frown changed to a smile. "But being an operator isn't necessarily bad. We have a project that could use those street smarts you've got. Why don't you sign this nondisclosure agreement so I can tell you what we have in mind? The rewards for helping us will be substantial. We need you for three or four months at the most. Then we'll get you an early, honorable discharge and a job on the ground floor of Wall Street."

"You will help me land a job on Wall Street?"

"No. We won't *help* you. We will *get* you the job. Some well-placed financial executives owe us favors. They'll gladly give you the chance to prove your worth."

Charlie weighed the pros and cons of signing the paper. The smart thing would be to give Bishop the cold shoulder. A secret job for the CIA could easily become unpleasant.

However, if he turned down the assignment, Bishop might indeed inform the colonel about Charlie's gambling operation. In that case, Charlie would be lucky if the colonel didn't ship him out to the Distant Early Warning Line in Alaska for the next two years.

But the clincher was Bishop's suggestion that he could put Charlie on the fast track for a Wall Street job. That was Charlie's dream. It would relieve him of spending the next two years reading Havana newspapers and interpreting Cuban radio messages. As he pondered the possibilities, the grandfather clock ticked in the corner of the room over Bishop's shoulder.

Picking up the pen, he added a sentence to the nondisclosure document. "If I take this assignment, Walter Bishop will use his good offices to find me a position in portfolio management."

He expected Bishop to rip up the papers. Instead, Bishop calmly signed both sets. His bluff called, Charlie signed the papers.

"What is it you want from me?"

3

Week of August 1, 1962

Tropic of Cancer

D MITRI LESNIKOV WIPED HIS BROW. He was the second captain on one of four Foxtrot-class submarines that had just crossed the Tropic of Cancer into the stifling heat of the Caribbean Sea. They were en route to escort a convoy of cargo ships to Cuba. Although he could only guess what those cargo ships carried, it had to be something critical to be escorted by four Foxtrot submarines. These were the largest subs in the Soviet Navy. Each one carried twelve powerful torpedoes to prevent American warships from attacking the convoy. At the moment, Lesnikov was covered in sweat as he bent over the rack of spare torpedoes in the forward torpedo room.

"Damn this heat," he muttered over his shoulder to Lieutenant Alexei Babel, who was standing as a lookout room's entry hatch. Always on the search for loyal, younger officers, Lesnikov had recruited Babel as a protégé. He had brought him to the forward torpedo room to keep an eye out in case the boat's political officer should come into sight.

"It's not just the heat that's making us sweat," said Babel. "It's what you and the first captain found out at the meeting just before we left Murmansk."

The top officers of the four Foxtrot subs were addressed at that meeting by General Issa Plyev, the commander of Russia's buildup in Cuba. "Along with its other torpedos, each boat will have one torpedo with a nuclear tip," Plyev told them. The subs were authorized to find a target and fire their nuclear torpedoes if American troops invaded Cuba or if they were instructed to do so by Soviet Premier Nikita Khruschev.

Was Khruschev crazy? The shock wave from an underwater nuclear blast would destroy any submarine that got too close. What would result if all four nuclear torpedoes detonated was unthinkable. Second Captain Lesnikov was too old for suicide missions.

"You know I'm due to retire next year," said Lesnikov, talking as much to himself as to the younger man. "And the pension is decent. Maybe Raisa and I can get a dacha near the Black Sea. You can visit us, Alexei. You can meet our sons. Two of them are also naval officers."

"It would be an honor, Captain."

"You must think it strange that you and I should be tinkering with these torpedoes without having told the first captain.."

"No sir," said Babel.

"It's not that I disobey orders, Alexei. In the Great Patriotic War, I saw men shot for that." He paused to assess the impact of this statement on the younger man. Babel had the misfortune to be descended from a man—the great writer Isaac Babel—who had been executed by firing squad during Stalin's purge in 1939. Unless the writer's reputation was restored, this lineage would put a ceiling on the younger Babel's career. The lieutenant kept his face bland, however, and showed no reaction.

"Of course," said Lesnikov, "I also saw men killed for blindly following stupid orders or doing stupid things. I myself suffered radioactive exposure five years ago, about the time that you graduated from the naval academy. Someone failed to close a valve near a reactor, and enough radiation blew into my face to give me this damnable cancer. And that, my dear Alexeivich, taught me a valuable lesson."

Lesnikov paused for his words to sink in.

"Accidents," he said, "need to be anticipated and prevented. If we are capable of putting nuclear torpedoes on our subs, we have to anticipate that the Americans are able to make nuclear depth charges. So we face the possibility of an accident of tremendous proportions."

Because of this aversion to accidents, he had dragged his young protégé into the cramped torpedo room to stand watch while Lesnikov, dripping with sweat, tried to find out which torpedo had the nuclear tip. The six torpedo tubes were each loaded with one torpedo, and the spare torpedoes, noses painted bright red, were stacked in a rack. Lesnikov approached the first torpedo in the rack and slowly swept its entire twenty-five-foot length with a Geiger counter. Since his radioactive accident, nobody begrudged Lesnikov's request for a Geiger counter when he wanted one. His hands were so sweaty from the heat that he had to grasp the instrument with care to keep it from slipping through his fingers. It gave no sign of any radioactivity. He swept the detector toward the second torpedo with no reaction, then the third, fourth, fifth, and sixth, all with no reaction.

Lieutenant Babel spoke up, "Maybe General Plyev was pulling your leg about the nuclear warheads."

Lesnikov looked crossly over his shoulder at the younger man. "General Plyev is not known for a sense of humor."

Having finished testing the spare torpedoes on the storage rack, Lesnikov approached the ones already loaded in the tubes. He edged as close as possible to the front of the number one tube. The Geiger counter burst to life with a cascade of clicking sounds much sharper than they would have been if the warhead had been properly shielded. That startled the captain so much that the instrument slipped out of his sweaty hands.

He sank to the metal floor and put his head in his hands. "Jesus," he said to himself. "Oh, my God, my God, my God."

Babel rushed over to pick up the Geiger counter and help the captain to his feet, but Lesnikov waved him off. "Come back to my quarters with me."

Stooping through the small hatch to the torpedo room, the two men went back to the officer quarters, inching past pipes and cables and seamen drenched in sweat. The stench of body odors pervaded the entire passageway. Lesnikov replaced his sweat-soaked shirt with a fresh one, pulled out the boat's roster, and searched through the list of crew members. Long ago, he had learned the value of knowing the people he worked with. Especially in the cramped submarine. And he had taken the trouble to observe the skills and weaknesses of the boat's seventy-seven crew members.

Technically, the best person for the task he had in mind would be the officer in charge of arming the torpedoes. But that officer would report any tampering to Deputy Political Officer Chernikov. He in turn would pass that information on to Moscow, and after that, Lesnikov could forget about taking his beloved Raisa to a dacha on the Black Sea. After scanning the list twice, he put his finger on one of the names and turned his head toward Babel. "What has been your experience with this one?"

"Very reliable," said the lieutenant.

Lesnikov picked up his phone and ordered Seaman Vladimir Vladivostok to come to the officers' mess room, which would be empty at this time of day. When the anxious seaman arrived, looking as though he feared being disciplined, Second Captain Lesnikov stared him in the eye. "Seaman, I have a job for you, but before giving it to you, I need to know if you are capable of following orders to the letter and keeping your mouth shut about what you did."

Unless the seaman wanted to be in the captain's doghouse for the rest of the voyage, there was only one acceptable answer. He replied, "Yes, sir."

"I mean absolutely shut. You can't tell anyone. Not your best friend. Not even your girlfriend. And certainly not Deputy Political Officer Chernikov."

The seaman gulped. Resisting an inquiry from Chernikov could invite banishment to Shostikov, if not worse. "What if he confronts me?"

"If you keep your mouth shut, he won't even know about you. But if by any chance he ever does question you, just say you don't know and refer him to me. Can you do that?"

"Yes, sir."

Lesnikov led the seaman through the officers' quarters to the forward torpedo room. "There is a problem with the torpedo in the number one tube, and I want to put it at the bottom of the rack with the spare torpedoes. Just in case we need to fire torpedoes, I don't want to have an accident. We don't want it to blow up in our faces. When we get back to port, I will have it repaired. Right now, though, I need your help to replace it with one of the spare torpedoes in the rack."

He pointed to the torpedo rack holding six of the twenty-five-foot-long missiles. "How long will that take?"

"About fifteen minutes to get the torpedo out of the tube if we use the block and tackle." He pointed to pulleys and ropes hanging over the torpedo rack. "Maybe another fifteen minutes to get a new torpedo into the tube. Then fifteen more to move them around so that the damaged one is down at the bottom of the rack where you want it."

"That's nearly an hour. Let's get started. If your chief asks where you were, tell him I had you on a special assignment swabbing the floors in here."

While Lieutenant Babel kept watch at the hatchway for intruders, the seaman opened the torpedo tube and slid the missile onto a holding tray. He swung the block and tackle above the exposed torpedo, threaded a sling under it, pulled on the rope dangling from the set of pulleys, hoisted the two-ton behemoth, and swung it over to the rack as easily as if he were moving straws. However, as he lowered the torpedo toward the rack, the pulley jammed. He tugged on the rope to undo the jam, and the nuclear-tipped torpedo dropped onto the rack with a thud.

Seaman Shostikov jumped at the sound of the torpedo clanking into place and glanced over his shoulder at Lesnikov and Babel, who looked startled. "Sorry, Captain. I forgot about the glitch in that pulley. You have to pull the rope at an angle to keep it from jamming."

"Well, remember it on the next one, Seaman. We don't want to kill ourselves," the captain said and then muttered under his breath. "Damn this boat with all its breakdowns. First the cooling system is out, and now a critical pulley doesn't work right."

The seaman attached the sling to the top torpedo in the rack, and Lesnikov helped him guide it into its tube. Then they rearranged the order of the torpedoes on the rack, placing the nuclear tipped one at the bottom. By the time they finished, both men were drenched in sweat.

The captain looked the younger man in the eye. "Thank you for your help, Seaman Vladimir Shostikov. Maybe nothing would have happened if that torpedo had fired, but our job is to avoid accidents, and you've performed a great service here. Keep this to yourself and let me be the one to tell the first captain and the political officer about it." He smiled. "I won't forget your cooperation." But he left vague what reward he had in mind for the enlisted man if he kept the captain's secret or what punishment might come if he let it slip out.

As he led Babel and the seaman out of the torrid torpedo room, Lesnikov felt pleased with his work. He had reduced the chance of the nuclear torpedo being launched by accident. However, he couldn't know if the other three subs had taken similar precautions with their nuclear torpedoes. He also couldn't know if the Americans had taken precautions to prevent an accidental launch of their nuclear depth charges, assuming that they possessed them. But those things were beyond Lesnikov's control, so he didn't worry about them. What did worry him was how he would explain his actions when Deputy Political Officer Chernikov found out that the torpedoes had been switched.

4

Week of August 1, 1962

ARLINGTON HALL STATION, ARLINGTON, VIRGINIA

WALTER BISHOP FILED THE NONDISCLOSURE agreement in his briefcase and left a copy for Charlie on the tabletop.

"Are you familiar with Senator Keating's warnings about Cuba?"

"Vaguely." Charlie recognized Kenneth Keating as a prominent republican senator from New York who was gaining public attention with his charges that the Kennedy White House was ignoring attempts by the Soviet Union to put nuclear missiles in Cuba.

"We think Keating is more realistic about this threat than the president is," said Bishop.

"What does that have to do with me?"

"With all this Cuban intelligence you've been scrutinizing, you haven't picked up any hints of this?"

"Mr. Bishop, I'm not free to tell you all the things that pass through here at Arlington Hall Station. This is the army's most hush-hush operation."

"Well, tell me what you can."

"The only thing that I could possibly talk about is a man I interviewed last month at that CIA base of yours just south of Miami. Since he was a Cuban linked to you rather than us, I guess it's okay to tell you about him. One night, he ran into a roadblock for a Russian convoy not too far from Havana. He reported seeing flatbed trailers carrying huge canisters he thought might be missiles. When I passed that on to my colonel, he saw it as one of those golden bits of intelligence he needs for promotion to bird colonel, and it put me in his good graces."

Charlie grinned. "In fact, until you showed up, he even stopped ragging me about my hair."

Bishop frowned. "We interviewed the same guy. It was a Russian SS-4 missile that could deliver a nuclear warhead as far as Washington, DC."

"Mr. Bishop, I don't know anything about nuclear missiles. If that is what you're looking for, you've got the wrong guy. How did you ever find me in the first place?" Charlie leaned back in his chair and waited for Bishop's response.

"Lieutenant," said Bishop, nodding like a teacher trying to be patient with a dense student. "We didn't pick you at random. We need somebody with several important qualities. Army Personnel has an enormous IBM computer out in Maryland, and we got a technician there to help us. He kept his computer sorting out every criterion we asked for. First, we need somebody quite smart, so we had it sort out everyone in the top quartile on the intelligence test you took when you first went into the army."

"That must have narrowed things down to a few hundred thousand." Charlie smirked.

"Don't sneer. This thing was a marvel, whirring away with its tapes spinning back and forth. We tell this guy what we want, and he sits down at a key punch machine and punches out a deck of computer cards that he feeds into the machine. And you're right.

They found 214,374 people for us."

Charlie laughed.

"We also need somebody fluent in Spanish. So we told him to narrow that list down to those who scored above the ninetieth percentile in the Army's Monterrey Language School. He spends another hour punching up another deck of cards and feeding them into the computer. Now we're down to a few dozen candidates. Next, because this is a sensitive assignment, we need someone we can trust. So we have the computer pull out all the names with top secret security clearances."

"A sensitive assignment?"

"A very sensitive assignment." Bishop tapped the desk with his fingertips. "Next, and this is critical, we need someone who scored as an expert marksman on the rifle range."

"Expert marksman?" asked Charlie, his pulse picking up.

"Now we're down to a handful of soldiers, enlisted men as well as officers. So we send out investigators to talk to your relatives and acquaintances. Many of them were the same people who were interviewed when you were vetted for your security clearance."

"Expert marksman. Fluent in Spanish. Familiarity with Latin cultures. Russian missiles. Walter, skip this cock and bull story about the IBM machine. Just tell me what you're talking about."

Bishop stood up, put his hands on his hips, like Superman, and peered down at Charlie. "Let's be blunt, Lieutenant. The possibility of a nuclear attack coming from Cuba is real. If Fidel Castro were gone from the scene, the threat would disappear. Once the message got out that Castro was removed because he was fucking around with Russian nukes, no other Cuban would be dumb enough to risk his life letting them put anything on the island."

Charlie slumped forward in his chair, grasping the edge of the table. "You want me to help you assassinate Castro?" He slowly drew out the words one by one and narrowed his eyes.

"No," responded Bishop. "We don't want you to help. We want

you to do it."

Charlie bolted to his feet. He wavered for a moment as he tried to calm himself. Struggling to control his speech, he said in a very slow voice, "You are out of your mind. I want nothing to do with this! You can do what you want with all those threats you've been making."

"Just hear me out. That's all I ask."

Bishop sat down, took off his glasses again, and gestured for Charlie to sit as well. He held the glasses by the frame as he leaned forward over the table.

"This mission is fully supported at the highest level of government, so you're not going out on a limb here." Bishop motioned again toward the chair. "It would be easier to converse if you sat down."

"The highest level of government?" Charlie muttered as he sank into his chair. "You're telling me that the president ordered you to kill Castro and pressure me to do it?"

Bishop said, "He doesn't know about you personally, of course. But some of those Cubans you've met must have mentioned the Operation Mongoose plan to overthrow Castro. The president set up that operation, and his brother, the attorney general, heads the committee that oversees it. They hold weekly meetings on it at the Justice Department. Every Tuesday."

"In that case, they're as nuts as you are."

"Let me ask you this. From your experiences interviewing Cuban refugees, do they deserve to be saddled with a monster like Fidel Castro?"

"That's irrelevant. We've got no right to go around bumping off people just because they're bad. Christ, there'd be no end to the number of people we'd have to target."

Bishop responded, "Think about it from the point of view of those people you've been interviewing. He took their property and forced them into exile. He convicted others in phony trials and executed them in front of cheering crowds in a public stadium. He threw hundreds, if not thousands, of others into prison. And the longer he stays in power, the longer this will go on."

"I don't need you to tell me how bad it is," Charlie blurted, his eyes narrowing. "The Cubans drill it into me every time I talk to them. Your problem, though, is that I'm no killer. Hire the Mafia. At least they'd know how to go about it."

"After Castro closed down the Mafia's casinos in Havana, they wanted revenge. So we approached them, but it never worked out." Bishop held up his hands as if to signify he had no control over what the Mafia had failed to do. "Neither did some other things."

"Such as?"

"That's on a need-to-know basis."

"Need to know?" Charlie's voice became shrill. "After you've botched all your other attempts, you want me to pull your chestnuts out of the fire. But you won't tell me why the other attempts failed. It seems to me I have a powerful need to know."

"All in good time," said Bishop. He began drumming his fingers on the tabletop again.

"Well, if the Mafia couldn't reach him, I certainly won't be able to."

"We'll train you," said Bishop, with another smile. "We can train any resourceful person to approach a target without being detected. What we can't train somebody to do is to acquire the courage and resilience you've already shown."

"How did I show that?" Charlie asked with a trace of amusement at the idea of Bishop finding him courageous and resilient.

"For one thing, you wouldn't expect a guy with a limp to be an expert sharpshooter."

Charlie scowled. "A guy doesn't shoot with his feet."

"Whoa, Charlie," said Bishop lifting his hands, palms out. "I'm not trying to insult you. I meant it as a compliment. It takes courage for a guy with a limp to apply for ROTC in the first place and resilience for him to succeed. An admirable resilience."

Charlie's scowl shifted to a grin. "It wasn't that hard. My dad did a lot of election work for the local political machine, and the boss persuaded the university to give me a chance at ROTC so I could get money for college. Once that happened, the rest was easy. I'd spent four years in my high school band playing the trumpet while we marched around in complicated formations. Compared to that, marching with the ROTC was a piece of cake."

Then, realizing that this show of exuberance did not help his argument, Charlie frowned. "Whatever you think of my qualities, Mr. Bishop, I'm not a killer. You can't train a normal person to be an assassin anymore than you can train your Mafia hit men to be Boy Scouts. I repeat, you can't train a normal person to be a killer."

Bishop slouched back in his chair, then slowly leaned forward with his head halfway over the table. "Nor would we want to train you to be an assassin. We just want to use that expert sharpshooting skill of yours to eliminate a target. A target that is causing unspeakable misery to his own country. A target that will, if not stopped, bring our country—your country—under the direct threat of nuclear attack."

"But, Mr. Bishop, you're asking me to operate beyond the law. As I told you, I can't do that."

"The police in your hometown might not look at it that way. A few years ago, you provoked an incident that left the police with egg on their face. If they knew what we know, they would probably reopen that case and take out a little revenge on you regardless of your family's political connections."

"Egg on their face!" Charlie shouted. "Jesus Christ, that cop shot my best friend."

"The police will think that you set him up for it."

"Set him up?" Charlie shouted again. "Where are you getting this stuff?

"Lieutenant," said Bishop, "We talked to everybody: the police, the members of that dance band you started, your school friends, your music teacher, your girlfriend."

"None of them could have given you this crap you're inventing."

"True, no single one of them said very much. Put all of these isolated little tidbits together, however, and a coherent picture emerges. Especially when added to by some things you yourself revealed in the lie detector test you took for your security clearance."

Charlie shuddered. That lie detector test had uncovered the darkest secret of his life. Beads of sweat were building on his lip. But wiping them might convey a sense of fear. So he forced his hands to stay still.

After a moment, Bishop continued, "You lied on your polygraph test when asked if you had ever had a homosexual experience."

Bishop stopped to let the words sink in. It took Charlie a moment to respond, and his voice was subdued. "I was sexually abused when I was fifteen, and I explained that once the polygraph picked up on my nervousness about the question.

"Besides," he added, his voice losing the subdued tone it had a moment earlier. His chin jutted forward. "The army has the same information you've got. If they had any doubts about my sex life, they would have kicked me out immediately. And this hogwash about the police is all hearsay that wouldn't hold up in any court in the land. So this threat isn't going to work any better than your attempt to blackmail me about my poker game."

Despite his bravado, Charlie's stomach churned. The point of Bishop's threat, he realized, was not to get him prosecuted or dishonorably discharged from the army. It was to make Charlie fear that Bishop could ruin Charlie's reputation among his family, friends, and girlfriend. Not to mention killing his chances for his dream job on Wall Street. He stared at Bishop.

"There is one other little matter that I had hoped we could avoid," said Bishop.

Charlie gulped, and he hoped that it didn't show. The beads of sweat on his upper lip were becoming more and more annoying with each moment. Jesus. Could this bastard have stumbled onto the one thing that really did worry him?

"You can be cavalier about the impact of these things on yourself, Lieutenant. But other people are touched as well. Your father, for example, has a problem with his booze."

"So what? Half the country has a problem with booze."

"But half the country doesn't do the reckless things your father does when he's tanked up."

Bishop pulled a newspaper clipping and a sheet of paper stamped secret, which looked like a notarized affidavit, from his briefcase. Charlie didn't have to read the newspaper clipping; he had read it a few years earlier. The affidavit, however, made him shiver as he took it in his hand. It was damning enough to send his father to prison. And perhaps himself as well. He had pulled his father away from the scene, driven him home before the police arrived, then helped his mother clean him up and put him to bed. He looked at the signature and recognized the name—his father's main antagonist in their local chapter of the United Auto Workers union. Those two hated each other, and Charlie could easily imagine his father being betrayed by the other guy.

He slumped back in his chair, deflated.

"Lieutenant," said Bishop softly. "All we want is your help in protecting the country from a nuclear threat. If you give us this help, we will relieve you of spending the next two years doing what you've already called drudge work. We'll get you out from under the thumb of your colonel, secure an early honorable discharge for you, and set you up in your dream job. Give us your help, and this will go in the burn bag." He pointed at the notarized testimony.

"How is that going to help me? Three years from now when you want my help on something else, a second copy of this crap will miraculously reappear, and once again you'll have me over a barrel."

"By then, the statute of limitations will have expired on this incident. You'll be working on Wall Street. Your father will be doing whatever it is that he does. And everyone will be untouchable. At that point, you'll be safe." Bishop smiled warmly, then added, "But you're not safe now."

Charlie pulled himself out of his slumped position and sat up straight.

"You've got me, Mr. Bishop. I hope to fuck you're proud of yourself. However, I want till Monday to make a final decision. And I want a couple of assurances from you."

Bishop motioned for him to continue.

"You have to be able to get me out of Cuba once you get me in. I will do whatever I can to keep my father out of prison. But even he wouldn't expect me to do it at the cost of spending the rest of my life in some godforsaken dungeon in Havana."

"What's the second thing?"

"If I do this, it's going to cause me a lot of expenses. You can't expect me to go broke. You've got to cover my expenses without me having to file a never-ending string of reimbursement requests. I don't want any paper trail that will link me to you guys."

"This is all possible." Bishop smiled. "We can discuss it at our next meeting Monday morning in my office. Can you give me a yes right now contingent on my figuring out a way to do those things? If I can't do that by Monday, you're free to walk away, spend the next two years reading Cuban newspapers, pacifying your colonel, and doing whatever you can to keep your father out of prison."

This at least gave Charlie some breathing room. Maybe he could think up a way out over the weekend. He nodded yes, and Bishop recited an address. As Charlie started to write the address on the affidavit, Bishop pulled the paper away and stuffed it in his briefcase.

"Commit the address to memory. Start the habit of remembering things rather than writing them down. You don't want to carry anything into Cuba that might identify you as American. We don't want to endanger you, and we don't want you to endanger the people there who will be helping you. Show up at eight on Monday in civilian clothes. Bring a bag with enough stuff for two weeks."

Bishop stood up, came around the table, shook Charlie's hand and clasped him on the shoulder. "Welcome aboard, Lieutenant."

Charlie walked through the doorway, placed his field cap on his head, stepped across the elegant banistered porch, and limped down the steps into the muggy heat of August. All his life he had been able to finesse people to get what he wanted. But doing that with Bishop was going to be a challenge. Finally out of the man's sight, he used his sleeve to wipe the nervous sweat from above his lip. Then he dropped the arm and let it swing freely as he walked. Try as he might, however, he couldn't stop his hands from shaking.

———

BISHOP's PARTNER, WHO WENT BY the name Mcgillivray, waited until Charlie had stepped out the door before he addressed Bishop. "He's a flippant son-of-a-bitch pushing that need-to-know shit! I'm glad you didn't tell him anything."

"He is annoying," agreed Bishop. "But let's face it. We don't want a milquetoast for this job. And at the end of the day, he's got the one advantage that nobody else has. His girlfriend ushers the president's visitors into and out of the Oval Office several times a day."

"She's only an intern, Walter. Nobody's going to tell her anything important."

"But even an intern picks up rumors, innuendos, and shifts in relationships. This is going to be like having a mole in the White House." Bishop grinned.

"Another thing," said McGillivray. "Why did you give him until Monday? We have a Mongoose meeting the next day, and I want to report that we've got something new cooking. I don't want Parnell backing out over the weekend and forcing me to tell the attorney general that we've had another setback." McGillivray shook his head. "God, that Bobby's an asshole."

Bishop looked up, startled. "You're not going to tell him that we're planning a liquidation?"

"Not unless he asks, which he won't."

"How do you know?"

"Plausible deniability. He wants Castro gone, but he doesn't want to know about it. I'll let him think we're planning sabotage. He loves sabotage, so I don't worry about him. What I worry about is that loose cannon Parnell. Why didn't you keep him here until he was broken?"

"He's already broken," grinned Bishop. "That happened the minute he saw that phony affidavit about his father that you cooked up."

5

Week of August 1, 1962

HAVANA, CUBA

MAJOR ESCALANTE WANTED TO DELIVER the good news in person. He walked to the newspaper offices of Revolucíon, where he found el líder máximo dictating an editorial.

Castro held a fresh cigar between the fingers of his left hand as he made gestures of emphasis toward the stenographer. He paused and turned to Escalante who stood in the doorway, grinning. "You have something?" said Fidel.

"It took awhile, but we got them all. The hotel manager planned to take off with the girl as soon as she sent the poison upstairs. If I hadn't ordered my corporal to bring the manager up to your suite, he would have fled the moment I left the room. By now they would both be in Florida, and we would have learned nothing about the rest of the gang."

"Was he tough to break?"

"I just tapped my baseball bat on the floor by his feet and reminded him that the fucking dictator Batista had let our men be tortured and murdered after they were taken prisoner at Moncada. Once that manager thought that the same treatment was in store for him, all I had to do was touch the fat part of the bat to his nose. It was so close he could smell the wood. He pissed his pants and sang like a bird." Escalante grinned at how easy it had been to break the manager.

"Where are they now?"

"We're holding them in Havana, except for the girl, who's still in Santa Clara where we picked her up. She was sitting in her mother's house, like she couldn't think of a better place to hide. Anyway, we'll keep her locked up until I can fly there and find out if she can add any information to what we already have."

"Good. What about their safe house?"

"I got the Committee for the Defense of the Revolution to put a team of volunteer watchers in the neighborhood so we can keep tabs on it day and night. "

"Anything else?"

Escalante bowed his head toward Castro but focused his eyes on the stenographer and nodded his head in her direction. Castro asked the woman to leave the room for a moment.

"None of the traitors knew very much beyond their own specific tasks. But one of them did say something suspicious. Right before he left Florida, a gusano and an American peppered him with questions about government buildings, roadblocks near the safe house, and storage places for rifle ammunition."

Castro looked puzzled.

"It was as if they expected to fail at this insane plot to poison you," said Escalante. "They were searching for places where they could hide equipment for a gunman, probably a sniper."

"An American? Or one of those Florida gusanos?"

"Probably a gusano. I have a man in Miami asking around about this, but so far we can't pinpoint anyone specific."

"The ones you've got, put them on trial immediately," said Castro. "That will embarrass the Americans and send a message to Cubans to stop cooperating with these plots."

"We can do that, Comandante. They certainly deserve it. However, we got criticized in Europe for those spies we executed last month. Maybe there's another way to send the message." He paused. "We could release them and let them have fatal accidents. Word of mouth about the accidents would spread among the Cubans and be a warning, but the Europeans wouldn't know what was going on, so we would be shielded from criticism by them. With this damned American embargo, we need some friends in Europe."

"It's in your hands, Major. I need to finish this editorial." He called the stenographer back into the room and began waving his cigar at her. He stopped in mid-gesture, turned his head, and said over his shoulder. "But before you let them go, find out everything you can about this new would-be assassin."

LANGLEY, VIRGINIA

"THAT LANSDALE'S AN IDIOT!" FUMED Bill Harvey, red-faced, agitated, and smelling of alcohol as he shifted his weight from one foot to the other. He waved a sheet of paper in front of his boss, CIA Deputy Director Richard Helms, who sat in a leather chair at a polished mahogany desk. A vista of the northern Virginia countryside showed through the window over his shoulder. Leaning back in his chair, Helms gestured with his fingers for Harvey to continue.

"Look what he's put on the agenda for the SGA meeting next Tuesday."

SGA, Special Group Augmented, was a committee chaired by Attorney General Robert Kennedy and responsible for overseeing the Operation Mongoose project. Mongoose was administered by Air Force General Edward Lansdale, the object of Harvey's current anger. Harvey jabbed his finger at the piece of paper. He leaned across

Helms's desk, thrusting the paper at his boss's face. The offending statement was an agenda item identifying Harvey as responsible for liquidating Cuban leaders.

"I want to get rid of Castro as much as anyone," stressed Harvey, "but we can't have this on the official record. What the hell's wrong with Lansdale? He's got this hyped-up reputation because of that counter-insurgency campaign he waged in the Philippines. And now he does a dumb-ass thing like this."

He paused for Helms to comment, but Helms stayed silent.

"I put a call into Lansdale and left a message for him to take this off the agenda. I will not go to a meeting that officially puts us on record for doing assassinations."

"What was Lansdale's response?" asked the deputy director.

"I haven't gotten it yet. But unless the agenda's changed, I won't go to the meeting."

Harvey waited for an objection from Helms, but it did not come. Harvey stepped back from Helms's desk and sat down in a hardback chair opposite it, seeming to relax after seeing no sign of disapproval from his boss.

"Have you mentioned this to John?" Helms asked, referring to his own boss, John McCone, the CIA director.

"No. I thought it would be better to go through you for something like that."

"Good," Helms replied. "Let's keep him out of this for the time being. We need his support, but we have to keep him in the dark about the details of any liquidations."

"What if he asks?"

Helms smiled. "No chance of that. People don't ask when they know they won't like the answer. Do you know what he said the last time someone talked about our bumping off Castro?"

"I heard about it," said Harvey, smirking.

"You know he's getting married and he's converting to

Catholicism. When the subject of assassination came up, he said, 'That could get me excommunicated.'"

Both men chuckled. Helms continued, "He's going off on a honeymoon cruise soon, so let's not bother him with this right now. By the time he returns, let's hope you've got the job done. And keep going with those sabotage projects. The attorney general is really jumping all over us about our not doing enough sabotage. You haven't lived until you've had Bobby Kennedy on your back."

"God, that guy's a prick," said Harvey. "Do you know what he did in Florida?"

"Tell me."

"He was touring our training facilities for the Cuban freedom fighters, and the son of a bitch strutted around like he ran the place. He tore a sheet of paper out of a teletype machine and started to walk out with it. I had to stop him and pull it out of his hands. He didn't even resist. He just left."

"That's what I heard too," said Helms. He leaned forward. "But remember this. We need his backing. He is the attorney general, after all, and in fact, he is the president's brother. If you alienate him, we're up shit creek." He paused. "Or more accurately, you're up shit creek."

ROSSLYN, VIRGINIA

CHARLIE STRETCHED OUT ON VANESSA'S bed. He wore nothing but his army-issued khaki shorts, and he propped his head against a doubled-over pillow by the headboard. His confrontation with Bishop kept popping into his mind. He cursed himself for not having probed more deeply about Bishop's implication that the president had in fact ordered a Castro assassination. Instead of giving a direct yes or no, Bishop had deflected the question with something about a vague Operation Mongoose.

He considered aborting the project, returning to his position at

Arlington Hall Station, and taking a chance that Bishop would not follow through with his threats. But it was too late for that, because he had already accepted his reassignment to Bishop. And he had stupidly signed a CIA agreement not to disclose anything about his conversation with Bishop. His only hope now was to play along with Bishop until an opportunity came up to wiggle out of the situation.

As he lay on the bed, a copy of *Life* magazine rested on his chest, opened to a cover story on H-Bomb tests being conducted in the Pacific. But Charlie's eyes watched Vanessa who sat with perfect posture at her vanity, nude from the waist up, her back toward Charlie. To see her breasts, he had to stare at her reflection in the mirror. She was stroking her long, blond hair with a pearl-handled brush.

"So was the dinner okay?" he asked in Spanish.

"Superb, Charlie."

"Sabroso?" he asked.

"Muy sabroso. It's sah BRO so, not SAB rose o."

"If my accent is so bad, why do you insist on us speaking Spanish?"

"Your accent is not bad. It's just that you tend to anglicize some words." Then she flashed him a toothy smile in the mirror and changed the subject. "But I don't know how you can afford a restaurant like that on a lieutenant's salary."

"On a lieutenant's salary I couldn't possibly afford it," he laughed. "I got a decent cut from my poker game this week."

She didn't respond, and he added, "I might have to shut it down for awhile."

"Why?"

"I'm starting to draw attention. And I want to avoid another run-in with my colonel in case anybody complains."

She set the hairbrush on the vanity, stood up, and dropped her half slip to the floor. She crooked one of her knees, tilted her head to the side, and thrust one arm down in a playful erotic gesture. Charlie smiled in enjoyment. She was tall, almost as tall as he was. As she danced slowly toward the bed, her thigh muscles rippled, a result of karate lessons she had been taking for three months.

She slid in beside him, and he could smell the faint scent of perfume. She propped up her head with her left hand, while she used the right index finger to trace lines up and down his chest.

"Somebody asked me something today," he said, "and I didn't have a good answer, not that the answer was any of this guy's business in the first place. But tell me again how you got your internship at the White House."

She sat up and drew her knees to her chest. "Things just fell into place. I told you about it before."

"Tell me again. I must have missed something the first time." He smiled.

"Charlie," she said without smiling. "You never miss anything. You pick up on things better than any man I've ever known. You're almost as good at it as a woman."

"Indulge me," he laughed.

"My faculty advisor at Barnard came from Boston where she knew Dave Powers's family. When she asked him if they had any internship openings, he said no. However, as a favor to her, Dave gave me a tour of the White House offices last spring."

"So it's Dave now?"

"Yes. Dave Powers. The president's assistant."

"The two of you are on a first name basis?"

"Of course. He's my boss. Dave showed me around. It was very exciting. He even introduced me to the president."

"But you're not on a first name basis with the president?"

"Not when anybody's around, of course, but in private Dave calls him Jack. Stop interrupting. Anyway, I went back to New York, and in June, Dave called to offer me an internship that had just opened up. So here I am." She grinned.

In fact, he remembered all of this. But he had been nagged by Walter Bishop saying he *knew* how she had *wrangled* the internship. Charlie pressed her for details.

"At the moment, your main job is ushering guests into the Oval Office?"

"Oh, yes," she beamed. "I go in along with the photographer. Afterward, I match up the right names with the right photos. You wouldn't want to mix up, for example, Billy Graham with Hugh Hefner."

"Hugh Hefner's been to the White House?"

"Of course not. I'm just using him as an example. But you have to stop interrupting me. Once the photographer is finished, I go outside by Mrs. Lincoln and wait for everyone to come out of the president's office. Then I help them gather their things and escort them to the exit."

"So the president's advisor is Dave, not Mr. Powers, but his secretary is Mrs. Lincoln, not Evelyn."

Vanessa frowned. "Everybody calls her Mrs. Lincoln, even Mr. Kennedy. I've been there for two months, and she's never invited me to use her first name. For some reason she doesn't seem to like me. In fact, I don't know if anybody there likes me. Except for Dave. If it weren't for him, I might have quitted."

"Quit," Charlie laughed. "The past of quit is quit, not quitted." Despite her nearly flawless English, she still had trouble with some sounds. The trait charmed him, but her affection for Dave Powers was annoying.

"Can you give me a tour?"

"I don't know if they'd want me showing my boyfriend around. You just want to see it because you've got this absurd admiration of Kennedy."

Not as much admiration as before he'd met Walter Bishop,

Charlie thought. But he said, "Regardless, it would be fascinating to watch you work. You're in a position to pick up the inside scoop. Do they ever mention Operation Mongoose?"

"What's that?"

"I'm not sure. It's something my Cubans talk about. They're never very clear on what it is, but they make it sound like the White House is involved."

"If they thought you were pumping me for information, they'd never give you a tour."

"Then don't tell them. Just ask Dave. He'll agree."

"We'll see," she said. Then she yawned. "Let's do something before I fall asleep."

6

Week of August 5, 1962

HAVANA, CUBA

ISABEL FERNANDEZ WATCHED AS MAJOR Oscar Escalante slapped a fistful of papers on his desktop. With long brunette hair framing her thin, oval face, she sat poker-faced with her feet flat on the floor. She forced her toes not to tap, worrying why she had been summoned.

"Señorita Isabel Fernandez Rodriguez," he read aloud from the papers. "Two years at the school of philosophy, but you did not graduate. Currently you work as administrative aide at the Ministry of Communications. One of your duties is translating materials from English. Is that correct?"

"Yes, Major," she replied, trying to show no unease despite his intense stare and the forbidding drabness of the room. Dirty green paint on the wall was peeling in spots. She returned his steady look, noting his bushy eyebrows that contrasted with his neat, short, military crew cut.

"Mother of a three-year-old daughter." He continued reading, then looked up, smiling. "Your daughter's name is?"

"Ángela. She is named after her father, Angel. He was a sergeant with the Revolutionary Armed Forces in Ghana, and we were to be married when he returned. But he died in a car crash." Although the new revolutionary ethos declared that single mothers be treated equally with married mothers, Isabel had received enough snide innuendos about her out-of-wedlock child that she felt obliged to explain her status.

"I am sorry for your loss, señorita. Your prometido was a hero to the revolution."

He glanced down at the papers and smiled once more. "This gets even more intriguing. You are a licensed pilot."

"I always wanted to fly. Even as a child. The birds always looked so free as they floated across the sky." She smiled for the first time. "For my quinceañera, my parents let me take flying lessons, and I earned a license for single engine aircraft. The revolution let me keep the license. Having a child, however, and working full time, I do not have much chance to fly today."

"Have you been told why we sent for you?"

"No, Major." Her burst of enthusiasm from talking about her flying dissipated, and her stomach began to churn again.

He pushed a document across the table for her to read. "This is a request from a newspaper, *The Irish Times*. They want us to let one of their stringers, a Mr. Michael Collins, prepare a series of friendly articles on the revolution."

He squinted. "What is a stringer?"

"It is a freelance reporter who is not on a newspaper's payroll but who gets paid for each story the newspaper uses. By using stringers, the paper can report stories from places where it cannot afford to maintain a staff. Havana, for example."

"The Ministry of Communications is going to assign you to assist this stringer. We want you to help him write positive stories about our revolution. Getting favorable publicity abroad will be good for us."

"I understand, Major," said the young woman. "But I would normally receive an assignment such as this from my supervisor at the Ministry of Communications. What is so important about this Mr. Collins that I get the assignment from el comandante's security chief?"

"Because there might or might not be a problem with this Mister Collins."

The major leaned forward. "I need your discretion on what I'm going to say next. It is very important that you do not talk to anyone about this. Can I trust you?"

"Certainly, Major." But her fingers tapped a nervous drum beat on her lap. She knew she could keep a secret. However, it could be dangerous to know the secrets of Castro's security chief.

"If this stringer is, in fact, who he says he is, the problem disappears. However," the major pointed a finger to the ceiling, "if he is not who he claims to be, there could be a problem. A big problem. A very big problem."

She furrowed her eyebrows, not understanding the issue.

"We believe the CIA is sending an assassin to kill el comandante. We don't think they would be dumb enough to send a gringo when there are so many Cuban traitors in Miami who would love the job. But when this *Irish Times* request arrives just as we are learning about a possible assassin, we have to be alert."

"I understand, Major. Has this reporter done anything specific to arouse our suspicions?"

"Only one thing. You will see on page two of those papers that he spent a summer in Franco's Spain." With his left hand, he slid the original in English across the desk to her, while he used his right hand to point to a line in the Spanish translation that he kept in front of himself.

Relieved to have something to do with her hands, she reached for the papers and flipped to the second page.

"I see your point, Major. Why would a man enamored with

fascist Spain want to praise our revolution? However," she added as she pointed at a line halfway down, "it also says here that he got expelled from Spain at the end of the summer. Maybe he wasn't enamored with the fascists after all."

She set the papers back on the desk and waited for the major to say something. When a moment of silence passed, she asked, "If this Mr. Collins poses any threat at all to the prime minister, why don't we simply deny his request for a visa?"

"There are several reasons," the major replied. "First, we will get good publicity from him whether or not he is the assassin. If he is not the assassin, we get the benefit of positive coverage. But suppose he is not an Irishman. Suppose he is an American CIA agent posing as an Irishman. In this case, we will put him on trial, which will embarrass the Americans and generate support for us around the world. If we refuse to admit him, we will lose an opportunity to present our case to the world. Furthermore, the CIA will find some other way to get him in, and the next time, he might be harder to find."

"So you want to let him in, but you need to find out whether he is indeed the assassin."

"¡Absolutamente!" The major jabbed his index finger in her direction. "And that's where you come in."

"Major," she squirmed in her chair. "I know nothing about spies or assassins. And it sounds dangerous. If I find out that he is an assassin, he will kill me to protect his own identity. My daughter will become an orphan."

Major Escalante leaned forward with a friendly, paternal look on his face.

"We don't want you to confront him or do anything dangerous. Until we are satisfied that he is a genuine reporter and not some pimp for the CIA, we have people who will keep him under surveillance. So we don't want you doing that. What we do want is for you to stay close to him. Get him talking English to see if his accent is indeed Irish."

"And how will I do that? I've never heard an Irishman talk. I don't know what they sound like."

"But you've seen enough movies to know what an American sounds like. If his accent sounds American, that will be a good tipoff for us. Or if he's familiar with American things, such as baseball, that an Irishman wouldn't know about. Report anything suspicious to me, anything that conflicts with what he's claiming to be. Does he actually draft stories for his newspaper? Have a meal with him and note whether he keeps the fork in the same hand like a European or switches it back and forth like an American? Give him some companionship and get as close to him as possible so he will let down his guard."

Her eyes flashed in anger. "Major, I am not a prostitute. I want to help you. But if what you need is someone to prostitute herself, you will have to find somebody else."

There was a long moment of silence as the major sat back, a stony look on his face. Despite her confident demeanor, she trembled for having talked so bluntly.

Finally, he spoke, "Perdón, señorita. I did not mean to imply that. You are absolutely correct. It would be quite wrong for a young mother to do such a thing."

Despite her confident look, Isabel shuddered. Was the major threatening her daughter?

"For several reasons," he went on, "you are the ideal person to assist this Mr. Collins and to keep me informed about what he is doing. I need somebody with courage, and it took courage for you to say what you just said. I need somebody who speaks English and who understands enough about journalism to figure out what this Mr. Collins is up to. If he is legitimate, I can stop wasting resources on him. But if he is indeed the assassin, el jefe's life is in danger. Will you help us?"

In truth, Isabel didn't care enough about el jefe's life to put her own at risk. She had joined the cheering crowds that greeted Fidel on his triumphant entrance to Havana almost four years earlier.

But since then, her revolutionary ardor had faded. She rarely got to spend an hour in the cockpit of a plane anymore. The system of neighborhood watchers repelled her. Their snitching had caused some of her college friends to be arrested. And recurrent food shortages left half the country underfed, including her daughter. Unconsciously, she tugged at the revolutionary fatigue shirt that hung on her thin body.

However, if she refused this assignment, the consequences could be unpleasant. At the very least, she would lose her job, and, much worse, her daughter might be rejected for admission to the schools Isabel had in mind. Her eyes wandered past the major's shoulder to a portrait of Fidel on the dingy wall.

"Of course, Major," she smiled, turned her eyes back to him. "It will be my honor to serve the revolution."

"Your first task will be to accompany me on a flight to Santa Clara in a few days. I want to test your flying skills. If you are still competent, I could use you as a backup pilot, and I might be able to get you an appointment as an observation pilot in the Revolutionary Armed Forces. You will also be spending a lot of time ushering this Mr. Collins around town. Can the Ministry of Communications give you a vehicle for that?"

"I have a motorcycle, Major. With a sidecar for a passenger."

"Why am I not surprised that an airplane pilot would also drive a motorcycle?" Escalante beamed a pleasant smile. "We will provide you a salary increase to cover your expenses during this assignment. Is there anything else you need?"

She paused, embarrassed to make a special plea. "My Angelita is very thin and needs more protein in her diet. If you could get an increase in our ration of chicken, it would help."

"Consider it done. And more rice as well."

He wrote his private phone number on a business card and handed it to her.

"Contact with this reporter will be handled through your

supervisor at the Ministry of Communications. Phone me as soon as you get the arrival information and be prepared to fly off to Santa Clara with me at a moment's notice."

Then he stood up to end the interview. She felt the sweat trickling down her side as she left his office and stepped into the sultry August air, her stomach still in knots. She welcomed the increase in food rations, but this promise of a pilot job made no sense. Even if the request came from Che Guevara himself, the Revolutionary Armed Forces would never let a woman fly its airplanes. And if this reporter did indeed turn out to be an assassin who succeeded in his mission, she could get the blame. She shuddered at what this might mean for Angelita.

Tysons Corner, Virginia

Bishop's office turned out to be a small shop among a shabby strip of stores along Leesburg Pike near Tysons Corner. Charlie parked his cherry-red Corvette in front of the door and pulled the canvas top closed. He entered a Spartan room with a few government issue gray metal desks and a several old wooden chairs. The room smelled of stale air. In contrast to the dim character of the room, the overhead fluorescent lights shone brightly and buzzed with an annoying sound.

"So how are you going to get me out of Cuba once this is done?" said Charlie as he plopped himself into the chair next to Bishop's desk. "This has been on my mind all weekend."

Bishop smiled, apparently with some pleasure, at Charlie's worries.

"I promise you, we've got a plan for that, and I'll go over it with you. But the first thing we have to do is find out if you still have your expert marksman skills. Then some training on how to put them to use."

Bishop pointed toward the door and got up to leave.

"Where are you going?"

"Where else can we find out whether you're still an expert marksman? The rifle range."

"One second," said Charlie, laying his hand on Bishop's arm. "There are a couple of things we haven't settled yet. Before we leave, I need a copy of those orders that reassigned me to you."

"I left them in my office at Langley. We'll get them when we come back."

"Mr. Bishop," Charlie objected. "Without those orders, I am effectively AWOL from Arlington Hall Station. I need them now."

"I told you. They're in my office at Langley. We'll get them when we return."

"On Friday you told me your office was here. Without those orders, I'm not going to any rifle range. Call your office, and you can have them delivered here in twenty minutes. But without those orders, I'd be better off heading back to Arlington Hall Station and hoping that the colonel thinks that I'm just late for work."

Bishop pursed his lips. He started toward the door and motioned for Charlie to follow. When Charlie refused to budge, Bishop said, "The other thing we learned from your background check was your tendency to be a pain in the ass."

Charlie smiled, "Better to be a pain in the ass than to be back on the colonel's shit list for going AWOL."

"Let me look in my briefcase. Maybe I left a carbon copy in there."

Bishop rifled through his attaché case, wadded the orders in his fist, and jabbed them in Charlie's direction. "What else?"

"My expenses. I told you that Friday. I don't want to go broke working for you guys. How are you going to reimburse me?"

"We'll put some cash in a safe-deposit box in Zurich. You can make arrangements with them for taking it out."

"How much?"

"Two thousand dollars."

"Ten thousand."

"Jesus Christ," Bishop screamed, then lowered his voice. "That's twice your annual salary."

"I've got huge expenses. Airline tickets, hotels, meals out, clothes, and who knows what? Plus, I'll be losing income from my poker game that I have to close down, thanks to you."

"Five. And that's it."

"Who's got access to this safe-deposit box?"

"It will be a secret Swiss account, open only to you and us."

"To you? I don't want a joint account with you."

"We have no choice, Lieutenant. That's the only way I'll be able to get this approved. We need some recourse in case you fail to keep your end of the bargain." He rose from his desk and spotted Charlie's flashy sports car outside the door. "Not a good idea to leave that little gem sitting here while you're gone. Give me your car keys so we can bring it over to your apartment."

Then he stepped toward the door and motioned for Charlie to follow. He turned the lock behind him before they got into a drab blue Pontiac sedan. The dreary colors seemed right for a spook, Charlie thought. He noted the black and white Virginia license plate number: A 312 279. He kept repeating it in his mind until Bishop looked to the left so he could merge into traffic. Then Charlie pulled a pen from his pocket and wrote the number in blue ink on the inside of his left thumb. He could transfer it to paper later. The number might or might not ever prove useful. But it couldn't do any harm.

"A few ground rules," said Bishop as he pulled onto the highway. "Don't mention anything about Castro. The people where we're going are there only to teach you the technique of being a sniper. They don't know what you're going to use it for. Or who you are. From now on, you're Michael Collins."

Bishop looked over at Charlie who repeated the name, "Michael

Collins?"

"Yes. The only one there who knows where you're going is your Cuban spotter, Flavio."

"Which probably isn't his real name either."

"Exactly," smiled Bishop. "You're catching on."

7

Week of August 5, 1962

Marine Corps Base Quantico, Virginia

A T THE FIRING RANGE IN Quantico, Virginia, a Marine Corps staff sergeant shoved a semi-automatic weapon into Charlie's hands. "This is what we'll train you on," he said.

Charlie frowned. "This is one of those old M-1 Garands from WWII. It's a relic that we've been phasing out for years. It doesn't even have a modern magazine, just that old eight-round clip. This would be the kiss of death in a firefight with people using AK47s."

"You're not training for a firefight, so an automatic rifle doesn't do you any good. What you need is to make a few well placed shots from two to three hundred yards out, and this weapon has been modified for that." He pointed out the detachable bipod at the end of the barrel and the telescopic sight that had been mounted on the rifle."

"Is it accurate at those distances?"

"Our Marine snipers have been using this for years and have no complaints about its accuracy. To get a baseline of your accuracy now, we'll start you out shooting at two hundred yards. Then we'll check your accuracy and keep moving you back to see where you maintain eighty percent accuracy with the scope."

The sergeant pointed to different sets of target areas. Each one featured a human silhouette with circles radiating out from the heart. A berm of earth served as a backstop for each, and the berms had furrows dug out from the thousands of bullets over the years. Farthest out and highest were the eight hundred yard targets. Closer in and lower were the targets for five hundred-yards, three hundred yards, and two hundred yards.

Charlie dropped to a prone position, balanced the rifle on the bipod, cradled the stock in his left hand to steady it, and pulled the butt tight against his shoulder. For an instant, he considered firing wildly so that Bishop would give up on the plot, thinking that Charlie had lost his sharpshooter skills. But Bishop was too smart for that, he realized, and Charlie himself couldn't resist the challenge to shoot for bullseyes. He peered through the scope, put the crosshairs in the middle of the target's chest, and squeezed the trigger, jolting backward at the kick of the rifle.

The sergeant raised a set of binoculars to his eyes and examined the target. "You're high and to the right. Turn the elevation screw down a couple of clicks."

He handed the binoculars to Charlie who inspected the target himself. He adjusted the screw on the scope before taking another shot. This time he had the correct altitude, but he was off to the right. He glanced at the triangular wind flag halfway down the firing lane to determine the wind's direction. As he started to turn the screws to adjust for the wind, the sergeant stopped him. "Don't adjust the screws for the wind. We'll teach you how to do that. Right now just keep your crosshairs set for zero wind and make adjustments in your aiming as you go along."

"Okay. This time it's for keeps." Charlie emptied the clip, pausing a few seconds between each shot. When he stopped, Bishop took the binoculars from the sergeant.

"Jesus!" said Bishop. He handed the binoculars to Charlie.

There was a huge hole in the center of the target's chest where three bullets had torn the paper apart. Another hole was in the lethal zone, and two more on the edge of it. Charlie felt a powerful sense of satisfaction. It was like the feeling he used to get when he played trumpet in his high school band and would hit the high notes nobody else could reach. He took the scope off the rifle and smiled over his shoulder at Bishop.

"Let me try a few rounds without the scope. If I'm out in bright sunlight, the scope might cause a reflection that will give me away. In that case, I might want to shoot without it."

He snapped a new clip into the rifle and took his first shot. Then he paused before taking the second.

"Don't pause," Bishop interrupted. "If you don't take your second shot immediately, you won't get the chance for it. The minute his security hears a bullet whizzing by, they'll knock him to the ground and cover him. You've got to get your second shot off immediately."

Charlie sneered over his shoulder. "Maybe you should do this yourself."

———

IN THE SERGEANT'S OFFICE, BISHOP poured coffee into two Styrofoam cups. He raised one in a toast. "Impressive. That eight-hundred-yard shot might be out of reach, but at two hundred yards, you're deadly."

The sergeant spoke, "The eight-hundred-yard shot is not particularly good with the M1. But we can definitely increase your accuracy at the three-hundred– and five-hundred-yard ranges. There are other things you need to learn as well. You need to know how to use a range finder to calculate distances. You also need to know how to track your target, work with a spotter, plan an escape, and avoid tails. Mr. Bishop has not given me a lot of time to teach you that. We're going to bundle it into a crash course over the next two weeks."

"You mean I'm going to be stuck here for two weeks?"

"Yes. Your last assignment," said Bishop, "will be a week from Friday. Then, if you're not in jail, I want you to meet me at the shop in Tysons Corner the following Monday morning. Eight o'clock sharp."

"Jail? Why would I be in jail?"

"Follow instructions, and you won't be in jail. If you have any problems, call me at this number." He held out a business card with a name and telephone number. No title or address.

"How am I going to get home?"

"Someone will give you a ride."

"And this last assignment will be what?"

"You'll see."

The White House

VANESSA FOLLOWED THE PHOTOGRAPHER OUT of the Oval Office, leaving the president alone with the foreign minister of Venezuela. She brought a tray of coffee and cookies to the Cabinet Room where the foreign minister's three aides waited for him. When they discovered that this blond, German-looking woman in the form-fitting paisley dress spoke perfect Spanish, they happily flirted with her as they waited for their boss. Near the end of the thirty-minute session, Vanessa followed the president's secretary, Evelyn Lincoln, to the Oval Office. Lincoln knocked softly on the door, pushed it ajar, and said, "Mr. President, your three fifteen is here."

Peering over Mrs. Lincoln's shoulder, Vanessa spotted a scale model replica of Kennedy's wartime PT-109 patrol boat on the mantel behind the president. His patrol boat had been run over by a Japanese destroyer, turning Kennedy into a decorated war hero. Next to the replica rested the coconut shell with the SOS he had carved in to rescue his stranded boat crew. "Just give us one more minute, Mrs. Lincoln," said Kennedy, making it sound as though he dreaded being cut short from his exhilarating time with the charming

Venezuelan. A moment later the foreign minister emerged, smiling as he showed his aides a PT-109 tie clasp the president had given him. Vanessa helped the foreign minister and his entourage retrieve their belongings. Then she escorted them to the White House exit, chatting with them in Spanish as they walked.

All in all, she reflected, everyone had gotten something from the visit. Kennedy got a photo clip for the evening news. He would look presidential, sitting in his rocking chair smiling down at his visitor slumped in a sofa. The foreign minister got the PT-109 tie clasp plus a photo of himself next to the American president. And Vanessa got the foreign minister's business card, with his private telephone number penciled in. "Call me the next time you're in Caracas," he had said. "I'll give you dinner plus a guided tour of the city." So it had been a win-win day. Vanessa smiled to herself as she walked back to retrieve her purse from the chair by Mrs. Lincoln's desk.

As she reached the secretary's station, the president stood by the desk talking to Mrs. Lincoln. He plucked a piece of candy from a dish she kept on her desk and popped it into his mouth. Apparently, there never had been a 3:15 appointment, and Kennedy didn't look displeased at being torn away from the foreign minister. Vanessa retrieved her purse and turned to head back to her own desk, when the president addressed her. "You did a very good job today, Vanessa. Would you care to grab a bite to eat about six o'clock in the Residence?"

"I would love to, Mr. President, but I don't know how to get there." She smiled.

"Dave Powers will bring you up."

Not just a win-win day, thought Vanessa as she headed back to her desk. A triple-win day.

––––––––

AFTER THE YOUNGER WOMAN WAS out of earshot, Mrs. Lincoln looked askance at the president. He gave her a coy smile.

"This one is very risky," she said. "You don't know if she is reliable. What if she blabs about this to Ted Sorensen's typist, who shares an apartment with a girl in Senator Keating's office? Keating would have a field day with that information."

Kennedy's smile shifted to a frown. "Ted's typist rooms with somebody from Keating's office?" He tapped his teeth with his fingernails. "Tell Kenny O'Donnell to reassign her someplace else, maybe in Jackie's office, and find Ted a new typist."

Tropic of Cancer

Second Captain Demitri Lesnikov's Foxtrot submarine had almost reached the convoy it would escort to Cuba. The boat's cooling system still malfunctioned, and the deeper they went into the tropics, the worse the heat became. Lesnikov was sitting at a table in the officers' mess with the boat's first captain and Deputy Political Officer Chernikov, interrogating the chief technician of a communications team. At the start of the voyage, the first captain had resented making room for the team on the already crowded boat.

That had been at the start of the voyage. Now, the officers listened with respect as the technician made his report. "NATO tracked us around Scandinavia and as far as Greenland. Then they lost us."

"The Americans lost us?"

"The Americans. The Canadians. Everyone. They know we're out here, but they don't know where. We're sure of that from tracking their transmissions."

"You mean," the captain said, "we have sailed the entire length of North America and we've eluded the American anti-submarine warfare apparatus. They don't know where we are?"

"Not with enough precision to do anything about it," said the technician. "We are certain of that."

The first captain turned to his left and smiled at Lesnikov and then to his right where Chernikov returned the smile. "Excellent work, Seaman," he said as he handed a bottle of vodka to the man standing in front of the three officers. "Here's a token of our appreciation for you to share with your comrades. Work like yours needs to be rewarded. But don't drink it all at once. We want at least one of you on duty and alert at all times."

The seaman ducked his head as he passed through the narrow hatch leaving the officers' mess. Once he was out of earshot, the captain tapped his fingertips on the stainless-steel tabletop. "If the Americans try to interfere with the convoy, we can pick off their ships like sitting ducks. And if we get a chance to fire that nuclear torpedo, we can wipe out their entire Caribbean fleet. Where is it in the firing line?"

Lesnikov shuddered at the first captain's eagerness to fire the nuclear warhead. But he was relieved to discover that the captain did not know that Lesnikov had altered the placement of the torpedoes. "Since the crew doesn't know that one of the torpedoes carries a nuke, I placed that one at the bottom of the torpedo rack. I didn't want it already in one of the tubes where in the heat of action, the crew might fire it by accident without your knowledge."

"Good thinking, Lesnikov. However, an occasion might arise when we will need to get at it quickly. You can leave it out of the tubes but put it at the top of the torpedo rack, where we can get it if necessary."

"But Captain, what if somebody makes a mistake and puts it into a torpedo tube without your knowledge?"

The first captain looked sternly at Lesnikov. "Comrade Captain, it is your job to make sure that such a mistake does not happen. Put it at the top of the rack and keep an eye on it."

THE WHITE HOUSE

KENNETH O'DONNELL'S ADMINISTRATIVE AIDE, MISS Flanagan, stopped in front of Vanessa's desk and stood staring down until Vanessa looked up. "Being a Barnard girl, I don't suppose there's any chance that you can type or take shorthand."

Vanessa reddened in anger. This was one more sign that she was disliked in the West Wing. Without saying a word, she inserted a sheet of blank paper into the IBM Selectric typewriter on a nearby desk. She tapped two sentences with dizzying speed, pulled the sheet from the typewriter, and handed it to the other woman.

Now is the time for all good secretaries to treat their interns with respect.

Now is the time for all good secretaries to treat their interns with respect.

"She not only types, but she's cheeky, too," snorted Miss Flanagan. "What about the shorthand?"

Vanessa took back the typewritten sheet, turned it over, and began scrawling shorthand strokes that spelled out exactly what Miss Flanagan had said.

"My father forced me to take a semester at business school before I went to college," said Vanessa. "But it came in handy once I got to college. Every now and then he'd become upset at me and withhold my allowance."

Miss Flanagan rolled her eyes at the mention of an allowance, but Vanessa continued talking without reacting.

"When he did that, I earned spending money by typing term papers for the other girls. And because the shorthand made me so good at taking notes, I also picked up money by going to the other girls' classes and writing down their professors' lectures. So yes, Miss Flanagan, Barnard girls can type and take shorthand."

If it had not been for the other woman's snide reference to her college, Vanessa would never have been so confrontational with Flanagan. Her boss, O'Donnell, ran the White House Office, and he could chuck Vanessa out at the slightest whim. However, she calculated, her new status with the president gave her protection.

"I need to find a new assistant for Ted Sorensen, and I guess you're it," said Flanagan. "Follow me."

"What happened to the old one?"

Without answering, Miss Flanagan led Vanessa to Sorensen's office. "I will introduce you to him, and he can tell you what he wants you to start on. When you get a break, stop by my desk. Since you'll be a staff member now instead of just an intern, you'll be on the payroll, and I have some paperwork for you to fill out."

At first, Vanessa worried that she would miss ushering guests into the Oval Office. After all, that was how she had come to Kennedy's attention. This new job, however, promised to be much more exciting. Sorensen was the president's speechwriter and most trusted counselor. As his assistant, she would be in the middle of everything. Maybe she would find out about that Operation Mongoose Charlie had mentioned.

She was bursting to share the news of her new responsibilities with him or someone—anyone. But she would have to be careful not to give in to Charlie's persistent demands for a tour of the offices. Better to keep him as far from the White House as possible. He might not understand that the president was just a fling. An exciting and pleasant fling, but nonetheless, just a fling. Charlie, on the other hand, might be a keeper.

She would also have to be more careful to take her Enovid pill every day. This was no time to get pregnant, and being involved with two men increased the risk of disease. Maybe she should switch from the pill to condoms. But how was she supposed to tell the President of the United States to wear a condom?

8

Week of August 5, 1962

Havana, Cuba

ISABEL FENANDEZ SAT IN THE back of the jeep next to Major Escalante en route to the Ciudad Libertad Airport, where the major kept a plane. Sergeant Ramos, the major's pilot, drove the jeep. He stopped at the airfield's main gate so a guard could check their identification. After the guard raised a red and white gate to let them in, Ramos drove to a parking spot and led them by foot to the Piper Cub they would fly to Santa Clara.

"Did you ever pilot a Piper Cub?" he asked Isabel.

"Yes, we used that plane in my pilot's lessons. But it was smaller than this one."

"This is bigger than the originals. They called this one their Family Cruiser," said Ramos. "We like it because it can carry four people and has a bigger engine. It cruises about 160 to 170 kilometers per hour."

"What's its range?"

"Nine hundred kilometers, more or less. Enough to get to Santa

Clara and back. Nevertheless, we will refuel there and once again when we return. Since the major sometimes flies out on the spur of the moment, I have to keep it fueled at all times."

He gave her a set of combination numbers to unlock a small safe inside the door of the hangar. "Inside the safe, you'll find several key rings. Pick the one for this plane." He pointed to the identification number on the tail of the Piper Cub. "We keep the planes locked so we don't have to worry about any gusanos breaking in to sabotage them."

Isabel fingered through several key rings until she found the one for the Piper Cub. The ring held two keys, and she flushed with an unexpected realization. If she could palm one of the two keys, an occasion might arise for her to flee Cuba with Ángela. Without pausing to think, she twisted one of the keys off the ring and slipped it inside her right shoe. She jogged back to where Ramos waited by the plane, the key biting into her skin with each step.

Her heart raced as she handed the key ring to Ramos. If he noticed a key missing and searched her, she could go to prison. Why had she done such a foolhardy thing?

"Hmm," murmured Ramos as he took the ring. "I thought this ring had two keys."

Isabel's pulse shot up, and she struggled to breathe normally as she watched him examine the key ring.

"No. That must have been the Cessna I was thinking of." He handed the key back to her. "Here. The major wants to test your flying skills, so you're the pilot today. I'll be the copilot in case you need me."

Taking the key, she walked around to the pilot's side of the plane. Her legs wobbled with fright, and she took slow deliberate steps so Ramos wouldn't notice her anxiety. She climbed into the cockpit to start the pre-flight check and was startled to see Ramos jump immediately into the copilot's seat.

"Don't you need to prop the engine?" she asked.

He laughed and pointed to a button in the middle of the instrument panel. "That Piper you flew before must have been very ancient. This one has an electric starter."

TWO HOURS LATER, APPROACHING THE airstrip in Santa Clara, Isabel pulled back on the throttle. She let the plane slow until the airspeed needle pointed to fifty. Then to double check that the controls still worked, she made several small back and forth movements of the rudder. She dipped the nose of the plane and lined herself up with the center of the runway, hoping to impress the major with a soft landing.

A last-minute gust of wind shook the plane and pushed the nose off course. From the corner of her eye, she saw a startled look come onto Escalante's face as the plane blew to the left. Sergeant Ramos, in the copilot seat, made no move to take over the controls. She pushed on the right rudder pedal to bring the plane back in line with the runway, let the plane drop to about three feet from the ground, and pushed the stick forward for her final glide to the ground. But the tail wheel struck first, then the right wheel, bouncing the plane off to the left again and ruining her hopes for a soft landing. She raised the left wing to steady the plane and finally got all three wheels onto the ground.

When they came to a stop, she turned to Escalante. "Sorry about the bounce, Major. I'm a little rusty."

Sergeant Ramos grinned and piped in. "You did well, señorita. Those last-minute gusts are always tricky, but you handled them nicely. Taxi over to that fuel pump so we can refill."

A jeep drove them from the airstrip to the center of Santa Clara. They stopped at the hotel to register and drop off their luggage. Then Escalante led the three of them to the police station. He turned toward Isabel as they walked the short distance.

"Last month, we interrupted an attempt to poison Fidel at the Hotel Habana Libre. We are holding the girl who dumped the poison into el líder máximo's coffee. Although she has been interrogated extensively, I want to talk with her one more time before we dispose of her case. To soften her up, we put her in a drawer cell yesterday."

Isabel shuddered. Everyone in Cuba knew about the infamous drawer cells that were pitch black and infested with cockroaches. They were so small that their inhabitants could not straighten their legs. Isabel dreaded the idea of witnessing what was going to be an unpleasant experience.

They entered a large interrogation room with grimy stucco walls and peeling dark paint. The room had one small dirty window that let in very little light. She smelled mildew, and the oppressive heat caused sweat to trickle down her sides. Escalante sat at a table and motioned for Isabel to sit as well. They faced a hardback chair that had a bright light shining down on it.

Isabel gasped at the sight of the girl as she was brought blindfolded into the room. She walked bent over, because she could not yet straighten her body after being cramped overnight in the drawer cell. Her snarled hair appeared not to have been combed for a week. She wore a tattered drab dress, and insect bites covered her dirty legs. The guard pushed her into the chair. He pulled off the blindfold, and she shut her eyes tight against the blazing light.

"Look at me!" commanded Escalante.

She tried to open her eyes but could not get past a squint. "Sir, it is so hard to see after having been in the dark for so long."

"Quiet! You have not been in the dark that long. You only spent one night in the drawer cell. Prior to that, you had a regular, comfortable cell."

The girl squirmed in the chair and tried to turn her eyes away from the blinding light.

"Sit still!" shouted Escalante so sharply that Isabel jumped. She couldn't imagine the impact on the poor girl.

Escalante softened his voice. "You were only put in the drawer cell because you wouldn't tell the truth. Prior to that, you were not mistreated in any way. Did anyone rape you or touch you indecently?"

She shook her head to the side.

"Answer me," snapped Escalante.

"No." She whimpered.

"You say 'No señor,'" he barked. "You don't talk to me like one of your grubby little friends."

"No señor." She whimpered again.

"Did anyone kick you?"

"No señor."

"Did anyone hit you or slap you or knock you down?"

"No señor."

"Did anyone deny you food or water?"

"No señor."

"Did anyone poison you the way that you tried to poison el líder máximo and his lady friend?"

She looked to the ground and tried to shake her head, tears building in her eyes.

"Answer me."

"No señor," she said in a muted voice.

Escalante paused and let a long silence build. Finally, he lowered his voice and said very softly, "If you tell me the truth, you will not be sent back to the drawer cell."

She exhaled a long sigh.

"But if you lie to me, you will spend the rest of your life there."

While Isabel watched in horror, Escalante picked a baseball bat from under the desk and handed it to Sergeant Ramos. The sergeant rose to his feet.

"Put your hands flat on the table."

The girl focused her terrified eyes on the baseball bat. In a swift motion, Ramos raised the bat over his head and smashed it on the table, just inches from the girl's hand. She recoiled.

"Do you know what happened to our brave soldiers who were captured at Moncada?"

She shook her head.

"The police tortured them to death. They lined up the soldiers so they all had to watch. They picked the first one and asked a question. Not liking the answer, they clubbed him. Another question, another clubbing, breaking bones each time. Blow after blow. When they had no more bones to break, they killed him with a vicious blow to the head. Then they went to the second soldier and to the next and the next, all the way to the end. The last ones trembled as they awaited their turns." Ramos touched the tip of the bat to the girl's cheek.

Escalante softened his voice. "We don't want this to happen to you. Or to anybody in your family. You have a small sister, do you not? Three years old? Nothing will happen to her if you tell us the truth."

The girl trembled, seemingly unable to talk.

"Speak, damn you! Speak!" he shouted. "Talk to me."

But the girl was paralyzed by fear. She was shaking and wringing her hands. Escalante turned to Isabel, who was herself on the verge of tears. "Do something. Tell her she must speak."

Isabel rose from the desk and put her arms around the girl, hugging her tightly. Then she pushed back from the girl and said in a soft and deliberate voice. "For the love of God, muchacha, tell this man what he wants to hear. Tell him before it is too late."

Then she walked to the back of the room, leaned against the wall, and folded her arms around her chest. The girl choked back another sob, and asked, "What do you want to know, señor?"

For thirty minutes, Escalante peppered her with question after question. Finally, he leaned back and lit a cigarette. After a deep puff, he pushed himself up from the table.

"Take her out and clean her up," he told a guard. "Give her a new dress. Then let her go."

Isabel dropped her arms to her sides in stunned surprise. Why would Escalante free the girl after she admitted her role in the plot to poison Castro? The girl's mouth dropped open. She rose from the chair, but before she could even say *thank you*, the major turned on his heel, walked over to Isabel by the back wall. He took her elbow and led her from the room, his cigarette dangling from his fingers.

"Señorita, you got more from that girl with one hug than I got with a whole night in the drawer cell and an act of melodrama with the baseball bat. You should have been an actress."

Isabel clenched her fists, fearing that she would vomit. "It was no act, Major. I just wanted her to talk so you wouldn't beat her." She shook her head. "I'm afraid I wasn't cut out for this kind of work."

The major let go of her elbow, stepped back, and looked at her without speaking.

"What did you learn, Major? And was it worth terrorizing her this way?"

"We confirmed that she got the poison from the hotel manager. She expected him to rush her to a safe house where they would be smuggled by a boat to Florida. However, that plan fell apart when I picked up the manager. She gave us the names of their helpers and the approximate location of the safe house. As she goes home, she will tell her friends and relatives about the drawer cell and the baseball bat. They, in turn, will tell the same story to their friends and relatives. The message will get out that people must not cooperate with these CIA assassination attempts. So, yes, it was worth it."

Isabel said nothing.

"Comrade, that girl tried to poison Fidel and his friend. Did his companion deserve to have her guts ripped out simply because she gave el comandante a few moments of comfort?"

Escalante edged closer to Isabel, towering over her with his immense bulk. His bushy eyebrows looked sinister. "Heaven forbid that one of these assassins should succeed. Suppose those gusanos in Miami come back to power. They will bring back the Mafia with their casinos and brothels. They will put you and me out of jobs, and, if we are unlucky, stand us up before a firing squad. So don't worry about that little slut who tried to bring all this about by poisoning el comandante. Worry about what will happen to your daughter if the gusanos come back. And worry about this reporter, Michael Collins. Is he truly an Irish journalist? Or is he a plant for the CIA?"

This entire speech spurted out in a rush, and the major had to inhale deeply when he finished. Isabel looked up defiantly at his eyes, but she said nothing. He flicked his cigarette butt to the floor.

"Go back to the hotel, señorita, and get a good night's sleep. I need you rested so you can fly us back to Havana tomorrow."

She followed him out to the front office of the police station. He took something from his pocket and passed it to the officer at the front desk, who immediately left the building.

Back in her hotel room, she removed the key from her shoe. It had been biting into her foot the entire day. Then she collapsed on her bed sobbing. As her sobs ebbed, she realized why Escalante wanted her at the interrogation. The message was meant for her.

———

THE NEXT MORNING, SHE PICKED up a newspaper from the hotel concierge as she took a café con leche before going to the air strip. She shuddered when she read a story on an inside page.

> *Señorita Maria Gomez, a waitress at the Hotel Habana Libre, was struck by a truck and killed yesterday afternoon as she left the Santa Clara central police station. She had just been released after having been detained on suspicion of anti-government activities. Several people witnessed the accident, but nobody could identify the driver, who fled and disappeared.*

9

Week of August 12, 1962

THE NATIONAL MALL, WASHINGTON, DISTRICT OF COLUMBIA

BLACK SEDAN SPED UP I-95 through the wooded Virginia countryside from Quantico to Washington, DC. At the wheel was a muscleman named Bob Gordon, who worked for Walter Bishop. In the back seat, Charlie and his Cuban spotter, Flavio, compared notes on the day's assignment and their previous two weeks of sniper training at Quantico. Working together, they learned how to elude tails, acquire targets, and blend into the surroundings like chameleons. They practiced making a getaway and being patient when one's adrenalin surged, and the body craved action. They began at six in the morning and trained until ten at night.

On Saturday, the sergeant gave them the evening off and they headed to Quantico's Officers Club to relax. The club hall was packed with single men in uniform celebrating the end of the week. Some had dates. Charlie and Flavio found a corner table where they could talk while they consumed their burgers and beer. As he had done all week, Flavio peppered Charlie with so many tales of Castro's oppression that he was beginning to weaken Charlie's qualms about the assassination.

"To Americans, Castro is just an abstraction someplace far away. But to me, he's a matter of life or death." He pointed to his skinny chest and stared at Charlie. His black hair was cut so short he looked like one of the sergeant's Marines. "Castro executed my uncle. My father managed an exclusive hotel, and he barely got the rest of our family out alive. Today, he works as a clerk in a K-Mart."

Charlie sat in stunned silence and twirled his beer can on the tabletop.

———

Now, IN DC, THEY WOULD find out if the lessons they had learned could be put into practice. Another of Bishop's musclemen Jim Wolsey had planted a bullet trap someplace in the capital. The trap consisted of a plywood box stuffed with rubber mulch which would catch the bullet Charlie intended to fire into it from 150 yards. He needed to do this without being caught by the DC police. If he and Flavio did get caught, they would be jailed for who knew how long before Bishop could spring them. Bishop was supposed to have cleared this exercise with the chief of police, but street cops and desk sergeants wouldn't know about that. The risk of arrest only made the caper more exciting to Charlie. The challenge consumed him so much that he almost forgot that the point of this exercise was training him to kill another human being.

Gordon dropped them off by the Lincoln Memorial. Charlie pretended to be a tourist, dressed in blue jeans, a button-down shirt, and a gray V-necked sweater. Hanging from his neck was a Leica 35-millimeter camera. To complete his masquerade, he had crammed his guitar into a bulky burlap sack and slung it over his shoulder. Also in the sack was the M1 he had broken down into three pieces—the stock, the barrel assembly, and the trigger assembly. No one looking at Charlie would guess that the sack slung over his shoulder contained a deadly rifle.

"What now?" asked Charlie.

"The trap is set up on the Mall on the other side of the Washington Monument," said Flavio, "a mile or more from here.

There's a two-seat Vespa parked over there." He pointed to a blue motor scooter on the far side of the Lincoln Memorial. "I'll drive to the point where I want you to set up for your shot. As you head there, take a break and sit on the ledge of the reflecting pool to change film in the camera. Strum something on that guitar. When witnesses are asked what they saw, we want them to remember a tourist with a guitar, not a gunman with a limp."

"After you cross 14th Street, you'll see a bunch of trees between the edge of the Mall and the place where I'll be parked on Madison Drive in front of the Smithsonian. Pick a spot that gives you some cover from the trees but also gives you an open shot at the trap. When you're finished shooting, walk quickly to the Vespa and hop on behind me. Walk on the toe of your left foot to hide your limp. Remember to walk. Don't run, or you'll draw attention, and it'll be harder to disguise your limp."

As Flavio headed toward the parked Vespa, Charlie pulled on a pair of surgical gloves. He took several photos, starting with one of Flavio getting onto the blue Vespa. Once he was alone, Charlie opened the burlap sack to snap a photo of the M1 rifle. Then he wandered along the Lincoln Memorial Reflecting Pool, snapping photos as he went. He took one of a peace activist passing out leaflets. The young man carried a placard that said SANE, the Committee for a Sane Nuclear Policy. At the end of the pool, Charlie sat on the ledge to strum his guitar, as Flavio had suggested. "This Land is Your Land," might appeal to the SANE activist who was still within earshot. Hearing it, the activist offered to take a picture of Charlie with the Washington Monument in the background.

As he crossed 14th Street, Charlie spotted the Vespa, the clump of trees, and the trap box in the distance on the other side of 12th Street. He was going to have to shoot across 12th Street and hope he could get off a shot between cars.

He picked a spot among the trees that gave him cover but also gave him a clear view of the trap. After glancing around to ensure that nobody was watching, he dropped to the ground and snapped together the three pieces of the rifle. Then he rolled onto his stomach, spread his feet for balance, and rested the barrel of the rifle on its bipod. His toes tapped nervously on the ground; he could easily shoot someone if he failed to fire carefully. He inhaled as he saw a car on 12th Street move into his line of sight. Just as the car passed out of the scope, he exhaled, held his breath for a second, and squeezed the trigger. The rifle jolted against his shoulder, and he returned to normal breathing.

Without a coach peering through binoculars, he had no way to know if he had hit the trap. But nobody near the target scurried around as they would have done if the bullet had ricocheted off the pavement. Just to make sure he had hit the target and Bishop wouldn't force them to go through the exercise a second time, he decided to take a second shot. Again, he had to wait for a car to pass by on 12th Street. He squeezed the trigger and dropped the rifle to the ground.

He limped swiftly to the Vespa, hopped on, and put his arms around Flavio's waist. They headed west on Madison Drive toward 14th Street where Flavio had to stop for a red light. Charlie tapped his toes on the pavement in frustration as they waited, hoping Bob Gordon retrieved the rifle, camera, and guitar before the police arrived. In the distance, a siren wailed as it came their way. A speeding squad car, with its red lights flashing, turned onto Madison Drive and skidded to a stop at the place Flavio and Charlie had vacated a moment earlier. When the traffic signal changed, Flavio drove south on 14th Street, crossed the Potomac, and exited onto a side street where a black sedan waited for them. They let the Vespa fall over as they piled into the sedan.

In the back seat, Charlie's adrenalin rush began to wear off. He slumped, dejected that the cops had shown up so fast. He replayed the scene in his mind. Had he failed to spot an onlooker? Was there a cop nearby who had seen the whole thing? And why had he forgotten to pick up his shell casings? Had someone heard the shots or seen the flash? If so, could Bishop get him a suppressor for the rifle?

Flavio nudged Charlie's arm and said in a voice low enough that the driver could not overhear. "I got someone who wants to see you, Michael."

"Who?"

"His name is Meyer."

"What's he want?"

"I don't know. He just said to meet him at eight tonight at Cecil's Deli and Café on 14th Street in the District."

"No way, amigo. I've got a woman I haven't seen for two weeks. We've got a dinner date. Afterwards, who knows? What can he offer to top that?"

"Meyer is not the kind of guy you want to screw around with, Michael."

"Neither was that sergeant down at Quantico who ran our asses ragged for the last two weeks. But we survived him. If your friend really wants to see me, tell him I'll show up at 9:30 in the morning."

10

Week of August 12, 1962

CECIL'S DELI, DISTRICT OF COLUMBIA

THE MORNING AFTER DOING THE trap shot on the National Mall, Charlie drove into Washington to keep the appointment Flavio had set up for him. He glanced around as he entered the air-conditioned, half-empty deli on 14th Street. A long narrow seating area stretched from the front door to the kitchen in the rear, and an alcove of tables was off to the right. Following Flavio's instructions, he set a dollar bill next to the cash register and said to the counterman, "Meyer asked if you could seat us at the back of that alcove section and not put anybody next to us."

The counterman snatched the dollar and led Charlie back to the corner. He dragged a "Section Closed" sign to the front of the entire alcove. Then he seated Charlie at a table. "Do you want coffee while you wait?"

"Yes," said Charlie, sweeping his eyes around the room. Whoever Meyer was, he obviously carried clout at the deli.

Thirty minutes passed, and Charlie scratched his chin as he pondered the events of the previous two weeks. If it weren't for the threat of his father going to prison, Charlie would have rejected Bishop's proposal at the start. As it was, he felt as though he'd made a deal with the devil—a deal that might be impossible to break.

On top of that, Flavio's repeated tales of woe and oppression were starting to wear down Charlie's moral scruples about carrying out the assassination. When they had been drinking beer at the Officer's Club in Quantico, Charlie had confessed his qualms about the project.

"Forget that, Michael. You're our only hope. Why is plugging that hijo de puta now any more wrong than letting him spend the next fifty years stealing people's property, torturing them, murdering them, and spreading this shit abroad. You're the only one who can stop it."

With this jumble of thoughts drifting through his mind, Charlie spotted a movement outside the front window. A man in a tailored blue business suit and fedora stopped in front of a drugstore across the street. Appearing to be in his sixties, the man lit a cigarette and stared into the drugstore's plate glass window. He appeared to be using it as a mirror to see what was behind him. Finally, he crossed the street, dropped the cigarette into the gutter, and walked into the deli. He was trim, of medium build, and had a thin craggy face. He couldn't have been more than five feet tall. He walked straight to Charlie, who stood to greet him. But the man waved him back down.

Without any excuse for being late, the man said, "Meyer Lansky." He slid into the chair across from Charlie and set his fedora on an empty chair.

Charlie raised his eyebrows.

The man's voice seemed deep for such a small man, and he spoke slowly. "You look surprised."

"Having read about you," said Charlie, "I would have expected someone built more like a linebacker."

"You complaining about my size?" Meyer scowled.

"Not me, Mr. Lansky. I spent most of my childhood pushing back against guys who ragged on me for my limp. So I never knock anybody's appearance."

Meyer's lips curled up in an attempt to smile but didn't quite make it. "You got class, kid. I like that in a young guy. Call me Meyer and tell me what your real name is."

Remembering that Flavio had been the one to set up this meeting and that Flavio didn't know his real name, Charlie said, "Michael."

Meyer sneered. "And I'm the king of England."

Charlie was about to retort that England had a queen, not a king. But one didn't get smart to a guy like Meyer Lansky, so he said in a nervous and stilted voice, "What is it that brings us together?"

Rather than reply, Meyer picked up the menu. "Let's order something before we get down to business."

When Charlie ordered the Reuben sandwich, Meyer commented, "You're going to eat a Reuben at ten o'clock in the morning?"

"Well, they don't have bacon and eggs."

"Bacon and eggs?" snapped Meyer. "It's a Jewish delicatessen, for God's sake. Why would a Jewish deli have bacon?"

The waiter poured coffee for Meyer, picked up the menus, and left the two men alone. Charlie said nothing. His foot, however, tapped nervously on the floor. It was not comforting to have been summoned by the guy who had been the Mafia's point man for gambling in pre-Castro Cuba. And was rumored to have helped run a Mafia operation called Murder Incorporated. Meyer pulled a Tareyton cigarette from a pack in his pocket.

"I don't mean to be inhospitable, Meyer," said Charlie, raising his hand, palm out, "but if you could hold up on that cigarette until we leave, I'd be greatly appreciative. I have a powerful aversion to cigarette smoke." Charlie hoped he had been sufficiently fawning.

Meyer frowned but stuck the cigarette back into its pack and slipped the pack into his pocket.

"So," he said, "last night you were so eager to get laid by your girlfriend that you couldn't come over here to meet me. Instead, you forced me to come out this morning."

Charlie shrugged.

"You made the right choice, kid. If I was a young guy and hadn't seen my girl for two weeks, I'd have done the exact same thing. But you don't want to do that to me twice." Meyer put his right hand over his left fist and cracked his knuckles. "Tell me about this trip to Havana."

"I never said anything about a trip to Havana."

"Your Cuban friend told me."

"I never said that to any Cuban friends."

"You didn't have to. He sees you dragged down to Quantico by some asshole from the CIA. You take a crash course from some asshole Marine on how to become a sniper. You apparently work for army intelligence, and you speak Spanish. You're obviously on your way to shoot that asshole Castro."

There seemed to be a lot of assholes in Meyer's world. But what the hell was wrong with Flavio that he had passed on this information?

"Meyer, I can't tell you anything about what I do. I can't tell anybody. As far as my travels go, the army is always sending me off to different places to do different things. Besides, how does Flavio even know you anyway?"

"So you know him as Flavio, and he knows you as Michael. Fascinating all these code names the CIA comes up with for you guys." Meyer smirked as he shook his head back and forth.

"You were going to tell me how you knew him," said Charlie.

"His father managed a hotel for me, and he got wiped out by Castro. But we keep in touch, and I told him to let me know if he heard about any Americans going down to Cuba. So when he told me about his kid going down there with you, I told him to set up a meeting."

"Flavio's blowing smoke."

Meyer paused as the waiter set their breakfasts on the table, the Reuben for Charlie and a cheese blintz for Meyer. He refilled the coffees. Meyer sliced into the pastry.

"Flavio said that you're a smart ass, and I can see what he meant. Let's cut the crap. You know you're going down there, Flavio knows you're going down there, and I know you're going down there. I need a favor."

"Meyer, how can I make you understand? I get in deep trouble with my bosses if I start telling people what I do or where I go. I can't talk about this."

Meyer paused again, a frown on his thin craggy face.

"Let me try this another way." His deep voice enunciated the words slowly. "Suppose for the sake of the argument that you might be going to this place you can't talk about. Would you do me a favor?"

Charlie grinned involuntarily at Meyer's clever way to get the information out of him. "I've got no reason not to do you a favor, Meyer. It would all depend on what it was, whether it was going to get me into trouble, and whether anybody was going to get hurt."

"Nobody's going to get hurt. Will you just listen for a second so I can give you some background?"

He stared with dull eyes until Charlie nodded his agreement.

"You've got to understand the chaos down there at the end. I put on this huge party to celebrate the success of our casino in the Habana Riviera on New Year's Eve. It was only open to the foreigners and the richest of Cubans. What a beauty, kid! Crystal chandeliers. A magnificent pool that rivaled anything in Vegas. Great cuisine. An elegant cocktail lounge where the hookers could sell their johns a drink before taking them upstairs. Then, that very day, President Batista flees the country, and police services collapse. Mobs of Cubans flood the place. They ransack everything. And I mean ransack. They rip the stuffing out of sofas, smash the mirrors in the gilded frames, piss on the floor, and make off with everything they can carry."

Meyer shook his head back and forth as he stared across the table at Charlie, then continued, "I hang on for another week, hoping that we can strike a deal with Castro. But everyone with any money at all is fleeing because the guy's a communist. Then I hear these stories that he's executing prisoners, and I realize I've got to get out. He's due to arrive in Havana on January ninth, so on the eighth, I pack everything that will fit into my Cadillac and head out to the airport. We got stuck in the worst traffic jam you ever saw. A mile outside the city, everything comes to a complete stop. If we really want to catch that plane at the airport, we're forced to leave our cars and walk with what little we can carry. You never saw so many abandoned Cadillacs in your life, kid. And Lincolns. Mercedes. Even a Rolls. And claiming all these abandoned vehicles are Cubans in rags who are coming out of the woodwork."

Meyer fidgeted in his chair and waved his hands as he told his story

"Damned Latinos are all alike," Meyer growled. "Criminals. They have to steal to subsist. The strangest thing I saw was this Cuban guy pushing a motorcycle he'd stolen—one of those old classic Harleys, a big bright red one. It had a sidecar, and he was just pushing it down the road toward town. It must have run out of gas, and he didn't have the brains to siphon gas from one of the deserted Cadies."

Charlie looked at his watch; he had promised Vanessa he'd be back by noon. "Meyer, is this story leading to something? What's this got to do with the favor you wanted?"

"Hold your horses, kid. All you kids are too impatient. I'm trying to tell you how hectic it was at the end, and why I couldn't get out with all of my possessions."

He sipped his coffee and paused while two women walked past the alcove and out the door. He took a bite of his bagel and continued talking with his mouth full.

"You know that the high rollers get staked for credit. Every now and then, however, they run into a string of bad luck that leaves them without enough cash to pay what they owe. So one night, I'm telling this guy that I don't take IOUs. He spins his wife around, unhooks this strand of pearls from her throat, and hands it to me. It must have cost a thousand dollars. The woman had tears flowing from her eyes. But what could I do? I can't just take his IOU and let him disappear into Houston or Hollywood, where I'd have to spend a fortune sending out somebody to find him. If he'd stiff his own wife, and she was a good looker, why would he not stiff me?" Meyer raised his hands palm up in a sign of helplessness.

"So I dropped the pearls into a five gallon empty gas can I had hidden in my closet that nobody knows about." He paused. "Except you."

Charlie gulped.

"Then somebody else gives me their golden wedding rings. Lots of people give me their wedding rings. And plunk, they're dropped into my jerrycan. Then Rolex watches, earrings, diamond studded tie clasps and cuff links, uncut stones they'd bought from HStern, even gold coins they shouldn't have had, because it's illegal for Americans to own gold. Diamond engagement rings. More diamond rings than you can shake a stick at. They all get dropped into the jerrycan. Then some guy runs into the club to avoid the police. In exchange for my help, he gives me something for the can. Or maybe a hooker finds some jewelry lying around, and I pay her to turn it in. We never steal from anyone, but people who cause an inconvenience have to expect a charge."

"And still nobody knows about the jerrycan," said Charlie.

"Not yet. Not even Jimmy Blue Eyes. But he was bound to find out if I didn't hide it."

"Jimmy Blue Eyes?"

"Yeah. We were like partners. Helped each other out. We worked well together, but I could never escape the feeling that Lucky Luciano had put us together so he could keep an eye on me."

Charlie gulped again. The world of top-ranking gangsters scared him.

"Lucky didn't trust you?"

"Well, he never said so. But the one I had to be careful about wasn't so much Lucky, as Carlo Gambino who ran the Genovese Family and still does. You see, I'm not Italian, and the made men in the families are. I'm useful to them and we work well together. But I'm Jewish, so I'm an outsider."

At the mention of the notorious Carlo Gambino, Charlie struggled for composure. How could this small gregarious grandfather-looking man across the table from him be pals with the mobster believed to be the boss of the bosses in the Mafia? Would helping out Meyer get Charlie caught between rival Mafia families? Equally intriguing was whether there was a rift between the Jewish and the Italian mobsters?

"But Jimmy Blue Eyes is Italian?"

"Yeah. His name is Vincent Alo, but everyone calls him Jimmy Blue Eyes. We got along well together. When I needed something from Lucky or Genovese, Jimmy Blue Eyes could usually get it for me."

"So you hid the jerrycan before Jimmy Blue Eyes could find out about it?"

"Exactly." Meyer grinned. "You're catching on."

"But a jerrycan is not an easy thing to carry around. You hid it all by yourself?"

"No. It was a two-man job. Somebody had to be a lookout while the other guy did the actual work. That was Greasy Thumb Scalio."

"That solves your problem, Meyer. Just get the Miami Cubans to insert Greasy Thumb into Havana so he can empty the jerrycan for you."

"Can't," said Meyer, turning down the corners of his lips in a sad look. "Poor Greasy Thumb loved the outdoors, and he got lost one weekend while he was snowshoeing in the wilderness in the Adirondacks. Somehow, he lost his snowshoes and couldn't make it back to civilization. By the time a rescue party showed up, he was dead."

Charlie felt a shudder in his shoulders but took a deep breath in hopes of seeming relaxed. He wanted to look cool before Meyer, not frightened.

"So you're my last hope, kid. I'm going to show you where the stuff is hidden, and you're going to bring it back with you when you finish off this mysterious assignment you can't talk about. Or better yet, abort this crazy assignment once they get you in so that you can concentrate on locating my jerrycan. You get twenty percent of what's inside it. And that can is holding at least a million dollars' worth of stuff."

Meyer reached into his jacket pocket to pull out a folded piece of paper. Although Charlie strived to appear unflappable, he jumped out of his chair. If Charlie read that paper and learned where Meyer had stashed the jewels, there could be no turning back. As he jumped up, he knocked the chair backwards, and it fell to the floor with a clang.

"Stop, Meyer!" he said too loud. Not quite shouting, but certainly loud enough for the counterman to hear. However, the counterman didn't look up. "This isn't my kind of thing. Get Flavio to do it."

Charlie picked up his chair, reset it at the table, and sat down again.

"You're not listening, kid," said Meyer. "I already told you that Latinos aren't trustworthy. They all steal. Flavio will grab this stuff and disappear into that Miami Cuban community, and I'll never be able to find him or his father."

Then Meyer put on a grandfatherly smile. "You, on the other hand, have a regular job, a Social Security number, an apartment, a girlfriend, and probably some living relatives. You're much more trustworthy."

"Wait, Meyer," said Charlie, pushing his hands out in a stop gesture. "I'm grateful for this generous offer. But I don't want to see that paper. If you open it, I'll walk out the door just so I don't have to look at it. Please do me a favor. Put it back in your pocket for a minute and give me a chance to explain myself."

Meyer's eyebrows narrowed onto the bridge of his nose. "Why are you so scared of a piece of paper?"

"Meyer, look at the logic of the situation from my point of view."

"A guy can go nuts worrying about other peoples' points of view."

"If I see that paper, I'll know where your jerrycan is hidden. If I come back without the jewels, it's only human that you'll think I stole them."

"So what's the problem? You make sure you bring back the jewels. I give you twenty percent. We part company and go on with our lives. What could go wrong?"

"A dozen things could go wrong. Maybe the customs agents find me and take their forty percent or whatever it is, and suddenly your million dollars has dropped to $600,000, minus my cut. Maybe I won't be able to find the jerrycan. Maybe someone else has already found it and emptied it. Maybe I'm only able to carry part of it instead of all of it. Maybe I'm being extracted from Cuba by boat, and the boat capsizes. Maybe someone steals it from me after I find it. Maybe I need to use some of it to buy somebody's help in getting out. Maybe some cop stops me, and I have to flee without it. After all, it's not going to be easy blending into the scenery of Havana if I'm lugging a five-gallon gasoline can. With all the stuff you've got inside, it could weigh 50 pounds."

"Thirty-seven point five."

"You weighed it?"

"Of course. How else am I going to know if I'm getting back the full amount?"

"If I come back empty handed, I could end up like your friend Greasy Thumb."

Meyer scowled. "You got a suspicious mind, kid. I already told you. Greasy Thumb died of exposure to the elements. I had nothing to do with it. If you don't go out skiing in the Adirondacks like he did, nothing will happen to you either."

Charlie was about to point out that Meyer's earlier version had sent Greasy Thumb snowshoeing, in the Adirondacks, not skiing. But he was deterred by the scowl on Meyer's face. They sat staring at each other for a full two minutes before Meyer stood up and walked over to the cash register. He tore a blank page from a pad of waitress order sheets sitting next to the cash register. The page read, "Cecil's Deli and Café."

"You got a pen?" he asked Charlie as he slid back into his seat by the table. Charlie pulled a ballpoint pen from his pocket, and Meyer tapped it against his teeth as he pondered what to write. Slowly, in very small letters, he filled up the backside of the sheet and pushed it across the table for Charlie to read.

August 18, 1962

> *I commission an army lieutenant that I know by the name of Michael to do a very important personal favor for me. As payment he will receive a generous fee. As long as he makes an honest effort to carry out his task, I guarantee that no misfortunes will befall him.*

Meyer Lansky

"You put this note in a sealed envelope and tell your lawyer to release it to the press in case you have any accidents after you get back. This insures you from being hurt by me, because the FBI and the press will be all over me if this note becomes public. I have a powerful interest in not letting that happen."

He tapped the slip of paper with his fingertips.

"In addition, I'm upping your share to thirty percent of whatever you bring back. That only leaves me with seventy. But seventy percent of something is still better than a hundred percent of nothing. From your point of view, as you put it, this is a great deal. You're going to make three hundred thousand dollars. Tax free. Which has to be fifty times more than what the CIA is paying you to try something that's probably going to get you killed."

Charlie was stunned. He mused aloud, mostly to himself, but loud enough that Meyer could hear, "A month ago, I'm sitting around minding my own business, trying to keep my girlfriend happy. Before I know it, I get the CIA on my back. Now I got the Mafia on my back as well."

"Mafia! What are you talking about?"

Meyer snorted and waved his hands in the air.

"There is no such thing as the Mafia. You've been listening too much to that arrogant punk, Bobby Kennedy. It's just you and me and a little side deal. Ask around. You'll find out that I'm a man of my word. I never welsh on deals."

Asking around in Meyer's circle of acquaintances might be even more dangerous than turning him down outright. It might get Charlie an ice pick through the ear, a favorite Mafia method of dealing with troublemakers.

"Meyer, you're very generous. But this stuff is beyond me."

Meyer sat perfectly still for thirty seconds. Charlie's fingers twitched in the silence.

"It's not generosity, kid. It's business. You're going to retrieve my property for me. As long as you don't try to cheat me or siphon off more than your share, you're safe. Your insurance policy is right here." He tapped the note which was still sitting on the tabletop.

Meyer's threat was so obvious about what he would do if he thought he was being cheated that Charlie's head bobbed forward.

"Meyer, my hands are going to be full as it is. If I try to take on this as well, I'm going to screw up everything. Get Flavio to do it. Or Jimmy Blue Eyes. Anybody but me."

He slid the order page across the table and looked up at the older man. Meyer folded the sheet into quarters, wrapped it in a dollar bill, then slowly pushed himself to his feet.

"I have to be someplace soon, kid, so I can't talk with you anymore at the moment. But you're my only hope. All you've got to do before you leave is let me show you where my stuff is hidden. Just think it over, and I'll get back to you in a week or so."

Meyer looked imposing for a man five feet tall.

"In the meantime, finish your sandwich. You haven't even touched it. Here's your insurance policy and a reimbursement for the tip you gave the waiter."

He bent forward to slip the folded piece of paper and the dollar bill into the breast pocket of Charlie's shirt.

"One other thing," he said. "I like the way you wouldn't tell me your name or what you're going to be doing in Cuba. It shows you can keep a secret."

"Before you take off," said Charlie, "what is Flavio's real name?"

"You ask too many questions, kid," he said in his deep slow voice. "Flavio's name is a secret. Just like this conversation is a secret. It never happened. If word gets back to me that you've talked about it to anybody, I will be unhappy. Very, very unhappy."

He straightened up and put his fedora on top his head. "Right now I have to get over to the National Gallery."

Although shaken by the warning, Charlie couldn't help but smile at the idea of Meyer Lansky visiting an art museum. "The National Gallery?"

"Yeah. They've got busts of Homer that they're selling for only $12.50. Get yourself some culture, kid. It'll make your life better."

Charlie smiled as he watched the man leave the deli. Meyer had given Charlie a brilliant idea

11

Week of August 19, 1962

TYSONS CORNER, VIRGINIA

WHEN CHARLIE ENTERED BISHOP'S DINGY Tysons Corner shop Monday morning, Gordon and Wolsey were sitting by the wall, staring vacantly into space. Wolsey, Charlie noted, had ears so big they stuck out like megaphones. Bishop sat at a desk, rolling back and forth over a patch of faded and cracked linoleum, grimacing each time the wheels got stuck. He waved a copy of *The Washington Post* in front of the lieutenant's face the moment he sat down.

> *An unidentified gunman fired two shots on the National Mall Friday afternoon. There were no injuries, and police have no indication of the shooter's motive.*
>
> *Witnesses reported seeing a man walk toward a motor scooter driven by a second man. They headed up Madison Drive to 14th Street and then across the Potomac, where they disappeared. The abandoned scooter was later found by the Alexandria police in a vacant parking lot.*

Washington Police are asking that anybody who witnessed the event call them with any information they may have.

"I know," said Charlie with a glum look. "I screwed up, but I don't know how. I've replayed this in my mind a dozen times, and I still can't recall a single person watching when I set up for my shot. I don't know how anybody saw it."

"Don't be so hard on yourself," Bishop advised. He seemed to relax once Charlie admitted something had gone wrong. He pointed out that Charlie had succeeded in putting both bullets into the trap and gotten away. He, along with Gordon and Wolsey, had been scrutinizing everything Charlie did, and they also hadn't spotted anybody watching. Maybe a cop just drove down 14th Street at the wrong moment. You can't control everything, but in the last analysis, he and Flavio had pulled it off.

"Do you think you're ready for Cuba?" said Bishop.

"I have some questions," said Charlie "Number one is blending in. At Quantico, they stressed that you have to blend into the environment and make yourself invisible. How is a tall, pale guy like me, with a limp, going to blend in as a Cuban?"

"You're not going to. You'll have a cover."

Bishop paused for Charlie to ask about the cover, but Charlie sat and waited.

"You're going to be a newspaper reporter for *The Irish Times* doing stories on the accomplishments of the Castro regime. You'll be one of their stringers."

"What's a stringer?"

"You'll find out next week when you take a crash course on reporting. Then you're off to Dublin to meet your contact. Since he owes us a favor, he was glad to take you on. If he can edit any of your dispatches into something publishable, it'll be a feather in his cap. And as far as your limp goes, it's an asset. Castro's security police won't look twice at a guy with a limp. It will also help with your getaway. As soon as you've finished your job, you'll put on a special pair of shoes we'll make to even out your footsteps. While they're out searching for somebody hobbling around, you'll walk away just like a normal guy."

Charlie snarled. "I've got news for you, Walter. I *am* a normal guy. It's you guys blackmailing people into doing your dirty work who aren't normal."

The CIA agent stayed stone-faced.

"Besides, Walter, my clothes all have American tags. Any cop who looks at them will know I'm not Irish."

"That's why you're going to Dublin first. Your contact there will help you buy an Irish wardrobe."

"However, he won't be able to give me an Irish accent or give me a feel for what it's like to be Irish. How is any of this going to fool the Cubans?"

"Do you really think Castro's goons can recognize an Irish accent? You're going to pose as the great-nephew of an historic Irish revolutionary, and that'll be enough for them. For icing on the cake, while you're in Dublin, wander around the city and gather impressions about places you can mention to the Cubans."

He held out an Irish passport with Charlie's photo but made out in the name of Michael Collins, born in Cork, in 1939. Charlie scowled.

"So you just dreamed up this person and forged a passport?"

"Of course not. He's an actual person born in Cork in 1939. Just in case anybody checks it out, we want it to be authentic. And he was quite willing to let us use his name."

"Let me guess. He owed you a favor."

Bishop chuckled. "Sort of. We paid off a gambling debt for him."

"What if he can't keep his mouth shut? Nobody's going to resist telling his friends that the CIA used his name on a forged passport in exchange for getting his debts paid."

"He thinks it was the Irish Republican Army, the IRA. No Irishman who wants to stay healthy is going to talk about them forging a passport."

"I thought the IRA was dead."

"Just dormant. You worry too much," said Bishop. "Everything is going to work out. Do you know anything about the real Michael Collins?"

"Very little."

"He led the move for Irish Independence forty to fifty years ago. He was tall, just like you. He was so tall, they called him 'the big fellah,' and he practically invented guerrilla warfare. The Cubans are going to love the idea of his great-nephew touting their revolution for a newspaper from a country that gave the finger to the British a long time ago."

"Walter, this is so off-the-wall it doesn't make sense."

"The trap shot probably didn't make sense to you either. But you followed our instructions and pulled it off. Why do you think it won't work this time? We've done this kind of thing before, and it always works."

"If it always works, then why is Castro still alive?"

Bishop pounded his fist on the dingy desk. "Nobody involved in those attempts ever got caught. And you won't be caught either. The big difference is that you're going to succeed. No success, no big reward." He narrowed his eyes. "And if you fuck it up on purpose, you and you father will be in deep shit."

———

BIG REWARD IF I SUCCEED; deep shit if I cop out. Charlie slapped the dashboard of the Corvette as he drove back to his apartment in Arlington County. What an asshole, that Bishop! If in fact his name is Bishop. Charlie pulled off the street into a strip mall parking lot, stopped at a pay phone, and dialed the number of his old office. He asked for Delroy Brown, the trusted platoon sergeant who had served under him at Arlington Hall Station.

"Virginia plate, number A 312 279?" repeated Delroy.

"Yes," said Charlie. "Tell them you're checking a security detail for army intelligence. But don't call my home phone. It's bugged. I'll call you back."

12

Week of September 16, 1962

Rosslyn, Virginia

FOR WEEKS, VANESSA HAD FENDED off Charlie's requests to visit the West Wing. She hadn't opposed the idea at first. Charlie was a good-looking guy, and it might be fun to show him off. But now that she'd slept with the president, she couldn't possibly let Charlie into the West Wing. What would happen if their paths crossed?

The problem was that Charlie kept coming up with new reasons why she should give him a tour. She laughed at the latest scheme he'd concocted. He laid it out for her one night after they had arrived at her apartment in Rosslyn, VA.

"You're telling me," she said, her eyes opening wide, "that because you and the president are both Irish-Catholic, you want to see the West Wing?"

"Yes," he said. "He's our first Irish-Catholic president."

"I've never heard you talk much about being Irish."

"I don't like to brag."

She rolled her eyes. "So far as being Catholic, you haven't gone to Mass during the entire time I've known you."

"So I'm not fanatic about it. What difference does that make? If the president were an Argentine immigrant, wouldn't you want to see the West Wing?"

———

VANESSA DECIDED TO SEEK PERMISSION for Charlie's visit from the most forbidding White House official she could think of. Then when she brought the rejection back to Charlie, he would stop bothering her about it. And as she made her request, Kenneth O'Donnell sat stern-faced at his desk, arms folded across his chest and the president's official portrait on the wall behind him. "By all means." He smiled. "Have Miss Flanagan put him on the list of visitors."

That evening she coached Charlie on the visit. "Wear your uniform," she instructed him. "The president tends to like military officers—as long as they're not generals or admirals."

"I'm going to meet the president?" His eyes widened.

"No! But the president's likes and dislikes filter down to everyone else."

She spread a set of photographs on the kitchen table. "Here are some people you might run into. I want you to recognize them so you'll know who's who. You shouldn't say anything inappropriate to any of them."

"Where'd you get these photos?"

"I borrowed them my first day on the job so I could study them. I wanted to be able to recognize the main people by sight so I didn't make any mistakes. Now this," she said, pointing down, "is my boss, Mr. Sorensen. He goes all the way back to Kennedy's first days in the Senate ten years ago. He writes most of his speeches. Next to his brother, the president trusts him more than anybody else. He's nice, but he's very introverted. So don't start any conversations with him."

"Who can I start conversations with?"

"Nobody." She pointed to a second photo. "This is Mrs. Lincoln. She's also been with him since the Senate. She's loyal, and she's a tough bird. When he decided to run for president, she was recovering from a medical problem, and he wanted to dump her for someone who would have more stamina."

"But he didn't."

"Word is he sent an aide to ask for her resignation. She supposedly replied, 'If he wants me to resign, let him tell me himself.'"

"It appears he didn't do it," said Charlie.

"It's a weird thing," said Vanessa. "He's ruthless at cutting off old friends and old contacts who aren't useful to him anymore. Apparently, there was a big flap last spring when he cut off Frank Sinatra. But he can't personally fire any of his employees."

She pointed to another photo, of a black-haired stern-faced man. "But Kenneth O'Donnell can. So don't do anything to upset him. He's been with the Kennedys ever since he and Bobby went to college together. He pretty much runs the White House."

Charlie pointed at the pile of photos. "Which one is the national security advisor?"

She pulled up the photo showing McGeorge Bundy with a receding hairline and plastic-framed glasses. "You don't want to talk to him either. Even if he starts the conversation."

"Why not?"

"He's arrogant." She turned up her nose. "Your work deals with Latin America, and he has no respect for those of us who are Latinos or those like you who work on Latin America. He once said about people like us, 'Second rate minds deal with second rate problems.'"

"Well," said Charlie, "better I should be a person with a second-rate mind than a person who's a first-rate asshole."

Vanessa stomped her foot on the floor. "Do you see why I don't want you talking to anybody there? If you say something like that to any of these people, I'll be put out on the street the next day."

13

Week of September 16

THE WHITE HOUSE

CHARLIE WORE A FRESHLY PRESSED khaki uniform when he showed up at the West Wing entrance the next morning, his garrison cap folded over his belt. Vanessa walked up to him, looking even more stunning than usual, in a white cashmere sweater and a tight, tweed skirt he had not seen before.

"Don't expect too much," she warned him as she led him into the building. "This is just like any other office. I need to run you by the president's secretary, Mrs. Lincoln, who is a command post for everything that goes on here."

On the way to Mrs. Lincoln's desk, Charlie spotted Tom McGillivray, whom he remembered from the day McGillivray and Bishop had recruited him. McGillivray followed a man Charlie recognized as Ted Sorensen into the Cabinet Room. For a brief second, Charlie and McGillivray locked eyes.

"Is that an Operation Mongoose meeting?" Charlie whispered to Vanessa and pointed to the men going into the Cabinet Room.

Her mouth dropped open in horror. "How did you know that? You're not supposed to know about that."

"It's something my Cubans talk about."

"Well, don't ever say that again," she warned, lowering her voice. "They'll think you got it from me, and I'll be out of a job."

She introduced him to Evelyn Lincoln, but they were interrupted before they could do any more than say hello. A pert, young, redheaded woman came out of the Cabinet Room and told Vanessa that Ted Sorensen needed something from her immediately. "I'll escort your lieutenant to the Fish Room, Vanessa, and keep him company there until you come out."

She took him by the arm and headed away from Lincoln's desk. As they walked, they passed two young women who smiled at Charlie. One said to the other, "Now that's a good-looking boyfriend. If it was me, I would have stuck with him." She spoke just loud enough that Charlie could overhear.

His redheaded escort marched him into the Fish Room and seated him at the end of a long shiny table. A portrait of Franklin Roosevelt hung across from Charlie, a huge grandfather clock stood in a corner, and behind Charlie, a huge sailfish was mounted on the wall. She served them each coffee in a China cup with a small presidential seal. Then, pulling out a chair from the side of the polished table, she sat primly erect.

Troubled by what he had heard, Charlie asked, "What did that girl mean, 'she would have stuck with me?'"

"Oh, dear," said the redhead, her smiled disappearing. "I don't think she meant for you to hear that."

"But I did hear it, and so did you. What did she mean?"

"Lieutenant, please don't put me in the middle of that. It would be better for you to talk with Vanessa."

Charlie's face flushed at the implication of what he had just heard. His eyes hardened as he said, "Who?"

The redhead continued looking Charlie in the eye. But she said nothing.

"Dave Powers?"

She shook her head no.

"Ted Sorensen?"

"Good God, no!" said the woman. "He's so straitlaced, even Marilyn Monroe wouldn't have been able to get a rise out of him. Not even if she had dressed in a tight gown and sung *Happy Birthday* to him."

"Then who?" he demanded, raising his voice again.

"Lieutenant, keep your voice down, and stop badgering me."

But she let her eyes drift back through the entrance to the Fish Room. Charlie followed her gaze out of the Fish Room toward a door to the Oval Office that Vanessa had pointed out earlier.

"Oh my god," he whispered hoarsely. "Get me out of here."

"Wait, Lieutenant. Give her a chance to explain."

"I'd explode if I talked to her right now. Please, just get me out of here."

———

He stopped at a Virginia liquor store on the way home to his apartment. Knowing very little about liquor, he bought a fifth of the only brand he could think of, Jim Beam. He poured a glassful and set it on the end table by his sofa while he went into the bedroom to change from his army uniform to civilian dress. As he finished, the phone rang. It was Bishop.

"What the hell were you doing at the White House? Don't you know you could compromise this whole operation doing something like that? How the hell could a guy as smart as you do something so stupid?"

When Bishop calmed down enough to listen, Charlie explained that his girlfriend had invited him over to show off her new job as

Sorensen's typist.

"She went into the Cabinet Room to check something with Sorensen, and that's when I made eye contact with your pal McGillivray sitting by the windows. But don't worry about it. I won't be going back. We're breaking up."

"Why?"

The phone Charlie held to his ear was starting to annoy him. Standing up while he held the phone annoyed him. And above all, Bishop's voice annoyed him. He snapped into the phone, "Never mind. It's personal."

"Don't be too hasty about breaking up, Charlie. Every relationship has its ups and downs. Give yourself a chance to patch it up. It might be useful for us to have a connection to Sorensen's typist."

"A connection!" Charlie shouted into the phone. "She might have pissed me off, but if you think I'm going to spy on her, forget it."

"All I'm saying is don't do anything rash. You've already got plenty to worry about, and you don't need the distraction of a romantic breakup."

"It's over, Walter."

"Charlie, take the day off, and check in with me at Tysons Corner tomorrow. In the meantime, get it out of your system. Get a bottle of booze and tie one on. Or go to a gym and beat up a punching bag. Just don't do anything hasty."

––––––––

CHARLIE DROVE TWENTY-FIVE MILES INTO the hilly Virginia countryside to the historic Bull Run battlefield. Looking down, pondering his predicament, and sometimes shaking his head, he wandered by the old cannons, the split log fence, and the statue of Stonewall Jackson. He felt a connection to those Union Army soldiers who had been so cocksure and unprepared as they marched into the disaster that Old Stonewall had prepared for them. Charlie had been so preoccupied that Bishop might betray him, he never anticipated a betrayal by Vanessa.

When he got back to his apartment in Arlington, he found her sitting on his sofa, wearing the same white cashmere sweater and tight tweed skirt she had worn in the morning. Her hair was still perfectly coifed, but her turned-down mouth and pinched lips gave her a haggard, haunted look.

"How long have you been here?"

"About an hour. You didn't answer your phone, so I came over." She pointed at the glass of bourbon on the end table. "How long has this been sitting here?"

"All day," Charlie said. He crossed the room and dropped into an easy chair opposite from her.

"Well, if you didn't touch it under these circumstances, I guess I don't have to worry about you becoming alcoholic."

"Alcoholic!" he screamed, lunging forward. "You're screwing that bastard Kennedy, and you think you can judge my drinking habits?"

"Please, Charlie," she pleaded, her face contorted. "I am sorry. I feel so humiliated at the office I might have to quit. And now I'm humiliated in front of you. Please forgive me. I never meant to hurt you. And I don't want to lose you."

"You never meant to hurt me? How could you think that it would not hurt me?"

"I'm sorry, Charlie. It didn't mean anything. I just got intoxicated with the surroundings and everything."

As she shifted on the sofa, her short skirt rose up on her thighs. Charlie's eyes followed the ascent of the hem. She reached back over her shoulders and started to pull up the cashmere sweater.

"Don't," he said.

"Charlie, I feel so bad about this. Please don't make it any worse for me. She finished pulling off the sweater, baring a naked upper body except for a flimsy, lacy bra. She hiked up the skirt and leaned forward to unhook her nylons from their garters. Then she slid the shiny stockings slowly down her legs.

Lying on his back and staring at the ceiling, Charlie reached over to shut off the alarm when it clanged. Vanessa pushed herself to a sitting position and rubbed her eyes.

"Charlie, I have to go home and change clothes for work," she said. "I'll shower at my apartment." She pulled on her clothes and stood for a moment looking back at the bed.

"You have to break if off with him."

She squinted at him. "Don't tell me what I have to do."

"Don't tell me what I have to put up with."

She stepped to the door, but before passing through it, she turned to him. "It will end."

Charlie lay in bed for another half hour after she left. She said she didn't want to lose him. But she had not given a forthright "Yes" about breaking it off. Her "it will end" could mean two or three things. Maybe it meant yes, right now. Maybe it meant next month. Maybe it meant she would hang on until Kennedy grew tired of her. And would she have any reason at all to break it off once Charlie had left the country for Cuba? A trip he hadn't revealed to her yet.

"Fuck," he said to himself as he swung his legs over the side of the bed. He was going to go out and treat himself to breakfast. Fuck Bishop as well. Charlie would show up for work when he felt like it.

Tysons Corner, Virginia

It wasn't until the next morning that Charlie arrived at Bishop's office. "I've been looking over the passport you gave me," he said as he dropped into the creaky chair by Bishop's desk. "Michael Collins has traveled to a lot of places I've never been. Paris. Spain. Prague. Zurich."

"Paris was your jumping off point. It's where you picked up the train for all the other places."

"And Prague?"

"The Cubans will be impressed that you went behind the Iron Curtain to do a complimentary article on restaurants there."

Bishop fished through a file cabinet and pulled out a restaurant review with the byline of Michael Collins. Handing it to Charlie, he said, "We sent this to the Cuban Ministry of Communications to establish your bona fides as a reporter. We had a lot of trouble finding a Czech who would say anything nice about the regime there, so memorize it in case anybody questions you about Prague."

"And Spain?"

"You spent a summer there to improve your Spanish."

"Spain is run by that fascist Franco. Anybody who went there will be a red flag to the communist Cubans."

"Franco declared you persona non grata and kicked you out. That will establish your credibility with Castro."

"Even if all this works, somebody is bound to recognize my accent is American, not Irish."

"How are they going to do that if you're speaking Spanish all the time?"

"That's another problem. I speak Spanish with a Cuban accent. How did I get a Cuban accent if I learned the language in Spain?"

"You didn't learn the language in Spain. Your Spanish instructor in Dublin was Cuban, so that's how you got the Cuban accent. In fact, it was your Cuban accent that made the Spaniards suspicious of you."

Charlie rolled his eyes.

"You worry too much, Charlie. It's good to have a little paranoia in this business, but you overdo it."

"What about my getaway?"

"Your spotter, Flavio, will pick up the M1 at Guantanamo and deliver it to you in Havana. Then you do it the same way you did on the National Mall in Washington. The instant you pull the trigger, you and Flavio take off on a motor scooter, probably a Vespa. It's the perfect getaway vehicle for two guys. It can go into all kinds of alleys and paths that a police car can't follow. He'll drive to you our safe house, which is on a bay west of Havana. There's a guy there named Pepe who will radio us as soon as you show up. We'll have a mother ship cruising well out of Cuban radar range, and as soon as Pepe calls, we'll send a speedboat to pick you up."

"Just like that? No backup plan."

"Just like that. We'll activate a backup plan if we need one."

Charlie felt unnerved by Bishop's lack of interest in a Plan B. But before he could object, Bishop asked, "When can you leave?"

"After the crash course in journalism, I need another week at least, maybe two."

Bishop grimaced.

"If I'm going to have any chance of trapping Castro, I've got to find out as much as I can about his habits. While I'm looking into that, I need a couple of things from you. Get me a flash suppressor for the M1. It might have been the flash from the shot in DC that alerted somebody to call the cops. Then get me another afternoon at the rifle range so I can test out the M1 with the suppressor attached."

"You've got it," said Bishop. "I've lined up all kinds of material on Castro for you to study. That should give you plenty of background."

"Let me see what I can find at Library of Congress first. Then I'll pore through your stuff. See if you can find any psychological profiles you worked up on him and anything showing where he spends his time."

"Lieutenant, you can't drag your heels forever. We're under a lot of pressure from the White House to get moving on this."

"I understand, Walter. But if you want this to succeed, you've got to cut me a little slack. You have to give me time to prepare."

He paused before raising the next issue, which he worried might make Bishop explode.

"There's one final thing I need from you. If I'm going to avoid the mistakes of your previous attempts, I need to know why they failed. You've got to document for me what happened on them."

"Impossible! That's classified information."

"Let's face it, I'm classified information. If you want me to risk my life for you, you've got to let me know why you failed these other times."

Bishop grimaced again. "A lot of the stuff isn't relevant. The Mafia's attempt never got off the ground, and some of the things were just proposals that we never took seriously. Let me see what I can find for you."

———

Leaving Bishop's Tysons Corner shop, Charlie headed into the city. He plugged dimes into a parking meter on a side street just off Independence Avenue, then walked to the magnificent marble and granite Library of Congress building. He felt dwarfed by the immense rotunda of the main reading room, with its ornate decorations, its arched windows, and its statue of Thomas Jefferson looking down on the patrons.

He used the card catalog and the Readers' Guide to Periodical Literature to locate human interest stories about Castro and his top lieutenants. He wrote what he wanted on request slips, brought them to the main desk in the center of the rotunda, and handed them to a woman with salt and pepper hair pulled back into a tight bun. Then he waited while she disappeared into the stacks and came back with a cartload of materials.

He spread the materials on a large reading table and scanned them for any items of human interest that could suggest a way to ambush Fidel Castro. When he finished with his first batch of materials, he returned to the main desk with a second set of requests. By 4:30, his shoulders ached from spending so much time bent over the table, and he left the building. A parking ticket stood prominently under the windshield wiper of his car.

He jammed the ticket into the glove compartment and headed out to Virginia for the town of Vienna, stopping on the way to pick up a burger and a cola. On Patrick Street in Vienna, he parked unobtrusively under a spreading maple tree where he could watch the entrance to a red brick apartment building. This was the address that his former sergeant, Delroy Brown, had found for Bishop's auto license number. As the sun began to set, Charlie sat munching his burger while watching the entrance. At 7:00, Bishop's blue Pontiac turned into the parking lot and parked in front of the entrance. Pretty modest wheels and digs for a mid-level bureaucrat. Whether this information about Bishop's living arrangements would prove useful, Charlie didn't know. He did know, however, that it couldn't hurt.

————

THE NEXT MORNING, HE WALKED up the magnificent steps to the library again. He started with the *New York Times Index*, and the clerk brought little rectangular microfilm boxes of the newspaper dating back to January of 1959, when Castro came to power. Inserting each spool of film into a microfilm reader, he turned a crank that advanced him day by day through the pages stored on the spool of microfilm.

Although he had learned a lot about Castro from his interviews of Cuban refugees and his reading of Cuban newspapers, that research had focused on political issues. His current look into Castro's personal life showed a much different picture. He loved scuba diving, which would make an excellent locale for a rifle shot, if Charlie could get advance information on where and when Castro would scuba dive. He was also crazy about baseball and fancied himself as a pitcher. But there'd be too many people on a baseball field to risk shooting him there.

Trapping him in bed would be difficult because he moved from one sleeping place in Havana to another precisely to deter assassination. He had a prodigious desire for female companionship and took different lovers throughout the week. At the beginning of his reign, the Habana Libre would have been an ideal site, because Castro went there every day. One could hide in a closet, wait for him to be alone, plug him, and sneak down the stairs before anyone found out what had happened. These days, however, Castro went there so sporadically that this approach would be impossible.

At 4:00, Charlie rubbed his eyes. He stuck a dime in a pay phone in the lobby and called Bishop's number. He wasn't in. Charlie left a message with his secretary that he would show up at the Tysons Corner office the next morning to go through whatever materials Bishop had found for him. "If you have any copies of *El Mundo*, have Walter bring those with him as well."

He leaned on the pay phone, musing over another thought that had been bothering him for days. Bishop had a plan for extracting Charlie from Cuba. But if that plan failed for whatever reason, there was no backup plan

He pulled another dime from his pocket and phoned his friend Sergeant Delroy Brown at Arlington Hall Station. Delroy might be able to help find another piece of information.

14

Week of September 23, 1962

Baltimore, Maryland

FOLLOWING THE DIRECTIONS FROM DELROY Brown, Charlie drove down a treeless Baltimore Street lined with dirty brick row houses. He pulled to a stop in front of the building with the number Delroy had given him. Three tough-looking teens stared at him from a stoop across the street where they were lounging. Charlie scuffed his feet nervously on the floorboards before he pushed open the car door and stepped over a pile of garbage at the curb.

A thin, black youth answered the door. "You the dude that wants to learn how to hotwire a car?"

Charlie nodded.

The young man held out his hand. "Twenty bucks."

Charlie handed him a ten. "You can have the rest when we're done."

They got into Charlie's car. The teens across the street hadn't bothered it. The man put a small tool kit on the floor by his feet.

"Go to the gas station on the corner first," said Charlie's passenger. "We need to buy a little gas and an old battery, if they've got one. After that, we go to the junkyard where we can practice without any cops poking their noses in."

He smoothed his hand along the dashboard. "Nice little Vette you've got here." He smiled. "Pricey?"

"I bought it used. They're a lot more affordable that way."

That was the extent of their conversation until they pulled up to a battered 1949 Ford in the junkyard. A key was in the ignition switch, but they had to hook up the battery that they had bought at the gas station. Charlie's new acquaintance turned the ignition key to make sure that the engine worked, then turned it off as soon as it started.

"Now, here's what you do." He sprawled lengthwise on the front seat, stuck his head under the dashboard, and pulled down a set of wires behind the ignition switch. Using a wire stripper, he cut two of the wires and stripped half an inch of insulation off the ends.

"How do I know which of those wires to cut?" asked Charlie.

Lying on his back with his head under the dash, the young man focused on Charlie. "Pick the one you think is coming from the battery and the one you think is going to the dashboard lights. What you're doing is bypassing the switch and sending juice directly to the dash lights. Watch."

He twisted the two wires together, and the dashboard lights came on. Pulling a third wire from behind the ignition switch, he stripped the insulation from it as he had done for the others. He looked back at Charlie with a conspiratorial grin.

"Now watch what happens when we touch the wire of this starter to the hot wires."

With his left hand, he touched it to the other wires. The engine turned over, he pumped the gas pedal with his free hand, and the motor began to idle. He scrambled back to a sitting position.

"That's all there is to it." He grinned. "Carry the battery over to that old Plymouth over there, and we'll see if you can do it."

As Charlie lifted the battery up to a spot where they could connect it, a dribble of acid spilled onto the blue slacks he wore. He got behind the steering wheel, and his companion pulled a screwdriver and a mallet from his tool kit. "Before you get started, let me show you an easier way that works sometimes." He jammed the blade of the screwdriver against the key slot of the ignition switch and slammed the mallet against the screwdriver, pushing the blade into the key slot. After three strikes of the hammer, he twisted the screwdriver to the right, and the engine jumped to life.

"Doesn't always work," he said, grinning. "But if it does, you save yourself a bit of precious time."

He pulled the screwdriver from the key slot and motioned for Charlie to duck his head under the dashboard. "Now let's see if you can do it the traditional way."

When they returned to his Corvette, Charlie handed over the other ten-dollar bill, and added a five. "You're a great teacher, my man. The public schools should have people who teach as well as you do."

Charlie grinned with elation. He now had the means to acquire a getaway car in Havana. But if Bishop's extraction plans failed, Charlie might also need a boat.

"But suppose it was a speedboat rather than a car that I needed to hotwire. How would I do that?"

"I don't know, man. The same way, I guess."

———

Dropping off the hotwire teacher at his row house, Charlie headed to Baltimore Harbor. The safe house in Havana was on a bay, Bishop had said. Maybe there would be a marina there where he could borrow a boat in case Bishop's plan fell through. He parked by the entrance to a boat dealer, calculating that he would be viewed as a serious potential customer by anyone seeing him step out of the shiny sports car. He strolled the yard and ran his hands along the smooth fiberglass exterior of a model with an inboard motor.

A salesman introduced himself and leaned on the boat. "What would the gas mileage be on this boat?" asked Charlie, letting his left hand drop down to hide the holes that had been burned into his blue slacks by the battery acid.

"On boats, we use gallons per hour, not miles per gallon."

"Well how many gallons per hour would this boat take?"

The salesman glanced at the placard next to the boat. "Let's see, a 200-horsepower boat. You'd get twenty gallons per hour at top speed. Maybe fifteen at cruising speed."

"How many hours would it take this boat to go 125 miles?" Havana to Key West was only 110 miles, but it would be prudent to build in a margin of error.

"Between four and six, depending on the sea and the wind and how fast you're going."

Charlie thanked him. The salesman stared at the three one-inch holes on the front of Charlie's slacks.

To be safe, Charlie would need 120 gallons of gas. Twenty-four five-gallon cans. He scanned the seating area of the boat. Maybe it could hold that many cans. But where would he get them in Havana?

15

Week of September 30, 1962

THE WHITE HOUSE

THE PRESIDENT'S SPECIAL ASSISTANT, DAVE Powers, came on the line when Vanessa picked up her jangling phone. "I need you to bring an envelope up to the Executive Residence."

Her pulse quickened, but she was wary. Her previous meetings with Kennedy in the family quarters had provoked a fight with Charlie in which they'd ended up snapping about what each one could and couldn't do. If it hadn't been for Dave guiding her up there the first time, she might never have slept with the president, and the rift with Charlie might never have occurred. Was it part of Dave's job to find women for Kennedy? "Oh, Dave. I'm not so sure that's a good idea just now."

"Jack says he needs that envelope, and you're the only one available. Just come over and pick it up. In ten minutes, you'll be back at your desk."

———

HER SHOULDERS TENSED AS SHE entered the family quarters on the second floor. Then she relaxed when she saw that the president was not waiting for her in his bedroom but was sitting at a desk in the West Sitting Hall. Over his shoulder was the elegant half-moon window with its valance curtains. Looming behind the window was the gray-stone Old Executive Office Building that Vanessa found depressing. She agreed with Mark Twain who once called it "the ugliest building in America." Kennedy motioned for her to take a seat on the couch by the window, while he pulled two one-page memos from the envelope she had handed him. He penciled a comment on one of the memos and set it on the coffee table.

"Did you really read it that fast?"

"You just saw me do it," he said, flashing a broad smile. "With the volume of stuff that comes through here, a person has to move fast to keep up. You should take a course in speed reading."

He sank into the couch next to her, and their hips touched. "How is your new job going? Is Ted treating you okay?"

"Mr. Sorensen is very businesslike," she said, flattered that the president knew she was no longer a mere intern. "But basically, he's nice. He's very nice."

Kennedy chuckled. "He is stern, to be sure, and he'll never be the life of the party. But he's solid. And loyal."

There was a moment of silence, and her pulse quickened as he inched closer. She hadn't come up here wanting to do this. But if she rebuffed him now, would she get another chance? And if she kept it secret from Charlie, would it really cause any harm? It was only a moment of pleasure with a handsome, charming guy. He undid the top button of her blouse, and she didn't back away. Instead, she lifted her hand to the back of his neck.

————

WHILE KENNEDY EXCUSED HIMSELF TO use the bathroom, Vanessa began putting on her clothes. Her eye caught the two memos sitting on the coffee table. They were irresistible. She reached for them. The first was from CIA Director John McCone and the second from Roger Hilsman, the head of state department intelligence. McCone insisted that we needed to determine if the Russians were indeed putting nuclear missiles in Cuba. He urged the president to restart flights of the high-flying U-2 surveillance plane over island. Hilsman argued against restarting the U-2 flights so soon. Up until now, the Russians had never installed nuclear missiles outside of eastern Europe, and the sites being built in Cuba were defensive anti-aircraft weapons.

At the top of Hilsman's memo, Kennedy had penciled in. "Ted, draft a persuasive statement for holding off the decision a little longer. One that will expose that nut Keating as an alarmist." It took Vanessa a moment to recall the senator from New York who claimed Kennedy was being naïve about the Russians.

The bathroom door clicked as Kennedy emerged fully dressed and let the door swing shut behind him. She slid the papers back onto the coffee table, but not before he saw her. Flustered, she pulled on her blouse and slip, leaving her underclothes exposed on the pillow.

"I'm sorry," she said, blushing. "I shouldn't have looked at them. I certainly won't say anything to anyone."

Kennedy pointed to the memos. "Since you're typing for Ted, you'll find out soon enough. So no harm done."

She felt awkward, standing half-dressed. In a comparable situation with anybody else she would have commented on the issue at hand, but Kennedy never discussed policy with her. She was in a compartment of his life that was separate from everything else. Nonetheless, the memos were jarring.

"It's very scary. It's a hard decision for you."

He gave her an enigmatic grin, then frowned. In a self-revealing moment she'd never seen before, he said, "All the decisions that come up here are hard. The easy ones get made down below."

He began pacing the floor and talking, as much to himself as to her. She felt as though she had simply become a sounding board for his reflections.

"What doesn't happen down below, or doesn't happen well enough, is anticipation of the consequences. When we went into the Bay of Pigs last year, none of those high-paid specialists at the CIA anticipated the disaster that resulted. Neither did the generals and admirals at the Pentagon. The consequences of a miscalculation now are much greater than they were at the Bay of Pigs. We temporarily suspended the U-2 flights in exchange for the Russians agreeing not to put any offensive weapons in Cuba or start trouble elsewhere, at least not until after the election."

He stopped pacing and looked over at her, where she still stood between the couch and coffee table. He clicked his fingernails against his teeth, a gesture she had noted before.

"If we restart the flights too soon, they will probably try to push us out of Berlin. We will then have to react to that, or our NATO alliance will go down the drain."

Vanessa nervously shifted her feet as she realized how easily a war could erupt out of all this. She also felt awkward and unable to help as she watched him. He clearly wasn't asking her advice.

"We're strong enough here that we could bomb everything they've got in Cuba, and there's nothing they could do to stop us. But we've gotten ourselves into a bind in Germany. For the past decade we've fallen behind on conventional weapons in favor of nuclear arms. They give us 'a bigger bang for the buck,' claimed Ike's defense secretary. But today it puts us in a bind. If the Russians invade West Berlin, our only effective response is nuclear. And who wants to start a nuclear war?"

Then, as quickly as he had delved into the issue of the U-2 flights, he changed the subject. "Are you okay?" he asked. "You look a little drawn. Are we all right?"

This was her chance to tell him about the trouble he was creating for her romance with Charlie. Instead, she said, "It's this U-2 business. It makes me nervous."

"Good," he smiled. "I'd worry about anyone who wasn't nervous about it." He put the memos back in their envelope and handed it to her. "Give this to Ted and tell him to draft something for me."

"With all respect, Mr. President, it might be a little embarrassing for me to bring this directly from here to Mr. Sorensen. Could you ask Mrs. Lincoln to do it?"

"Of course," he said. "I don't want to cause you any embarrassment."

———

VANESSA'S FEAR OF EMBARRASSMENT TOOK a backseat to the flurry of activity in following days. Kennedy's dispute with Keating erupted in the television news. And she had to admit to herself that the white-haired and distinguished Keating certainly looked impressive when he stood on the Senate Floor to complain that the White House was failing to counter Russian aggression in Cuba.

"In August alone," Keating claimed, "Soviet vessels unloaded 1,200 Russian troops and 5 torpedo boats at the Port of Mariel."-

Kennedy was fuming at Keating's speech the next time Vanessa saw him. He charged that the numbers had been leaked to Keating by the CIA to pressure the White House into restarting the U-2 flights. "I'm going to get those bastards," he told Vanessa.

However, he still refused to restart the surveillance flights. Then Keating raised the ante. He charged that the Soviets were installing missile launchers on the island that could sling a nuclear warhead well into the U.S.

Vanessa didn't believe Kennedy could continue to ignore the Soviet buildup. He needed hard intelligence on the issue of the missiles. Yet she didn't hear of any action until a week after October 9, when she finally received word that he had ordered the resumption of U-2 flights over Cuba.

Tyson Corner, Virginia

Charlie slapped the Castro dossier down onto Bishop's desk. "This is going to be harder than I thought, Walter."

He leaned back in his chair and stared at the peeling paint on the ceiling of the Tysons Corner office. Bishop looked up from a book of crossword puzzles. The Castro file Charlie was reading was classified material that Bishop would not permit Charlie to read unsupervised. So while Charlie had spent the previous three days searching for patterns to Castro's movements, Bishop sat at his desk with little to do. At the beginning he used the time to catch up on paperwork. Then he leafed through magazines and newspaper articles strewn around the room. Today, he worked crossword puzzles.

"All I need," said Charlie, "is some pattern to the places Castro visits on a regular basis. Then I can scout them out to find one that gives me a clean shot with the best concealment. I wait there and zap el líder máximo when he shows up."

"El líder máximo?"

"That's what his toadies call him. But, Walter, I'm finding nothing helpful about his patterns. First I spend two days at the Library of Congress poring through *The New York Times* and news magazines. Then I spend the rest of the week looking at your stuff. And there's nothing. Nothing. Zilch. Nada! Nada! Nada!"

Bishop shook his head impatiently but said nothing.

"I thought maybe I could hide out where he goes home every night, but he never goes to the same bed twice in a row. He seems to spend more time sleeping in cars on his way to meetings than he does sleeping in a house."

Charlie picked up one of the dossiers, eyed it blankly for an instant, then dropped it back on the table.

"Most men go back to the same one or two women where they would be easy prey for an ambush, but this guy is like a rabbit. He just bangs whoever is available. The only long-term affair you've discovered is the one he had with that woman Marita, and one of you tried to get her to poison him. Whose bright idea was that?" He looked sharply at Bishop.

Bishop frowned. "Don't be so snarky," he said.

Charlie rolled his eyes. "She hid the poison capsules in her cold-cream jar, so she could pop them into his mouth after he fell asleep. By that time, however, the pills melted, so she couldn't use them. She concocted an idiotic story about confessing to Fidel that she had been set up to poison him. But she loved him so much that she just couldn't go through with it. So Fidel, behaved like a starry-eyed teenager, made love to her, and let her walk away scot-free."

He pointed at Bishop. "And you guys believed that? This guy who executed hundreds of people suddenly got misty-eyed and let his intended assassin go free because she had been such a wonderful piece of ass?

Bishop rose and began to pace the floor. "Jesus Christ, Lieutenant, have some patience. Nailing down a guy like Castro isn't as simple as getting a date to the spring prom."

Lieutenant? Yes, he was definitely getting on the man's nerves. Whenever Bishop got annoyed with Charlie, that's when he called him, lieutenant. Charlie smirked as Bishop stepped in front of him and stared him down.

Bishop huffed. "I have to go take a leak."

As Bishop headed to the restroom at the rear of the office, Charlie ripped two pages from the report on Marita and stuffed them in his pocket. He returned the report to the middle of the pile of documents that would go back to CIA headquarters.

When Bishop returned, Charlie picked up with his complaints. "So then I looked for a headquarters where Castro conducts his business, and that's as helter-skelter as his love life. One day he went to the Havana Hilton, or the Habana Libre as they call it now. Then he inspected the underground bunker they're building for him. Then he visited the Russians at their el Chico headquarters. Or he thought up a brilliant idea, so he headed to the newspaper Revolucíon to get it on page one. Or he inspected troop sites, Anna Betancourt schools, or anti-aircraft batteries." He sneered at Bishop. "With that huge budget you've got, couldn't you hire anybody capable of finding someplace where this guy stays put on a regular basis?"

"So what's your plan?"

"Maybe the Russian headquarters at el Chico, depending on how far the perimeter fence is from Punto Uno. That's where Castro stays when he's there. I could just stake out there for a few days and wait for him to show up. It would be nice if you had some mole who could tip me off on when he's headed out there, but you don't seem to have such a mole."

"Maybe Flavio could find that out."

"No!" shouted Charlie, remembering that Flavio had blabbed to Meyer Lansky earlier. "Flavio's a spotter, not a mole. He needs to get the rifle to me, escort me to the safe house when it's all done, and signal you to send in that boat to get us the hell out of there. If he goes around asking questions about Castro's whereabouts, he's going to get us in trouble."

———

As CHARLIE DROVE AWAY FROM his meeting with Bishop, he grew increasingly worried. Too many pieces of Bishop's plan were questionable. He had no backup extraction plan. He was too willing to use the talkative Flavio as a mole. He held a naïve belief that the Cubans could easily be fooled about Charlie's English and Spanish accents. It was hard to believe that an agency as competent as the CIA could be so slipshod.

Maybe it wasn't the agency that was slipshod; maybe it was just Bishop. Maybe he did not have the approval from the highest levels of government he claimed. Maybe this was a rogue operation. Charlie would be the perfect pawn in such a game. If he succeeded in bumping off Castro, Bishop would become a hero in the agency. If Charlie failed and got picked up by Cuban security forces, Bishop could deny he knew anything about it. Charlie would be hung out to dry in the Cuban justice system. Hell, even if he managed to escape

Cuba, he could be hung out to dry in the American justice system.

Charlie pulled his car to the curb as he pondered what to do. This was the perfect out he'd been waiting for. If Bishop was running a rogue operation, he had no ability to follow through on his blackmail threats. Charlie could blow the whistle on him. Unless Bishop could demonstrate that he did indeed have authority from the highest levels of government, Charlie was going to abort this whole operation. He could hardly wait to take this up with Bishop.

16

FALLS CHURCH, VIRGINIA

CHARLIE WANTED TO HOLD HIS confrontation with Bishop in a setting other than Bishop's office. He didn't want to worry about being recorded, having somebody else sit in, or being put in the subordinate position of sitting in a side chair looking at Bishop behind his desk. He needed a meeting place that provided privacy and neutralized Bishop's advantages. He scouted out bars, cafés, and pizza parlors in the Tysons Corner area of Arlington. He poked his head into several establishments and finally settled on a bar and grill with a long narrow dining room and an isolated booth at the rear. He used the pay phone to call Bishop.

"I need your input on something, Walter. Could you meet me for a bite to eat after you get off work?"

"I'm booked all night.

"How about lunch tomorrow? Angelo's Bar and Grill òn Chain Bridge Road right before you get to Tysons Corner."

Bishop sounded annoyed. "A bar? All this time I've been hanging out with you, and you've never had so much as a beer. Now you want to meet me in a bar?"

"All the time you've known me? We just met a month ago."

"Doesn't matter. We'll talk when you come in tomorrow morning."

"I've got a big dental appointment that's going to take up the morning. Just meet me at Angelo's for lunch. I'll pay for the pizza."

CHARLIE ARRIVED EARLY AT ANGELO's. He headed to the back booth and ordered a Coke. Remembering something he'd learned from Meyer Lansky, he offered the waiter a dollar to keep customers out of the neighboring tables.

Bishop slid into the dimly lit booth. Spotting Charlie's empty glass, he signaled the waiter and said, "I'll get us a couple of drinks. What do you want?"

"Just a Coke."

"If you want to fit in where you're going, you'd better get used to something a little stronger than Coke."

"Okay," said Charlie. "Pick something."

They sat without talking until the waiter came back with two martinis. Charlie took a sip and made a face. "No wonder I never developed a taste for gin."

After the waiter left, Bishop asked, "What's so important that you had to drag me out to this dump."

"Let's suppose I'm able to zap Castro like you want, and let's suppose you do get me out of Cuba afterward. Or suppose you fail to get me out, but I manage to get out anyway." He paused to see Bishop's reaction to the implication that Charlie might have his own getaway plan. But Bishop remained stony faced. "There's still another problem. Every left-wing journalist in the country will be talking to every Cuban in Miami, including Flavio, trying to find out who did it."

"You don't trust Flavio?"

Charlie took another sip of his martini, managing not to grimace this time. Bishop said nothing more and let his own drink sit on the Formica tabletop while he waited for Charlie to continue.

"If what I'm doing is just a rogue operation cooked up by you and McGillivray without any higher authorization, I'm in deep trouble. I could end up in prison."

"I've already told you that this has been approved by the highest level of government. What more do you want?"

"Some documentation of that."

Bishop slapped his hand down on the tabletop. "Jesus Christ, Parnell! Why don't you just ask us to phone it in to the *New York Times*?"

Bishop held up his hands. "I don't run this agency, Lieutenant. I only manage one little operation. Nobody would ever allow me to give you written authorization for this. Here's the best I can do. I'll see if I can get my boss to talk to you. He's the CIA liaison to the Bobby Kennedy committee that oversees Operation Mongoose."

"What's his name?"

"Let me see if he'll talk to you first. Then we'll tell you his name. I'm going to use that phone on the wall over there."

Bishop slunk over to a pay phone next to the men's room, stuck coins into the slot, and turned to face the dirty wall while he talked, as though someone might read his lips if he looked back into the room. The conversation took five minutes. Bishop strolled back to the booth but didn't sit down. "Bad luck."

"He won't see me?"

"Yeah, he'll see you. I tried to get you in tomorrow morning. But he wants to see you right now. Ride in my car with me. It'll be easier to get through the gate in my car. Afterwards, I'll get a driver to take you back here."

"So why is this bad luck?"

"Let's just say he's a morning person."

LANGLEY, VIRGINIA

"THIS GUY IS LEGENDARY INSIDE the Company," said Bishop as he drove out the picturesque, tree-lined George Washington Memorial Parkway toward Langley. "Kennedy called him 'our James Bond.'"

"High praise. What did he do?"

"High praise, if that's what he meant it to be. The trouble with Kennedy is that you never know when he's being sincere or sarcastic."

Charlie laughed, and Bishop asked, "What's so funny?"

"You guys worrying whether somebody else is sincere."

Bishop clammed up, and they rode in silence until he turned onto Dolly Madison Boulevard.

Charlie said, "You were going to tell me how he became a legend."

"He put the finger on a mole in British Intelligence who was passing our stuff on to the Soviets, a guy by the name of Kim Philby. The Brits couldn't find enough proof to prosecute him as a spy, but they did sack him from his job. Getting rid of a Soviet mole in itself was enough to make his career." Bishop beamed with apparent pride, as he turned his eyes toward Charlie. "All your bitching about CIA screw-ups; here was a concrete success. A couple of years later, he had an even bigger success. He dug a five-hundred-yard tunnel into the Russian sector of Berlin and tapped into a communication cable of the Russian army. Took the Russians a couple of years to discover the tap, and in the meantime, we got a heads up on all their plans. The only reason I can tell you about it is that it isn't active anymore. Hell, if it was still active, it would be so *top-secret* that I wouldn't know about it myself."

"Okay, I've got that. But what's his connection to Castro?"

"He interfaces with Operation Mongoose and heads a program

we call ZR/Rifle, which is responsible for our executive action operations."

What the hell does executive action mean? Charlie asked himself. But he refused to give Bishop the pleasure of explaining it to him.

They turned off the parkway and passed through the security gate. Bishop parked a short walk from a concrete canopy floating on slender legs, abutting on a white seven-story building. They stepped over a CIA seal in the glossy stone floor in the lobby to a desk where Bishop got Charlie a visitor's pass.

He led Charlie to an office overlooking an inner courtyard, but the office was plain, with a standard-issue gray metal desk and hardback chairs. The office seemed much too modest for a man who had been so highly praised by the president.

Nor, to Charlie's eye, did the occupant fit the image of James Bond. He was squat and balding with bags under his eyes. He held a lit cigarette between yellowed fingers, and several cigarette butts were stubbed out in an ashtray on his desk. The stale smell of cigarettes hung on him, along with the smell of alcohol.

"Charlie, meet Bill Harvey," said Bishop, as he directed Charlie to a hardback chair in front of Harvey's desk.

"So, you're the nervous Nelly who wants to see authorization for your assignment?"

He had a slight slur to his speech. Shocked by the man's coarse bluntness, Charlie couldn't think of a good reply. He muttered, "Yes, sir."

Harvey glanced at Bishop, who stood off to the side, beneath the official portrait of the president. "Have you explained to him what we do in ZR/Rifle?"

"No, Bill," said Bishop.

"Let me lay it out for you," he told Charlie, giving him a stern look before pulling two sheets of paper from a file cabinet behind his desk. "Look at this."

He waved the first paper in front of Charlie. "This is from a presidential memo dated November 3, 1961. It lays out the objective of Operation Mongoose as helping 'the people of Cuba overthrow the Communist regime.' Take a look at it."

He handed the paper to Charlie. When Charlie finished reading it, Harvey took it back and waved the second paper in front of him. "This is the agenda for a policy meeting of the Mongoose committee that took place this past August 14 at 14:00 hours in the office of General Edward Lansdale, the operational director of Mongoose. You will see that it makes me responsible for 'liquidation of leaders.'" Harvey paused, as if to emphasis the term liquidation.

Charlie felt very uneasy, but he stiffened his back to keep from squirming in the chair. Harvey actually seemed proud of being responsible for liquidating people. He handed the paper to Charlie.

"I am taking the extraordinary measure of letting you see this," said Harvey to Charlie. "But you cannot take notes on it."

I don't need notes, thought Charlie, handing the paper back to Harvey. I've memorized the date and the key phrase.

"Does that satisfy you?" asked Harvey, sarcastically.

"Partially. It doesn't actually say that the president himself authorized Castro's assassination."

Harvey banged his desk, hitting it so hard that the ashtray jumped. He inhaled and exhaled slowly in order to speak calmly. "Lieutenant! Don't start splitting hairs like those Kennedy fags. No president is going to leave a paper trail on this. But you've seen the clear directive on Operation Mongoose stationery that puts me in charge of liquidations. Remember, Mongoose is chaired by that fucking Bobby. And nobody is closer to the president than Bobby."

Nobody said anything for a full minute. Then Harvey addressed Charlie in a very soft and solemn voice. "Lieutenant, you are taking on a very important task that might—no, probably will—prevent a nuclear attack on the United States. We will get you in and get you out. It's up to you to figure out where and when to do it. You're a brave man, and you're being asked to do a job that nobody else can do right now. We appreciate that. But don't be a hero. Just take a good clean shot, and then get to that safe house so our man can radio us to come and pick you up."

With that, Harvey turned back toward the file cabinet to return the two documents to their folders. Bishop's eyes followed Harvey's movements, leaving Charlie unobserved for an instant. He reached onto the desk for a small memo pad with the heading, "From the desk of Bill Harvey," tore off the top pages, and slipped them into his pocket.

Bishop guided Charlie out of the office. "I'm going to get you a ride back to your car."

"Kennedy fags. That fucking Bobby. Splitting hairs. Is he always like this?" asked Charlie.

"Only after lunch," said Bishop.

"And you expect me to take orders from a guy who's half drunk in the middle of the afternoon."

Bishop scowled and jabbed his finger at Charlie's face. "You take orders from me, Lieutenant. And you've seen the authorization for them. So cut the bullshit, now."

17

Week of September 30, 1962

Havana, Cuba

"**N**ADA!" MUMBLED MAJOR ESCALANTE, HIS hands clenched in frustration as he stared at the single sheet of flimsy paper on his desktop, a paper bearing the letterhead of the Russian el Chico command post. The major had come up with nothing in his search of Cuban intelligence records for information on Michael Collins. The only Michael Collins they could find was an Irish revolutionary from forty years earlier. So, Escalante had followed up by asking the Russians to search their records for something. Anything! But they, too, had come up with nothing—nada.

But what did nada mean in this case? Did it mean that the Russians actually possessed nothing about the man? Or did it mean they found nothing that they would share?

The Russians were nearly as difficult as the Americans. They dressed almost as badly as Cuban peasants, certainly more shabbily than Americans or Western Europeans. They refused to learn Spanish, and so he had to talk with them through interpreters. They smelled bad, according to the prostitutes. And they bitched about everything: the heat, the humidity, the bugs, the snakes, the food. If it weren't for all those weapons they were bringing in, Escalante believed they should all go home.

Most annoying to Escalante at the moment, the Russians could tell him nothing about this Irish reporter. But the major had to find out something. He was, after all, Castro's security chief, and so far, he had not found a single lead to follow up on, aside from the report from his spy in Miami that the CIA was planning to send another assassin to Cuba. In the absence of other information, Michael Collins was his main suspect.

He phoned the office of Isabel Fernandez to find out if she had any news yet on the reporter's arrival. He grimaced when told that she had stepped out. So he left a message in the most commanding tone possible that Señorita Fernandez should call him immediately.

Escalante wanted Isabel by his side as Collins passed through customs. Not that he expected Collins to be packing a murder weapon. No professional assassin would be dumb enough to try that. However, what you find in a man's pockets can tell a lot about him. Any American coins, for example, or any clothing tags from stores in the United States, would be dead giveaways. Conducting this search would slow down the process enough to make Collins sweat, and it was useful to observe how people act when they are nervous. He also wanted Isabel Fernandez to observe Collins at that moment, so that he could gauge her reactions. She might spot something suspicious that the major failed to see. Then she could go meet him as he came through immigration, put a big smile on that skinny but not-unattractive face, and pleasantly escort him to his hotel. Escalante would assign a car and driver to her for that purpose.

Following his phone call to Fernandez, Escalante summoned his administrative aide, Sergeant Ramos. He asked Ramos to contact their Miami spy and order him to redouble his efforts to find out if any of the Miami Cubans had heard anything new about assassination attempts.

ARLINGTON, VIRGINIA

HAVING GOTTEN NOWHERE IN HIS attempt to find out that Bishop was running a rogue operation, Charlie feared that he would become the fall guy if the operation went bad. He needed to act on the idea he had picked up from Meyer Lansky two weeks earlier. Lansky had written out what he had called an insurance policy that would protect Charlie from retribution in case anything went wrong. He needed something like that to protect himself from Harvey and Bishop.

Accordingly, Charlie spent the next few days compiling twelve-inch manila envelopes of materials. When he finished, he drove his Corvette to a Peoples Drugstore and entered the phone booth. He stuck a dime in the slot and dialed a Boston number. After it rang ten times, he hung up and slipped the coins back into his pocket. An hour later, he tried calling the same number from a different phone, but still, no one picked up. Finally, at eight p.m., someone answered.

"Louis, it's Charlie."

"Charlie, my man. It's been a long time. How'd you get my number."

"Your mother gave it to me. She sounded good."

"She's doing well. I miss those times when you'd come over and we'd jam together. You still playing that trumpet?"

"Not really. I switched to the guitar; it's more versatile. Look Louis, I need to buy some insurance."

Louis laughed. "Insurance? You got the wrong guy, Charlie. I'm in medical school, not business school."

"You can handle this. I'm going to be gone for a few weeks, and I need someone to hold something for me. Could you do that for me? For old times' sake."

"What is it?"

"Just a fat envelope. The army's got me doing something a little risky, and I need some insurance in case anything goes wrong. What I'd like is for you to put it in a safe-deposit box. Then, once a week, you're going to get a postcard from the places I'm visiting."

"A postcard?" said Louis. "Where are you going?"

"I can't tell you yet. The postcards won't be addressed to you, but they will be forwarded to you by someone else."

"Who?"

"I don't know, yet. Probably somebody in Ireland, and I will be signing the postcards with the name Michael Collins. If a month passes without a new postcard arriving from Michael Collins, hop on the shuttle to New York and bring the envelope to Tad Sulz who is a reporter at the *New York Times* for Latin America. If he is out of town, give it to his editor. I'll include enough cash with the envelopes to cover your costs."

"This sounds spooky. What are you up to?"

"I can't tell you that yet; I'll fill you in when I get back. Will you do this for me?"

"Of course, Charlie. Drop it in the mail. But you're worrying me."

"Don't worry. You're safe. Nobody knows about you."

"It's your safety I'm worrying about, not mine."

"The best way you can protect my safety is to do what I'm asking."

———

CHARLIE HOPED IT WOULD BE as easy to bring Vanessa on board as it had been with Louis. After all, Louis was his oldest friend, one of the survivors of that teenage moment Bishop was using to blackmail him. With Vanessa, he wasn't sure where he stood anymore. Her affair with Kennedy had thrown a huge monkey wrench into their relationship. Nonetheless, she would be a perfect person to hold the documents.

They went to a movie. She wanted to see *To Kill a Mockingbird*, which, she said, was going to become a classic. But Charlie insisted on something less heavy. They settled on *The Music Man* playing at the Old Town Theater in Alexandria, an art deco establishment not far from her apartment in Rosslyn. In his two-seater Corvette, after the movie, he sat behind the steering wheel without starting the engine.

"Let's go, Charlie," she said.

"We have to talk about something first."

"We can talk when we get to my apartment. We can relax and talk over a glass of wine."

"No. We have to talk here, just in case your apartment is bugged."

Her head jerked up. "Why would anybody bug my apartment?"

"Partly because you're working for Sorensen now, and that makes you interesting to both the CIA and the FBI. But mostly because you're close to me, and my apartment is bugged. I'm going to be dispatched abroad for a few weeks, and I need your help on something. Your job with Sorensen puts you in an ideal position to help me."

Since he worked in army intelligence, she was used to him travelling on temporary duty assignments. But she gasped when he mentioned a danger of being trapped overseas with no way to get home. "Where are you going, and why can't get you back safely?"

"I'm not free to tell you that."

"I understand that you can't tell me everything you do in army intelligence, just like I can't tell you everything I do for Mr. Sorensen. But this is different. You want me to use my position with Sorensen to pull you out of danger. Think of it from his point of view. How is he going to help you if I can't tell him where you are, why you're there, who put you there, and why they can't get you back? It's not going to work this way, Charlie."

She had backed him into a corner, and he had to tell her something. Swearing her to secrecy, he acknowledged that he was being sent to Cuba masquerading as a newspaper reporter from

Ireland. While there, he would assess the Soviet presence in the country. Although this was not an outright lie, he failed to mention that his true assignment was to kill Castro. If she knew that, he thought, she would drop him on the spot. She would probably jump out of the car immediately and look for a taxi.

He handed her a sheet of paper. "These are the phone numbers and the home address for my CIA control officer who goes by the name Walter Bishop. That's probably a code name, and they might deny they have anybody there by that name. But if you insist that it's about Cuba, the missiles, and Michael Collins, they'll put somebody on the phone. You'll know it's Bishop if he can tell you something about me that he could only know if he knew me personally. The color of my eyes, whether I'm left- or right-handed, which leg I limp on, or anything else you can think of. This guy is a dangerous snake, so don't go anywhere near his home."

"If you don't want me to go there, why are you giving me the address?"

"In case you ever need it for whatever reason."

"Isn't it unusual for a spook to tell you where he lives?"

"He didn't tell me. I pulled in some favors at Arlington Hall Station to get it. Let me tell you what he looks like. If you see anybody like this, run in the other direction."

He spent a minute giving her a description of Bishop. His height, his muscular build, his squat appearance, his horn-rimmed glasses, and his drab Pontiac sedan

"You mentioned a Michael Collins. Who's he?"

"That will be me when I get to Cuba." He showed her his Irish passport.

She shook her head in dismay.

"Bishop also has a few CIA sidekicks. One is Tom McGillivray. He was in that meeting with you in the Cabinet Room the day you showed me around your offices. You can find out his real name by looking over the roster of people who showed up for that meeting."

She squirmed.

"If anything happens to me, these are the guys you have to lean on to get me back safe and sound."

"And how am I going to lean on these super spooks who don't even have real names?"

He reached into a box in the space behind the car seats and pulled out two envelopes. "These are your leaning tools." He gave her slightly different instructions from the ones he had given to Louis. "Put the first envelope in your safe-deposit box. Don't read it. Just put it in there for safe keeping in case you need it."

"How will I know if I need it?"

"When I get to Ireland, I will find somebody to relay a postcard from Michael Collins to you. I will send them to him in a par avion envelope so that they will go out fast, and he will forward them to you in a different par avion envelope. As long as these postcards keep coming, you will know I'm safe. But if a month passes without you receiving one, you will know that I'm in trouble, and Bishop needs to do something to get me out."

He paused. "At that point, make an anonymous call to his office and threaten to give this envelope to *The Washington Post* if he doesn't deliver me to the West Wing gate at the White House. They will do anything you ask of them."

"Why?"

He shook the packages. "I can't tell you the details until I get back. But Bishop and McGillivray and some others have a powerful incentive not to let these documents become public. They will do anything you ask in order to keep the *Washington Post* from finding out about this."

"If they'll do anything, they might decide to bump me off."

"They can't. Bumping off a presidential staffer would cause a scandal that would blow the entire CIA out of the water. Since Lincoln's time, nobody has ever tried to assassinate a presidential aide."

He added, "This is also where the second envelope gives you added protection. If Bishop shows up, tell him that you have put this second envelope someplace in the West Wing where it will get immediately delivered to your boss, Ted Sorensen if, for whatever reason, you don't show up for work the next day. That will scare Bishop almost as much as *The Washington Post* finding out about it. If Sorensen hears about the plot, he will have to cancel it to keep the White House from losing plausible deniability. For that reason, Sorensen will stop the plan and ship the perpetrators to CIA oblivion, wherever that is."

She looked skeptical.

"You are in the safest position of anyone involved in this whole story."

"What's to stop Bishop from grabbing you now and torturing you so that he gets the envelopes back before you leave."

"He doesn't know about them yet. I won't tell him about them until the last minute, right before I'm ready to board my plane."

They sat quietly in the dark car, barely illuminated by a dim street light overhead.

Finally, she responded, "Charlie, this is horrible. How did you get involved in this?"

He paused, not wanting to admit the full truth. "I was blackmailed."

Then he turned the ignition key to start the engine. As he pulled from the darkened King Street parking spot to the brightly lit Jefferson Davis Highway, she angrily slapped the two envelopes on her lap. "I'll take these, Charlie. But if this guy Bishop shows up with his goons, don't expect me to be a hero."

The bad feelings over the envelopes carried into the evening. Vanessa told him that she needed to be alone for awhile. At the door, she gave him a wan smile and just a peck of a kiss. "I'm sorry for being so bitchy. Those envelopes have blown my anxiety off the charts. Let me come by to fetch you in the morning and maybe we can go to the Farmer's Market or something."

————

At nine the next morning, Charlie was putting away his breakfast dishes when someone rapped on the door of his apartment. Vanessa must have had a big change of heart to show up so early. He limped over to the door to unlatch the deadbolt and let her in.

It was Meyer Lansky.

18

Week of September 30, 1962

ARLINGTON, VIRGINIA

CHARLIE SWUNG THE DOOR WIDE open for Meyer. "Come in," he sighed. "I'll get you a coffee. Then let's go sit at the picnic table outside."

"Your apartment's bugged?"

"I think so," said Charlie.

Once they reached the picnic table, Meyer lit a Tareyton cigarette and inhaled a deep breath of tobacco smoke.

"How the hell did you find out my name and where I live?" said Charlie.

"Easy. When you left Cecil's Deli, I followed you to your car and copied down your license number. You really need to do a better job of looking over your shoulder."

Meyer took a long drag on the Tareyton. "Well, have you decided to help me?"

"Do I have a choice?"

"You've always got a choice, kid. I never hurt anybody just because they can't do business with me."

He took another puff of the cigarette and blew out a stream of smoke. "Of course, I do have a long memory, just in case the guy displeases me down the road."

While staring Charlie in the eye, he set an envelope on the picnic table. "This is a map showing you exactly where the can is stashed. You can study it later. After you've memorized it, destroy it." He paused. "When you get there, just go to the Colón Cemetery. You're gonna like this place, kid. It's got to be the classiest cemetery I've ever seen."

"When I think of classy, I don't think of cemeteries."

"You will with this one. When you get there, look for the tomb of Dolf Luque."

"You put the jewels in his grave?"

"No. He's too prominent. Too many people stopping by to see it. Luque was a great baseball player, and you know how the Cubans love their baseball. They called him the Pride of Havana. When I was young, I once went to Ebbetts Field to see him play for the Brooklyn Dodgers. He was going downhill by then, but he still pitched a complete game. Damned near pitched a shutout."

"But the jerrycan's not in his grave?" Charlie tried to get Meyer back to the subject.

"No. Walk around Luque's tomb until you find the tomb for Alfonso Martínez. The map will show you where it is." He pointed toward the envelope he had set on the picnic table. "Martínez was prominent enough that I don't have to worry about him being disinterred."

Noting the puzzled look on Charlie's face, Meyer explained. "This cemetery is so crowded with graves that they have to dig up old graves to make way for the new ones. So when you bump off el líder máximo, they'll have to dig up somebody else's grave to make room for him. Locate Dolf Luque's grave and then look around for a tomb that looks like a big casket with a couple of stone slabs on the top. That will be Martínez's tomb. Push the first slab aside, and underneath it, you'll find the jerrycan."

"Move a big heavy slab of stone? How am I going to do that?"

"Kid, if I could do it, you certainly can do it."

"Meyer, you put a million dollars' worth of jewels right out in the open where anybody can find them?" Charlie raised his eyebrows. "And you did this in broad daylight?"

"I did it at night. You want to do your part at night, too. Somebody sees you walking out of that cemetery with two heavy medicine bags, they'll get suspicious."

"Medicine bags? You said you put them in a jerrycan."

"The jerrycan's too cumbersome. Empty half of the jewels into this bag." He raised up a black bag of the type that doctors carried. "And the other half into this one. With one bag in each hand you'll be balanced, and they'll be a lot easier to carry than the jerrycan." Meyer smiled at his ingenuity.

"And how am I going to smuggle two medicine bags into Cuba?"

"You're not going to smuggle them," said Meyer, with a coy grin. "Use your imagination. Put your clothes in these bags and use them for suitcases. That way, everybody who sees you will think you're a doctor on his way to see a patient, and they'll treat you with kid gloves."

Charlie had to smile at Meyer's ingenuity. He opened one of the bags to peer into it and then turned it upside down to look at the bottom.

"I'll take them," he said. "But they've got 'Made in America' stamped on the bottoms and my cover has me coming from some other country. So I'll replace them with medicine bags from that country."

"And what country is that?" Meyer asked.

"That, I'm not free to tell you."

Meyer raised his hands as if to say he understood.

"But Meyer, you have to remember that it has been four years since you stashed the jerrycan in that tomb. It might not be there anymore. If it isn't, you're going to think I'm the one who stole it."

"I already wrote out your insurance policy, kid. All you can do is try. And if I don't see any big changes in your lifestyle when you get back, I'll take you at your word. But if you all of a sudden trade in your little Corvette for a Mercedes or you buy yourself a big house out in Chevy Chase, that's going to make me suspicious."

He turned his head to the side and blew a smoke ring. It drifted away in the breeze. "There's another thing we got to talk about. How do you plan to get out of Cuba?"

"My handlers have a plan for that. So my problem won't be getting out as much as it will be keeping them from nosing around in the medicine bags. Even though it's none of their business if I happened to find a million dollars' worth of jewelry in a cemetery, they certainly will spend a lot of time asking me about it during my debriefing. And if that happens, you won't get your share very quickly. Worse, if they force me to go through customs, the government will take its cut, meaning that both of our shares are going to be a lot smaller than what we thought."

"You need an escape plan that sidesteps your handlers. Not only will they fuck around with my jewels; they might also decide to drop you in the ocean just so they don't have to worry about you ever talking about what you did for them. And with you out of the way, my jewels are gone forever. Find some way to signal me, and I'll hire a team of Miami Cubans to pick you up in a speedboat."

As Meyer said that, the image of Greasy Thumb Scalio freezing to death in the Adirondacks popped into Charlie's head, and he shivered.

"You don't trust me, do you?" said Meyer, evidently having spotted the shiver. "I never should have told you about Greasy Thumb Scalio. It feeds right into that suspicious mind of yours. How many times do I have to tell you that he just had an unfortunate accident that had nothing to do with me? If he hadn't gone snowmobiling in subzero temperatures in the wilderness, he'd have been perfectly okay."

Meyer's head bobbed back and forth as he said this, as though the physical gesture would convince Charlie of Meyer's sincerity. But Charlie recalled that Meyer's first rendition of Greasy Thumb's escapade had him snowshoeing in the Adirondacks. The second rendition had him skiing. And this one had him snowmobiling. Did Meyer have a bad memory? Or was he sending Charlie a message?

"Even if I do trust you, Meyer, I can't trust the Cubans. You told me that yourself. If my handlers would dump me overboard to shut me up, the Cubans would certainly dump me overboard to get the jewels in those medicine bags. Even if you came along to watch over things, they would dump you overboard as well."

They were quiet for a moment until Charlie said, "But using those the medicine bags is a great idea. How do I contact you when I get home?"

"Call Cecil's Deli and ask for David. He's the counterman. Give him your phone number and say the words 'Washington Senators.' Nothing else—just 'Washington Senators.' Then wait for David to call you back and tell you what to do."

"Wouldn't it be simpler if I just called you directly and you indicated a place for us to meet?"

"Do that only as a last resort. The FBI spends so much time eavesdropping on my phone it's a wonder they've got any time left to chase real criminals. They'll pick up everything we say."

He slid the envelope with the map across the table to Charlie.

"But here's what I'd like to see you do, kid. Make a getaway plan of your own. Then scrap this crazy business of trying to shoot Castro. Not that I mind somebody rubbing out that son-of-a-bitch. He deserves it. But if Castro gets shot, the whole Cuban army will be on a manhunt, meaning that you probably won't escape. If you don't get away, I don't get my jewels. So once they get you into Cuba, just concentrate on finding the jewels, and let those CIA bastards find somebody else to do their dirty work."

"I can't do that, Meyer. They've got me by the balls."

———

CHARLIE RETURNED TO HIS APARTMENT while Meyer stayed behind to finish off another cigarette. Moments later, a key turned in the apartment's door lock, and Vanessa came in.

"Charlie, the strangest thing just happened. I'm parking my car in the shade across the parking lot, and this ugly little man is sitting at the picnic table smoking a cigarette. He says, 'Good morning, Vanessa,' just like he knows me, and then he gets up and walks away without saying anything else."

"Well, if you see him again, run in the opposite direction."

———

THE NEXT MORNING—SUNDAY—CHARLIE SKIPPED CHURCH for about the hundredth consecutive time and lay in bed with Vanessa. At noon, she left to attend a Sunday afternoon dinner with her parents. "This is a family tradition," she said, but she did not invite him to come along. He took advantage of the free time to check on flights to Miami. He was in luck. A plane would leave Washington National Airport at 6:30 the next morning and arrive in Miami at nine o'clock. He needed an hour to pick up a rental car and drive about forty miles southwest to the city of Homestead where he needed another few hours to conduct his business. That left him plenty of time to catch the four o'clock flight back home. By the time he got back to Virginia, the rush hour would be over. With any luck, Bishop wouldn't even notice he'd been gone.

———

TO AVOID ANY TAILS BISHOP might have put on him, Charlie made several abrupt turns as he drove out the next morning. Once he was confident he was not being followed, he headed straight to Washington National Airport.

It took longer to get out of the Miami airport than he had expected. Consequently, it was eleven in the morning by the time he arrived at the First National Bank of Homestead on Krome Ave. An assistant banker helped him fill out the forms to open up a safe-deposit box.

"Which size box do you want, sir," asked the banker.

"One large enough to hold these," said Charlie, holding up the black medicine bags Meyer Lansky had left behind.

"I think you will need two boxes, sir."

Into one of the safe-deposit boxes, Charlie stashed $500 in ten-dollar bills along with photocopies of his passport and the official army orders assigning him to Bishop's CIA unit. He slipped the safe-deposit box keys along with his Virginia driver's license into a small white envelope, signed his name where the flap seals against the envelope, and put Scotch tape over his signature. He put that envelope inside a larger manila envelope and did the same thing, signing it and sealing the signature over with Scotch tape. Nobody could possibly open either envelope without marring his signature and thus letting him know that someone had looked inside.

He headed to Cantina Latina, a bar and grill outside of the Homestead Air Force Base. In his previous job with army intelligence, Charlie had frequently visited the air base to interview Cuban immigrants. He had treated so many of them at the Cantina Latina that he had become friends with the owner, a Mexican American named Eduardo Delgado. Eduardo's cantina somehow managed to serve people of different ethnic backgrounds without running afoul of Florida's segregation statutes. How he pulled that off was a mystery to Charlie. But it made the cantina an ideal place for Charlie to bring those of his refugees whose black and Hispanic appearances would get them barred from other restaurants.

"Hola, Charlie," said Eduardo, as Charlie took a seat at the bar. "It's been a long time. What brings you back? Another batch of refugees you need to interrogate?"

"I never told you I did anything like that," said Charlie.

"You didn't have to. Every time you come down here, a new batch of Cubans shows up." Eduardo laughed.

"I missed breakfast this morning and I'm starving. Could I get a coffee and some of your huevos rancheros? Then I need you to tell me about your charming wife and those handsome sons of yours. And I need a favor."

Once served, Charlie dipped a piece of toast in the egg yolk and savored the taste. He needed to make these for Vanessa sometime.

"What is this favor you need?" asked Eduardo.

Charlie handed Eduardo the envelope containing his drivers' license and the keys to his safe-deposit boxes.

"I need you to hold this for me until I come back to get them. Don't let anyone open them. In fact, put them in your safe so that they don't get lost. Can you do that for me?"

"Por supuesto," said Eduardo. "I'll do that right now."

19

Week of September 30, 1962

DULLES INTERNATIONAL AIRPORT

AN HOUR BEFORE BOARDING HIS flight to Dublin, Charlie marched to a secluded pay phone in the futuristic looking Dulles International Airport, not far from Langley. After almost two months of being manipulated by Walter Bishop, Charlie was about to turn the tables. He rubbed his hands together as he imagined the indignation Bishop would show at the news.

When he heard about the documents Charlie had hidden away, Bishop shouted into the phone, "You conniving bastard! You're blackmailing us."

"Blackmail is such a harsh word, Walter. Think of it as insurance that you get me back safe and sound. Once I'm back and you've set me up on Wall Street, I'll destroy those documents."

"Who's holding them?"

"You'll never know, and you'll never find out."

"That girl who's been two-timing you with Kennedy?"

Charlie kept his voice calm. "Give me credit for a having a few braincells, Walter. She'd be the first person you'd suspect, so I'd be a fool to give them to her. They're someplace else."

"I have people who can pry that information out of you."

"It's too, late, Walter. I'm just about to board my plane for Dublin. Besides, if you arrange for someone in Ireland to beat it out of me, you'll leave me half dead and incapable of doing the job you want. The Irish police will find my fake Irish passport, and they'll be pissed. Once again, you'll have an international incident on your hands. You'll have to go back to Bobby and admit to another screw up."

"That would be better than your publicizing the documents."

"You're not listening! I have no intention of publicizing them. Other than assuring me that you're actually going to bring me back home, the documents are no good to me. If they became public, no reputable person would hire me for anything, much less a Wall Street job. You, on the other hand, would probably go to prison. So just get me back safely so we can both put this behind us."

———

As the stewardess on the Boeing 707 set a dinner on the small tray hanging from the seat in front of him, Charlie realized how cramped he was going to feel on the overnight flight. He should have flown first class, especially since Bishop was covering the expenses. He declined the offer of a drink from the stewardess and leaned back in his seat to ponder what was happening.

He was delighted that he had been able to get help from his trusted friend Louis, but he felt guilty about roping in Vanessa. She would almost certainly be visited by Bishop's goons. Even though she was tough and smart, they would scare her out of her wits. Hell, they'd scare anybody out of their wits. But they could not cause her any physical harm. Bishop needed secrecy, not a news story about a CIA assault on a White House aide. In fact, things would work out okay even if she just gave the documents to Bishop. He would see how dangerous they were to him, and he would realize that Charlie had probably hidden another set with somebody else. Bishop could not risk letting any misfortune befall either Charlie or Vanessa.

He drifted off to sleep, and when he awoke, the sun was rising. His ears began to pop as the 707 started its descent.

DUBLIN, IRELAND

CHARLIE STROLLED ALONG DUBLIN's COBBLED streets. The damp air helped clear his mind as he walked away from the *Irish Times*, where he had met his contact. The man appeared edgy about the task that Bishop had given him. He showed none of the Irish charm or warmth that Charlie had expected. When Charlie asked for help picking out some Irish clothes, the contact simply directed him to Clerys Department Store and sighed with apparent relief as Charlie headed off in that direction. Bishop had apparently paid the guy enough to be helpful but not enough for him to relish his job.

In contrast to his taciturn *Irish Times* contact, Charlie found a gem when he wandered into Trinity College to seek out a guitar teacher. Séamus McDonald was a graying and rotund sixty-five-year-old widower who looked like Santa Claus without the red suit. He wore rumpled gray flannel pants and a traditional hand-knit pullover sweater.

"Séamus, I'm familiar with music, and I've played the guitar for six years now. But I need help on some Irish songs, especially singing them with an Irish accent. I'd be glad to pay fifty dollars if you could give me lessons each day for the next week."

"What songs did you have in mind?"

"Well, 'Kevin Barry,' certainly, and 'Minstrel Boy,' plus any others you can think of."

"Let's start with 'Kevin Barry,' sure. Can you come back at half-three?"

So Séamus spent an hour each afternoon that week showing Charlie how to strum those songs and sing them with an Irish accent. "No! No! Michael," he nagged Charlie. "Not 'Early on a Sunday morning.' It's 'Aharly on a Sunday mornin'.' Dubliners tend to drop the final g."

At the conclusion of the first lesson, Séamus led Charlie to a nearby pub for a pint of Guinness Stout. Charlie would have preferred a Coke, but he did not want to offend the older man. With his wife passed away, Séamus was happy to kill an hour of loneliness by telling Charlie the story of his life.

The next day he led Charlie up O'Connell Street, the city's main thoroughfare, which had served as a focal point for so many battles in Ireland's long struggle for independence. The rain had stopped, and the clouds parted. Séamus looked up at the clear sky and commented. "It's a grand day, sure. That sun feels good."

He pointed out Nelson's Pillar, the towering monument to the great British admiral. "This is an insult to every self-respectin' patriot," said Séamus, giving the finger to the statue. "One of these days we will get rid of it."

He showed more enthusiasm toward the statue of Charles Stuart Parnell and the General Post Office, which had been a focal point of the 1916 Easter Rebellion. As Bishop had instructed him, Charlie tucked these pieces of information into the back of his mind so he would have something specifically Irish to talk about once he got to Cuba.

Dragging Charlie into the Abbey Theatre, Séamus cajoled him into buying tickets to a production of Séan O'Casey's famous play about Irish Independence—*Shadow of a Gunman*. The next day they strolled in the other direction to St. Stephen's Green and stopped in the Horseshoe Bar at the Shelbourne Hotel. They sat quietly in a leather booth, as a waiter set their pints of Guinness on a glass top table.

"A bit pricey here," said Séamus, lifting his glass to toast Charlie. "But I had to show it to you. This is where your namesake, Michael Collins, drafted the Irish constitution. 'Tis a great name your parents gave you, Michael. And I know you're proud to be named for the Big Fellah."

He went on to give Charlie more details about the big fellah's role in Irish independence than Charlie could keep straight. Out of curiosity, he asked, "What did Michael Collins do after independence? Did he become prime minister or what?"

The older man squinted and frowned. "You don't know?"

Charlie shook his head.

"I should think your Da would have told ya."

Charlie didn't reply.

"He was assassinated," said Séamus. "Shot by a gunman."

The answer to his question stunned Charlie, and for a moment they sat in silence. He stared out over the elegant horseshoe-shaped bar, skeptical that what he was learning from Séamus would persuade Cuban police that he was indeed from Dublin. Any tourist could talk about statues, an elegant hotel, and a long dead revolutionary. If he wanted to give a convincing imitation of being Irish, he needed to know something about their day-to-day life.

"Séamus," he said, "there's something else I need to know. What's it like for the average guy here in Dublin? His wife and their kids? All of Dublin can't be as shiny and polished as this place."

Séamus twirled his half-empty beer glass on the tabletop as he stared quizzically at Charlie. Then he stood up. "Come," he said, stepping around the table toward the door. He led Charlie to a bus stop, where they climbed to the top of a double-decker bus heading up to O'Connell Street. One of the springs must have been sagging, because the rear of the bus tilted to the left. Several passengers made the sign of the cross when they passed a church. As they crossed the River Liffey, Charlie spotted an abandoned shopping cart and other debris in the muck by the side of the river. The river smelled bad. Finally, reaching the other side of the river, Séamus led them off the bus and east toward Montgomery Street.

"So it's the gritty side of Dublin you want to see," he said, stopping and pointing at a dirty brick building. This is a Christian Brothers Industrial School for Boys."

"What's so gritty about a school for boys? It seems like an admirable thing to have."

"Several years ago, my nephew spent eighteen months in this school, after he was caught takin' a loaf of bread from the Gresham Hotel. His weight dropped by a stone."

"A stone? How much is that in pounds?"

"Fourteen."

Charlie whistled.

"He lost weight, because the bigger boys bullied the smaller ones for their food. He was beaten on a regular basis by the staff, and he said he was sexually assaulted by one of the brothers. Raped, he was. And nobody believed him. Today he's afraid of his own shadow. He only works at pick-up jobs, and what little money he makes he spends on Guinness or Jameson. There are dozens of industrial schools in Ireland, and Lord knows how many lives they've destroyed."

"Séamus," said Charlie, grimacing. "I am so sorry to hear that. I don't know what to say."

"There's nothin' you can say, my boy."

Séamus led him up the street to another dirty brick building.

"This area used to be called the Monto. It was the center of prostitution until after independence. The British army barracks were right down the street, and they provided overwhelmin' demand for prostitutes."

"And this was a brothel?" asked Charlie, pointing at the building.

"No, this is a Magdalene Laundry. It is where wayward girls were originally put. This one is run by the Sisters of Mercy, and today it houses not only prostitutes, but unwed mothers, their children, and orphaned girls."

"So the sisters are helping these girls get their lives back in order."

Séamus looked up into Charlie's eyes and frowned.

"The girls provide grindin' labor for free so that the Sisters of Mercy can make a profit. Like the boys at the industrial schools, the girls here are poorly fed, beaten, and practically imprisoned. Unlike the boys, they don't get out for a long time. We think that some of them are imprisoned here for their entire lives."

Charlie's mind flitted from the nephew of Séamus being raped to the busload of passengers he had seen making the sign of a cross as they passed by a church. He started to ask why those devout, church going people failed to put an end to the abuse of children in the Magdalene laundries and the industrial schools. But he remembered something that happened now and then in his dealings with Cubans when he would criticize some injustice in their social circles. They often responded with a blistering criticism of the treatment of Negroes in America. Although Charlie agreed with that criticism, he did not want to get sidetracked into a discussion of it with Séamus. Instead, he asked, "Why do they name it Magdalene Laundry?"

Séamus, without smiling, looked up at Charlie. "Mary Magdalene was history's most famous prostitute."

They were going to love this story in Cuba, Charlie thought. At least they would if they're true communists and want to believe the worst of capitalist countries. But whether they did or they didn't, the story would reinforce his cover as an Irish reporter enchanted with the Cuban Revolution.

After his guitar lesson the next day, Charlie pulled Séamus to a bench outside the room where Trinity College kept its historic *Book of Kells*. This was one of the first treasures that Séamus had shown to Charlie. It was a painstaking illustration of the gospels done by monks a thousand years earlier. Charlie's eye caught an image of Mary, the mother of Jesus, in a flowing blue and white robe.

"Séamus, I need to hire someone to do something for me. It'd be worth a hundred dollars if you would do it."

Séamus's eyes lit up. "What is this assignment that is worth so much?"

"It's not an assignment, just a very important favor."

He pulled two postcards from his guitar case. "I will mail these to you when I get where I am going. They will come in a par avion envelope so that they'll get to you fast. Throw out that envelope, put the cards in these two envelopes, and mail them." He handed Séamus one airmail envelope addressed to Vanessa in Virginia and a second addressed to Louis in Boston.

"I will send you two post cards like this once a week. Here are several pre-addressed envelopes for you to put them in. We can go to that historic post office you showed me and buy postage stamps. But I have to stress how important it is that you send these out as soon as you get them."

Charlie paused and stared Séamus in the eye for an instant. "If you don't get them out on time, all hell will break loose."

"Michael, you're startin' to worry me. What are you up to?"

"Séamus I can't tell you that yet. You'll have to wait until I get back. As long as you follow these instructions, nothing can be traced to you, so you're safe. And there's nothing illegal in what you are doing. However, I desperately need your assistance. Will you help me on this?"

"And what is the point of all this subterfuge?"

"The people who sent me to Dublin are now sending me off to another place. These post cards are my insurance policy that they will bring me back home. When I no longer need them, I'll send you a telegram telling you to stop. But until you get that telegram, keep sending out these postcards as soon as you get them."

"And where is this place where my postcards will come from?"

"I can't tell you yet."

Séamus laughed. His fat cheeks shook. "Michael, the envelope you send me will have a post mark on it. You can't keep it a secret, so you might as well tell me now."

A woman in high heels walked past them as they sat on the bench, her heels clicking on the floor. Charlie had to wait for her to pass before talking again.

"Cuba."

Séamus whistled. "Cuba, secret messages, dressed in Irish clothes, wanting to mimic an Irish accent, visibly upset at the play about a gunman. And named after the most famous gunman in Irish history. Hmm."

Sitting on the bench by the *Book of Kells*, they stared at each other. I should've known he'd figure this out, Charlie thought.

"Séamus, I can't tell you any more right now. It's just that I don't trust the people in charge of me, and I desperately need your help. Will you help me on this?" He stared as somberly as he could into the older man's eyes.

"I will, my boy. But when this is over, I want an explanation of what this is all about."

"I promise," said Charlie, shaking the older man's hand and draping his left hand over his shoulder. "It's the least I can do to thank you for all your help."

"It's not 'thank' my boy—it's 'tank.'" Séamus flashed a coy grin. "If you want to pass as a Dubliner, you must pronounce 'th' as 't'. Unless, of course, you're some rich guy tryin' to impress a Brit."

Having nailed down Séamus as his go-between for the postcards to Vanessa and Louis, he needed to do one more thing before leaving Dublin. He bought a tweed Irish flat cap with a visor, like the type sometimes worn by Ireland's great writer, James Joyce. Using a razor blade, he cut a slit in the lining and inserted two thin sheets of cardboard inside. Between them he sandwiched in fifty twenty-dollar bills. He found a tailor to sew up the slit. Afterward, Charlie turned the hat over and over so he could view it from all angles. The tailor had done the job so well that the cap looked completely unaltered.

———

FINALLY, HE CAUGHT HIS FLIGHT to Paris. Again, he declined the stewardess's offer of a drink. He'd consumed more alcohol in his one week with Séamus than he'd consumed the previous two months.

One of their conversations over pints of Guinness echoed in his mind as he leaned back in the plane's seat. After watching the play *Shadow of a Gunman* at the Abbey Theater, they found an empty table at a nearby pub. The play had left Charlie shaken. Had he signed on with the CIA as a warrior for his country or as just a gunman? The same could also be asked of Michael Collins. Charlie had challenged Séamus. "How were the bloody actions of Michael Collins any different from ordinary murder?"

"My boy, it was a war, for a noble cause. Without it, the country never would have become free. The British army would still be usin' the Monto as their whorehouse."

"So, the end justifies the means? If my end is noble, the means are okay?"

Séamus spoke in a soft voice "Not usually, my boy. The end doesn't usually justify the means. But sometimes it does. Sometimes it does."

Maybe Séamus was right, Charlie thought as his plane sped over the Irish Sea. Maybe there is a greater good. And maybe Flavio was right. If I don't bring about that greater good, who will?

20

WASHINGTON, DISTRICT OF COLUMBIA

ONCE THE SEATS AT HIS conference table were filled, Attorney General Robert Kennedy strode into the room. He set his briefcase on the floor, draped his suit coat over the back of his chair, and rolled up his sleeves. He scowled as he swept his gaze across the men in the room.

He's doing a slow burn, thought Tom McGillivray as he watched Kennedy take his seat. He looks like he's going to pop a cork. McGillivray sat by the wall instead of at the table. He held a briefcase stuffed with documents he could pull out quickly if requested by his boss, CIA Director John McCone. McCone sat directly across from the frowning attorney general.

Kennedy raised his hand and jabbed his index finger back and forth. "Things are moving too slow. We need some action."

He fixed his eyes on U.S. Air Force General Edward Lansdale, the operational director of Operation Mongoose. "Ed, you ran a great counterinsurgency operation when you were in the Philippines some years ago, but we're just not getting the same action on Cuba."

McGillivray looked over with sympathy to Lansdale who was being put on the spot. It wasn't that Lansdale was sitting on his hands, McGillivray realized. In March he had presented Kennedy with an ambitious six-phase operation to overthrow Castro. An escalating campaign of sabotage would degrade the country's power supply and other infrastructure, while psychological operations would turn the Cuban people against the regime. All of this would culminate in October when a specially trained brigade of Cuban exiles would invade the island, and the population would rise up in rebellion.

But October had arrived, and Operation Mongoose had little to show. Castro had set up a police state that neutralized Lansdale's proposed psyops program. Several sabotage attacks fizzled. The soldiers in Lansdale's brigade of exiles were growing restless as they waited in South Florida for the invasion order that never came.

Kennedy continued speaking. "We need better sabotage in Cuba," he said, tapping his index finger on the tabletop. With his Boston accent, Cuba came out like Cuber.

What a crock! McGillivray said to himself. The reason for the lack of sabotage lay within the White House itself. The Kennedys objected to any sabotage that could be traced to the United States. More specifically, anything that could be traced to the White House. Noise level, they called it. Sabotage activities had to have a low noise level.

That the other people in the room felt the same as McGillivray became evident in the feet shuffling on the floor and men squirming in their chairs. McGillivray, himself, did not intend to be the one to blame the ineffective sabotage on White House timidity about noise levels. Doing so would subject him to one of Bobby's tirades. The attorney general would almost certainly remind him that some of these very same people in the room had advised the president the previous year to undertake the Bay of Pigs Invasion of Cuba that ended in disaster. The incident had left Kennedy and his brother Robert with a deep mistrust of both the CIA and the top military brass.

To raise this issue of noise level required someone of the highest stature, and that was CIA director John McCone. "Sir," he said, "we can certainly do more sabotage. But it is impossible to make it effective unless we accept a higher noise level."

McGillivray held his breath, expecting a rousing reaction from Bobby. But the attorney general simply said, "Go on. What do you have in mind?"

Once McCone raised the issue of noise level without objection from the attorney general, other members chipped in with their ideas. We could infest Cuban waters with mines that would disrupt commerce but not be traceable to America. We could provoke an act of sabotage somewhere in the world, blame it on Castro, and use that to justify a U.S. invasion of the island. Another person suggested blowing up an old U.S. Navy warship in international waters and blaming it on Castro. Another suggested committing sabotage on U.S. soil and blaming that on Castro as well.

By the time Kennedy called an end to the meeting, he hadn't made clear how much noise he would tolerate. He had, however, accomplished his main goal. The participants agreed to step up sabotage activity designed to overthrow Castro.

McGillivray smiled as he left the room. With his demands for more sabotage, Kennedy had unwittingly provided McGillivray with the perfect justification for Lieutenant Parnell to assassinate Castro. Assassination was simply the ultimate sabotage. It would lop the head off Castro's entire regime. McGillivray needed to urge Bishop to speed up the timetable.

21

Week of October 7, 1962

ROSSLYN, VIRGINIA

ANESSA COULD CONTAIN HER CURIOSITY no longer. If Charlie's materials were as dangerous as he had hinted, she had a right to know what they contained.

Taking the materials to the sofa in her living room, she slit open the two sealed packets. The contents were identical. Each one contained four smaller sealed envelopes that were labeled Photos, Documentation, Supporting materials, and Narrative. A short note explained that the first three envelopes provided supporting evidence for the truth of the narrative.

In the Photos envelope, she found pictures of a rifle, the Lincoln Memorial, a young man on a blue Vespa motor scooter on the other side of the Lincoln Memorial, a SANE peace activist passing out leaflets by the reflecting pool, and Charlie himself holding a guitar as he sat on the ledge of the reflecting pool with the Washington Monument over his shoulder in the background. She couldn't see how any of the photos would be evidence of anything in his favor.

The second envelope contained a set of army orders reassigning

Charlie to temporary duty to a unit in Northern Virginia, which an accompanying note identified as a CIA outfit headed by Charlie's recruiter, Walter Bishop. A second paper, signed by both Charlie and Bishop, promised that Bishop would intervene to get him an early discharge and set him up with a Wall Street firm as a portfolio manager.

Vanessa whistled. This was Charlie's dream job, the one thing he talked about more than any other, and he would be good at it. The stock tips he had given her had outperformed the widow and orphan stocks in the professionally managed trust fund set up for her by her father.

The third envelope contained bits of memorabilia with no inherent meaning to her. They were things he had held onto, said a note, in case he ever needed evidence that would support the claims in his narrative statement. They included a SANE leaflet apparently handed out by the activist at the reflecting pool, a page torn from the phone book of the Marine Corps Base Quantico with a date penciled in, a page from a CIA document about somebody named Marita, again with a date penciled in, and a page from a memo pad with the title "From the desk of Bill Harvey." Two typewritten notes described documents he claimed to have been shown by Bill Harvey while in Harvey's CIA office. The first described a White House order dated November 3, 1961, that established the special group augmented to oversee the Operation Mongoose plot to overthrow Fidel Castro. The second described an agenda for an August 14, 1962 Operation Mongoose meeting that, Charlie claimed, named Bill Harvey as responsible for the CIA plot to assassinate Castro.

That Charlie could remember all these details did not surprise Vanessa. Over and over, he had shown an ability to recall precise details. She had always admired the deviousness she had seen in him. She had the same trait, herself. But this carefully planned collection of photos and seemingly innocuous items, gathered just in case Bishop ever tried to renege on his promise, showed a level of guile that she had never imagined. Was he paranoid?

Before tackling the fourth envelope, she refilled her coffee and returned to the sofa. She slit open the envelope and pulled out ten sheets of single-spaced typewritten pages. The title startled her so much that the cup jiggled in her hand and she spilled coffee on the end table. *Narrative of a CIA Plot to Assassinate Fidel Castro.*

Reading carefully, writing notes on a separate pad as she went, and backtracking repeatedly to double check earlier statements, she spent an hour going through the ten pages.

Her first reaction was fury—fury at Charlie for misleading her about his role in this sordid mess. He hadn't outright lied to her, but he had never let on that he was participating in a plot to assassinate Castro or that he would actually be the one to pull the trigger. She punched the edge of her sofa. Not that she cared two hoots whether Castro got bumped off. The world would be better off without him. But how could she possibly continue being intimate with the guy who did the deed?

Her fury increased when she read about Bishop blackmailing Charlie so blatantly. Threatening to give local prosecutors information that could send Charlie's father to prison.

When she read about Bishop's threat to expose Charlie's teenage homosexual abuse, tears welled in her eyes.

Charlie had always been warm and considerate, despite his cunning. She didn't want to lose him, but this was a lot of baggage. Would he really go ahead with this outrageous plan? Or, more likely, did he plan to finagle his way out of it at the last minute, the way he usually wiggled out of unpleasant situations? The only saving grace was his final sentence. "In the last analysis, I don't know if I'm willing to do it." But that might be just a ruse to make himself look like the aggrieved victim of CIA blackmail. She and he needed to have a talk.

In the meantime, Charlie's narrative was explosive. The little pieces of evidence he had accumulated made the entire story believable. How could he have taken Bill Harvey's memo pad unless he had been in the man's office? How could he have a scrap of paper from a CIA document about a woman called Marita if that document did not exist?

If any of this became public, reporters would crawl all over everybody connected in any way with the CIA. High level officials would be scrambling to prove that Harvey and Bishop were running a rogue operation on their own. If that claim didn't stick, there would be hell to pay throughout the capital. It would touch everyone: the highest levels of the CIA, the whole Operation Mongoose establishment overseen by the president's brother, the attorney general, the various cabinet heads, and high level military officials who attended Mongoose meetings. Maybe even the president himself, although Charlie made no allegations about the president. The president was the one person in the whole sorry mess that Charlie had a personal reason to point fingers at. Yet he made no claim of the president's involvement.

The only point of the documents was to ensure that Bishop bring Charlie back from Cuba. Once that was done, the documents would have to be destroyed, because they could ruin Charlie's reputation as well as everyone else's. In the meantime, the papers were so threatening to Bishop that he would do anything to get them back.

And that realization filled Vanessa with fright. Her breathing quickened and her hands trembled.

22

Week of October 7, 1962

PARIS, FRANCE

CHARLIE'S MOOD DARKENED AS HE reached the City of Lights. He strolled the Champs-Élysées toward the Louvre in the distance, expecting a lift in his spirits. As a boy, he had been warmed by an impressionist painting of Paris in his local museum. He would gaze at it and ponder the lives of the people there. Now he was in the world's most famous museum, in that very city, and standing before one of its greatest treasures the Mona Lisa. But he felt no warmth. The enigmatic eyes and lips of Mona Lisa pointed out his own ambiguous situation. Murder wasn't something he wanted to do. "But if the end is noble," Séamus had said, "then the means are justified." And, as Flavio had pointed out, if Charlie failed in this assignment, Fidel would continue oppressing Cubans for decades to come.

Leaving Mona Lisa, he went out to the cool October air and rode the Metro to the Sacré-Cœur Basilica. Despite the crisp weather, street performers were plying their crafts. Charlie sat on a stone wall watching a young woman dressed in blue and white, as Little Bo Peep, stare into a mirror and apply her makeup. When she finally closed her makeup case and tucked it into a hidden nook, she turned and smiled. "You look sad, Yank," she said in French-accented English.

Shocked at being addressed in English, Charlie took a second to respond. "I have to do something that I dread."

Her lips flattened into a caring look, and her hand came up to her chest. "I have to work now," she said. "But I will be back at five if you want to talk about it."

Then she went off, her blue and white skirt rustling as she walked away. Charlie felt alarmed. How had she recognized him as American? If he couldn't fool Little Bo Peep in Paris, what hope did he have of fooling the police in Havana?

He went down the steps from the basilica and limped through the narrow streets to Moulin Rouge where he gawked at its big red windmill. He entered the nearby Metro station and rode to the Trocadero stop, where he was stunned by the vista when he emerged from the subway. Beyond a big white palace and across the Seine, the girders of the Eiffel Tower soared above a majestic green park.

He ascended the enclosed stairwell to the top of the tower. Fantastic, he thought, as he looked out over the city. But Paris was a lonely place to tour by himself. Vanessa popped into his mind, and he missed not having her there to share it with him. How good it had been with her before she got into that business with Kennedy.

He wandered through the gardens beneath the tower, and a beautiful young woman stopped him. When she touched his arm, he had no doubt that she was a streetwalker, and he felt himself getting aroused. Since Vanessa had cheated on him, would he not be justified in spending an hour with this girl? But an image of the girls in Dublin's Magdalene Laundry came into his mind. If he took this woman's offer, would he not be just as bad, in the mind of Séamus, as those British soldiers in the Monto in Dublin? He turned away. Just why it would be so much worse to pay for sex with that girl than it would be to assassinate Castro, he couldn't say. He shook his head in disgust at himself.

Nevertheless, he craved human contact. He hurried back to Sacré-Cœur, arriving about half past five. But Little Bo Peep had gone. He looked in the spot where she had stashed her makeup kit, but it too was gone. Nor did she appear the next day when he wandered back up the hill to the basilica.

He could wait no longer, since he was scheduled that evening to take the overnight train for Zurich.

ZURICH, SWITZERLAND

ARRIVING IN ZURICH AT EIGHT the next morning, he felt stiff from sitting up all night. Next time he would travel first class. He registered at a hotel near the train station and popped into its restaurant for coffee.

———

ON THE THIRD FLOOR OF the Seidenhof Hotel on Zurich's Bahnhofstrasse, Bishop's assistant, Jim Wolsey, sat staring out the front window. For four days, he and Bishop's other assistant, Bob Gordon, had taken turns at the window. Suddenly, Wolsey sat up straight. "Thank God, there he is—finally."

Gordon peered out over Wolsey's shoulder. Wolsey lifted the 35-millimeter Leica camera with a long telephoto lens and snapped several photos of Charlie limping up Bahnhofstrasse, stopping in front of Credit Suisse Bank, and going in through the main entrance. An hour later, Charlie emerged from the bank entrance and went straight to a waiting taxi. The taxi drove away.

"Let's go," said Wolsey. "At last, we can get out of this dreary burg."

They crossed the street, entered the bank, and asked to see an account officer.

"I wish to close this account," Wolsey said to the officer as he gave the account number and handed over his passport for identification.

The manager rifled through several folders before pulling out the one for Wolsey's account.

"We would normally give you a check for the balance." He set a dollar bill on the desk, in front of Wolsey. "But your joint account holder, Michael Collins, just withdrew all but one dollar. He took it all in cash—fifty one-hundred-dollar bills."

"That thieving son-of-a-bitch!" Wolsey swore.

"But sir," said the manager, "Mr. Collins is co-owner of the account. It *is* his money."

———

CHARLIE HAD THE TAXI DRIVER make several turns into and out of narrow streets before returning to the Bahnhoffstrasse several blocks away from Credit Suisse. Once he was confident he wasn't being followed, he left the taxi and darted into a small family-owned bank.

"I wish to open a numbered account with a small deposit," he told the accounts manager. "Will this be sufficient to open the account?" He laid forty Ben Franklins on the desk in front of the manager. He kept ten of them to convert to Cuban pesos for his trip to Havana.

"That will be more than sufficient, sir," said the manager.

"Am I correct that this account is completely secret? That no one but me has access to the account—not friends, not any government, not even the Swiss government?"

"That is correct. Swiss banking laws protect the privacy of every account."

"Wonderful." Charlie smiled. "I want a safe-deposit box where I can put my valuables, and I want to put the cash in an interest-bearing account. I also want instructions on how I can have you wire cash to me if I need it."

Bishop would be pissed, he realized, when he discovered that Charlie had withdrawn the money. But leaving that money in the joint account would allow Bishop to withdraw it himself and make

Charlie beg for any funds he might need.

Confident that none of Bishop's henchmen had any idea where he had deposited the money, Charlie ambled down Bahnhofstrasse amid the upscale shops. He was determined to spend time sightseeing, considering what he had to look forward to in Cuba. He bought two postcards to send to Séamus in Dublin. Then he stopped in a women's accessories shop and bought a pair of elegant leather gloves. For a fee, the clerk agreed to mail them directly to Vanessa Perez in Rosslyn, Virginia.

Charlie spent Saturday wandering the Zurich streets. He popped into the Swiss National Museum housed in a fairytale-like castle near the train station. He stopped in several art galleries to imagine what he might buy if he ever did get Meyer's jewels out of that Havana cemetery.

That evening he dined at an elegant fondue restaurant recommended by the hotel's concierge. He spent an hour at a jazz club listening to a Dave Brubeck imitator. He reminisced fondly about the dance band he and his friend Louis had founded when they were teens. Finally, he returned to the hotel and turned in early so that he would be fresh for his flight to Havana the next morning.

HAVANA, CUBA

CHARLIE'S PLANE TOUCHED DOWN AT the José Martí International Airport in Havana at seven p.m. on Sunday, October 14. Boarding the plane in Zurich, the weather had been drizzling and cold. Havana, by contrast, felt hot and muggy when he stepped onto the tarmac. Toting the medicine bags he'd bought in Dublin and draping the guitar case strap over his shoulder, he joined the line of people heading toward Customs Control. With the heat, the humidity, and his fear of getting caught, sweat ran down his sides and drenched his shirt.

He strained not to fidget as the customs agent pored meticulously through his bags, opened the guitar case, pulled out the instrument, and peered into it. The agent ran his fingers along the felt lining inside the case but failed to notice its false bottom. He told Charlie to empty his pockets, which Charlie did, pulling out his wallet, a comb, the Cuban pesos he had bought in Zurich, and the Swiss-manufactured range finder he'd gotten at Quantico. The only thing the agent noted was the range finder.

"That's for my camera," said Charlie, pointing at the 35-millimeter camera sitting among his other belongings. His heartbeat sped up. The customs agent must surely know that a range finder could also be used to gain accuracy in shooting a rifle. The agent turned his head toward a dirty window behind him and held up the range finder toward the window. Behind the window a huge man in a military uniform stood next to a thin, frail-looking woman. The soldier waved his hand at the customs agent who dropped the range finder back into the guitar case. Charlie's eyes followed the unspoken exchange between the two men. He hadn't yet entered the country, and already he was being watched.

"El bonete, por favor," said the agent, pointing toward Charlie's head. The agent's stern face and his unblinking eyes sent Charlie's pulse racing. If the agent spotted the twenty-dollar bills hidden behind the lining, Charlie was done for. He held his breath as the agent ran his fingers around the inside of the cap before dropping it on top of the guitar case. Again, the agent looked over his shoulder at the dirty window where the soldier stood next to the skinny woman. Seeing no signal from behind the window, the clerk used white chalk to mark the baggage and then turned to the next person. Charlie exhaled slowly as he moved on to Passport Control.

———

MAJOR ESCALANTE FROWNED IN DISAPPOINTMENT. Other than Michael Collins rubbing his chin in a gesture of nervousness when the customs clerk asked for his hat, the reporter's composure seemed normal. Even the most innocent of passengers demonstrate some anxiety in the face of Cuban authority, the major thought. More interesting was the expression of his colleague, Isabel, when the reporter came into view. Her lips twisted slightly up into the beginnings of a smile. The major nudged her arm with his elbow. "Well, what do you think? Anything suspicious or worthy of note?"

"Nada, Major. Nothing at all."

"Interesting," suggested the major. "Tall and trim, with good posture. Except for that bushy hair on his head and that strange limp, he almost has a military bearing. But not a bad-looking guy."

She wiped the smile off her face and gave the major a blank look. "If you like that type," she said. "I'd better get up front so I can meet him as he comes through Immigration Control."

The major watched her walk toward the exit, stepping lively enough to suggest that she did not dread the prospect of meeting this young man. Escalante thought he spied a wiggle of her hips through the baggy uniform as she walked away. She was certainly showing more enthusiasm for this assignment today than she had the day he recruited her. It might not be a bad idea to increase the surveillance on her as she kept an eye on Collins. He made a note to himself to have his administrative aide get in touch with the Committee for the Defense of the Revolution (CDR). They should put a neighborhood watcher near Isabel's home to keep an eye on her. Whoever thought up this idea of neighborhood watchers for the CDR was brilliant. He deserved a medal.

23

EDWARDS AIR FORCE BASE, CALIFORNIA

A s CHARLIE WAS WINGING ACROSS the sea, Air Force Major Richard Heyser finished off an enormous breakfast of steak and eggs. The sun had just risen. It would be almost nightfall before he could eat again, so he needed a considerable amount of food. After breakfast, a doctor checked his pulse, blood pressure, and body temperature as well as the openness of the air passages in his nose and throat. These needed to be perfect for the major's task that day.

"Everything looks good," the doctor informed him. Then he turned to Heyser's backup pilot, thirty-five-year-old Major Rudolph Anderson. "So I guess it's no go for you today, Rudy."

The backup pilot smiled. "Glad you passed your physical, but I really wanted to be the first one for this."

Five days earlier, President Kennedy had ordered the resumption of U-2 surveillance flights over Cuba. But there was so much cloud cover over the island the next few days that the plane's reconnaissance cameras were useless. Heyser, Rudy, and the other U-2 pilots sat around playing cards and passing time as they waited to see which one would get the nod to resume the flights. It wasn't until Sunday, October 14, that the skies cleared up enough for the U-2 cameras to do their work.

Heyser attended a briefing on his mission, where he was instructed to circle out over the Gulf of Mexico and approach Cuba from the southwest. He was shown all known locations for Russian surface-to-air missiles (SAMs) along his route, and he was reminded of the evasive tactics to take in case any of those missiles were fired at him. After the briefing, he reported to his ground crew and put on a bulky pressure suit. If the U-2 plane lost air pressure at its 70,000-foot altitude, his blood would boil unless his pressurized suit inflated.

As Heyser went through his pre-flight preparations, backup pilot Rudy Anderson rode a jeep out to the plane, where he conducted a pre-flight inspection of the aircraft. He checked the plane's entire outside surface for any abnormalities. Then he got into the cockpit to test the electrical system and avionics. Finally, he drove back to the ground-crew room.

"The plane is A-OK," he reported. He gave Heyser a thumbs-up as Heyser got into the jeep to be driven out to the plane. Even without being inflated, the pressure suit was still so cumbersome that he could not climb the ladder to the cockpit. Two ground crew members put him into a harness and hoisted him up to his seat. They connected the pressure suit to the various belts, cables, hoses, and communication wires that would be his lifeline, once in the air. Heyser closed the cockpit canopy and worked through his own pre-flight checklist before turning on the jet engine. The flight crew removed the safety pins from the temporary wheels, called pogos, near the tips of the wings. The wings drooped so much they needed the pogos to keep the wingtips from dragging on the ground when the plane taxied along the ground.

As soon as the wings generated lift, the pogos dropped off, and Heyser rose off the runway, climbing into the sky at a staggering rate of almost three miles per minute. Even at 500 mph, it took five hours to circle the Gulf of Mexico and reach Cuba. His target centered on San Cristobal, near the western end of the island. He clicked on the camera switches, and they snapped photographs for the seven minutes that he was over the target. He scanned the sky below for telltale signs of any surface-to-air missiles being fired at him. Fortunately, nothing came his way.

Upon leaving Cuban air space, he flew to McCoy Air Force Base in Florida.

Landing the U-2 was one of the trickiest parts of the flight. Even at slow speeds, the long spacious wings kept giving the plane lift, leaving it vulnerable to cross winds. Forty-five minutes out from the airport, he hit the speed brakes to start slowing the plane for a landing.

As the plane came in, another pilot waited in a chase car at the end of the runway. Heyser passed over him at an altitude of about ten feet. However, he could no longer gauge his altitude and distance accurately. Spending so much time at 70,000 feet had skewed his depth perception. The chase car sped after the U-2 as it sailed over the runway, and the backup pilot called out the plane's altitude for every two feet of drop. At two feet above the ground, Heyser hit stall speed, and the tail wheel touched the runway. He felt a sharp bump as the two front wheels hit ground, and he struggled to keep the plane level. Even as it coasted down the runway, the plane's capacious wings generated enough lift to make it roll from side to side. Heyser struggled to keep the wings from crashing into the runway. When he had slowed enough, he let one of the titanium wingtip skid plates gently touch the ground, then the other. The plane came to a complete stop, and workers attached new pogos to the wingtips so Heyser could taxi to a hangar.

Two ground crew teams rushed out to the plane. The CIA crew unloaded the film with the 928 photos that were snapped during the seven minutes over the target. They took the film under armed guard to the CIA's National Photographic Interpretation Center in Washington for analysis. The air force ground crew was responsible for the plane and the pilot. They lifted the pilot out of the plane. Having been cooped up in the cramped cockpit and the pressure suit for eight hours, with little room to stretch his arms or legs, Heyser was exhausted. He entered the operations room for a detailed debriefing.

Heyser had no way to know what a crucial role his photographs would play in events over the next two weeks.

24

Week of October 14, 1962

HAVANA, CUBA

THE AGENT AT IMMIGRATION CONTROL barely glanced at Charlie's Irish passport. He stamped it and waved Charlie into Cuba.

Passing into the airport proper, Charlie's pulse had just settled down when he was approached by a woman with curly brown hair. She looked to be in her early twenties, and she wore the dark green military uniform of the Castro revolutionaries. It hung loosely on her thin body, making her look underfed. Was she the woman who had been standing behind the dirty window watching him go through customs?

"Mr. Collins?" she asked in English.

"Soy yo," Charlie replied, wanting to avoid any English, lest she recognize his accent as American.

"¿Usted habla español?

"Si, señorita. Lo hablo."

"¡Qué bien!" she said and continued in Spanish. "I am Isabel Fernandez. I work for the Ministry of Communication and have been assigned to give you any assistance you need for the articles you are writing."

"I was told that I would have an assistant," he grinned, "but I had no idea she would be so stunning."

Isabel smiled as she led him outside the building. They got into a 1951 Ford waiting at the curb, a driver behind the wheel. The car had a hole in the muffler, and the old V-8 engine growled with a throaty roar as the chauffeur drove them out of the airport. Smelly exhaust drifted up through the floorboards into the car. It was a short distance to downtown Havana, and the driver dropped them off at the Habana Libre Hotel. It had been expropriated by the revolutionary government and was now used to house government guests. She led him into the twenty-five-story building, one of the tallest in the city, and watched as he filled out the registration form.

He gawked at the lobby and the two-story atrium. Taking his room key, he turned to her and asked, "Who are all those girls in school uniforms?"

"They are teachers in the Ana Betancourt schools. It is a revolutionary program to ensure that all girls receive an education. They're holding a convention here this week." She swept her hand toward a banner attached to a far wall near the young women. Then she bade him goodbye. "I will pick you up tomorrow after breakfast," she said matter-of-factly. "I did take the liberty of scheduling one interview for you at a medical clinic outside Havana so you can see the care that we provide our people. After that we can go over your schedule. There are several places of interest you might want to see. In the meantime, enjoy your visit. If you have any energy left from that long flight, feel free to wander around this evening and see the sights. Unlike many big cities, Havana is perfectly safe. I will stop by about 9:00 tomorrow morning."

She handed him an envelope. "Here are the credentials you need as a reporter in order to file stories back to your newspaper." The words poured out of her mouth like a well-rehearsed speech.

With that said, she shook his hand, turned, and left.

———

WHEN ISABELLE SHOWED UP THE next morning, she arrived on a bright red Harley-Davidson motorcycle with an attached sidecar. Charlie ambled around the vehicle, running his hand over the embossed arrowhead logo on the gas tank. "Where in God's name did you get this?" he asked in Spanish with a big grin. "A classic hog."

"A hog?" she asked. "You call a motorcycle a hog?"

Jesus, thought Charlie. He had barely met her, and he'd already started to blow his cover. He stammered, "It's just something that the kids in Dublin call a Harley Davidson because it's so big. But this one has a sidecar and everything. Where did you get it?"

"My father wheeled it home the day before Fidel came into Havana. He bought it from some American who was on his way to the airport. Because of an engine problem, he had to push it home instead of riding it. But that didn't matter because he got it for such a good price."

Recalling Meyer Lansky's story about Cubans confiscating the abandoned vehicles on the road to the airport, Charlie thought, yeah, zero is indeed a good price. That sidecar might be a big help for toting around his guitar and the M1 rifle.

She changed the subject. "Bring your guitar," she said. "It might help us break the ice where we are going. And you can leave your hat behind. It's going to be warm today."

However, Charlie did not want to leave his hat behind where it could be examined by anybody who might search his room. When he returned with the guitar, he continued wearing his flat hat. She drove them into the countryside for an hour to a small town west of Havana, Nuevo Mariel. Arriving at the town, she slowed to a crawl and inched her way through the dusty streets to the health clinic. It looked austere to Charlie, and the physician seemed overwhelmed by the long line of people in shabby clothes. Waving his hand in the direction of his patients, the doctor said that he would not be free for an interview until afternoon.

Charlie and Isabel wandered through the streets of one- and two-storied stucco buildings, most covered with dirty pink, blue, or brown paint. As they walked, he scanned the surroundings for potential sniper sites. The best spot was directly across from the clinic, where a deserted building sat in front of a wooded area. If Isabel could persuade Castro to visit the clinic, and Flavio could get the rifle into the building, Charlie could think up an excuse to wander into the building and take his shot. Then, in the momentary confusion that would follow the shot, he would hop onto Flavio's Vespa, and they would flee to the safe house. From there, Bishop would have the two of them whisked out of the country.

He was so lost in these thoughts that Isabel had to nudge him in the side to get his attention. She wanted to visit a nearby elementary school while they waited to go back and interview the doctor.

The school principal showed them around the building. "Until now," she said in English, "very few children went to school. Now all children go to school, girls as well as boys." They visited a classroom with six columns of students, seven rows deep.

"This is a lot of children in one class," Charlie said in Spanish.

"We still have a shortage of teachers," said the principal in English. "Speak English with me Mr. Collins. I need to practice."

Out of politeness, he replied in monosyllables, trying to say as little as possible, lest either the principal or Isabel recognize his American accent. Finally, he smiled as charmingly as he could. "But Profesora," he said in Spanish, deliberately mispronouncing the words, "I need to practice my Spanish even more than your need to practice your excellent English."

Isabel pointed to Charlie's guitar. "Being from Ireland, maybe Mr. Collins could play an Irish song for the children."

The principal asked the teacher if she would permit this diversion from her study plans for the day, and she nodded her head yes. She guided Charlie by the elbow to the front of the room and introduced him to the children. Charlie draped the guitar strap over his shoulder, made a point of tuning the strings, and rested his hip in a half sitting position on the teacher's desk.

"This is an Irish revolutionary song from almost fifty years ago," he said in Spanish. "Ireland was fighting for its independence from the British, just as Cuba fought for its independence from Spain. Let me sing it in English, and then I'll tell you what the words mean." As he strummed the mournful chords of the song, he sang in a tenor voice, enunciating the dreary words just as he had been taught by Séamus McDonald.

> *Aahly on a Sunday mornin'*
> *High up on a gallows tree,*
> *Kevin Barry gave his young life*
> *For the cause of liberty.*
>
> *Just a lad of eighteen summers,*
> *Still there's no one can deny,*
> *As he walked to death that mornin',*
> *Kevin held his head up high.*

Charlie then translated the mournful words into Spanish and explained that it had become a rallying cry for Irish revolutionaries in the wake of Ireland's famous Easter Rebellion. On Easter Sunday, 1916, Irish rebels made coordinated attacks on British-held positions in Dublin.

"But it failed," said Charlie, "much like Fidel Castro's attack on the Moncada Barracks failed in 1953. When the British army executed Kevin Barry, Irish public opinion turned against the British. People sang this song throughout the country. It became so important in building public support that without it, Ireland might still be ruled by the British."

Isabel and the principal beamed happily as Charlie responded to questions from the children.

"Why do you wear that funny hat on a warm day?" one of the children asked.

"I am an Irish writer," Charlie smiled, taking the cap into his right hand and waving it. "Writers and artists and musicians need what in English we call a persona, which has a meaning slightly different from the same word in Spanish. In English, persona is a symbol of identity that people will recognize. So when you see a hat like this, you will remember me. Our most famous writer, James Joyce, often wore a hat like this. So I wear one as well, to bring me luck with my writing."

But knowing that his limited knowledge of Ireland could easily betray him as in fact not Irish, he cut the questions short. "Let me play another song. The words of this one are from one of Cuba's greatest writers." Both Isabel and the principal beamed again as he strummed the chords of "Guantanamera" and sang the opening stanza in his tenor voice. When he reached the chorus, he called out, "¡Cantem!" and motioned with his hands for them to sing along.

Guantanamera. Guajira Guantanamera.
Guantanamera. Guajira Guantanamera

At first, only a few children sang, but the powerful beat of the song drew in the rest, and by the end, the other three adults in the room had joined in as well. Charlie ended with a full bow from the waist. He looked over at Isabel and the principal who were clapping for him.

"Thank you," he grinned. "I haven't had this much fun in weeks."

Isabelle's reaction, standing misty-eyed and clapping loudly, confirmed his belief that he had done the right thing in taking the music lessons from Séamus. If he ever got back to Dublin, he would take him to dinner at that fancy hotel on St. Stephen's Green. Whatever worries Charlie had about Isabel accepting his authenticity as an Irish journalist sympathetic to the Cuban revolution, that worry was now resolved.

When they arrived back at the medical clinic, the doctor was treating his last patient, a baby screaming from an ear infection. Charlie snapped a picture of him treating the child as well as some other pictures of the clinic. "If only we had more equipment and medications, we could do a much better job of treating our patients," the doctor said during his interview.

Riding in the motorcycle sidecar on the way back to Havana, he watched Isabel's curly brown hair blow in the breeze. It would be nice, he thought, to sit behind her with his hands around her waist, rather than being scrunched into the sidecar.

"Do you think you could get Fidel to visit that clinic?" he asked Isabel when she brought the Harley to a halt in front of the Hotel Habana Libre. "A photo of him with the patients would do wonders for his image around the world."

"I'll call to find out."

She drove off, and Charlie went into the hotel to draft his article about the health clinic in Nuevo Mariel. How in hell he was going to make it look like a convincing newspaper story, he didn't know.

————

As soon as she dropped Charlie off at the hotel, Isabel phoned Major Escalente to request that Castro visit the clinic. The major's gleeful reaction surprised her.

"Aha!" he exclaimed, "the first sign that our Mr. Collins is not what he appears to be."

"How so? He needs a photo of Fidel for his story."

"Tell Mr. Collins that I will have el comandante at the clinic at 11:30 this Friday morning."

"Don't you have to check with him first?"

"Señorita, you leave that to me. Your job is to make sure that Mr. Collins shows up, and then you must get the hell out of the way, in case he has a grenade or a gun and he tries to use you as a shield."

"Major, I have spent two days with this man. Whatever he is, he is not an assassin. No assassin could have played the guitar and sung Guantanamera the way he did with the children at the school. He even sent postcards to his friends in Ireland. Assassins don't send out postcards."

"Anybody can sing Guantanamera or send out postcards. Just remember to step away from him when I show up with el jefe."

She hung up the phone and slumped back into the chair at her desk. She felt confident that Michael Collins was not an assassin. But from the poor quality of the dispatch he had filed back to the *Irish Times*, he clearly was not a reporter. What was he? Was he in anyway a threat to her and Angelita? Or was there some way he could get the two of them out of Cuba?

25

Week of October 14, 1962

The White House

EARLY ON TUESDAY, OCTOBER 16, National Security Advisor McGeorge Bundy strode through the West Wing. With a stern, determined grimace on his face, he headed toward the family quarters, and he held a big package in his hands.

President Kennedy was reading the morning newspapers when Bundy entered with a stack of photos taken by Major Heyser's U-2 spy plane two days earlier.

Kennedy pointed at a grainy photo. "It looks like a plowed-up football field to me," he said

"I assure you, Mr. President, CIA's photo experts have established beyond doubt that we are looking at construction sites for nuclear missile launchers. These missiles are big enough to reach well into the U.S." He pointed toward the telltale signs that the photo experts had marked on the photos: launching pads, control bunkers, nuclear warhead storage sites, and a convoy of trucks with trailers long enough to carry a medium-range ballistic missile.

Kennedy was stunned. He had been double-crossed by Soviet Premier Nikita Khrushchev. Khrushchev had pledged that he would not introduce offensive weapons into Cuba while U-2 flights were suspended.

"That fucking liar!" sputtered Kennedy. "He can't do that to me."

———

EVELYN LINCOLN SUMMONED VANESSA. HANDING her a list of names, Lincoln said, "I need you to phone these people. I can't call them myself because the president's got me busy on something else. The president wants them in the Cabinet Room at 11:45 this morning. No excuses. This is so important that they should cancel anything else on their schedules."

Vanessa glanced at the list. It contained all the members of the National Security Council plus a handful of critical officials.

"What do I tell them when they ask me why?"

"You don't know why. Just tell them to be here. If any of them needs a heads up before hand, the president will phone them himself."

From the urgency in Mrs. Lincoln's voice, something big was up. Given the determination with which McGeorge Bundy had sped through the hall earlier, Vanessa wagered that this had something to do with those memos she had seen in West Sitting Hall more than a month earlier.

As she finished making the calls, Ted Sorensen told her that he wanted her to attend the meeting so she could take notes for him. "I will be glad to, Mr. Sorensen. But why do you need my notes when the president will already have someone taking minutes, and he has a tape recorder to record everything that goes on in the room?"

"A tape recorder?" Sorensen looked alarmed. "Who told you that?"

"Nobody," she said. "The other day in the Cabinet Room, I dropped my pen on the floor. When I bent over to pick it up, I saw a microphone and a switch under the table right where the president sits. The only conclusion is that he tapes some of his meetings."

"If you ever repeat this to anybody, even to me, you will be fired," Sorensen barked. "Do you understand?"

"Yes, sir," she said, jolted by Sorensen's snappish tone. He was normally very staid when talking with people. "I'm excited to be involved in this, but I still don't understand why you need my notes."

"Redundancy," explained Sorensen. "We can check your notes against the minutes against the recordings. The microphone won't pick up everything clearly. Besides, I won't be able to sit in on every meeting, so I need a pair of eyes and ears in the room."

Sorensen paused for a moment, then stressed, "You must maintain complete secrecy about this assignment. You have a top-secret security clearance, and so do many other people in government. But having a top-secret clearance doesn't authorize them to know what you will learn on this assignment. You can talk about it only with me or the other people in the room. Can you do that?"

"Yes, sir," she said.

When Sorensen told Evelyn Lincoln to alert Kennedy that Sorensen wanted Vanessa to sit in on the meeting with him, Lincoln objected.

"Is she trustworthy?"

"Well," said Sorensen, "she is a frequent visitor to the family quarters, and from all appearances, she hasn't mentioned it. As far as I can tell, she hasn't even talked about it with Fiddle or Faddle, who, I understand, have also been frequent visitors to the family quarters."

Lincoln shook her head. Fiddle and Faddle were the nicknames for two White House secretaries who had also attracted Kennedy's attention.

"Besides," said Sorensen, "she already works as my typist and stenographer. So she's going to know what's going on in that room soon enough. With her at the meetings, I can do a better job of helping the president."

THE MEETING OF THE ExCOMM, as the Executive Committee of the National Security Council came to be called, lasted into the early afternoon. Then the members returned for a follow-up meeting at 6:30. By the time Vanessa got home, she plopped onto her couch in a state of physical and psychological exhaustion. Charlie was trapped someplace in Cuba, which was dotted with nuclear missiles. Ex-Comm had been divided into two groups. One urged a blockade of the island until Russia removed the missiles. The second, including all of the military advisors, argued that this could easily lead to war if the U.S. Navy sank any Russian ships that tried to run the blockade. They favored an immediate wave of air strikes lasting nearly a week, followed by an invasion of the island.

And there was no one she could talk to about it.

26

Week of October 14, 1962

HAVANA, CUBA

WEDNESDAY MORNING, CHARLIE WATCHED ISABEL rumble her Harley up to the Hotel Habana Libre. Instead of her customary fatigues uniform, she wore a wide, blue-colored skirt that allowed her legs to straddle the motorcycle freely. She said, "This will be a good day to show you some of the lore of Havana, so you'll have background for your newspaper stories."

"Before we go off on this sightseeing tour you've set up,"—he smiled—"could we stop by the Agence France-Presse? I worked out an arrangement for them to file my stories back to the Irish Times."

He dropped off his story at the agency and had her make a detour to a post office, conspicuously slipping two postcards into an airmail envelope.

"Why don't you mail the postcard directly and save a few centavos?"

"It gets there faster this way," he replied, inserting the envelope into the mail slot before she could see the addressee. Having her watch him send postcards back to Ireland would solidify his cover as an Irishman, but he did not want to make it easy for her to find out where Séamus McDonald lived.

He hopped back into the sidecar, setting his 35-millimeter camera on his lap and spare rolls of film on the floor along with his flattop hat. He leaned back, pondering how he was going to avoid her prying eyes long enough to search out Meyer Lansky's jewels and to ambush Castro. She drove down Avenida 23 to the Malecón, Havana's concrete breakwater that stretched for miles along the sea front. She rolled the bike to a stop.

"The first thing you have to see is the Malecón. Then we'll bike to the Prado and do a walking tour through Old Havana."

The air was noisy and smelly, because a parade of old cars with leaky mufflers drove along the street that paralleled the breakwater.

She pointed out the massive Hotel Nacional. "I thought of putting you up there, because that's where most of the foreign journalists hang out. But it's a little pricey, and I didn't know what kind of budget your paper provided for stringers."

Thank God, thought Charlie. Hanging around inquisitive foreign reporters would almost certainly blow his cover.

But he responded to her with, "Where you put me is fine."

He leaned against the concrete wall of the Malecón while she walked across the street to pick up a newspaper from a vendor. Waves of water crashed on a beach of rocks beneath the wall, and a cool mist fell upon him. He didn't bother to move, because it was a hot morning, and the mist felt good.

A teenage girl in very short shorts approached Charlie and coyly stuck out a hip in a provocative pose. Before she could say a word, Isabel came back from the newspaper vendor. She snapped at the girl in an angry Spanish that flew by so fast Charlie missed almost all of it. The girl fled.

Isabel drove a short distance to Chinatown where she parked the Harley near an archway with a pagoda motif. A street sign said Zanja, and below the sign was some Chinese lettering, a dragon's head, and a circular-shaped lantern. She took a thick chain from the sidecar and fastened the bike to a pole. They strolled down a long narrow street walled in by three-story apartment buildings with occasional shops and storefronts at the street level. All were marked by peeling paint in pastel colors: blues, pinks, and yellows. A din of honking taxis, loud conversations, bongo drums, and children at play echoed off the buildings. The smell of car exhaust mingled with roasting chicken and occasional clumps of rotting garbage. Laundry had been draped over the railings of small balconies to dry. Throughout, there were colorful collections of flowers: a pink and white hibiscus plant, an orchid, and a plant Charlie did not recognize. He pointed toward it. "What is that big white flower that's on so many balconies?"

"That is the mariposa. It's our national flower. Even on Calle Zanja they have the mariposa."

"Calle Zanja?"

"Yes. Other than the schools, Calle Zanja this is Fidel's greatest achievement."

"Isabel," said Charlie, with a sweep of his hand toward the run-down storefronts. "This doesn't look like an achievement. It looks like a slum. A slum with lots of pretty flowers, but nonetheless a slum."

"It doesn't look like an achievement, because, gracias a Dios, you never saw it before the revolution. This whole street was the brothel capital of the Western Hemisphere. It was one of the dirtiest, ugliest, and most degrading places you could think of."

She paused to stare at him, and he noted for the first time that the deep brown color of her eyes matched the brown of her hair. He didn't know how to respond. His introduction to the Magdalene Laundry back in Dublin had colored his view of brothels and prostitution. He didn't want to discuss this subject with her. But she plowed ahead, oblivious to his reticence.

"Men from all over the world, but especially the United States, came here for their pleasure, leaving behind babies, disease, and girls whose lives they ruined."

Charlie nodded.

"When Fidel outlawed prostitution and kicked out the American mafia that ran the brothels, he did more for Cuban women than anyone in the history of the human race."

"What about that girl on the Malecón that you snapped at? She looked like a prostitute."

"It's impossible to eliminate it all. There is too much poverty in Havana and a lot of hunger due to the American embargo. They won't buy our sugar, our chocolate, our cigars—anything. So there are many girls who have to pick up a little money any way they can. When that girl saw you in your European clothes, she saw a man who could not only pay her money, but, if she really got lucky, take her home as a bride. That girl you saw is what we call a jinetera."

"Jinetera? A jockey?" He narrowed his eyebrows in a puzzled look.

She laughed. "Use your imagination, Michael. A jockey is paid to mount a horse. A jinetera is paid to mount a man or let a man mount her. So these girls are the jineteras, the jockeys."

Before Charlie could reply, she pointed toward a dilapidated building. "Take a photo of that for your newspaper," she commanded. She put her hand on his bare arm and pulled him forward for a better view of it. The touch of her hand on his skin sent a short, warm wave of pleasure through him.

"That was the Shanghai Theater. It was the biggest cesspool in the city. It featured live sex shows every night. Europeans and Americans came looking for something they couldn't see at home. The Americans were the worst. At home they treated their Negroes like slaves. Here they could get what they wanted, a Black Cuban girl, and the younger the better. If it hadn't been for the revolution, my own daughter might have been destined for a place like that."

Charlie snuck a look at her left hand but saw no ring. "You have a daughter?"

"Ángela Fernandez." Her mood softened. "Or Angelita, as I call her. She's almost four. She is beautiful." Isabel smiled warmly.

She led him out of Zanja Street, past the capital building, and into a park where Charlie stopped, spellbound by the scene. A dozen or more young men stood shouting at each other, and their hands flew through the air in animated gestures. One emaciated young man, red-faced with anger, pushed his face just inches from another man's and screamed. Halfway across the park, Charlie heard the scream, and his head snapped back.

Isabel laughed at his response. "They're arguing about baseball. In Cuba, as you must know, we are crazy about baseball. So all day long, men gather on this corner and argue about the greatest pitchers, the greatest hitters, the greatest teams. We call this Esquina Caliente."

"The hot corner." He grinned. "Tercera base."

Isabel's eyebrows went up immediately, and Charlie froze. As an Irishman he should not have known that third base was called the hot corner. Only an American or a Cuban or somebody familiar with baseball would know that. Before he could think up an excuse for what he had just said, she took his arm again and tugged him toward Avenida O'Reilly.

"You have a street named after an Irishman?" he asked.

"Sort of," she said. "Alejandro O'Reilly was an Irish-born Spanish general who lived in Cuba for a time. But what I want to show you is at the end of this street."

She led him down the street to the Hotel Ambos Mundos, a five-story 1920's building in pink stucco, having balconies adorned with flowerpots. "This is charming," he said. "But what is so special about it?"

She pulled him into the lobby and across to the elevator, where she directed the operator to the fifth floor.

"The famous writer Ernest Hemingway lived here during the 1930's. As a writer yourself, you might want to see it."

They walked down the corridor to room 511, Hemingway's room, which the hotel now maintained as a small museum for the famous author. His typewriter and other mementos sat on tables as though they were waiting for the master to return and start working. Charlie took several photos of the room and got a tourist to take a shot of Isabel and him standing next to the number 511 on the door.

They left the hotel and retraced their steps up Avenida O'Reilly. She smiled up at him. "I thought you would enjoy seeing that."

"I did," Charlie smiled back. "Thank you very much."

He looked at his watch. "It's well past noon," he said. "Can you think of some place where a stringer could buy you a bite to eat?"

"I most certainly can," she replied. "I have just the place for you—another Hemingway haunt."

To Charlie, the stone exterior of El Floridita did not look distinct from other buildings along the street. The inside, however, captivated him. It was packed with customers of all nationalities. Red-coated waiters bustled about serving people. While they waited for a table, Charlie strolled the aisle and examined celebrity photos on the wall.

"My God, there's Graham Greene." He pointed at the photo of the famous British author. Photos of Americans John Dos Passos and Spencer Tracy also adorned the wall, but Charlie did not draw her attention to them. No point in being overly enthused about Americans.

She smiled. "Graham Greene used the Floridita as a setting for Our Man in Havana, that marvelous spoof about British spies."

A waiter found them a table in the middle of the room, and as they pondered their food choices, Isabel continued talking.

"In addition to being a place where spies meet, they claim to have invented the Daiquiri here, so you must try one. And they are famous for their seafood, so you must try that as well."

Fearful that he would betray himself as American by inadvertently shifting the fork back and forth between the left and right hands, Charlie ordered shrimp that he could pick up with his fingers and dip into the sauce.

A huge Cuban military officer nodded at Isabel as he passed their table.

"Who is that?" asked Charlie.

"Major Escalante. He's my boss."

"You work for the army?" Charlie stiffened.

"It's a temporary job, in addition to my duties at the Ministry of Communications."

It took him a moment to process what she was telling him.

"When I came through Customs Sunday night, were you standing behind a window, observing me?"

"Yes. The major and I were both there."

"So you're my watcher while I'm in Cuba?"

"Michael, don't look so shocked. Do you imagine that the Americans or the British would fail to watch a Cuban reporter in their countries? Wouldn't your own government in Ireland do the same?"

"Be serious, Isabel. We're neutral. We didn't even join NATO."

She tilted her head down and looked up at him from the corners of her eyes, with a coquettish smile.

"Peace, Michael. Watching you has been the nicest assignment I've had in a long time. I don't get to visit places like this every day or hang around charming guys like you. When the major realizes that you're not some spy for the CIA, he will lose interest in you. And I will be out of your hair. So let's enjoy ourselves while we are here."

Was this the truth? he asked himself as they left the restaurant and ambled back toward the Harley. Was she just pretending to keep tabs on him but actually reporting nothing important to the major while she was out on a lark with Charlie? Or was she reporting his every move back to the major? In either case, he couldn't do anything that would make her suspect that he was working for the CIA.

He might, however, be able to enlist her help in scouting out Meyer Lansky's jewels. Doing so, however, would be risky. When they got back to the Harley, he decided to take a chance. Palms sweating, he said, "This is going to sound weird, but there is one thing I would like to see while you're showing me around."

She looked down at him in the sidecar. She straddled the leather seat of the big Harley, and her blue skirt rose up her legs. Charlie tried not to stare.

"Hable, hombre," she laughed. "What is it?"

"This is going to sound a little strange, but people have told me about a famous cemetery you have."

She grinned. "El Cementério Cristóbal Colón. Yes, you must see that. It is one of the most ornate cemeteries in the world."

She kicked hard on the bike's starter pedal, and the engine roared to life. She weaved through the narrow streets of Old Havana, then through a posh residential neighborhood, and then up to the cemetery entrance. Again, she chained the cycle to a post, and they walked toward the entrance. He snapped a photo of her beneath the massive arch at the entrance. Then he imposed upon a young woman to photograph the two of them beneath the arch.

"¡Acérquense!" said the woman, motioning with her hands for them to move closer together. Isabel's shoulder pressed against Charlie's arm as they looked into the camera.

As Isabel pointed out graves of important Cubans, they came to the most elaborate tomb Charlie had ever seen, a seventy-five-foot high monument to firefighters who lost their lives in an1890's Havana fire.

"Where is the grave of Dolf Luque?" asked Charlie.

"Dolf Luque? It's right over there," she pointed. "But why do you care about Dolf Luque? I didn't know that the Irish played baseball."

"We don't," he said. "But my grandfather spent time in New

York thirty years ago when he was young. He keeps talking about this Negro Cuban who played for the Brooklyn team. I don't remember the team's name."

"Dolf wasn't Negro," she said. "The Americans didn't know what to do with him when he first arrived, and he got caught up in that crazy prejudice the Americans have. They would only let Cubans play in the Negro League. It wasn't until late in his career that he got into the Major League. I think the Brooklyn team was called The Dodgers."

"That's it!" Charlie beamed. "When I told my grandfather I had gotten permission to come to Cuba, he told me he wanted a photo of Dolf Luque's grave."

Her eyebrows narrowed in a skeptical look, but she led him through a maze of lanes and pointed to a gravesite that looked quite bland compared to its neighbors. In most American cemeteries, Dolf's tomb would be viewed as elaborate, Charlie thought. Here it looked quite modest. He lifted his camera and looked at the film counter.

"¡Mierda!" he exclaimed.

"What's wrong?"

"I'm out of film, and I left my spare roll on the floor of your sidecar. I hate to ask this, but would you get it for me? I've never seen gravestones like these, and I would like to have a few moments to wander around looking at them. If you get the film, you won't have to stand around waiting for me."

He gave her the most ingratiating smile he could muster, and she walked off toward the gate at the entrance. Charlie immediately glanced at each headstone near Dolf Luque's until he found the one for Alfonso Martínez. It was topped with three stone slabs. The slab at the head of the grave was only two inches thick, but it did not budge when he pushed on it. There must be a wedge, he thought, that fits against the walls of the crypt to keep the slab from slipping off. He bent his knees and pushed up with his legs and arms with all the power he could muster. Finally, the slab broke free from the sides of the vault, and Charlie pushed it aside.

In another stroke of luck, down in a corner of the vault, next to Alfonso's casket, was a five-gallon gasoline tank with peeling olive drab paint, just as Meyer Lansky had said. Charlie's pulse shot up.

He reached his right hand into the tomb to lift the jerrycan, but it was too heavy. Bending over the edge of the tomb, he used both hands to muscle the jerrycan up to the top of the casket, where he let it rest on its side. With some effort, he twisted open the cap. He reached his fingers into the can and jiggled it to shake its contents toward the opening. He finally touched what felt like two round stones joined together by some kind of string. He fiddled with the stones until he hooked his middle finger under the string and pulled it out of the can.

Oh my God! A foot-and-a-half long necklace of matching pearls. Meyer had told the truth.

Leaving the jerrycan on top of the casket, he tucked the pearls into his pocket and walked to the other side of the tomb so he could push the stone slab back into place. Just as he bent his knees to push the slab, he heard footsteps coming up the gravel path. Isabel was back! Lark or no lark, if she saw that he had opened a tomb, she would be obliged to report it to the major. But the slab was hard to move, and her footsteps were drawing closer. Again, with his pulse racing, he bent his knees and pushed the slab as hard as he could. He was gasping for breath by the time it locked into place. He stepped over to Dolf Luque's crypt and took several deep inhales to slow down his breathing, just as Isabel got there.

Taking the fresh rolls of film from her, he rewound the spool of used film, opened the back of the camera, and replaced the used cassette with a new one. Then he clicked three shots of Dolf Luque's grave. As they walked to the exit, she once again let her shoulder brush against his arm.

In the sidecar he stretched out his legs and leaned back in relief. From all appearances, she didn't suspect a thing. But now he really did have two jobs. Getting the jewels out, for which he was going to need her help. And shooting Castro, of which he had to keep her ignorant. Was it possible to do both jobs? If not, which should he choose? Finking out on recovering the jewels made no sense. Assuming that Meyer kept his word, Charlie's share of the jewels was worth more than anything Bishop could do for him. The problem, however, wasn't what Bishop could do for him. It was what Bishop could do to him. He could ruin Charlie's reputation and probably get his father prosecuted.

27

Week of October 14, 1962

HAVANA, CUBA

CHARLIE CHECKED TO SEE IF Flavio had contacted him yet. If Flavio could get the rifle to him before Castro showed up at Nuevo Mariel, Charlie could finish off this whole business. He went over in his mind how they could do it. Flavio would set up the rifle on the second floor of the abandoned building across the street from the clinic before Castro showed up. As an excuse for Charlie to walk over to the building, he would say that he needed to relieve himself. Since there was no public restroom in the area, nobody would think twice if a man went behind an empty building to urinate. He would run up the stairs, aim the rifle, squeeze the trigger, then run downstairs to whatever escape vehicle Bishop had provided for them. They would speed to the safe house before anyone realized where the shot had come from.

This was a risky plan, he realized, so they would have to be ready to abort it at a moment's notice. The major might put his own snipers in the building or order a soldier to follow Charlie when he walked off to relieve himself.

Their arrangement for establishing contact was straightforward. Flavio would tie or tape a phone number to a brick which he would hide in a predetermined spot at Revolution Square. Charlie walked the short distance from his hotel to the plaza. It was dominated by a towering memorial to the great Cuban patriot José Martí. A landscaped stone wall sloped away from the memorial, and Charlie took a seat at the end of the slope. He watched for anyone who might be looking in his direction. Seeing no one, he ran his hand along the back of the stone wall, feeling for Flavio's brick. However, he felt nothing. Glancing one more time at the walkway to make sure no one was watching, Charlie twisted around to look behind the wall. No brick was in sight. A sudden terror surged through him. Some cop must have intercepted the message. Then he calmed down. If the message had been intercepted, security police would have picked him up the moment he sat down on the wall.

When Isabel picked Charlie up Friday morning, she was back to wearing her green fatigues uniform, and the sidecar was missing from her Harley. "What happened?" he asked.

"It got a flat tire. The mechanic took off the sidecar so I could still drive around while he is fixing it. You'll have to sit behind me."

They rode west on the Carretera Panamericana parallel to the beach, Charlie behind her, his hands around her waist and his chest pressed against her back. She wound the Harley through the dusty streets of Nuevo Mariel to the clinic they had visited earlier. The doctor gushed with appreciation for Isabel's having arranged Castro's visit.

"Thank you so very much," he said, smiling broadly. "When el comandante sees how many things we need, he will get them for us."

Women swept the floors and wiped down the bare walls, doing their best to spruce up the Spartan clinic for the visit. Finally, about 1:00 p.m., dust appeared on the eastern horizon, and in a few minutes, half a dozen vehicles pulled into view. Major Escalante directed two squads of soldiers who hopped out of trucks and headed straight for

Charlie. They pinned his shoulders to the wall and patted him down, turning his pants pockets inside out. They dumped the contents onto the ground, including his pens and his reporter's tablet. Seeing no weapons, Major Escalante grabbed Charlie's 35-millimeter camera from his hands.

"Stop!" Charlie shouted. "If you open that, you'll ruin the film, and you won't get any pictures of Castro."

The major handed back the camera and turned to Isabel, "El bolso, por favor, señorita."

She handed him the purse. Instead of dumping its contents onto the ground as he had done with the stuff in Charlie's pockets, he simply opened it and fingered through it. Not finding a gun or a knife, he handed it back to her.

"You will pardon me, Señor Collins and Señorita Fernandez, but I am responsible for the prime minister's safety."

With that he signaled to a sedan at the end of the convoy that it was safe for the rider to get out. The tall bearded form of Castro emerged, toting a long, lighted cigar between the fingers of his left hand. Major Escalante allowed Charlie to take several photos of the leader as he walked around the clinic, conversed with the doctor, and greeted patients. Charlie snapped an especially poignant shot of him smiling while he touched a small boy on the cheek. Throughout, the major placed himself between Charlie and Castro.

"Can I get a statement from him?" Charlie asked. The major stepped aside and allowed Charlie to approach Castro. Charlie was almost six feet tall, but he had to look up to make eye contact with Castro, who was six three..

"Señor Castro, soy periodista de un periódico europeo. ¿Me permita unas pocas preguntas?"

Between puffs on his cigar, Castro graciously responded to Charlie's questions. At one stretch, he rambled for five minutes blaming the American embargo for hindering his attempts to improve Cuban health care. He spoke so fast that Charlie couldn't get it all written down. Major Escalante was stomping his feet impatiently, and Isabel approached him.

"You didn't have to inspect my purse, Major. I am not a spy. Are you finally satisfied that Mr. Collins is not your assassin?"

The major looked down at her, frowning. "It is my job, señorita, never to be satisfied about that. However, I have to admit that even the CIA wouldn't send a cripple to assassinate el jefe."

"A cripple?"

"You didn't notice that he limps?"

She frowned at the major. But before she could express her contempt for his remark, Castro stopped talking. The major hustled him back to his car, and once again, the entourage formed a convoy. As quickly as they had roared into town, they stormed out, heading back to Havana and leaving a cloud of dust in its wake.

"That hijo de puta!" exclaimed Isabel.

"Castro?"

"No, the major. He had no need to look into my purse. I'm no threat to anyone. He must be a pervert who gets his kicks out of looking into a woman's private things."

They returned to the motorcycle, and Charlie said, "We haven't eaten since breakfast. Could you find a café where we could stop, and I'll treat you to lunch?"

"I know just the place."

She drove west a few kilometers into the port city of Mariel. Charlie enjoyed the feel of pressing against her back and smelling her hair. They rode into town on a narrow, roughly paved street lined with many drab one-story houses. They passed through a small grimy industrial area dominated by a cement factory and an electric power plant as she drove them to a pleasant neighborhood called La Boca. It was at the tip of a small peninsula where the huge bay joined the ocean. She stopped at a small house with two tables outside the front facing the water. Across the street, a grassy area led down to the beach. Their table gave them a panoramic view of the bay.

"There aren't many of these left," she said.

"Many of what?"

"Private restaurants. The government nationalized the big restaurants and drove any restaurant owners tied to former President Batista out of the country."

"So how did this one stay private?"

"There are not enough government restaurants to meet the demand, so small places like this are allowed to stay in business. They're usually family affairs operated out of somebody's house."

Charlie narrowed his eyebrows. This was the first time all week that she'd said anything even mildly critical of the revolution.

"Wow," she said, looking at a sheet of paper, "they have frutas del mar."

"Let's do it."

She ordered a beer, and Charlie ordered a coffee. As they waited for their food, she sneered and said, "That wasn't Castro."

Charlie opened his eyes wide. "What do you mean? He has a double?"

"He has to," she replied, "given all the attempts by the CIA to kill him."

"All those photos are worthless then."

"Not necessarily," she replied, smiling for the first time. "If you and I couldn't tell the difference, how will your newspaper know?"

"But how do you know? He looked authentic to me."

"I was suspicious when the major was able to arrange for Castro to be here on only two days' notice without checking his schedule first. Then, the double waited too long to get out of his car. Castro is very impetuous, and ever since the rumors that he abandoned his troops after Moncada, he's very much afraid of looking cowardly. I think he would have brought that car roaring right up to you and jumped out even before it came to a complete stop. But this was the clincher."

She got to her feet, picked a newspaper from the neighboring table, and handed it to Charlie. "I saw this right before we sat down." She pointed to a small headline about Castro inspecting an anti-aircraft battery at Matanzas that morning.

"Matanzas must be 150 kilometers from here. Even Fidel can't be in two places at the same time."

Charlie stiffened at this knowledge. He had barely steeled himself to the task of killing the tyrant, and now he might end up killing Castro's innocent stand-in. Before he could say anything, she smiled and asked, "Did you ever hear the joke about Castro's double?"

"No."

"Since he has to maintain his weight to match that of Fidel, and Castro's not underweight, the double is the only man in Cuba who's not on a forced diet." She pulled at the baggy uniform hanging loosely over her abdomen, indicating that the forced diet had kept her so thin.

"Won't you get in trouble for telling Castro jokes?"

"Are you going to report me?" she quipped.

"No way," he laughed. "Don't worry about that."

The waiter came and placed two plates on the table. Before they picked up their knives and forks, Isabel smiled and said, "Show me how to use that camera and I'll get a picture of you behind that plate of seafood. It'll give you a memento you can take back to Ireland."

Charlie set the F-stop and the shutter speed for her and posed behind the food while she took his photo. Then he snapped one of her, and the waiter snapped one of the two of them together.

"What was this rumor of Fidel abandoning his troops that you mentioned?

"As you know, Fidel started the revolution in 1953 by attacking the army's Moncada barracks in Santiago. Most of his soldiers were captured, brutally tortured, and executed, but Fidel got away. He was caught by an honest policeman who locked him up rather than killing him. His opponents have always charged that he fled the scene as soon as the shooting started instead of sticking around to fight and protect his men. The charges aren't true, but because of the rumors, he feels that he must always do whatever makes him look brave, no matter how foolhardy it might be. So at the Bay of Pigs Invasion, for example, he went right up to the front lines to take part in the fighting."

She stopped talking and smiled as he picked at the seafood on his plate, trying to separate the antennae and the eyeballs from the pieces he would eat. Then he saw her staring at his hands as he shifted the knife and fork back and forth between his right and left hands. Jesus! He was eating like an American, and she seemed to have picked up on it. He clutched the fork in his left fist and kept it there. To divert her attention elsewhere, he pointed out toward the picturesque bay. Fishing boats were moored at weathered wooden docks, and men floated on big inner tubes, trailing fishing lines into the water. "What is that big building over there?"

"Something for the Russians, I imagine. They bring a lot of supplies in through this port."

Charlie set down his utensils, rose to his feet, and crossed the street to get a closer look at the water. He walked along a fence separating the grassy area from a construction project.

"Michael, stop! That's prohibited."

Cautiously, she followed at a distance. She caught up with him at the end of the fence. An armed sentry was patrolling around the building. The moment he disappeared around the corner of the building, Charlie said, "Wait here."

Grasping the fence post with both hands, he swung around it, ran to a bush overlooking the project, and crouched down. Isabel swung around the fence post the same way that Charlie had and slid in behind him just as the sentry reappeared. From their position they saw a very long shed covering an inlet of water lined by a walkway that wound around it in a U-shape. Next to it was another shed just like it.

"What are they?" she asked.

"My guess is that it's a repair shed for boats. The water lanes inside are too narrow for big ships like that one out in the bay." He pointed to a freighter. "And it's bigger than it needs to be for small boats."

"So what is it, then?"

"There's only one kind of vessel that's long and thin and sits low enough in the water to fit under that roof." He pointed his camera at the shed and snapped several photos.

She looked at the details he had pointed out. "Submarines," he said.

"And look at that!" He pointed his camera toward a construction project across the bay. Tall girders looked ominously similar to missile launchers he'd seen at Cape Canaveral in Florida. He cursed himself for not having brought a telephoto lens. On the ground, not far from the girders lay a long black tube.

"Missiles!" he said.

"So what?" she asked. "The Russians have given us lots of anti-aircraft missiles. And why wouldn't we have them here? This is a major port? If the Americans try to invade us, Castro will blast them out of the sky."

"Those missiles are bigger than any anti-aircraft missile I've heard of. And look at that Russian freighter out in the bay and those big nose cones spaced out on the deck. No one would ever waste anything that big just to shoot down airplanes. These are long-range missiles."

He pointed his camera, hoping that the missiles and the nose cones would show up in the picture. "Kennedy's going to explode when he sees this."

She gave him a sharp look, and Charlie gasped. "I mean when his spy planes discover this."

She didn't respond. He grabbed her hand to pull her to her feet, but just as they got up, the sentry came into view. Charlie knocked her harshly to the ground behind the bush. Once the sentry disappeared around the side of the building again, he jerked her back to her feet.

As they reached the Harley, he apologized for treating her so roughly. "I'm sorry for knocking you to the ground like that, but if that sentry had seen us, we would have had a lot of explaining to do."

She didn't respond.

"Let's get out of here," he said.

———

WHEN THEY REACHED HAVANA, ISABEL drove directly to her apartment. She wanted to show him typical living quarters, she said. She lived alone with her daughter, her parents having died two years earlier, and that was the main reason, she explained, why she had been unable to finish her college studies.

"Where is your daughter?" he asked as they came in the door.

"She's sleeping over at a friend's place. I will pick her up in the morning."

There wasn't much to show in the apartment. It was a small unit on the ground floor of a two-story building. The outside was tan stucco, with the walls splattered by dirt and dust where they rose from the ground. Inside, a few posters hung on whitewashed plaster walls. Bare electrical wires came out of the wall, and other wires were taped to them to bring electricity to a table lamp by a sofa and to a bare bulb hanging over an old scarred wooden kitchen table. A bare gas pipe came out of the wall and connected to a small stove with two burners. A bathroom and bedroom stood behind the kitchen.

She prepared two cups of tea, and they stood side by side looking at photos on the wall. Two were of her deceased parents and her as a child. Another photo showed her smiling as she held a small cinnamon-complexioned girl on her lap. Her shoulder brushed against his arm. Slowly, she took both cups and set them on an end table. She stood in front of him, misty-eyed, and he raised his hands to her cheeks.

In seconds, they wrapped their arms around each other. She led him through the kitchen into the bedroom where she stripped off the drab olive-colored uniform.

———

AFTERWARD, CHARLIE FELL ASLEEP. HE awoke with a start and realized that he had been dreaming of Vanessa. But it was Isabel pressed against him on the narrow bed, and he felt a pang of guilt. The room was dark, except for a moonbeam shining on the sheets, and Isabel was wide awake. She was lying on her back, her eyes open, staring at the ceiling. She looked over at him and smiled as she saw his eyes open.

He felt awkward. "I hope this doesn't get you in trouble."

She laughed. "You seem to worry a lot about me getting in trouble." She bent toward him and gave him a peck on the lips. "I don't know what it's like where you come from, but no Cuban is going to get in trouble for showing a little passion."

"¡Que bueno!" he replied.

"English," she said. "I want to practice my English. We've been speaking Spanish all week, and I need to practice my English."

He stammered something in monosyllables.

"It is fascinating," she said in English, "that you speak so eloquently in Spanish, which is not your native language. But you seem almost tongue-tied in English, which is the language you grew up with."

Still lying on her back, she turned her head sideways to look at him.

He said nothing.

"What is your real name?"

"Collins, Michael Collins."

"Señor Collins," she said, reverting to Spanish and clenching her fists in apparent nervousness. "I am going to take a great risk with you, a risk I probably should not take. But I cannot go on pretending.

I have to take the risk and I want you to take the same risk with me." She paused to let her words sink in. "You're not Irish, and judging by that story you filed, you're not much of a journalist."

"How do you know what was in that story. I didn't show it to you."

"Agence France-Presse held onto it long enough before sending it out for us to take a look at it. Michael, everything that goes out of Cuba is censored. If it is offensive, it doesn't go out."

She sat up in the bed and pulled her knees up to her bare chest. "You use American slang to describe my motorcycle. You have too much interest in a dead baseball player. You eat lunch with the wrong hand. You know too much about missiles and submarines. And you have photographs that you're going to send to Kennedy. Who are you?"

Charlie was stunned. He also sat up. He hadn't even been here a week, and his cover was blown, completely blown. Now what?

He asked, this time in perfect American English, "Was bringing me here just a ruse to expose me?"

"No, this was not a ruse," she replied in Spanish. "My cycle didn't have a flat tire. I just had the sidecar taken off so that you would have to ride behind me. And you were driving me crazy pressed up against me, breathing on my neck, and holding your hands on my waist. You have been so nice, and so available. It wasn't a ruse, Mr. Whatever-your-name-is. I loved it, and I wouldn't give it back for all the tea in India."

"In my country we say, 'all the tea in China,' not 'all the tea in India.'"

"So you are American? Not Irish?"

He nodded. "However, I really am a stringer for the Irish Times. Somebody in the U.S. government thought it would be a brilliant idea to get a reporter admitted to Cuba from a European newspaper so he could do a hatchet job on the revolution."

"But that story you filed on the clinic was not a hatchet job. If you were supposed to do a hatchet job, why didn't you chop up the clinic?"

"You told me that the clinic didn't exist until Castro took power. Until then, the people had no clinic. The doctor was so sincere and so overwhelmed with sick people that I couldn't chop him up. Especially not after watching him handle that screaming baby with the ear infection that could have easily been cured with an antibiotic if he'd only had one. But he doesn't, I suppose because of the U.S. embargo. I couldn't do it. I still don't like Castro or this revolution of yours, but that doctor deserved respect."

They lay quiet for a moment before he asked. "What now? Do you turn me in?"

"I should," she said, "unless I want to end up in a drawer cell."

"A drawer cell?"

She described Major Escalante using the baseball bat to terrorize the bent-over girl who couldn't stand up straight because of the night she'd spent in the drawer cell. Then, in what seemed to him to be an abrupt change of subject, she asked, "How did you plan to get out?"

"Of Cuba?"

"Yes. You'll never be able to get on a commercial flight with those photos you've been snapping of submarine pens and missile batteries."

He paused before responding. "They'll send a boat for me. But I can't tell you anything about who or where or how."

They lay on their backs staring at the ceiling. He turned on his side to look at her.

"I wish I had met you some other way. I would have liked to know you better. And meet your daughter, Angelita."

Her eyes began to tear up, and she sobbed softly. "How could two people be put into such a horrible situation?"

He remembered Bishop's instruction that he should kill anyone who discovered his identity. But that was impossible. He swung his legs out of the bed and reached for his pants. "Before you run in to tell the major what you've discovered about me, would you give me an hour's head start to get out of here?"

She didn't move.

He motioned with his hands for her to respond, but she still didn't move. He gestured again in exasperation. "What is it? What do you want from me?"

"I want you to take Angelita and me on that boat. I want you to get us out of Cuba."

28

THE WHITE HOUSE

TED SORENSEN SCOWLED AS HE returned to his office. When he finished dictating his notes, Vanessa understood the scowl. He had just left a meeting of the president with the Joint Chiefs of Staff. They demanded surprise air strikes to take out the Russian missiles in Cuba. This would be followed by an invasion. One hundred forty thousand troops were now positioned to invade the island, and a contingent of marines had already practiced an amphibious landing in Puerto Rico. A blockade, the chiefs argued, was much too risky. It would fail to get the nuclear missiles out of Cuba, and it would open up the danger of a direct naval confrontation with the Soviets at the blockade line that might escalate into a nuclear exchange.

When his dictation got to the comments of the Air Force Chief of Staff, General Curtis LeMay, Sorensen shook his head in disgust. LeMay had scorned the blockade as being "almost as bad as the appeasement at Munich" and had left the president seething. Sorensen looked up at Vanessa. "He must be my least favorite human being. That was a punch below the belt."

"I understand that Munich refers to appeasing Hitler before World War II," she said. "But why is that hitting the president below the belt?"

"The president's father," Sorensen explained, "destroyed his own political future while serving as ambassador to England in 1940. He opposed resisting Hitler's aggression, even after Hitler began bombing London. By his Munich reference, Le May was threatening to publicly brand the president as an appeaser like his father."

"After you type up my notes, take the rest of the day off. I can cover ExComm this afternoon, but I will need you fresh and alert tomorrow. The president is flying to Chicago to campaign for candidates there," Sorensen finished.

"He's going to campaign? With all this going on?" Dumbfounded, she scratched her head.

"We need things to look like it's business as usual around here until we decide on our response to the Soviets. If the press finds out about it beforehand, we lose control over our options. He wants Bobby and me to bring ExComm to an agreement by the time he returns on Sunday. That means I'll have a lot of work for you all weekend. So go out and relax this afternoon because the next few days will be grueling."

As if she could relax in light of the latest turn of events. As if anyone could relax. She wandered zombie-like up to her desk on the second floor of the West Wing to type up the dictation. From her top desk drawer, she pulled out the sealed manila envelope with Charlie's documents inside and read the thick black words she had printed on it.

Personal papers of Vanessa Perez

If I fail to show up for work tomorrow, give this immediately to Ted Sorensen.

She drew a line through the previous day's date, wrote in the current date—Friday, October 19—and put it back in her desk drawer. She had worked out an arrangement with a fellow secretary that each would check the other's top desk drawer for any unfinished business if the other failed to show up for work. That would protect each of them from letting anything urgent slip through their fingers. She grabbed a sweater from the back of her chair and left.

The fifteen-hour days since the creation of ExComm on Tuesday had become a drain, not only on Vanessa, but on everyone. It showed in the clenched jaws and stooped shoulders of the men on the committee and the growing tension among them. She recalled stories about a clash between Attorney General Robert Kennedy and Secretary of State Dean Rusk. Back when the CIA began pressing the president to restart the U-2 surveillance flights over Cuba, Rusk had strongly objected. "What's the matter, Dean?" the attorney general had chided, "No guts?"

She was glad to be out of the pressure cooker for the afternoon. She headed toward the Shaw Community Defense Center for a Friday workout with her karate instructor. Charlie had laughed at her when she had told him about the karate class. But she had retorted, "This city isn't safe for a woman, Charlie. If somebody tries to mug me, I want to know how to kick him in the face."

When Sorensen had mentioned the president's trip to Chicago, she had hoped for a brief second that she might be invited along. She had never been to Chicago. But on reflection, she was glad to be left out. She had accompanied him on an earlier trip, but it had been a disappointment. Rather than flying on Air Force One, she was put on the backup plane with reporters who peppered her with innuendoes about why a mere White House intern was travelling with the president. Then at the hotel, she was ordered to stay in her room out of sight while the president conducted his business.

Late in the evening, Dave Powers escorted her to the president's suite. Kennedy had returned, but his back was in agony. She helped him out of his back brace. The brace made his spine so rigid that he could not even bend enough to untie his shoelaces, so she did that for him. If he ever needed to bend forward in a hurry, thought Vanessa, he would be in trouble. Once out of the brace, he began a set of exercises prescribed by his orthopedic physician. Lying on his back, he raised each leg in turn, clasping it by the knee, and pulling it to his chest. The exercises seemed to ease his pain because he started to talk. "I usually do these with some background music. See what you can find on the radio."

She searched through the FM stations until she found one playing Broadway show tunes.

"That's good," he said.

Marilyn Monroe was singing "Diamonds are a Girl's Best Friend."

He asked for a glass of water and a pain pill from a bag of medications he carried. She was shocked at the number of pill bottles in the bag. The pain killers were not prescribed by his physical therapy doctor, because he didn't believe in pain killers. Those came from another physician some White House aides called Dr. Feelgood. Whether these two doctors ever discussed the president's health with his official White House physician, Vanessa didn't know. But she did know that the little black bag contained an excessive number of pills.

Ever since that trip, however, and her appearance as Sorensen's aide at the ExComm meetings, Kennedy had become somewhat distant with her. He continued being gracious when they came into contact, but he seldom invited her up to the family quarters, and his telephone calls became less frequent. The urgency of the missile crisis had changed everything.

With Kennedy backing away from her and Charlie out of the country, she felt abandoned. Not that male companionship would be hard to attract. Even in a city as overpopulated with single women as Washington, Vanessa drew attention from men. However, she had no desire to scout out a new lover. She would do that only if it became impossible to repair the rift with Charlie. She didn't understand why he had been so hurt. The affair with Kennedy was only a fling, and Charlie ought to realize that. What girl wouldn't jump at the chance to spend an hour in bed with a president as handsome as Kennedy?

And it wasn't as though Charlie was above reproach. This new assignment of his raised a huge question. Did he truly intend to shoot Castro? That would end their relationship faster than anything else she could think of. Or, as seemed more likely, had he accepted this assignment to buy enough time to think up a way to prevent Bishop from carrying through with his blackmail threat against Charlie's father? Once he figured a way out, would he pull a fast one on his CIA handlers by aborting the attempt to assassinate Castro? It was a dangerous game to play, but he was, she knew, capable of such deviousness. A little deviousness in a potential mate is desirable, to be sure. Straight arrows don't get very far in this world. But this latest venture of Charlie's was over the top.

Rosslyn, Virginia

Vanessa was half daydreaming as she returned from the karate workout, parked her car, and wandered toward her apartment entrance. Just as she reached the door, two muscular men trapped her. One was huge; like a linebacker in the National Football League, and his ears popped out like megaphones, just as Charlie had described.

The smaller one said, "Miss Perez?"

"Yes?"

"We have some news about your friend, Lieutenant Parnell. Could we go someplace private where we could talk?"

"It's private right here," she said. "Nobody is in sight." She struggled to keep her voice from quaking. This day was bound to come, and she had been dreading it since the moment she had read Charlie's documents. When the men made no effort to start a conversation, she added, "Do you gentlemen have any identification?"

Both men held up FBI identification cards, but they flashed them so fast she couldn't make out the names. But it didn't matter. Smith looked exactly like Charlie's description of Walter Bishop—squat, mid-thirties, crew cut, and horn-rimmed glasses.

"We would really like to talk in private," said Bishop. "Could we go up to your apartment?"

"I would have to be nuts to let two total strangers into my apartment."

"You've already seen our FBI identification," he replied. "This is a government investigation, so we're not exactly strangers. You are perfectly safe."

Before she could reply, they each grabbed an arm and pushed her through the door into the building. Recalling a trick from her karate class, she slammed the hard sole of her shoe onto Bishop's instep, causing him to recoil and let go of her arm. But the other man tightened his grip. Even though she squirmed and tried to break free, she was no match for his strength. She cursed her recklessness for having rented in a building without a security guard. They led her to the elevator and pushed the button for the third floor. Leaving the elevator, they strongarmed her to the door, but she refused to pull out her key to unlock it.

"You can either unlock the door yourself, or we'll break in."

When she hesitated, Bishop's assistant pulled a pick from his pocket, wiggled it into the key slot, and, in less than a minute, pushed the door open. Bishop shoved her into an easy chair, then bent over to rub his sore instep. "You're too gutsy for you own good."

Although terrified, she blurted, "You're going to manhandle a White House aide? You must be crazy!"

Smith squatted in front of her as she sat in the easy chair.

"We don't plan to manhandle you, Miss Perez," he said in a soothing voice. "We want those documents that Lieutenant Parnell stole from the government and gave to you. As soon as you give them to us, we will leave."

"I don't have any documents," she shouted. "Get out of here! I don't know what you are talking about."

Smith turned on the TV set, adjusting the volume loud enough to drown out her voice but not loud enough to bother neighbors. He picked up an airmail envelope sitting on the end table by the easy chair.

As he read it, he smiled. "Interesting. You know nothing about any documents. But here is an envelope mailed from Ireland. Inside the envelope is a postcard signed by Michael Collins, which is your boyfriend's alias. But there is no address for your Ireland contact."

"Go to hell!" she shouted.

Bishop's assistant turned the TV volume up another notch.

"It would be better if you cooperated, Miss Perez. Your friend has made off with classified materials that we want back."

"Go to hell," she repeated, but in a weaker voice.

Smith paused. "You might want to think about the welfare of your parents, who are in a very vulnerable position. For example, they would not want the IRS to find out about that illegal bank account your father has in the Cayman Islands."

Smith nodded toward the telephone sitting on the end table. He picked up the hand set and held it out to her. Not knowing what else to do, she dialed her father's number.

"I have in my apartment an asshole and a son of a whore from the CIA." Since she was speaking in Spanish, she figured they wouldn't be able to identify the insulting language or her pronunciation of the word CIA. "They're threatening to tell the IRS that you have an illegal bank account in the Cayman Islands."

A loud torrent of Spanish came through the phone's earpiece. She lowered the handset and said to Smith, "He says he closed out that account a long time ago and already reported to the IRS."

Grabbing the phone from her hand, Smith shouted into the mouthpiece, "Listen, you wetback. If you know what's good for you, you'll tell your daughter to cooperate."

"It's too late," said Vanessa, smirking. "He already hung up."

Bishop twisted the receiver end of the handset to his ear and heard nothing but the dial tone. He snapped over his shoulder to his buddy, "Bring her to the bathroom. True, we can't leave any bruises on her. But I'm sure we can show her the reasonableness of what we want."

He strode to the bathroom and filled the tub with cold water. The assistant followed, dragging Vanessa with him. While Bishop pushed her down so that her back was against the rim of the tub, the other man knelt on her ankles to prevent her from kicking her way free. Without a word, Bishop forced her head under the water. He held her there long enough for her to panic, then pulled up her head. She coughed and gasped for breath. Her eyes widened and her mouth dropped open in a panicky look of terror.

"That was fifteen seconds. You can either give us what we want, or you go under for twenty seconds. And then twenty-five, and so on until you give it to us."

She said nothing, and Bishop forced her head under for a full twenty seconds before pulling her up. She spat in his direction, and Bishop plunged her back under the water.

They could do this to me, but they couldn't kill me, she said to herself, gathering her courage as she was jerked up and then thrust under the water again. If she held out as long as she could, maybe he would give up. But her time underwater grew longer and longer. Never in her life had she ever been so much under somebody else's control. With Bob kneeling on her ankles, she couldn't even squirm out of Smith's grip. She looked pleadingly at him when he pulled her up, but he pushed her back under.

The final plunge only lasted sixty seconds, but it seemed like forever. Her chest began heaving so strongly that she couldn't keep her mouth closed. By the time Smith pulled her back up, water was already draining into her lungs. She coughed and sputtered. "My safe-deposit box."

"See how easy that was," smiled Smith. "And you could have saved yourself that unpleasantness if you had cooperated. Now put on some dry clothes so you look normal when we go to your bank." He threw a bath towel at her.

Bishop followed her into the bedroom.

"Give me some privacy," she snarled.

"Can't," he said. "You might have a gun in that dresser."

Toweling herself dry, she weighed her chances of attacking Bishop with a karate kick to the face. He was very powerful, but she would have the element of surprise, because he would be distracted by the sight of her pulling off her wet underclothes. He would never expect a sudden karate kick to the face. With the hard-soled shoes she was wearing she could easily break his nose. She had practiced that kick often enough at the gym that she could pull it off. Then she could go to the living room, catch other one by surprise, and do the same thing to him. However, it wouldn't do her any good. After the shock of getting their noses broken, they would recover, and they would still be in her apartment. Even if she got them out of the apartment, they would just send two different thugs the next day, and eventually she would have to give up the envelope.

———

AT THE BANK, BISHOP WALKED Vanessa toward the entrance. He grabbed her arm and warned her. "You're going into the safe-deposit room by yourself. But if you tip them off in any way that anything at all is wrong, there will be hell to pay. The next guys who come after you won't be as nice as we have been."

Bishop sat alone in the lobby while Vanessa checked in to visit her safe-deposit box. He was still sitting there when she emerged carrying the large manila envelope. She thought of telling him that he had accomplished nothing, because a second envelope was sitting in Ted Sorensen's office. But she decided it might be better to withhold this information. She motioned for Smith to stay seated as she slid into the chair next to him.

"The only thing I want," she said, staring coldly at Bishop's eyes, "is for Charlie to come back safely. You'd better make sure you do that."

"He'll be back. You don't have to worry about that," Bishop said as he reached out for the envelope. She pulled it back toward her lap, waited a second, and then tossed it on the floor. "Now get the fuck out of here and let me walk home in peace."

29

Week of October 14, 1962

Havana, Cuba

WHEN MAJOR ESCALANTE ARRIVED AT his office on Saturday morning, he found a rumpled older woman sitting in the dirt by the front door. She was resting her back against the mud-spattered pink stucco of the building.

"Buenos dias, Doña Clara." He smiled, then unlocked the door and motioned for her to enter. She took a seat in a hardback wood chair while he walked behind the desk to his swivel chair.

"She had a visitor last night, señor major—a man, the whole night."

"This visitor, what did he look like?"

"A gringo. Very pale, tall, and slim. A head of bushy hair, and he walked with a limp. Why would she entertain a gringo who limps? A gringo showing off that gold wristwatch the way he did?" Doña Clara raised her nose.

"What about the daughter? This all took place in front of the daughter?"

"The daughter was gone. She has some place to leave the daughter when she wants privacy."

"Thank you, Doña Clara. Please see if you can find out where she puts the daughter." He handed her some peso notes. "This will help cover the costs of coming over here this morning. Are your rations okay?"

"I could use more rice, señor, and perhaps a little more chicken."

"I will talk to the rationing committee," he replied, as he ushered the woman to the door. "It should show up next month. If it doesn't, let me know."

He sank back into his swivel chair. Thank God for the Committee for the Defense of the Revolution, with its network of grandmother spies. After the previous day's encounter at the health clinic, Major Escalante had come to doubt that Collins was the assassin. Then he and Fernandez disappeared for the rest of the day, only to reappear and spend the night together.

A month ago, she had insisted that she was too good to sleep with Collins in order to help the revolution. Now she has no trouble taking him in for the night to further her own agenda, whatever that is. He rubbed his chin. Escalante had no objections to a young woman sharing a moment of passion with a young man. But this particular young woman had two years of college, held a semi-professional job, and had a three-year-old daughter to protect. Would such a woman take the risk of jumping into bed with a possible killer simply out of passion? Just days after she had met him? There must be another motive.

Once again, the major put Collins back to the top of his list of potential assassins, and Isabel Fernandez entered his list of suspicious people. He didn't know what he suspected her of, since he was not even certain that Collins was an enemy. However, something didn't smell right. The next time he saw her he would find out what she had to say about this and where she hides her daughter when she wants to be alone. Finding the location of the daughter was the key to keeping the mother in line.

"BEFORE ANYTHING, YOU MUST MEET Angelita," Isabel told Charlie as they prepared to leave her apartment on Saturday morning.

"Where is she?"

Instead of responding, she led him out the door to unchain her motorcycle from its post. He hopped on behind her, and they drove off. After a kilometer, she stopped along the road, across from a school. She twisted around to face him while she balanced the cycle by touching her toes to the ground. "She's hidden with a santera, a priestess in the Santeria religion of the Afro-Cubans."

"Hidden? Why?"

Isabel set the cycle on its kickstand, and they both got off so they could stand facing each other.

"So that Major Escalante can't kidnap her," she said.

"Why would he kidnap a three-year-old child?"

"To keep me in line."

"But from what you told me about the girl in the drawer cell, he already has plenty of threats to keep you in line."

She grimaced. "Oh that poor girl, Michael. She was a wrecked animal, she could barely function. Then after he pretended to set her free, he had a truck run over her." At that point, she got interrupted by an army jeep that sped past them and kicked up dust.

"Jesus. I should have kept my mouth shut last night. If he suspects any of those things I told you, you're done for."

"I was done for anyway. I'd already figured out you're not Irish and not a journalist. But if I turned you in, I would lose my only hope of Angelita and me escaping Cuba."

He grinned with admiration. "You're a gutsy lady. I understand why you hid Angelita, but why with a santera?"

"Because she is safe there. The santera conducts her worship in a house of saints, sort of like a Christian church or a Jewish synagogue. Except that in this case, the house of saints is her own house."

The sun was higher in the sky now, pouring off its heat, and sweat trickled down Charlie's back under his shirt. Noises of children at play drifted toward them from a yard across the road.

"There is no one at the house of saints who reports back to the CDR you told me about—that Committee for the Defense of the Revolution?"

"Oh, yes. The government frowns on all religion. They have placed a grandmother spy among the members."

"A grandmother spy?"

"The CDR gives money to old ladies to keep watch on what happens. We call them grandmother spies. But the grandmother spy at this house of saints won't report anything that the santera says to leave alone."

"The grandmother spy is not afraid of the CDR?"

"Of course she is. The CDR or Major Escalante could kick her out of her apartment, cut her food rations, and turn her into a beggar. But she believes that the santera"—Isabel held up a finger for emphasis—"has the power to send her to hell. Forever."

CHARLIE AND ISABEL RODE THE Harley into a small compound near a bay west of Havana and parked by a shack. A small tan-skinned girl ran toward Isabel with squeals of delight.

"Mucho gusto," said Charlie when Isabel introduced him to the santera, an older Black woman with a gnarled face and a warm smile. He became an object of curiosity at the house of saints. "¿Americano?" a pair of teens guessed. With his pale complexion, Charlie stood out among the people there, who were mostly Black. When he responded that he was from Ireland, they peppered him with questions about European attitudes toward Cuba. Charlie made up answers.

"We admire what you have done for education and health," he said.

"What about our music and our dance? The conga?" One teen got behind the other to do a few steps of the dance and the kick.

"That, too," said Charlie, grinning. He lined up behind the teens and joined in.

After a few steps, he left and joined Isabel, who was sitting at a table watching Angelita play with some other children. "I'm curious about something," he said. "It's none of my business, so you can tell me to butt out if you want to. I understand why you keep Angelita hidden, but why do you do it in a place where almost all the other people are Black?"

"Her father was part Black, and he died in Africa, so she also is part Black. I want her to keep a connection to him and to the African part of her background."

———

SHORTLY AFTER LUNCH, ISABEL SAT next to Charlie on the ground, where he leaned against the trunk of a tree. The pleasant smell of frying plantains lingered in the air. Angelita came over to sit on her mother's lap. She pointed to the flat top hat on Charlie's head. "What is that funny hat?"

"He always wears that"—Isabel laughed—"even on the hottest days." She put the hat on the girl's head.

Charlie tried to look relaxed as he leaned against the tree and fingered an unlit cigar that someone had given him. His other hand was clenched anxiously into a fist. Confiding in Isabel had been risky. In this topsy-turvy world of Cuba with its grandmother spies and drawer cells, could he trust anyone? She lay her hand on his clenched fist.

"How long will it be?" she asked.

"Until we can leave?"

She lifted Angelita off her lap. "Honey, Momma has to talk with Michael for a minute. Go play with the children over there." She pointed to two girls playing a game that looked something like hopscotch. Charlie pulled the flat-topped hat from Angelita's head before she ran off to join the other girls.

"Unless I want to make the major suspicious, I'll have to show up at my job on Monday. But the longer I stay, the riskier it gets," said Isabel.

"There are two things I have to do before we go, and you could help with one of them."

She raised her hand, palm up, in a gesture for him to continue.

"You say that the police don't bother the santera, and that she can keep things from the grandmother spies."

"That is true," said Isabel.

"There is something I want to take with us when the boat picks us up. Would she let us hide it here until we are ready to leave?"

"I am sure she would."

"And she wouldn't look into it herself or let the grandmother spy know about it?"

"I am certain of that," said Isabel. "But what is it?"

From his pocket, Charlie pulled out the strand of pearls he had extracted from the jerrycan in the cemetery."

Isabel's eyes widened, and her jaw dropped. She took the pearls from his hand. "These are real?"

"As far as I know."

"I haven't seen anything this beautiful in years," she said, draping the pearls across her hands. "This is what you want to hide?"

"No," he said. "These are yours to keep. Somebody asked me to pick up some jewelry he put in a hiding place just before he fled Cuba. If you drive me there at sunset, we can move the rest of the jewelry here."

"That stone you were pushing on top of that tomb next to Dolf Luque's grave. That's where you got this." She held up the pearls in front of his face. "How much jewelry are we talking about?"

"A lot," said Charlie. "Probably fifteen kilos. But I have two bags we can put it in so that we can carry it back here. We won't even need the sidecar on your bike."

Charlie left the house of saints and spent four hours walking back to the Hotel Habana Libre, where he picked up his two black doctor's bags. At 7:00 p.m., he walked to the rendezvous spot where Isabel had promised to pick him up.

She found an opening in the cemetery fence which they drove through. The sun had set, and dusk was beginning to settle in, but a bright half-moon lit the sky. Charlie pushed aside the stone lid from the grave and struggled to move the heavy jerrycan from the top of Alfonso Martínez's casket to the ground. He shoveled half the jewelry from the jerrycan into the first bag and half into the other. Then he locked them.

"Let's get out of here," she said, "before somebody sees us in this moonlight."

"Wait." He tossed the jerrycan back inside the tomb and pushed the stone lid back in place. "No point in advertising that we were here."

He looped a short rope through the handles of the bags to make a sling that he draped over the back of his neck. This left the bags hanging, one on each side, as he got onto the back seat of the motorcycle and held on to her waist with his hands.

The Santeria ceremony had already started when they got back. Isabel pushed the medicine bags under a cot in the room she shared with her daughter.

"I should take you back to the Habana Libre. You will raise suspicions if you stay here overnight."

Charlie looked out from the room, mesmerized by the scene in the yard. The santera had changed clothes. She now wore a multi-colored smock and a turban-like headdress. An altar had been fashioned on a table, with a saint's statue as the centerpiece. In front of the statue was a glistening roasted chicken and a lush arrangement of bananas, orange slices, mangos, and other fruits. Four lighted candles sat at the corners of the altar. The smell of the candles and roast chicken mingled with the aroma of incense. Scattered on neighboring tables were crucifixes, holy pictures, medallions of the Virgin Mary, and images of Nigerian orishas. These were gods or saints; Charlie did not know the difference.

A thin older man with white stripes painted on his black chest, glowed in the image of two lighted candles he held in his hands. A woman, with white gauze wrapped around her head sat on the ground puffing a huge cigar. The santera sat in a chair, holding in one hand a lit cigar and in the other a baton that she seemed to be using to direct the activities. At her feet on the ground sat Isabel's daughter, Angelita. In front of the santera, a dozen people in various costumes danced to the vibrant beat of drummers slapping the palms of their hands on homemade drums. A teenage dancer began to shriek and raise her hands to the sky. She twirled faster and faster as she danced. Then she slowed, bent over and bobbed her head as she continued shrieking. Finally, she fell to the ground, and began to twitch with convulsions.

Charlie's eyes widened. "Is she all right?"

"She received the saint," said Isabel, as she grabbed Charlie's forearm and tugged him toward the exit.

He resisted. "I want to see this."

"You can see it next time. Right now, we have to get you back to the Habana Libre. Sit at the bar for a couple of hours so that your other watchers will learn that you were there when they come around tomorrow asking about you."

30

Week of October 21, 1962

HAVANA, CUBA

REVOLUTION SQUARE WAS EMPTY ON Sunday when Charlie checked for a message from Flavio. He reached behind the stone wall beneath the towering José Martí monument, and his fingers touched a brick. A piece of twine was wound around the brick, securing a small placard of cardboard. He slipped it out from under the twine. It read, "97 5662 at 1:30."

He strolled through the park, then down several side streets, but saw no one on his tail. Finding a pay phone, he dialed 26 6579, the reverse of the numbers written on the cardboard. Charlie and Flavio had agreed on the precaution of writing the phone number backward and the time three hours later than scheduled, in case security police intercepted the message. That way they would arrive to arrest Flavio three hours too late at the wrong address.

"It's me," said Charlie when Flavio answered.

"Make sure you're not followed. Then meet me in front of the Floridita."

Flavio was lounging against a wall, watching a woman drive a pedicab past the restaurant. When they made eye contact, Flavio strolled away from the restaurant. Charlie followed, as Flavio made several turns to double-check that no one had followed them. He came to a stop before an out-of-sight doorway in the middle of a narrow street.

"This is a private restaurant," said Flavio. Then he nodded at a teen-age boy. "And this kid here will get us some lunch."

The boy led them up a flight of stairs where he sat them on the floor of what looked to be somebody's living room. It was nearly as barren as Isabel's apartment. After a moment, the boy brought them each a chicken drumstick.

"Is it safe to talk here?" asked Charlie.

"As much as any place in Cuba," replied Flavio, grinning. "We don't report the owner for running an illegal restaurant, and he doesn't report what we talk about."

"Man, I thought you'd never get here." Charlie smiled.

"You're looking eager to get started."

"We could have done it Friday, if you would have just been here. We'd be on the way home now. Where's the stuff?"

"It's buried in the backyard at the safe house."

Charlie's head jerked up with a start. "Buried? That'll ruin it!"

"Don't worry," laughed Flavio. "It's wrapped in an oilcloth. It'll work like it's brand new."

"I want to check it out."

"Let's finish lunch. Then I'll take you out there and introduce you to Pepe. He's the radio operator."

"Is it far?

"Fifteen kilometers, maybe. I'll run you in and out on a scooter that Bishop got for me."

"You should have asked for a jeep. It would be a lot easier to cart our stuff around."

"Too conspicuous," said Flavio. "Speaking of which, tell your girlfriend that she stands out like a sore thumb with that big flashy Harley she's got."

"She's not my girlfriend. She's the escort that Castro uses to keep tabs on me. But how do you know this? You been spying on me?"

"I suspected you'd be at the Habana Libre, so I loitered on the street until I saw you come out."

Flavio followed the same route to the safe house that Isabel had followed two days earlier on the way to Mariel. They got off the highway at the town of Santa Fe, just west of a bay that Flavio said had been the locale for Hemingway's masterpiece, *The Old Man and the Sea*. Given the many boats at the marina, it would be a promising place for Bishop to put a small boat ashore to pick them up. If that failed, Charlie could hot-wire one of the boats in the marina and drive back to Key West himself. Of course, they could only do this if Flavio could find a boatload of five-gallon gas cans.

They continued around the bay to its western edge. They wandered through several side streets until they were satisfied that they weren't being followed and came to a halt at a small, isolated house a few blocks in from the beach. Across the street was a small thicket of woods.

Only one person was home, an emaciated middle-aged man named Pepe, who scratched his arm nervously when Charlie came into the room. He promised to radio for the pickup boat as soon as they instructed him. "When will you need me?" he asked.

"We don't know yet," said Flavio. "A week, maybe. Two at most. Is that a problem?"

"The sooner the better," said Pepe. "If you two guys hang around here very long, that grandmother spy at the end of the street is bound to notice. You,"—he pointed to Flavio—"are okay, because I've been talking about my nephew coming to visit. She'll just think that's you. This guy, however,"—he pointed at Charlie—"is obviously a gringo.

If he stays here, I'll be done for."

Flavio took Charlie to the point in the backyard where he had buried the M1. Charlie knelt down to brush the dirt away with his fingers. Flavio got him a machete from the house.

"What the hell is Pepe doing with a machete?" asked Charlie.

"Cubans cut sugar cane." Flavio shrugged. "Lots of people have machetes."

"Not the world's greatest digging tool, but it'll work." Chopping into the ground, Charlie dug up the rifle. He put both it and the machete in a gunny sack he had brought.

"I've got it," said Charlie. "Now I need you to take me someplace on the scooter."

He instructed Flavio to find the road to San Antonio de los Baños. Traveling south on that road, they crossed the East-West Highway, and Charlie looked for a side street heading east. The only one he found had a guardhouse with a soldier standing in front, a rifle slung over his shoulder. A kilometer down the road, Charlie told Flavio to reverse direction and slow down after they passed the guardhouse on the way back. A few hundred meters past it, they found a very small lane headed east, parallel to the road with the guardhouse. They turned onto the lane and wound around until they came upon a big open space facing a complex of buildings in the shape of a quadrangle.

"Turn off the engine so they don't hear us," said Charlie. "Then we'll hide the scooter behind that clump of bushes."

"It's just the boys' reform school," said Flavio as they peered into the quadrangle from the bushes.

"It might have been a reform school at one time," said Charlie, "but according to Bishop, it's now the Russians' el Chico headquarters for their Cuba operations."

Charlie dumped his burlap sack on the ground and used the machete to dig a hole where he could bury both the rifle and the big knife. He left the rifle in the oilcloth and stuck it in the burlap bag.

Then he swept dirt over the hole and piled grass and leaves on top of it.

He pulled out his camera, inserted a new roll of film, and began snapping pictures of everything he could see—long dormitory-type buildings by the perimeter of the complex, a few free-standing buildings, a squad of young men being led through a calisthenics drill, and the Soviet hammer-and-sickle flag flying over the main building. Two men in civilian clothes with rifles slung over their shoulders patrolled the perimeter inside a chain link fence.

"Brilliant spot for a headquarters," Charlie said. "It's close enough to Havana for easy access but secluded enough that it presents no security problem. When Castro comes out here, he stays in a building called Punto uno, but I can't figure out which one that is."

"It doesn't matter," said Flavio. "At some point he'll have to walk over to that main building with the Soviet flag, and he'll be a sitting duck for you. It's barely a hundred meters away with nothing obstructing your line of fire."

Charlie continued clicking through the thirty-six-exposure roll of film, wound it back into its cassette, and removed it from the camera.

"Do you have a way to get this to Bishop?"

"I have a contact who goes back and forth to Guantanamo. He'll pass it on for us."

Charlie handed the cassette to Flavio, then pulled two other film cassettes from his pockets. He looked at them carefully, handed one to Flavio, and kept the one with the photos of Isabel and him at the cemetery.

"Send this one along as well. Bishop is going to love it. It's got submarine pens at Mariel, anti-aircraft batteries, missiles, and a Soviet freighter carrying warhead cones. These missiles here are much larger than anti-aircraft missiles. And the Russians wouldn't use ones this big for conventional warheads. This confirms what Bishop told me. When he turns in these photos, he's going to be the biggest hero the Company's ever had."

"What about the other one?" Flavio said, pointing to Charlie's pocket where he had returned the third cassette.

"Never mind about that one. Have your contact tell Bishop there's one more roll of film he gets after you and I are safely back home. It's sort of an insurance policy for us."

———

FLAVIO DROVE THEM TO THE house of an old acquaintance in the city not far from Hotel Habana Libre. For fifty pesos, the acquaintance let Flavio hide the scooter inside a shed on his property and agreed that Charlie could pick it up any time he wanted. Flavio and Charlie embraced and then parted. As Charlie watched Flavio walk away, he pondered about his own relationship with Flavio. He didn't think Flavio would betray him. However, he did worry about Flavio's ability to keep secrets. Only a few weeks earlier, he had compromised Charlie's identity by putting him in contact with Meyer Lansky. If he let anything slip about the safe house or the M1 rifle or their stake-out spot at el Chico, Charlie would be in danger.

As soon as Flavio disappeared from sight, Charlie returned to the shed. He drove the scooter back to el Chico to dig up the M1. Inside the oilcloth, he placed the film cassette he had held back from Flavio. He slipped his flat top hat with the money in the lining into the oilcloth as well. Then he reburied everything in another spot that Flavio wouldn't know about.

Once back at Flavio's friend's house, he wheeled the Vespa into the shed. He took a screwdriver from a workbench and unscrewed the scooter's small license plate, which he stuffed into his pocket. Without a plate the scooter was unlikely to be driven off by anybody else, and it would still be available for Charlie when he needed it.

He began the slow, half-hour walk back to his hotel. Early in life, Charlie had learned to handle his anxieties by keeping busy. But ambling along in the dim moonlight, he had no busywork to take his mind off his current fears. Terror seemed to lurk behind every building. He jumped into the shadows each time a car came down the road. He detoured around a street corner where four young men were drinking something and laughing loudly. Eager to get to the safety of his hotel room, he struggled to keep his imagination from running wild.

31

Week of October 21, 1962

THE WHITE HOUSE

UNNERVED BY HER ORDEAL WITH Bishop on Friday, Vanessa drove to her parents' home in Chevy Chase. She phoned Sorensen, claimed to have gotten ill, and asked to have the weekend off. He reluctantly agreed to give her Saturday off, but unless she was on her death bed, she should definitely come in early on Sunday at dawn if possible. She should also pack an overnight kit in case they worked so late Sunday evening she had to sack out on a couch.

Secure in the comfort of her parents' house for the next two nights, Vanessa's sense of terror about Bishop began to dissipate. In its stead, a powerful rage built up within her. Never again would she let herself be so defenseless. And she needed to send Bishop a message. She phoned her karate instructor to request a special tutorial. But the soonest he could see her was 7:30 Tuesday morning.

THE SUN HAD BARELY RISEN when Vanessa checked in on Sunday morning and discovered that the president was already back from his Chicago trip.

"We had to call him back early," Sorensen told her as he gave her assignments for the morning. "He's the only one who can break this deadlock on ExComm between the military who want an invasion and those of us who think that a blockade would work better. If this isn't resolved immediately, it's going to become public, and the pressure for invasion will become overwhelming."

"How can I help?" she asked.

"Start by phoning all these people." He handed her a list of the home phones for the ExComm members. "Tell them we're sending a car to pick them up for a meeting with the president at 9:30."

"Wouldn't it be faster if their chauffeurs just drove them in?"

"Reporters will get suspicious if they see a bunch of limousines arriving on a Sunday."

She had completed the calls and started on a typing assignment when Sorensen called her down to the Cabinet Room. As the ExComm members took their places on the black leather chairs at the table, they commented on the car-pooling arrangement. Some complained about having to ride in a cramped Chevrolet, while others laughed about it. Two cabinet members rode in a car so crowded that one of them had to sit on the other's lap.

"Bring some coffee and donuts to Averell Harriman," said Sorensen. "He's sitting just off the lobby."

"*The* Averell Harriman?" Vanessa recognized the name of the revered grand old man of foreign policy advisors. "Why isn't he in with ExComm where he's needed?"

"We're using him as a decoy to keep the reporters from realizing there's a critical meeting going on over here. Do what you can to mollify him."

He started to turn away, then turned back to face her. He grinned. "After you take care of Harriman, bring some coffee and donuts to the reporters as well. That will give you an excuse to stop in every now and then to eavesdrop. Find out if they're talking about anything we need to react to."

Harriman snapped at Vanessa when she brought his coffee. "I don't need coffee. I need to see the president. Tell him I need to see him now."

"I'll inform him immediately, sir. In the meantime, is there anything else I can get for you?" She set a copy of the *New York Times* Sunday edition on his table. It was thick enough to keep him busy for hours.

She spent the morning running back and forth between Harriman, Sorensen's office, her typing station, and the reporters. In midafternoon, she brought them more pastries and parried attempts of two of them to flirt with her.

"They know something's up," she reported to Sorensen. "They're talking about a buildup of ships and planes around Florida, as well as troop movements and military leaves being cancelled. They know that the marines have already practiced an invasion somewhere in Puerto Rico and that we have 140,000 men on alert to invade Cuba. They even know the operation code name, Operation ORTSAC. One of them sneered when they pointed out to me that ORTSAC is Castro spelled backward."

As she reported this, Vanessa had mixed feelings. She tingled pleasantly at being on the inside of this. But at the same time, she trembled with the knowledge that Charlie was in Havana. What would happen to him if an invasion took place on top of air strikes? And how did reporters find out all this stuff? She had been at the beck and call of the president's right-hand man all week, but the reporters knew more than she did.

"Thank you for your attentiveness," said Sorensen, in his normal unflappable tone. "I'll get this to the president. He's pretty much decided what he's going to do, and he'll lay it out in a speech tomorrow night. Maybe he can get the *Post* and *Times* to hold off on this until after his speech."

By the time Sorensen went home, it was ten o'clock at night, and Vanessa was glad she had brought an overnight kit. Exhausted, she sacked out on the couch in his office. She hated wearing the same clothes on Monday that she wore on Sunday. But with the tension so high in the West Wing, nobody would notice her wardrobe.

Monday began even more tensely than Sunday had. But Vanessa knew nothing about the most stressful moments.

GUANTANAMO BAY NAVAL BASE, CUBA

SARA JAMES WOULD NEVER FORGET that Monday morning. The telephone jangled her awake at 4:30. A naval duty officer was on the phone, ordering her husband back to work immediately. Two hours later, a navy seaman in battle dress pounded the door of her bungalow. "Grab your kids and report at once to that bus on the corner."

Looking down the street, Sara saw five buses. Neighboring wives, with suitcases and children, were already headed toward them. "What's going on?" Sara demanded.

"Just move! If you want to live, get to that bus as fast as you can."

An hour later, Sara's bus pulled up to the dock where naval launch boats were shuttling people to a destroyer anchored in the bay. Carrying a suitcase in each hand, she led her two children to a neighbor standing on the dock. "Bev, what the hell is going on here? Do you have any idea?"

"We're being evacuated."

"I can see that. But why?"

"It's got something to do with the Russians and Cubans," said Bev, "but that's all I know."

"I'll bet it's those FROGs my husband, Karl, has been tracking," said Sara.

"FROGs?"

"They're outdated MiG fighter planes that are radio-controlled. The Russians packed them with explosives and moved them to the perimeter of the base. 'We call them FROGs,' Karl said, 'for Free Rockets Over Ground.'"

"He told you this?"

"He wasn't supposed to, but he thought we were worrying too much about them. Their accuracy is so bad they couldn't do any real damage to the base."

"But what if the Russians armed them with nukes?" asked Bev.

Oh Jesus, thought Sara, as she led her two daughters from the dock onto the launch. Bev followed with her own three children. The smell of the salt water drifted toward them as the launch pulled away from the dock. If only one of the FROGs contained a nuclear device, it could wipe out most of Guantanamo. Long after the destroyer carried Sara and her children to safety, her husband would be at ground zero.

———

FOUR THOUSAND MILES AWAY, AT Eielson Air Force Base in Alaska, in the pitch-dark night, the duty sergeant shined a flashlight into the eyes of Airman Ramón Sanchez. "Get your crew to the hangar, Sanchez. It's a crisis."

Ramón met his crew at the F-102 Delta Dagger, an American interceptor aircraft they serviced. They opened the weapons bay under the fuselage and removed the plane's conventional missiles. Other crews did the same thing to the other F-102s at the base. Why he was ordered to do this made no sense to Ramón, because these were homing missiles that had demonstrated extraordinary accuracy. The F-102s stationed in Alaska were the first line of defense against any wave of Russian bombers flying to the U.S. from Siberia. With the F-102s defanged, what could stop the Russians from bombing West Coast cities from San Diego to Seattle?

No sooner did they get the conventional armaments off the plane than they received a new order. Replace the conventional armaments with a single nuclear tipped air-to-air missile.

———

BY MID-AFTERNOON, KENNEDY'S SECRETARY, EVELYN Lincoln, became so busy that she called on Vanessa for help. She pointed to a document with the president's signature and instructed her to transmit it immediately to General Thomas Powers, director of the Strategic Air Command (SAC). The paper authorized Powers to raise the defense preparedness level to DEFCON 3.

"Does this go along with it?" Vanessa asked. She lifted up a second page summarizing the practical impact of the decision. The contents of it made her hands shake. DEFCON 3 authorized SAC Director Powers to put twenty-three hundred nuclear weapons into position to be fired at a moment's notice. More than two hundred were on intercontinental ballistic missiles (ICBMs) and spread across the northern tier of the United States. Another two-hundred were loaded on B-52 bombers that were in the air around the clock awaiting the order to drop their bombs on targets in The Soviet Union and China, civilian as well as military. And a hundred and fifty were ICBMs in submarines. The rest were stored at air bases around the world.

Lincoln took the second sheet back from Vanessa. "No. We'll keep that here. Powers already knows all of that."

Vanessa spent much of the afternoon escorting different groups of people into the Oval Office or the Cabinet Room for presidential briefings. Some of these briefings went more smoothly than others. In mid-afternoon, she escorted the National Security Council members. If they were asked to comment on the crisis, Kennedy said he needed them to state their agreement with the plan of action he would outline that evening in his televised statement. He wanted them all to sing one song.

At 4:00 p.m., he met with his cabinet members, most of whom knew nothing of the brewing crisis. They too pledged their support for the president's course of action.

At 5:00 p.m., Vanessa ushered a group of Democratic congressional leaders into the Oval Office. She hadn't even gotten out of the door of the office before she heard them complain that Kennedy's response of a quarantine was too timid.

When she wasn't escorting people to meetings, Vanessa spent most of the afternoon typing revised versions of Sorensen's speech for the president. She would no sooner type one version than Sorensen would check it out with Kennedy, then come back, change it, and have her type the new version. By the time she finished, she knew it by heart she had typed it so often. Five times, she thought.

At 6:45 she sat on a sheet of canvas that had been laid on the floor to protect the Oval Office carpet. She was sandwiched between chairs set up for the news reporters and a jumble of television cameras, electric cables, and shabbily dressed television camera people. Having worn the same clothes for two days, she felt shabby herself. A snag on her nylons had opened up an embarrassing hole, and her hair was a mess. Just before 7:00 p.m., the president entered the room and sat behind his desk. He looked into a TV camera and waited for the on-air signal. In a slow, grave voice, he began to tell the American people his plans to protect them from the recently discovered missiles in Cuba—missiles that threatened to sling nuclear bombs at a great number of cities in southern and eastern U.S., including the nation's capital, Washington, DC.

32

Monday, October 22, 1962

Havana, Cuba

C HARLIE HAD TO TAKE A risk he had avoided so far. Few things were more likely to expose his true identity than showing up at the bar at Hotel Nacional de Cuba where the foreign correspondents hung out. His American accent, or his minimal knowledge about the craft of reporting, or just some mannerism was bound to betray him. But he felt desperate to hear President Kennedy's speech on the Cuba crisis. The Hotel Nacional de Cuba's bar was the one place in Havana where it was certain to be broadcast.

Throughout the city, people were on edge, expecting an invasion. The morning edition of the newspaper Revolución had come out with big headlines:

> *Planes and Warships Head Toward Florida*
> *Preparations for Yankee Aggression*

Charlie went to the hotel, posing as a reporter from Argentina. As long as he didn't talk with any Argentines, he thought he could pull it off. A tall, pale-skinned man would fit right into the image most people had of Argentines. He limped up to the big concrete building with the twin square turrets on top. He passed under towering palm trees toward the entrance and headed to the Galería Bar where a radio was turned on for the gathering crowd of reporters.

What would an Argentine drink? He spotted a large bottle of Johnnie Walker Scotch behind the elegantly curved bar. Half the Cubans he had met did not get enough to eat, but foreigners at the bar could still get Scotch. He ordered one on ice, ignoring Bishop's warning not to drink the local water. Most of the reporters in the room held drinks with ice cubes, and no one looked to be suffering from the water they contained. He found a seat in a white wicker chair next to one of the round pillars that dominated the room. Hanging from the wall next to him was a birdcage, and a small wren chirped peacefully.

Charlie was stunned by the sharpness of Kennedy's tone. He would "regard any nuclear missile launched from Cuba against any nation in the Western Hemisphere as an attack by the Soviet Union on the United States, requiring a full retaliatory response upon the Soviet Union."

"Invasión!" cried one of the reporters in Spanish. "Ellos van invader Cuba!"

"No!" shouted someone else. They're blockading the Russians from sending in more nukes. And if the Russians react, they're going to incinerate Cuba."

"In either case," said a third, "Castro's done for."

As fascinating as this argument promised to be, Charlie needed to avoid getting drawn into it. He slipped out the front door and went back to his room at the Habana Libre. Within an hour, Isabel came pounding on the door.

"You have to get out of here. They're going to round up all the foreign journalists and put them in protective custody until this crisis is over."

"How do you know that?"

"Michael, don't argue with me. I work for the Ministry of

Communications. It's part of our contingency plan in case of an invasion."

"All the foreign journalists?"

"All except the ones they trust."

"Well, they can trust me. Major Escalante himself slammed me against the wall to vet me, and I filed a very complimentary story about that clinic."

"Listen to me, Michael. You're going to be locked inside a hotel room and interrogated until they get what they want out of you. The only Western journalist they will allow to keep working is that one you Americans call the Tokyo Rose of Cuba."

Charlie slipped on the special shoes the CIA had made to hide his limp. They headed to the elevator, but by the time they reached the ground floor, an army truck with a squad of soldiers had come to a halt in front of the hotel. Isabel pulled him toward a rear exit where she had taken the precaution of hiding her Harley. She drove through back streets slowly so as to lessen the loud roar of the bike's big engine. When they got well away from the hotel, she sped toward her apartment. But two blocks away, she pulled to a sudden stop.

"Dios mío!" she exclaimed. "They have two police cars there. They're after me too."

"No," Charlie said. "It's me they're after, not you. Just go back home as if nothing's happened. I'll hide out in one of these dark side streets until they're gone."

As he started to slide off the rear seat of the bike, she turned to grab his arm. "Wait," she said. "Let me get us out of the street light before you do anything."

She pulled the Harley into a darkened lane. Once she stopped, she exhaled slowly, as though she had been holding her breath during the tense ride.

"Michael, I took a big risk going to your hotel to warn you, and for me this is what you Americans call the moment to fish or cut bait. I need you to be honest with me. Can you really take Angelita and me out of Cuba? If you can't, I have to go back to Major Escalante and report you missing, hoping that he won't suspect me of anything."

His own pulse was racing, and he took a second to catch his breath. How much could he tell her? Maybe this was just a ruse. What if he told her the plan, and she passed the information to Major Escalante? However, if she wanted to betray him, all she needed to do was to keep driving to her apartment, where the police were waiting to arrest him.

"There's a CIA safe house where someone will radio for a boat to pick me up. They'll send in the boat at night. All we need to do is put you and Angelita into the boat first, and then I'll hop in after you. Five hours later you're in Florida."

"One other thing," she said, glancing over her shoulder to see if anyone was coming up the darkened lane. "What is your real name?"

"Charlie," he said. "Charlie S. Parnell."

"Charlie," she smiled, pronouncing it "Sharlie." "I like that."

"There's one other thing you have to know," he said. "And now I'm the one taking the enormous risk. That American the major is looking for—it's me." He couldn't bring himself to utter the word assassin.

"I figured that out some time ago," she said as she edged the Harley out of the lane, glancing toward her apartment building to see if anyone looked in their direction. Once she determined that they hadn't, she turned away from the apartment.

"Where are you going?"

"To hide out at a friend's house while we make plans. We have to get off the streets before we get picked up. We need to figure out how to get to your safe house."

She pulled the Harley into a dimly lit alley where she banged on a door. No one answered. She pounded the door a second time and shouted, "¡Helena, abra la puerta!" She pounded again, her thin frame rocking back and forth as her palm slammed on the door.

The door cracked open, and a thin fearful-looking woman peeked out. Recognizing Isabel, Helena pulled the door open and backed up so Isabel could enter. Isabel blocked the door open and motioned for Charlie to roll the cycle into the room.

"No!" yelled Helena. "You can't bring that in here."

"I can't leave it outside," said Isabel. "Someone will steal it."

Isabel introduced Charlie as a distant cousin from Spain who feared he would be deported because of the crisis. If he could hide out until the crisis calmed down, he would be okay.

"No! Isabel. No!" Helena cried in alarm. "The grandmother spy will report any strange people to the police. He has to leave."

"When your boyfriend was beating you," snapped Isabel, "I took you in until he went away. I helped you, Helena, and now I need your help. Just until morning," she pleaded. "We'll be gone by the time it is light. But right now, we have to get off the streets. Anybody out after dark is bound to get picked up."

"You can stay until morning, and then you have to be out of here. At six!" she said.

She sat Charlie and Isabel on a padded bench–sofa in the small drab living area. Deeper into the room was a kitchen area and a bathroom. By the kitchen, a sheet draped down from the ceiling, marking off a makeshift sleeping area.

Helena sat on a stiff-backed kitchen chair across from them and twisted her hands in her lap. She lit another cigarette. After a few moments she went to the sleeping area behind the sheet and returned with a blanket. "The only place I have for you to sleep is on the floor," she said in a softer tone than she'd used earlier. You can make coffee before you go. But you have to leave before it gets light." She pulled out an old wind-up alarm clock and set it for 5:30.

Finally alone, Charlie stared at Isabel for several moments before asking, "You said you figured out some time ago who I was. How did you do that?"

She put her finger to her lips, moved closer to him, and

whispered, "We've already established that you're neither a reporter nor Irish. And a lot of your behavior didn't make sense. At Nuevo Mariel, you kept studying the buildings across from the doctor's clinic and even seemed to be sizing one up for something. At the cemetery, you showed too much interest in Dolf Luque. Then you sent me off on an errand that felt like something you contrived to get me out of the way for a moment. So, if you're not Irish, and you're behaving strangely, who are you? And why are you here?"

Charlie didn't respond.

"The only answer I can come up with is that you're the American sent here to kill Castro. I was terrified the other night that you were going to kill me when this subject first came up."

"But you're not terrified now?"

"Terrified?" she snarled. "I'm shaking in my boots, I'm so terrified. I'm terrified that we are going to get caught and that you're going to be executed after you've been beaten senseless with a baseball bat. Terrified that I'm going to be shoved into a drawer cell, and that my daughter is going to lose her mother."

"Then why did you take me in for the night?"

She paused before responding. "Because I want to get Angelita out of Cuba so she can grow up with some kind of normal life. And you're the only one who can do that for me. Besides, I don't believe that you are a killer. A man who could use his guitar to connect with those children at the school the way you did could not possibly be a man who would shoot Castro in cold blood—even if he deserves it for all the misery he's caused."

"You'd better understand that I've got to make the attempt. If you and I want the CIA to get us off this island, I have to make them believe that I tried."

She made no effort to roll away from him, and as they lay on their sides, facing each other, the soft warmth of her body began to overpower him. He moved his hand to her breast and slid his fingers slowly back and forth over the nipple.

"We're running for our lives. And you want to do that at a moment like this?"

"If I failed to bring you some comfort when I can," he quipped, "God might never forgive me."

"On this stone floor?" But she smiled as she said it.

"You can be on top."

33

Tuesday, October 23, 1962

SHAW COMMUNITY DEFENSE CENTER

PROMPTLY AT 7:30, VANESSA SHOWED up at the Shaw Community Defense Center on 9th Street. She wore sweats and carried her work clothes in a garment bag draped over her arm. She always felt nervous in that neighborhood, but she shook her head at the irony of her situation. The only violent assault she'd suffered in her life had been by a middle-class man in suburban Virginia not by any tough youths in a Washington ghetto. In any case, who better to teach her how to protect herself from Bishop than an ex-marine sergeant?

"Malcolm," she said to the tall, muscular instructor with the shaved head, "I'm improving at that kick you taught me. But I've got this guy who's stalking me. What else can I do?"

"Call the police."

She rolled her eyes. "Just help me, Malcolm."

"Well, you're very strong, and you're starting to snap that chest kick out like a piston rod. That'll stop most stalkers in their tracks."

"But maybe I'll slip on wet grass when he attacks, and the kick will be weak. Or maybe he'll duck, and my foot will glance off his shoulder. Or, worse yet, maybe he'll grab my foot and throw me off balance. What do I do then?"

"How big is this guy?"

"My height, but a lot more muscular."

He led her from the office to a thick mat on the workout floor. Surrounding the mat were barbells and various pieces of exercise equipment. The room smelled of men's dried sweat. Vanessa loved it.

"Let's go over your kick first," he said. "Show me how you react when I threaten you."

He held a protective mitt in front of his face as he snarled and moved toward her. She planted her left foot on the mat and snapped her right foot into the middle of Malcolm's mitt. If it hadn't been for the mitt, she would have broken his nose.

"Nice," he complimented. "Even though I'm a good two or three inches taller than you, you reached my face with no trouble. You're also very fast, so I don't think he'll be able to block your kick or grab your foot. But you did make one mistake."

She furrowed her eyebrows quizzically.

"Unless you had hit me squarely in the face, you wouldn't have stopped me. That's because you hit me when I had both feet planted on the ground. Try timing the kick so that it hits me when I'm off balance with all my weight on the forward foot. If you do that, you're going to knock me on my ass. You won't even have to hit me in the face. With the speed and strength you've got, you can hit me anywhere above the waist and knock me over."

They resumed positions, and it took Vanessa four kicks before she caught Malcolm off balance and knocked him over.

She grinned. "That was nice, Malcolm. But all I've done is knock you down. You can still get up and attack me."

"Let me show you some follow-through moves that will help.

You be the attacker this time, but make sure to hold that mitt at arm's length. I don't want to smash those beautiful white teeth."

Just as Vanessa stepped forward, Malcolm's right foot smashed into the mitt and knocked her down to a sitting position. Then he kicked her on the kneecap, jerked her head by the hair, and pulled her onto her back. He chopped his left hand down toward her throat, stopping just inches before striking her.

She rolled back to a sitting position, shaken. "Wow!" she said, rubbing the knee where she had been struck. "How do I do that?"

"You can't," said Malcolm. "At least, not yet. But here's what you can do in the meantime. Carry a purse big enough to hold a twelve-inch metal pipe. When you see that guy, pull out the pipe. He'll either back off or try to grab it from you. The instant that he's on one foot, knock him over with that kick. Then use the pipe to whack him on the kneecap. Grab his hair and roll him onto his back the way I did with you. Don't hit his head or throat with that pipe, though. Just threaten it. You don't want to kill him. You just want to scare him away."

They switched positions and practiced the moves several times, using a rolled-up magazine as the twelve-inch pipe. By the time they finished, Vanessa dripped with sweat. As she wiped herself dry and changed into her work clothes, she felt an exhilarating sense of power. She could hardly wait for Bishop to show up again.

Havana, Cuba

Isabel rolled off Charlie, and he lay on his back gazing dreamily at the ceiling. He turned his head toward her. She was lying on her side, her head propped in the palm of her hand, a satisfied smile on her face.

"A woman like you could grow on a guy."

"You're nice, Charlie, and I hate to spoil the mood. But what do we do in the morning?"

"We have to get to el Chico," he said, "but your Harley is a dead giveaway. Every cop in the city must be looking for it. We can trade it for a scooter at a place not far from here."

He told her the address and added, "Another giveaway is your uniform. The cops will be looking for that."

"I'll borrow something from Helena."

She peeked behind the bedroom drape to see if Helena was awake, and Charlie heard them chatting. When she emerged, she had on a baggy yellow blouse and a pair of denim pants. Gesturing ta da, she grinned. "Any better?"

THE WIND-UP ALARM CLOCK RANG at 5:30, and Charlie rolled away from Isabel's soft body. He stood up and stretched his arms toward the ceiling. Helena handed them each a coffee and a small loaf of bread.

"Do you have any more food we could take with us," asked Isabel. "We might be the entire day without food. My cousin can pay you."

Charlie passed a ten peso note to Helena. She handed over two more loaves of bread and a bottle of water.

Outside, Isabel kicked down on the starter pedal. Charlie swung his leg over the rear fender as he mounted the seat behind her. She kept the headlight off as she drove slowly down the dark lane to the main street. Five minutes out, she spied a blockade of soldiers and vehicles. With her headlight off, she was invisible to them. She searched for a detour around the roadblock, but the first side street she took came to a quick dead end. As did the second. She tried a third street, little more than an alleyway, and it led to a baseball field.

Turning into the field, she tried to drive around the barricade. She drove very slowly, hoping to avoid going into any ruts that would upend them. But in centerfield, the front wheel suddenly dropped into a big hole, dumping the two of them to the ground. They started pushing the cycle out of the hole. However, as it came over the rim of the hole, the drive wheel came loose from the ground and revved loudly before Isabel could twist the accelerator off. Fearing detection, Charlie tugged the cycle back into the hole and pulled Isabel to the ground, just in time. At the sound of the engine revving, a soldier at the barricade pulled his rifle off his shoulder and peered into the field. But he failed to spot Charlie and Isabel laying in the hole. After a moment, the soldier put the strap of the rifle over his shoulder and returned to the barricade.

Isabel rose, grabbed the handlebars of the Harley and began to push it forward.

Charlie pushed on the rear fender until they were out of sight and hearing distance from the barricade. Isabel started the engine and headed away from the soldiers. When they reached the main street, she stopped and turned to face Charlie.

"Oh my god! I thought we were goners," she said, breathless.

He nodded and gripped her tightly around the waist to keep his fingers from shaking.

The morning sky was beginning to lighten by the time they reached the house of Flavio's acquaintance. Charlie had to bang on the door several times before a disheveled sleepy-looking man appeared.

"I'm Flavio's friend," Charlie reminded the man, "and I've come to get the motor scooter I dropped off the other day."

"It's not here," said the man.

Charlie's jaw dropped. "Not here? Let me see!"

The man opened the shed next to the house. Charlie followed him inside, and Isabel wheeled the motorcycle inside behind Charlie. As the man had said, the scooter was gone.

"What happened?" asked Charlie.

"Flavio picked it up yesterday. He didn't say why."

"Shit!" Charlie exclaimed in English. Catching himself, he said in Spanish, "¡Mierda!" He scuffed his feet on the dirt floor to distract the man as he tried to think of something they could do.

"We hate to bother you," he said to the man, "but we cannot leave until this afternoon." He deliberately did not ask for permission to stay. That would be easy to deny. Then to make it worth the man's while, he said, "If you let us stay here until about five and find us something to eat in the meantime, it's worth fifty pesos. Also, get us some food we can take with us that will last for two days." He pulled the banknotes from his pocket.

"Sixty," said the man.

Charlie added ten more pesos. "And a couple of canteens for water."

"Seventy," said the man.

Clutching the cash, the man walked off to find the provisions. Charlie retrieved a screwdriver from a workbench. He took the license plate off the Harley and replaced it with the plate he had taken from Flavio's Vespa two days earlier.

"That will at least keep us from showing up on any list the cops might have."

When the man came back with a package of food, they ate a serving of the rice. They wrapped four chicken thighs and bread loaves in a newspaper, which Isabel tucked inside her purse. At 5:00 p.m., Charlie mounted the Harley behind her, and she pulled out onto the street. He directed her toward the road leading to el Chico.

Just before they reached the turnoff lane to el Chico, an army lieutenant in a jeep pulled out of a side street and stopped them.

"What are you doing with this motorcycle, señorita? Don't you know that all vehicles must be lent to the revolution until this crisis is over?"

"Yes, comrade," she replied, staring him in the eyes. "But we are on official business for Che Guevara. We're carrying a message from him to our Russian allies at el Chico. We have come all the way from Camaguay where he is mustering our defense forces."

Charlie lifted the bag of his belongings as though it held the message for Che. Isabel continued. "Please let us pass. We need to reach the Russians and get a reply back to Che as fast as we can."

The lieutenant seemed impressed that she knew el Chico housed the Russian headquarters. "One moment," he said. He pulled a sheet of paper from his jeep, looked at the license number on the Harley, and then ran his finger down the page.

"Your license is okay, but who is this man riding with you?"

"He is a civilian assistant to Che. He has to get a response from the Russians."

"What is it that you do for Che?" asked the lieutenant.

From his own military experience, Charlie could sense the lieutenant's indecision. He probably doubted that two people in civilian clothes would truly be messengers for Che. Not having a radio, he had no way to check out their story. But there would be hell to pay if he arrested them, and they did, in fact, turn out to be Che's emissaries.

"I am his personal consultant," said Charlie.

"And where are you from, señor?"

"Oriente Province, the City of Banes," Charlie said, just as Isabel had instructed him.

"Banes? That must be why you have that strange accent." He paused, as if unsure what to do next. "Would you come over to that tree with me, señor, so we can speak in private for a second?" He wandered to a tree a dozen paces away.

Charlie looked quizzically at Isabel, and she nodded for him to go ahead. He walked over to the tree, but when he got there, the lieutenant turned and walked back to the motorcycle.

"What the hell is this all about?" Charlie demanded. "I'm on business for Comandante Che, and I don't have time for games."

"My apologies, señor. I just had to check your walk. We're looking for a gringo who walks with a limp and a Cuban woman in a uniform."

Before the soldier could say more, a whoosh of wind rushed in on them. Seconds later, two American fighter planes roared in barely above the treetops and sped over el Chico. The two had no sooner passed than two loud booms trailed behind them, cracking through the air. Once past el Chico, the jets climbed almost straight up, banked to the right, and began a wide U-turn that would take them back to their base.

"What the hell was that?" shouted the soldier. "Are they bombing something?"

"No," said Charlie. "They're supersonic planes. What we heard was the sonic boom."

"You have to let us pass," Isabel shouted. "We must get Comrade Che's message to the Russians. He wants them to shoot down these hijos de puta the next time they fly through."

The guard let them pass, and she drove up the road. "Incredible," she said, "that they could fly so low so fast. One little mistake and they would have crashed. What are they up to?"

"Reconnaissance, I guess. They'll snap photos of everything the Russians have on the ground. Fidel must be going nuts. He has to show up here to persuade the Russians to shoot them down."

Charlie directed Isabel to drive up the road and stop. Not wanting the guard to see where they were going, he waited for the lieutenant's jeep to move off. While they waited, she twisted in her seat to look at him. "You did fantastic with that bit about Banes, Oriente. To have him mistake you for a Cuban from Banes is the ultimate compliment to your Spanish." She smiled. "But how did you hide your limp?"

He grinned, raised his left foot and pulled up the pant leg so that she could see the elevated heel built into the shoe. "The Company made me a special shoe that hides my limp. It worked like a charm."

By the time they reached Charlie's ambush spot outside el Chico, the sun was setting. She parked the Harley out of sight behind a large bush overlooking the compound. They sat by the bush and ate half of the food that she had tucked into her purse.

"I have to dig up something while it's still light enough to see what I'm doing," he said, rising to his feet. He paced off several steps away from her and dropped to his knees by the hiding spot he had dug earlier. Using his hands to scrape away brush and dirt, he lifted out the burlap bag containing the M-1 rifle and the machete.

She sat watching as he assembled the pieces of the rifle, clicking them into place. Her hands jumped slightly with each click. Lifting the rifle to a shooting position, he peered through the scope at the Russian compound, barely one hundred fifty yards away. He extended the weapon to her.

"Did you ever look through a scope?"

She turned up her nose. "I don't even want to touch it. Why don't you just put it back in that hole so we can leave? We'll pick up Angelita and your jewels and go to your safe house and get that boat to pick us up."

"I can't," he said. "Unless I take a shot at Castro, my handlers will cause all kinds of problems—for you as well as me. I'm not planning to miss, but in case I do, you will be my witness that I actually took the shot."

"No problem," she said. "I'll tell them you shot at him, and the reason you missed was because he ducked at the last minute. Now let's get out of here."

"They'll give you a polygraph test and find out that you're lying. We've got no choice but to wait until I can take that shot. Just crank up that motorcycle the moment I plug the bastard so that we can get out of here with a head start."

34

Wednesday, October 24, 1962

THE WHITE HOUSE

O N WEDNESDAY, TED SORENSEN SENT Vanessa to the ExComm meeting in the Cabinet Room to take notes for him while he worked on a statement for the president. Despite her excitement at being involved with ExComm, she had never felt comfortable in the all-male enclave. To discourage the men from sneaking looks at her legs or breasts, she took a seat by the window overlooking the Rose Garden, tucked her legs under the chair to keep them from sight, and slouched forward to minimize the shape of her breasts. But the tension in the room was so overwhelming that she needn't have worried about anyone paying her much attention.

A Russian convoy of twenty-two ships was approaching the naval blockade line that Kennedy had formed around Cuba, and one of the ships was transporting nuclear missiles. What would happen when these Russian ships came in contact with the armada of American naval vessels was anybody's guess. These powerful men around the conference table seemed to expect the worst. They slumped in their chairs.

In mid-morning, a messenger from the Office of Naval Intelligence handed a note to CIA Director John McCone. His mood perked up dramatically as he scanned the note and then announced to the group, "The Russian ships stopped dead in the water. Most of them reversed course and are headed away from Cuba."

The men around the table bolted upright. Secretary of State Dean Rusk said, "We were eyeball to eyeball, and I think the other fellow just blinked."

Vanessa also straightened up from her slumped position in a chair by the windows overlooking the Rose Garden. She couldn't help grinning. Maybe this was a signal that the Russians were willing to negotiate an end to the crisis.

The generals, however, continued to press for an invasion. They reminded the president that even though the quarantine might stop new missiles from coming in, it did nothing to get rid of the ones that were already there. Immediate air strikes were needed to destroy the missile sites. When Kennedy asked whether air strikes could take out all the missile sites, the Chairman of the Joint Chiefs, Maxwell Taylor, replied tersely, "No!" Massive air strikes against every missile launcher were just a start. They needed to be followed by an invasion. Even if the president was reluctant to invade, it was critically important that he make the Russians believe an invasion was imminent. Otherwise, they had no incentive to withdraw their nukes.

As quickly as Vanessa's spirits had soared, they sank. If the generals got their wish, but even one missile site survived the bombardment, the Russians could retaliate by flinging a nuclear warhead at Washington. The room she was sitting in could be incinerated in a flash. Moreover, Charlie, in Havana, would be stuck in the middle of a massive bombing campaign followed by an invasion.

ONE MAN IN THE CABINET Room did pick up on the opening the Russian reversal had made for negotiating a solution to the crisis.

But he also knew of something going on that would torpedo any negotiations. He would put an end to it as soon as he met with the Mongoose oversight committee.

35

Friday, October 26, 1962

DEPARTMENT OF JUSTICE

TOM MCGILLIVRAY NOTED THE CHANGE in Attorney General Robert Kennedy the moment he came into the room. In their two previous meetings, Kennedy had harangued the Mongoose committee to step up sabotage in Cuba. Now, however, he announced that all sabotage must cease. Sabotage activities at this point would undermine any chance of negotiating a deal to get the Russian nukes off the island.

Across from Kennedy, the CIA liquidation director, Bill Harvey, fidgeted nervously. He had just sent three six-man sabotage teams to Cuba.

Kennedy was irate. "How could you go off on a half-assed operation like this without my prior approval?"

Unfortunately for Harvey, the meeting was being held in the afternoon, and he had consumed a few drinks at lunch. He mumbled a vague response, and Kennedy reddened as his anger rose. "Stop rambling. Tell me what you're going to do to remove those sabotage teams."

When Harvey continued to mumble, Kennedy demanded, "Recall every one of those teams right now!" Then he stormed out of the meeting.

———

McGILLIVRAY SPED TO LANGLEY AS fast as he could. If sabotage had become a threat to peace negotiations, the assassination of Castro might provoke World War III. With a hint of desperation, he told Bishop of Robert Kennedy blowing up at Bill Harvey during the Mongoose meeting.

"If Parnell kills Castro now, the Russians will never trust Kennedy enough to negotiate a settlement. The hotheads in the Pentagon will get the invasion they want. And who knows how the Russians will respond to that? We have to stop Parnell."

Bishop sat behind his desk and gulped. "Parnell's gone underground," he said. "He's out of touch."

"Send a message to his spotter, Flavio. He can stop Parnell."

From his desk, Bishop pulled out a copy of a codebook he had given to Flavio. It took only a few minutes to encode a message instructing Flavio to stop Charlie from shooting Castro. He sent the message to a communications officer and ordered him to transmit it right away.

While they waited for confirmation that the message had been radioed to the safe house in Havana, Bishop and McGillivray made small talk. Bishop said, "Too bad Parnell didn't send us those photographs of the submarine base and the missiles at Mariel a month earlier. He'd have been a hero."

"True," said McGillivray. "But right now, he's a menace. He's got to be stopped."

Bishop's phone range. He listened, then frowned. "Our contact in Havana, Pepe, isn't answering our call. The message can't get through."

"Damn!" said McGillivray. "Keep trying. Around the clock until you reach him. Better yet, get hold of that contact person Flavio has at Guantanamo, the one who sent us those photos from Mariel. Send him to the safe house to find out where Parnell is. He's got to stop Parnell at all costs. Shoot him if necessary!"

36

Friday, October 26, 1962

VIENNA, VIRGINIA

VANESSA DAWDLED AT HER DESK that Friday afternoon. The fear of getting manhandled again by Bishop made her nervous every time she ventured into the streets. And it was all because of those damned envelopes Charlie had given her. Not only did the envelopes make her vulnerable to Bishop's goons, but they also added a new danger that Charlie hadn't thought of. If Bishop's plot to assassinate Castro became public and Vanessa continued to hold documentation about the plot, she could be prosecuted for withholding evidence of a crime. The more she thought about it, the more she believed that Charlie had probably stashed packets of the documents with other friends. Her envelope was redundant. One by one, she tore the pages into pieces and stuffed them into the burn bag. Now there would be one less piece of evidence that could get her in trouble.

But she still faced a danger from Bishop. He might think that Vanessa knew who else had gotten packets from Charlie, and he might pressure her into giving him the names of those people. The thought of being submitted to another round of potential drowning terrified her. She needed to convince Bishop to leave her alone.

But how?

———

When Vanessa got home, she started her preparations. She replaced her elegant skirt with a pair of black tights. Then, thinking better of it, she took off the tights and replaced them with a very short skirt she wore when playing tennis. The tights would have kept her legs warm, but they would slow her down if she needed to change clothes fast. Over the blouse she pulled on a loose sweatshirt, which could be discarded swiftly. Then she drove to the address that Charlie had given her for Bishop's home in Vienna. She parked on Patrick Street, where her car could not be seen from the entrance to the building. Leaning back in the car, she waited. As the sun went down, a pale blue Pontiac came to a stop by the entrance. Bishop emerged from the car and went into the building.

An hour later, he came out the door and drove off. Vanessa pulled on a pair of surgical gloves and picked up a foot-long, half-inch-thick iron pipe from the passenger's seat. Leaving her car unlocked, she ambled to the building entrance, hobbling slightly because she was wearing two different shoes. For traction and a solid footing, her left foot wore the gym shoe that she used for workouts at the Shaw Community Defense Center. On her right foot was a hard-soled man's moccasin she had bought at a K-Mart. Walking past a large bush by the front door, she went into the entryway.

What a dump! She expected a mid-level spook could afford better. It had neither an elevator nor carpeting. The floor and steps were covered with dull, brown asbestos tiles. Six steps led up to a landing where the stairs made a U-turn and climbed to the second floor.

Leaving the building, Vanessa sat behind the big bush by the entrance to wait for Bishop's drab Pontiac to return. When a woman emerged, Vanessa tensed up and clenched her fists. She moved into a crouch so she could run away if she were spotted, but the woman failed to notice her. Relaxing, Vanessa sat down again.

Her legs got cold and wet as she sat on the ground. Maybe she should have worn the tights, after all. Maybe she should have stayed home. What if she stumbled or slipped when she made the kick? What if Bishop grabbed her foot when she was off balance? Bishop was very strong, and he could do her a lot of damage if he got his hands on her.

Finally, at 10:30, Bishop's blue Pontiac pulled into the parking lot. Vanessa scrambled from her hiding spot behind the bush, ducked into the entryway, and positioned herself out of sight at the top of the first set of stairs. The outer door opened, and she heard Bishop's footsteps click on the tile floor. Her heart pounding, she peeked around the corner of the stairway wall and waited until he reached the third step. She jumped to the top step, braced her left foot against the riser, brought her right leg into kicking position, and snapped out her right foot as fast as she could. It caught him in the face while he was off balance with all his weight on the forward foot. Blood gushed from his nose as he tumbled backward. He bounced off the bottom step, and his head thudded against the tile floor. She whacked the metal pipe against his knee, just as her karate instructor had taught. Then she slammed the pipe against his throat. She looked at the two apartment doors, fearing that someone would have heard Bishop fall, but no one came out. Bishop was gasping for breath as she bent over his bloody face and whispered, "Don't you ever again fuck with me or any other woman."

She dropped the pipe and raced out of the building. The bloody moccasin fell off her foot as she ran to her car. Before getting into the car, she used the sweatshirt to wipe blood from her legs. Then she stuffed the bloody sweatshirt into a plastic bag along with the surgical gloves and her gym shoe. She put on a loose blouse and sped out of her parking spot. As she turned onto the main highway, she heard police sirens. She stopped at a strip mall on the way home and tossed the plastic bag into a trash can.

The volume of blood flowing out of Bishop's nose was unnerving. So was his gasping for breath after she'd smashed the pipe into his throat. At home, she poured a glass of bourbon, spilling quite a bit of it on the counter. Then she sank into her easy chair and forced herself to drink the bourbon. It took an hour for her hands to stop shaking.

She got even more unnerved the next morning, eating breakfast at her kitchen table, while she read the regional section of The Washington Post.

Man Murdered in Vienna.

> *Residents of a Vienna apartment building called police after they found Walter Bishop on the floor of the building's entryway. Rescue squad workers brought him to the emergency room at George Washington University Hospital where he was pronounced dead on arrival.*
>
> *The cause of death was either a massive head injury sustained when the victim fell down the steps or a crushed trachea. A bloody twelve-inch pipe found at the scene was apparently used to smash the trachea.*
>
> *None of the neighbors saw the assailant, but police believe that it was a medium sized man. They found a blood-stained man's size nine shoe nearby.*
>
> *Neighbors described Bishop as a quiet man who stuck to himself and caused no trouble. Bishop, 37, was a sales representative for Tesagon Devices, a supplier of medical equipment. Anyone with information about the incident is asked to call the Fairfax County sheriff.*

Vanessa read the article three times and stared blankly at the newspaper. Damn! She should have taken his wallet. The police would have thought it was a robbery, and that would have deflected attention away from her.

37

Saturday, October 27, 1962

SIBERIA

JUST AFTER LIFTING HIS U-2 reconnaissance plane off the runway at Eielson Air Force Base, Alaska, Captain Charles Maultsby turned north to collect radioactive samples from H-bomb tests the Russians were conducting above the Arctic Circle. As he neared the North Pole, Maultsby passed beyond radio communication with his home base and began navigating by the stars. Alone in the dark, he oriented himself by glancing at charts of the polar sky he had fastened to his right thigh. He used a sextant to measure the angles between the stars.

After collecting his radioactive samples, Maultsby reversed direction to head home. So far, so good. Then a brilliant display of purples and greens and yellows burst into the sky as the northern lights opened up a spectacular show. He strained to see the stars he needed for navigation, but the stunning show of the northern lights obliterated them. Even his compass didn't help. Because it pointed to magnetic north, rather than true north, it gave misleading directions this close to the north pole.

It was then that he heard the music from a Russian radio station and knew that he had drifted into Soviet airspace.

Oh, Jesus, he thought. I already spent a year and a half in a POW camp after getting shot down in Korea. I sure as hell don't want to end up in a Russia prison.

EIELSON AIR FORCE BASE, ALASKA

THE FIRST PERSON TO DISCOVER something was wrong was an Air Force captain in charge of monitoring Russian Air Force radio transmissions. One of his radio operators brought him a Soviet battle order sending six MiG fighter jets in pursuit of a plane flying over Siberia at 70,000 feet. Only one plane could fly that high—the U-2. When he called Eielson Air Force Base in Alaska, he found out that their U-2 had not yet come home.

"The Russians are going to shoot that son-of-a-bitch down."

"Sir, we have to tell that to the pilot," said the airman.

The captain, however, hesitated. He lacked authority to contact the plane, and everyone was jumpy over the high drama crisis going on in Cuba. He could short circuit his career if he took any unauthorized initiatives. Instead, he placed a call to the Director of the Strategic Air Command, General Thomas Powers.

"This better be important," Powers barked into the phone. "I'm out on the golf course having a great round, and you're interrupting."

The captain explained what had happened and asked, "May we tell the pilot that he's got six MiGs on his tail?"

"No. That will tip off the Russians that we're able to read their battle instructions."

"Sir, if we don't alert him, the MiGs will shoot him down."

"Drop it, Captain. I'll take it from here."

Flight controllers at Eielson finally made radio contact with Maultsby. Guessing that he was headed south and deeper into

Siberia, they ordered him to make a ninety-degree turn left. Eielson Air Force Base also sent out two F-102 Delta Dagger interceptor planes to protect Maultsby from the MiGs. Only five days earlier, the conventional arms on each of these same F-102s had been removed and replaced with a nuclear tipped air-to-air missile.

STRATEGIC AIR COMMAND OPERATIONS CENTER, OMAHA, NEBRASKA

GENERAL POWERS WATCHED A GIANT tracking screen as it showed the MiGs gaining on Maultsby's U-2 from the west and the F-102s approaching him from the east. The Russian fighter jets were on a collision course with two American interceptors whose only armaments were nuclear air-to-air missiles. The American pilots were authorized to fire those missiles only if ordered by the president. And presidential permission had not arrived. If the Russian MiGs shot first, would the F-102s defend themselves and fire their nuclear missiles even though they lacked permission? Powers stared intently at the tracking screen.

THE QUARANTINE LINE

A SIGNIFICANT FLEET OF ANTI-SUBMARINE warfare planes patrolled a huge area from Bermuda to Cuba. In addition, an elaborate underwater Sound Surveillance System, called SONUS for short, regularly tracked Russian subs as they entered the western Atlantic. They had, however, lost track of Captain Dmitri Lesnikov's Foxtrot-class submarine.

Finally, at 5:50 p.m. on Saturday, October 27, a spotter on one of the American tracker planes broadcast into his radio transmitter, "We've got him."

Several warships steamed toward the location. It was pitch black by the time the first destroyer reached the coordinates.

"Do we drop depth charges?" asked one destroyer's second in

command.

"No," said the captain. "Unless he takes offensive action, our orders are to bring him to the surface."

"Sir?" said the second officer, "that sub could sink us and a couple others."

"Our orders are to bring him to the surface," repeated the captain, "and that's what we're going to do. Launch the practice grenades."

At the stern of the destroyer, two seamen tossed five stick-shaped grenades into the ocean. Called practice grenades, they were designed to detonate with a loud noise that would be a warning to the sub to come to the surface. The White House had communicated to the Kremlin through the U.S. Embassy in Moscow that this was how it was going to signal Soviet subs to surface. If the boat surfaced, no real depth charges would be dropped. However, if the sub took any offensive action, the destroyer would fire real depth charges that would kill it. After the initial launch of the practice grenades, the destroyer's captain waited for a response.

When the sub failed to surface, the captain ordered, "Drop five more."

———

THE EXPLODING PRACTICE GRENADES RATTLED throughout Lesnikov's sub, terrifying him and the crew. Frightening as the explosions were, however, they did not cause any damage, and the sub's officers concluded that the Americans were trying to force them to surface.

The first captain flew into a rage at the humiliating thought of being driven to the surface by the Americans. "We will not dishonor the Russian Navy," he shouted. "Arm the nuclear torpedo!"

38

Saturday, October 27, 1962

THE WHITE HOUSE

I N THE CABINET ROOM, VANESSA sat by the windows curling her toes tightly to keep her feet from tapping a drum beat on the floor. She couldn't get the image of Bishop's bloody face out of her mind, and the drama working out in front of her in the Cabinet Room was unnerving. She forced her personal worries into the back of her mind. To be of any use at all to Sorensen and the president, she had to keep a clear head and take accurate notes.

EARLIER THAT MORNING, A U-2 reconnaissance plane flown by Major Rudy Anderson had disappeared over Cuba. It wasn't until mid-afternoon when Defense Secretary McNamara announced to ExComm that the plane had been shot down by a Russian anti-aircraft missile. Not only had the U-2 been shot down, but Russian anti-aircraft batteries had also opened fire against low level reconnaissance planes flying over Cuba.

We must take out the missile batteries immediately, demanded National Security Advisor McGeorge Bundy. The military officers around the table nodded their agreement.

President Kennedy asked whether the shoot-down had been ordered by Moscow or by local commanders. If the order came from Moscow, it was a deliberate provocation that deserved a response. If it came from local commanders, it might have been a communications gap, in which case no harm would be caused by delaying a response. "We need to know which it was before we act."

Air Force Chief of Staff Curtis LeMay vehemently disagreed. "The Russians shot down an unarmed American plane," he said in a huff. "We must retaliate by taking out all their anti-aircraft sites and their nuclear missile sites. We have to do it by Monday. Then we have to invade."

The only glimmer of hope for a peaceful outcome was a conciliatory private cablegram Russian Premier Nikita Khrushchev had sent to Kennedy. The message said he would withdraw all nuclear weapons from Cuba if the Americans would promise not to invade. However, this conciliatory offer was undone a few hours later when Khrushchev broadcast a bellicose message over Radio Moscow blaming the Americans for the crisis and promising to meet force with force. He upped the ante for withdrawing his missiles from Cuba by saying that the U.S. must also withdraw its Jupiter nuclear missiles from Turkey.

National Security Advisor McGeorge Bundy argued against swapping the missiles in Turkey for the ones in Cuba. "If we remove those missiles under pressure, the Turks and the Europeans will think that we don't mean business when it comes to protecting Europe. NATO will become meaningless."

The president pointed out that he had been planning to remove those Jupiter missiles for months. Inaccurate and vulnerable to attack, they had been rendered obsolete by a nuclear submarine now stationed in the Mediterranean Sea. It carried sixteen accurate ICBMs that could be launched at a moment's notice. "We're not giving up anything by taking out the Jupiter missiles. To any rational man, this will look like a very fair trade."

"We still have to invade Cuba," argued Maxwell Taylor, the

chairman of the Joint Chiefs of Staff. "Unless we get irrefutable evidence that the Soviets are going to dismantle their nuclear weapons in Cuba, we should start the invasion Monday morning."

"Once the shooting starts," stressed Kennedy, "we lose control over what happens. We all know how quickly everybody's courage goes when the blood starts to flow."

The president held off on approving a decision to invade. Instead, he ordered Robert Kennedy and Ted Sorensen to go to the Oval Office to draft a response to Khrushchev.

Vanessa felt emotionally drained as she followed Sorensen out of the room. "Do you want my notes now? Or should I type them up first."

"I need them now, while Bobby and I are working on that response to Khrushchev," he said. "But I can't read your shorthand, so type them immediately. Then bring them down to me. Don't stop to correct typos, and don't let anything interrupt you. I'll alert Mrs. Lincoln to let you into the Oval Office."

"But Mr. Sorensen," she asked, as she clutched the legal pad to her chest, "suppose he tells the generals not to bomb Cuba, but they do it anyway? What happens then?"

HAVANA, CUBA

AT EL CHICO, ISABEL WAS damp and stiff and hungry. She sat leaning against a tree. Their food had run out that morning, and they were down to one canteen of water as they sat waiting for Castro to show up. Her mind drifted to Angelita. What would become of her if Isabel ended up in prison because Charlie's crazy plan backfired? The moment that Major Escalante had pressured Isabel into her job as a watcher, Isabel had seen dangers. Just in case anything happened to her, she had arranged for the santera to raise Angelita. Isabel's only hope now was that this tall, thin American with the limp and the stupid flat-top hat could actually succeed in getting her and Angelita out of Cuba.

He was driving her nuts with his nervous energy. Three times he had dismantled the rifle and wiped all its pieces free of any grit that might impede its firing. He had cursed himself for failing to bring a tool to clean out the bore. The longer it took for Castro to appear, the more agitated Charlie became. He had been in constant motion for the previous hour: standing up, sitting down, kneeling, lying down, then standing up again, all the time pointing his rifle at the compound, switching his aim from one imaginary target to another.

She could think of only one saving grace for all this annoying nervous energy. Maybe he was having second thoughts about killing Castro. Maybe they could leave before the shooting started.

She watched him focus on the el Chico parade ground where, for the first time, something was going on. Men began to line up in military formation. A group of older men gathered on the steps of the main building with the Soviet flag. A guard opened the gate to the compound, and a string of vehicles pulled in.

"It's Castro!" he said. She leaned forward to peer over his shoulder. "This time it's the real Castro, not his double. And the Russians are coming out to give him a welcome." She watched Charlie drop on his stomach and focus the scope on Castro's sedan as it moved into the compound. He pressed his right eye against the scope, a grim look on his face, a brown stubble on his chin. He hadn't shaved in days.

Seeing the determined look on his face, Isabel put their last water canteen and the machete into Charlie's burlap sack. She carried the bag to the motorcycle, swung her leg over the seat, and put her foot on the starter pedal. Once Charlie took his shot, the two of them would roar away from el Chico before anyone in the compound had a chance to react. With a big enough head start, their pursuers would never catch up. They could pick up Angelita, go to the safe house, and be on their way to Florida. If they were lucky.

39

Saturday, October 27, 1962

Strategic Air Command Operations Center, Omaha, Nebraska

IN THE SCREENING ROOM, SAC General Thomas Powers watched his team of airmen chatting as they tracked blips of the Russian MiG fighter planes approaching the American U-2 reconnaissance plane. Also on the screen were the blips of the two American F-102 Delta Dagger interceptor planes from Alaska coming to protect the U-2 from the MiGs.

"Jesus, those MiGs are moving twice as fast as that U-2. The F-102s are never going to reach him in time. He's a goner," said one of the trackers.

"But he flies at 70,000 feet. The MiGs can't get anywhere near that, even with their afterburners blasting away," said another.

"Afterburners use a hell of a lot of fuel. They might run out of gas before they get close enough to shoot."

As the gap between the MiGs and the U-2 kept getting smaller, the trackers stopped their chattering. One airman unconsciously raised his hand to his mouth and gnawed at his nails. General

Powers, overlooking the scene, clenched his fists.

Then, as if to confirm the tracker's comment about running out of gas, the blips of the MiGs slowed down, reversed direction, and apparently returned to their base. The airmen let out a loud cheer. General Powers smiled broadly, made a military about-face, and left the room.

SIBERIA

CAPTAIN CHARLES MAULTSBY STILL DIDN'T know he had been chased by MiGs. He followed instructions from his flight controllers in Alaska to turn the U-2 leftward, hoping that would head him east and out of Siberia. He felt heartened as the Russian radio music station faded out and then elated when the glow of sun began rising in front of him on the eastern horizon.

However, Maultsby had a new problem. His own fuel was running low. To conserve it, he turned off the engine and went into a long, slow glide. His U-2 could glide up to 250 miles, and that might be enough to get him to the Bering Strait, where he would be out of Russia. He also decided to turn off his radio and lights so they wouldn't drain the battery and prevent him from restarting the engine.

Shutting down the plane's power, however, also turned off the cockpit's air pressure. His pressurized suit began to inflate. It became so bulky he could barely move his arms. Furthermore, the expanding suit pushed up his helmet so that it blocked his vision. It took several minutes to wrestle it back into its correct position. Finally, with a wave of relief, he spotted the two F-102s approaching him from Alaska. Rather than flying side-by-side to escort him back to Alaska, however, they made giant circles around the much slower U-2.

Maultsby restarted the engine at 25,000 feet, the pressure suit deflated, and he landed on an ice airstrip on the western coast of Alaska, just above the Arctic Circle. A ground crew pulled him from the cockpit and told him that he had been ordered to leave immediately on a flight to SAC headquarters in Nebraska. There he would face the wrath of General Powers for having drifted off course and potentially setting off a nuclear exchange.

"I have to do something else first."

After nine hours in the cramped cockpit, the pressure on his bladder was powerful. He staggered to a snowbank to relieve himself.

HAVANA, CUBA

ON SATURDAY AFTERNOON, FLAVIO'S RADIO operator, Pepe, turned on his radio for the first time in three days. Within moments he got a signal that Bishop had an urgent message for him. Flavio was in the musty safe house with Pepe. He loomed over Pepe's shoulder as he watched the older man write down letters in tune to the di-dah-dit sounds of Morse code. The letters came through in blocks of five characters per set. When Pepe finished, he handed the sheet to Flavio who pulled a code book from his pocket. He proceeded to decode the meaningless sets of letters into English. Even after decoding, it took a moment for him to translate the five-character blocks into a coherent message.

DON'T—SHOOT—. GAM—E OVE—

R. T —ELL C—OLLIN—S S—TOPH

—IM AT— ALL —COSTS

"Jesus," he said, staring at Pepe. "They're calling it off! Why the hell would they do that after we've gotten this close? All we have to do is wait for Castro to show up so we can put a bullet through his chest." Then another, more upbeat thought came to him. "This must mean they're going to invade after all, and our liquidating Castro would somehow interfere with that." Getting rid of the whole regime was a million times better than just bumping off Castro, he thought. "I must get to el Chico and stop Collins."

"How are you going to get into el Chico?" asked Pepe. "It's guarded."

"I don't have to get in. A kilometer before you get to the guardhouse on the highway, there's a small, abandoned lane that goes up to the fence around the compound. That's where I'll be with the gringo." He dropped the decoded message to the floor and moved toward the exit, talking over his shoulder to give instructions to Pepe. "You know the signal for them to send in the boat to pick us up. Radio them immediately so they can get that boat here tonight. If you have any questions, you know where we'll be. Come and get us if you have any problems."

The possibility that the Americans might actually invade Cuba elated Flavio. He hoped the CIA boat could extract them before the invasion started. That would give him time to join the Cuban brigade that had been training outside Miami. He pictured himself going ashore and leading the charge to overthrow the regime.

But the phrase "at all costs" bothered him. If Collins insisted on shooting anyway, how could Flavio stop him? Collins was the one with the rifle. Flavio was weaponless.

With these thoughts racing through his mind, Flavio pulled his Vespa from its hiding spot down the road from the safe house. No sooner had he done so than two jeeps roared up. He watched as four soldiers hopped out of the first jeep and burst into the safe house. Dios mío, thought Flavio. There'll be no way now for Pepe to send a message for that boat to extract them. Flavio not only had to stop his friend from shooting, but he now had to get both of them out of the area before the soldiers found out from Pepe that Charlie and Flavio were planning to ambush Castro at el Chico. He sped down the road.

———

MAJOR ESCALANTE FOLLOWED THE FOUR soldiers into the shack. They trained their rifles on Pepe who had been tapping out Morse code with his transmitter key. He raised his hands over his head.

Sergeant Ramos picked up the sheet of paper that Flavio had dropped on the floor, but he didn't know English. He handed it to Major Escalante who shrugged his shoulders. "I recognize the word

Collins, but the rest is gibberish. Where is that translator bitch when I could use her?"

He grabbed Pepe by the shirt front and slammed him against the wall of the shack. "What does this say? What is that gringo Collins up to?"

When Pepe hesitated, Escalante motioned for two of his soldiers to take the older man outside. They backed him against a palm tree, pulled his arms behind him, and held him tightly against the tree trunk.

"I don't know," said Pepe.

Escalante pulled a baseball bat from his jeep and tapped Pepe on the forehead. "I don't have time to screw around with you, old man. Unless you want me to smash your head, tell me what this message says, and whether that gringo Collins was here."

"They went to el Chico," said Pepe, staring at the bat only inches from his face.

"They? There's more than one of them? Did he have a woman? A skinny, brown haired little bitch?" shouted Escalante.

"No woman," said Pepe, still staring at the bat. "Just the gringo and a Cuban. They forced me to copy this stuff off their radio. They have a rifle and a machete. They went to el Chico."

"El Chico? El Chico is guarded. How do they expect to get in?"

When Pepe hesitated, the major swung the bat against his cheek, and causing blood to spurt from his mouth. Pepe shrunk back even more tightly against the tree to escape the next blow. "There's a lane, a kilometer before the guardhouse on the highway," he mumbled through his injured jaw. "Just go in there."

The major turned to Sergeant Ramos. "Secure this place. Take this guy to our jail, but don't let anything happen to him. We want to interrogate him later. I'm going to take a driver and a rifleman and the other jeep to el Chico."

"You should take the full squad, Major," said the sergeant. They have a rifle and a machete."

"No. Too many men. Someone will get nervous and start shooting blindly. Then all hell will break loose. I want those two pendejos alive. They are the mother lode of information about the CIA and the gusanos. They're no good to me if they're dead."

Escalante climbed into the jeep with the two soldiers and sped off for the hidden lane to el Chico.

40

Saturday, October 27, 1962

THE QUARANTINE LINE

ESNIKOV GASPED AT THE FIRST captain's order to arm the nuclear torpedo. "Sir, we will start a world war if we fire that torpedo. And we have no way to escape. If we detonate a nuclear torpedo, we have to assume that the Americans will have nuclear depth charges that they will use in retaliation."

Lesnikov looked toward Political Officer Chernikov for support. Chernikov was sweating profusely.

"We've been out of contact with Moscow for a long time," said Lesnikov. "We do not know what is going on above us. Maybe Khrushchev and Kennedy have made peace. Or maybe we're at war. Unless the Americans attack us or unless they invade Cuba, we do *not* have authorization to launch that nuclear torpedo." He looked again at Chernikov who never liked to do anything without approval. Several seamen stared wide-eyed at this open disagreement between their top officers. Finally, Chernikov nodded yes. "Let's get close enough to the surface to establish radio contact with Moscow and ask for instructions."

The sub's conning tower popped through the water into a blinding glare of search lights on the surrounding U.S. naval vessels. When the first captain of the sub opened the hatch, it was obvious that the war hadn't started yet. One of the nearby destroyers had a band on deck, playing "Stars and Stripes Forever."

The sub finally made radio contact with Moscow. "Throw off your pursuers and fall back to a reserve position," came the order. The first captain turned his sub around, closed the hatches, and submerged. The sub headed east, away from the quarantine line.

Havana, Cuba

"Charlie," Isabel called out, "someone is coming up the lane."

Charlie was too focused on the encampment to hear her. In the compound, two squads of soldiers hopped out of the trucks and lined up in a double-row formation, holding their rifles before them in the port arms position. Castro's sedan came to a stop, and he stepped out in front of the soldiers.

"Oh, shit," said Charlie out loud. "That line of troops is blocking my view. I'll have to stand up."

Shooting from a standing position made it harder to hold the rifle steady. Even more important, it left him in full view of the compound. He would only have time for a single shot. The soldiers held their rifles in a port arms position facing Castro. But the instant they heard the bullet whiz by or strike a target, they would turn, spot Charlie, and send a hail of bullets toward him and Isabel.

Charlie traced Castro's slow movement through the scope, waiting for Castro to come to a stop where he would make a perfect, stationary target. Castro was so tall he stood out above the two rows of soldiers, but Charlie wanted to wait until the commandante was a little further away from them. He didn't want to risk hitting one of soldiers instead of Castro.

"Charlie!" Isabel shouted this time. "There's something coming up the path."

Startled, Charlie looked over his shoulder. "Oh, thank God," he said, "it's Flavio. He's come to give us a hand. Oh my God, what a relief."

He turned his attention back to the scene in the compound and failed to hear Flavio shout, "Stop! Stop, Michael! Stop! They called it off!"

Charlie felt naked, standing and sweating in the hot sun as he peered through the scope. A trickle of sweat caused a nervous itch on his forehead. But he couldn't scratch it without disrupting his aiming the rifle. He could see Castro's head over the line of soldiers. "Thank God that son-of-a-bitch is so tall." He placed his crosshairs on Castro's skull.

He lifted his eye off the scope for an instant when a sudden movement on the porch of the headquarters building distracted him. A woman came out of the building and stood behind a line of Soviet officers waiting for Castro to join them. Maybe she was a maid or the wife of the Russian commander. She wore a long blue and white dress that came down to her ankles.

The colors of the dress triggered an image in Charlie's mind: the girl by Sacré Coeur in Paris who had dressed as Little Bo Peep. That nursery rhyme image had given him one of his few contacts with normalcy in the previous two months. She had invited him to come back to Sacré Coeur when she got off work to tell her about the thing he was dreading. But she was gone by the time he had returned.

"Shit!" he whispered. "Screw this. Let Bishop turn somebody else into a killer."

But he had to shoot something. Bishop would submit Flavio and Isabel to lie detector tests. If they told him that Charlie had failed to pull the trigger or had deliberately misfired, Bishop would make good on his threat to expose Charlie's father to prosecution. Flavio and Isabel truly had to believe Charlie had tried to shoot Castro—that he had missed only because he was forced to shoot from an unsteady standing position. He raised the crosshairs until they rested on the windshield of the automobile just behind Fidel.

He squeezed the trigger, and the windshield splintered around a hole the size of a quarter just above the steering wheel.

A rock hit him in the back, and then Flavio crashed into him from behind, knocking him to the ground. Charlie's elbow landed on a rock, and the rifle flew away from him. Isabel jumped off the bike and ran to retrieve the rifle. She drifted back toward the bike but kept the rifle pointing at Flavio, who wrestled on the ground with Charlie.

"What the hell are you doing?" Charlie yelled at Flavio as he rolled away from him and sat up.

"It's over, amigo," said Flavio. "They called it off."

"Who called it off?"

"Bishop. The CIA. That whole batch of pendejos."

"Why?"

"I don't know why. Just get your ass out of here. Now! A squad of soldiers invaded the safe house, and there won't be any rescue boat. By now, Pepe will have told them where we are."

A Jeep roared into the clearing and rolled over Flavio's scooter, Major Escalante at the wheel. Two soldiers jumped from the Jeep when it stopped and grabbed Flavio and Charlie. As they struggled with the soldiers, Escalante raised his pistol and waved it back and forth between the two men.

"Stop resisting!" he commanded.

Unnoticed by the major and his soldiers, Isabel lifted the rifle to her shoulder, braced herself, and pulled the trigger. She almost fell over from the rifle's kickback. Her bullet struck the earth at the major's foot.

"Drop that pistol," she shouted, recovering her balance and pointing the rifle straight at Escalante's chest.

He let the gun fall to the ground.

"Let them go," she shouted at the soldiers. The instant the soldiers released them, Flavio ran toward Escalante's jeep, hopped in, and raced out the lane. Isabel stomped on the starter pedal of the motorcycle, and the engine roared to life. Charlie grabbed the burlap sack and hopped onto the bike behind her. She dropped the M1 to the ground and turned the bike toward the lane that led out of the clearing. Escalante picked up his pistol, but by the time he fired it, Isabel and Charlie were halfway down the lane, and Escalante's bullets thudded into trees.

By that time, the soldiers on the parade ground had figured out where the gunfire originated. They rushed the fence and fired wildly at the motorcycle. But their bullets also went wide and thumped into the trees.

"What are we going to do?" Isabel screamed over the wind rushing around them as the bike picked up speed. Her voice was panicky. "Did you hear what that man said? They can't send in a boat for you. Castro is going to kill us."

41

Saturday, October 27, 1962

THE WHITE HOUSE

TED SORENSEN, ROBERT KENNEDY, AND three others followed the president into the Oval Office. The president told his brother and Sorensen what he wanted in the message to Khrushchev. He would follow up on Dean Rusk's suggestion to reply to Khrushchev's conciliatory message and ignore the bellicose one. If the Russians removed all their nuclear arms from Cuba, Kennedy would pledge not to invade the island. But he wanted nothing in the statement about the missiles in Turkey. Kennedy then addressed his brother. "You're on good terms with the Russian ambassador. Call him into your office so you can give him the message personally and press on him how urgent it is for him to get a quick response out of Khrushchev."

"If I know Anatol," said the attorney general, "he'll ask about our missiles in Turkey. What do you want me to tell him?"

"As the generals pointed out all afternoon, we can't withdraw those missiles now, without making the Turks and our other NATO allies think we betrayed them. Tell the ambassador we'll remove our missiles from Turkey after Khrushchev gets all his nukes out of Cuba. However, he cannot mention anything about the Turkey missiles publicly. If he does, the deal is off."

A big problem, they all agreed, was that it would take too long to get this message to Khrushchev if they stuck to normal diplomatic channels. The State Department would want to edit it. That would take time. Translating it into Russian and transmitting it would take more time. Then it would take additional time for the Soviets to receive it and double check the translation before it finally reached Khrushchev.

"I'll broadcast the message over Voice of America," said Kennedy. That way, Khrushchev would get it immediately, which would deter him from taking any immediate hostile action. The rest of the world would see the Americans as reasonable and conciliatory.

Robert Kennedy and Sorensen moved to an adjoining room to draft a statement. They returned to the Oval Office by 6:30 p.m., when the attorney general had to return to his office for the meeting with the Russian ambassador. Before leaving, he said to Sorensen, "I have to make the ambassador understand how critical it is for Khrushchev to get those nukes out immediately. The Joint Chiefs of Staff are adamant about starting air strikes by Tuesday at the latest. If Khrushchev doesn't act right now, I don't know if Jack can hold them off any longer."

After Bobby left, the president penciled in a few edits to the statement that Sorensen had given him. He then recorded the statement and sent it to Voice of America for broadcast around the world.

UNTIL KHRUSHCHEV RESPONDED, THERE WAS nothing more to do. Kennedy invited his old sidekick, Dave Powers, up to the Residence for a late-night dinner. Having been with Kennedy since his initial election to Congress sixteen years earlier, Powers was one of the few people with whom Kennedy could relax.

They were eating roasted chicken when the attorney general

returned and gave a very pessimistic report on his meeting with the Soviet Ambassador. The Kennedy brothers discussed this latest development while Powers quietly ate his chicken. Khruschev had no incentive to dismantle his nukes in Cuba unless he believed the U.S. would launch airstrikes against them and invade the island. But if he truly believed that was going to happen, he might launch the nukes in a preventive strike.

The president looked over at Powers picking up a piece of the roasted chicken. "Good God," he said jokingly, "the way you're eating up all that chicken and drinking all my wine, anybody would think it was your last meal."

"The way Bobby's been talking," replied Powers, "I thought it *was* my last meal."

Bobby left. Kennedy and Powers watched a movie, *Roman Holiday*, with Audrey Hepburn.

HAVANA, CUBA

"FIND SOME PLACE TO DITCH this bike!" Charlie shouted into Isabel's ear. "The whole Cuban army will be looking for it by now. Ditch it, and we'll walk back to the santera's house of saints where we can regroup."

Just before they reached the East-West Highway, she found a copse of trees and dumped the bike. As they piled branches over it, Charlie asked, "How far to the house of saints?"

"Maybe another ten kilometers."

The sun was high in the sky, which made them visible to any soldier who might be looking for them. They had barely left the bike and returned to the road when the rumble of army trucks came their way. They ducked back into the trees and crouched until the convoy passed. Charlie swatted a mosquito and used his sleeve to wipe sweat from his forehead. Both of their shirts were stained dark with sweat.

"God, it's muggy. Doesn't this place ever cool down?"

Isabel ignored his complaint. "I can get us out of Cuba," she said, chewing her lip, "but there's a small problem."

"*You* can get us out of Cuba? How?"

"You forgot," she snorted. "You should pay better attention. I told you before. I'm the backup pilot for Major Escalante. I know where he keeps his plane, and I can fly us to Florida."

Charlie lifted his hand to his chin, skeptically. "Doesn't he keep it locked up?"

"I have the key. But I can't get into the airport with Angelita and take the plane by myself."

"You're right. Stealing his plane from a guarded airport is a small problem," he said, dismissively waving his hand. There is another small problem. Between here and Florida, the American Navy has a massive armada of trigger-happy ships just looking for something they can shoot at. And you're going to fly between them?"

"Do you have a better idea?"

He didn't. They left their hiding spot once the convoy passed and resumed their walk toward the city, energized by the possibility of flying out of Cuba in Escalante's Piper Cub. They eventually reached the outskirts of the city and were soon passing many buildings along the way. Suddenly she stopped, grabbed Charlie's arm, and pointed toward a bridge over a river. Three soldiers guarded the bridge. Isabel and Charlie ducked behind a tree before the soldiers could spot them.

"It's the Rio Jaimanitas," she said, "and this is the only crossing."

"It's pretty secluded. Let's go upstream so we can get out of their line of sight." He took her hand and led her deep enough into the trees to shield themselves from the soldiers at the bridge. The river flowed slowly with very little current, but it was at least twenty yards wide.

"It's so muddy, I can't tell how deep it is," she said.

"We'll test it." He pulled the machete from the burlap bag that was still draped over his shoulder. "I'll cut us a couple of poles from these branches on the ground to help us steady ourselves."

The denseness of the surrounding trees muffled the sound of the machete hacking through branches, and none of the soldiers looked in their direction. Charlie fashioned two poles, each about five feet long. Draping the burlap bag over his shoulder, he stepped into the water. His feet sank immediately into a muddy bottom. Isabel followed him and nearly toppled over until she used her pole to regain her balance.

As they neared the opposite shore, he stopped so that Isabel could pass in front of him. She struggled onto the riverbank, mud clinging to the denim pants she had gotten from her friend Helena. She turned to look back, and suddenly she began to jump up and down, a look of horror on her face, as she pointed upstream, waving her arm to make sure that he looked where she was pointing. A huge crocodile was moving steadily toward Charlie, opening and closing its large mouth. Charlie's pulse raced and his mouth went dry. He dug harder with the pole against the muddy bottom, pushing himself forward as fast as he could. But the crocodile gained steadily on him. He breathed a sigh of relief when he finally stepped out of the water onto the shore.

However, the croc did not stop. It walked out of the water and kept coming toward him. Panicky, he slapped his pole against the animal's head, but the croc kept coming at him. Its mouth opened wide, as though it were ready to take a bite. Charlie jabbed the point of his pole into the soft tissue of the croc's mouth. The croc stopped moving forward. Charlie pulled back on the pole and jammed it once more into the croc's mouth. Finally, the croc turned around and walked back to the water. Charlie collapsed on the muddy riverbank and stayed there until he caught his breath. "I've never been so scared in my life. I thought I was done for."

"There shouldn't be any crocodiles up here," said Isabel. "They're all in the swamp on the other side of the island."

"Tell that to him."

Once they recovered from the scare, they moved forward and

entered the thick of the city. They mingled in crowds as much as possible so they wouldn't stand out. But it was hard, given their muddy clothes. When the crowds thinned, they edged along the streets close to buildings. By the time the santera's house of saints came into sight, the sun was setting. They each took a last swig from the canteen, but the tepid water barely wetted Charlie's parched throat. He tossed the empty container onto a pile of trash.

"You never told me about the problem with your plan," he said.

"If I had been as sarcastic to you as you were to me, would you have told me anything you'd thought of?"

Jesus, he thought. We almost got shot by Escalante and eaten by a crocodile, and her nose was out of joint because of his sarcasm. But, he could tell, she was indeed angry. And hurt.

"I'm sorry," he said. "It won't happen again. Please tell me the problem."

"We've only been walking for two hours, but I'm so tired I could collapse. All this tension is wearing me out."

"Me too. But what's the problem?"

"The major's plane is at a military airfield called Ciudad Libertad. It will be another two-hour walk from the house of saints. We'll have to carry Angelita and your two satchels, which are heavy, plus anything else you want to bring. I can't walk for two more hours, Charlie."

They turned onto a side road a few blocks from the Santeria.

"Problem solved," said Charlie, grinning as he pointed to an old Plymouth sedan parked on the street a block from the entrance. "Get me a screwdriver from the santera, and we'll borrow that car."

The Saturday night Santeria ceremony was going full blast when they arrived. Isabel found a screwdriver for him, and he pulled a gold bracelet from the medicine bag so she could leave a thank-you gift for the santera. Isabel lifted Angelita into her arms while Charlie slung his burlap sack over his shoulder and picked up the two satchels stuffed with jewels. With everyone focused on the ceremony, nobody saw them leave. But when they reached the spot where they had seen the old Plymouth, it was gone.

"Oh God," murmured Isabel. She collapsed into a sitting position on the ground, her feet spread-eagled in front of her and her shoulders slumped forward. Angelita stood up to give her a hug.

"¿Mamá, qué te preocupa?"

Isabel pulled the girl tightly to her chest, then looked to Charlie. "What now? I can't walk another two hours."

He too was depressed. "We'll try again tomorrow as soon as it gets dark. If the car's here, we'll borrow it. If not, at least we'll be fresh enough for the walk."

42

Sunday, October 28, 1962

HAVANA, CUBA

E ARLY SUNDAY MORNING, THE SANTERA called Charlie and Isabel to her room. Grinning, she showed off the gold bracelet Isabel had given her as she pointed to her radio. Nikita Khrushchev had announced over Radio Moscow that he had accepted a deal with the Americans. He promised to withdraw his nuclear weapons from Cuba, and Kennedy, in turn, promised not to invade the island.

"Fidel's not going to like losing those nukes," said Charlie.

"True," said Isabel, grinning. "But Charlie, just think. No invasion. No war."

Cubans crowded the streets to protest the perfidy of the Russians. The Ministry of Communications produced placards denouncing the Russian treachery and distributed them to mobs of people. Havana raged with turmoil all day. Crowds gathered at the Soviet embassy and shook their fists at the Russians.

Amid the chaos, Charlie and Isabel had no way to reach the airfield. Finally, after dark, the city began to calm. Charlie ventured into the street to see if the Plymouth sedan had returned to its parking spot. It had, and no people were in sight. "We can ride," he told Isabel with a grin. "I just saved you a long walk."

Charlie, Isabel, and Angelita walked out to the dark street, with little more than their clothes, the machete, and the black medicine bags filled with jewels. Draped around Isabel's neck was a cloth sling she had fashioned so she could carry Angelita if necessary.

Just a mere sliver of moon hung in the sky, but Charlie felt as though they were walking through a searchlight as they approached the old Plymouth. He smashed a large rock against the driver's side window, but it didn't break. He smashed it again, and Angelita stared wide-eyed, holding her mother's hand. Finally, Charlie had a hole large enough to insert his arm and unlock the door. He dropped the two medicine bags in the back seat along with the burlap sack containing the machete. Isabel crawled into the passenger side and set Angelita next to her on the bench seat.

Charlie grinned as he realized that this was the same type of car on which he had learned hot wiring back at the junkyard in Baltimore. He also recalled his instructor's tip to try the screwdriver method first. "If you're lucky, it'll work and save you a bit of precious time." He jammed the screwdriver into the ignition slot and whacked it with the same big rock he had used to smash the window. He whacked it again, but the ignition key slot would not turn. He whacked it a third time and a fourth, but it still wouldn't turn. Isabel drew a deep breath. On the fifth whack, the screwdriver blade dug into the slot, and finally, it twisted. The engine kicked over, and Isabel exhaled with a whoosh.

Charlie drove with the lights off, sticking to back streets as much as possible. But a mile from the airfield, the streets funneled into a main road. Two blocks in front of them, a squad of soldiers manned a roadblock. Turning around instantly, he drove up an unlit alleyway that contained few houses. As they continued, the houses disappeared and the lane dead-ended at the edge of a wide field. The control tower of the airport stood on the far side of the field.

Angelita had fallen asleep. Without waking her, Isabel wrapped her in the sling, draped the narrow end of it around her neck, and lifted her from the car. Charlie knotted the burlap sack so he could drape it over his shoulder, and he picked up a black medicine bag in each hand. Before they moved, Isabel opened one of the bags and reached inside. She pulled out a Rolex watch and dropped it on the front seat of the car.

"What was that for?" asked Charlie.

"Whoever owns this car is going to go through a lot of misery trying to prove he had nothing to do with the theft of Major Escalante's plane. And when he gets his car back, he will need to get his window repaired."

That watch would be long gone by the time the owner gets his car back, Charlie thought. But he kept that idea to himself as he led them into the field that abutted the airstrip. In moments, they reached the chain link fence around the perimeter of the airbase. As far as they could see, the top of the fence was covered with barbed wire.

"I cannot risk lifting Angelita over that," said Isabel. "Can you dig a tunnel under it with the machete?"

"Before I start digging, let's find out if that fence is electrified."

He balanced the machete on its blade and let it fall against the wire fence to see if sparks would flash. None did. He grabbed the machete, raised it over his head and jabbed it at the ground. They only needed a shallow passage, which Charlie was able to dig in a few moments.

"You first." He motioned for Isabel to slide through the hole. One of her pant legs snagged on the rough ends of the fence, and Charlie had to rip it free. When she reached the other side, Charlie very gently lowered Angelita into the depression, taking care to keep her face and clothing away from the chain-link edges. When she was halfway through, Isabel grabbed her under the armpits and pulled her out. Then Charlie fed the two medicine bags through the hole. Finally, he lay on his back and dug his heels into the ground to push himself through the slot.

Standing in the airfield now, they had no tall grasses or bushes to hide their movements. Charlie looked up. "At least there's not much of a moon. Let's get to your plane as fast as we can. We've got to get out of here before the sun comes up."

With Isabel carrying Angelita and Charlie lugging the heavy medicine bags, it was slow going to reach the Piper Cub. It sat in front of the hanger. A hundred yards away, by the control tower, a jeep sat in the dark. She unlocked the plane with the key she had pilfered three weeks earlier. He tossed the medicine bags on the floor and helped her fasten Angelita under the seat belt in the back of the plane. "I didn't know these Pipers had a back seat."

"This is their Family Cruiser. It was because it had a back seat that Major Escalante bought it." She motioned for him to stop talking. "We can discuss airplanes later, Charlie. Right now, we have to get this thing moving before anybody spots us."

Charlie used the machete to sever the ropes tethering the plane to hooks in the ground. He climbed into the cockpit, pulled the door shut, and adjusted his safety belt. He glanced at his watch—5:30 a.m. The night was passing too quickly. It would be touch and go whether they could reach Florida before the sun came up and made it easy for them to be spotted.

Isabel pushed the starter button on the dashboard, and the engine jumped to life. In the silence of the night, the noise was deafening.

"It'll be a miracle if nobody heard that," she said as she began to taxi across the tarmac. "Because the wind is blowing in from over the hangar, I have to taxi all the way to the end of the runway, turn around, and then take off in this direction."

She taxied out the runway so fast the tail began to lift, and she had to slow down. It felt to Charlie as though they were inching along, and he stomped his feet. When she finally reached the end of the runway and turned the plane around, headlights were already moving toward them. Isabel pushed in the throttle, and the Piper Cub inched forward, gradually picking up speed. The headlights also seemed to pick up speed. Charlie could feel the tail wheel lift, but the front wheels stayed firmly on the ground. He stared out the windshield in horror at the oncoming headlights speeding in their direction.

The plane's main wheels took several bounces before the plane lifted and they finally were airborne. A flash of rifle fire came from the vehicle below just before it passed from sight. A bullet smashed through the windshield, whizzing between Isabel and Charlie and tearing through the cloth fabric on the ceiling. Charlie jumped to the right and Isabel to the left. Her foot jammed down on the rudder pedal, sending the plane off course to the right. Charlie held his breath until she steadied the plane. She took it up to a thousand feet, banked, and turned until she got the compass needle pointing to five degrees from north. Charlie looked into the rear to make sure Angelita was still secured by the seatbelt. When he looked out the window, there were very few lights shining below. Isabel would have to navigate in the dark.

"I have to get high enough that we won't be spotted from the ground. But once we're out over the sea, we'll drop down and hope that we can fly under the American radar."

"What about the Cuban radar?"

"Once we're out over the water, it won't matter anymore if the Cuban radar picks us up."

They passed over Havana without incident, and darkness enveloped them as they moved out to sea. Isabel inched the stick forward and the plane slowly descended. Angelita stirred in the back seat. When Charlie turned to look, she was sitting up rubbing her eyes, staring at her mother in the unfamiliar position of the pilot's seat. The plane kept descending until it was barely above the crests of the waves. As Isabel leveled off, a gust of wind caught the Piper Cub, pushing it up and off course. Then, as the wind changed into a downdraft, the plane dropped just as suddenly as it had risen a moment earlier.

"Wee," Angelita shouted in Spanish. "That was fun! Do it again, Momma."

Charlie braced his feet against the floor, expecting to splash into the water, but Isabel regained control and brought the plane up to fifty feet.

"It would be harder for the Americans to see us if I stayed down at the wave-tops. But these little planes are so sensitive to wind gusts we need to fly higher to have a margin of safety."

More than once, they spotted warships along their route, including one aircraft carrier. They were almost on top of the carrier before Isabel saw it and swerved to the left. Charlie looked out the window to see if they'd been seen, but no flares shot up from the deck of the ship and no fighter planes took off after them. For Charlie, who liked to be in charge, it was unnerving just to sit and watch as Isabel guided the plane through the dark around the warships. He turned to check on Angelita, who was lying down again, her eyes closed, and her thumb in her mouth. He adjusted the seat belt so that it ran the length of her body and would hold her in place if they hit more turbulence.

Less than an hour into their flight, a faint, blinking dot of light appeared on the horizon, and it grew larger as the plane moved forward. Isabel shook Charlie's arm and pointed out the windshield. She had a huge smile.

"That's it," she shouted over the engine's noise. "Key West! That's the only thing it can be."

"Give it a wide berth," said Charlie. "Somehow, you've weaved us through the entire Caribbean fleet without being seen. You're like the best broken-field runner in the history of football."

"What's a broken-field runner?"

"I'll explain later. Right now, stay as far out to sea as you can without losing sight of the shore lights. Then just follow that string of islands up the coast until you get to Key Largo."

"How far?"

"A hundred miles from Key West, maybe."

"In kilometers."

He paused to make the calculation. "One fifty, more or less."

"Where do you want to land?" she asked.

"I want to get as close to Homestead as possible. The last island in the keys will be Key Largo. As you pass from Key Largo to the mainland, I want you to pick a remote spot to land on the beach."

"On the beach?" she shouted. "We'll kill ourselves. We have to land on the highway."

"We can't. Someone will spot the plane immediately, and we'll be arrested. However, if we strand the plane on the beach, it won't be discovered for hours. That will give us plenty of time to get where we're going."

"You can't land a plane on the sand, Charlie."

"The Florida sand is as hard as concrete. Up in Daytona they hold automobile races on the beach sand. That's how hard it is."

Half of the sun had popped up on the eastern horizon by the time they reached Key Largo.

"Do you see that highway going north out of Key Largo?" he shouted.

She nodded.

"That's called the Dixie Highway. It will take us to Homestead. But before that, it will veer off to the left. When you reach that point, find a stretch of beach as close by as you can."

"This is crazy. I'm going to land on the highway."

"If you do, the police will pick us up immediately, and you will find yourself in a bureaucratic jungle of immigration officials that will make the Cuban bureaucracy seem almost rational. Angelita will be put in a foster home, and it'll be weeks before you see her again."

This was an enormous exaggeration, he knew. Cuban refugees gained legal status immediately. But if she and he were picked up by the police and turned over to customs authorities, Charlie would be stripped of the million dollars of jewels and probably charged with smuggling. "This will work. Trust me. The sand is as hard as concrete."

He crossed his fingers and took a quick look back at Angelita to make sure she was secured snugly under the seat belt. Isabel shot him a skeptical look, then turned her attention back to following along the shoreline.

"Look," Charlie pointed out the windshield. "There's the turnoff to the left. And there's an empty stretch of beach just beyond it. That will be perfect."

She let her air speed drop. The plane sank lower and lower until it was only a few feet from the ground. When the air speed indicator reached fifty mph and the plane began to stall, she cut the engine and the rear wheel touched down on the sand.

But it was not as hard as concrete.

FLORIDA

THE TAIL WHEEL DRAGGED THROUGH the sand, slowing the plane, then bringing the front landing wheels down with a hard slam. They dug into the sand and rolled only a few yards before plowing to a stop and pitching the nose of the plane into the ground. The propeller dug into the sand and snapped off.

The seat belts kept Charlie and Isabel from flying through the windshield. Angelita, who had been lying asleep in the back seat, woke up when the landing jammed her against the seat belt covering her lengthwise. She screamed, "¡Ayúdame! ¡Ayúdame!"

Partially hanging from the seatbelt and pitched forward, Charlie pushed one hand against the instrument panel to lift enough weight off of his seatbelt so that he could unlatch it. He twisted around until his feet caught a firm hold, and he turned his attention to Isabel. He pushed his shoulder into her midsection, pushed up with his legs, and moved her body enough to release the weight on her seatbelt.

"Brace yourself so you don't fall forward when I undo the buckle," he said. She pushed her hand against the instrument panel for support.

The instant she was free, she turned toward Angelita who was hanging from her seatbelt, screaming. She lifted the girl's weight off the seatbelt, unclasped the buckle and took her daughter in her arms.

"Let's hope the door didn't jam shut," said Charlie as he twisted the lever and pushed outward. The door swung open. He crawled out and motioned for Isabel to hand Angelita to him. The girl was squirming and kicking and screaming so much he could barely hold her.

Once out of the plane, Isabel took her daughter back in her arms and hugged her tightly to her chest to calm her. "It's all over, my baby. You're okay," she murmured over and over, soothing Angelita, and stroking her hair. "You're okay now."

Charlie reached inside to retrieve his flattop hat which had fallen off his head during the crash landing. He dropped it on the ground, then reached back into the cockpit to pull out the two medicine bags and the machete that had wedged itself under the seat. "It's a miracle this thing didn't fly around during that landing," he said, touching his thumb to the edge of the blade. He dropped it next to his hat.

Then, as he realized how extraordinarily lucky they had been, he wrapped his arms around Isabel and Angelita and lifted them off the ground.

"We did it," he shouted and set them down. "We made it. Isabel, you were magnificent! You were beautiful! You got the plane into the air before that guy in the jeep could shoot us down. You flew right through the middle of the U.S. Navy without being spotted. And you got us down to the ground."

Once more, he wrapped his arms around the two of them and lifted them off the ground. "No more drawer cells. No baseball bats. No sniper rifles. By the time this day is over, you and Angelita are going to be legal immigrants on the path to citizenship." He set them back on the ground and gave them each a big smile.

"What now?" she asked.

"We get as far away from this airplane as we can before it's spotted. And we hitchhike to Homestead."

"Hitchhike?"

"I'll show you when we get to the highway. We're going to my friend Eduardo's cantina for breakfast and a shower. We'll borrow his car so we can stow these bags in my safe-deposit box in the city."

"Borrow the way you borrowed that car outside the house of saints?"

He grinned. "No. I couldn't do that to an old friend. This will be a traditional borrowing. Afterward, we'll buy some fresh clothes, and I'll call my CIA controller to pick us up. When they finish debriefing us, we'll be as free as the birds."

He set the flattop hat on his head and stooped to pick up the medicine bags. Then he led them inland toward the highway.

43

November 1965

Greenwich Village, New York City, New York

MAJOR ESCALANTE HAD STUFFED ISABEL into a cage. Charlie rushed to her aid, but he could barely move because his feet were stuck in quicksand. He himself was sinking as he tried to hold Angelita above the muck. He gasped for breath until he finally woke up with a start, drenched in sweat.

This nightmare hadn't bothered him for months, but now it was back. As consciousness returned and he could move, he sat up, shook his head to loosen the cobwebs, and looked down at Isabel. She, too, suffered from similar dreams. But tonight, she slept soundly. The clock on the nightstand read 5:30 a.m. Too late to go back to sleep, but too early to get up. He got up anyway.

It had been three years. It was now 1965, the last workday before Thanksgiving. He walked to the window and stuffed a tee shirt against the crack to keep out the cold November air. Taking Isabel and Angelita to the Greenwich Village apartment had seemed so romantic when he first thought of it. In truth, the unit was drafty in the winter and sweltering in summer. Its paper-thin walls made them a party to the neighbors' noises. And presumably their neighbors were a party to noises that he and Isabel made. Having been raised in crowded Havana, none of this bothered her like it bothered him. Outside the window, a siren wailed as an ambulance made its way to St. Vincent's Hospital, half a mile away.

Charlie put coffee into the percolator basket. When Isabel woke, she would want café con leche, but he was satisfied with a percolated cup. He took it back to bed, slipped under the covers, pushed his hip against her, and sipped the brew as he pondered what they had been through.

———

SETTLING MATTERS WITH THE CIA took longer than he had anticipated. James Marley, assistant to CIA Director John McCone, had been assigned to pick up the pieces of Walter Bishop's program. Marley balked at setting Charlie up in the Wall Street job Bishop had promised.

"You were out on a rogue operation," he told Charlie. "CIA Director McCone did not know about it. Consequently, the agency had no obligation to honor Bishop's deal. And now," added Marley, "the poor man cannot explain his actions, because he was murdered."

"Don't blame me," Charlie retorted. "The night he was killed, I was stranded in Cuba, trying to find a way out after you screwed up the extraction plan."

Charlie smirked to himself, knowing Marley held a weak hand of cards. He could not send a disgruntled Charlie back to his old army unit. It was inevitable that some night he would go drinking with his army buddies and brag about his exploits in Havana. He also couldn't let Charlie walk around Langley where he would pitch himself as the anti-hero who would have liquidated Castro if only the planning directorate had not flinched at the last minute. And it was too late to liquidate Charlie. He was involved with two different women, each of whom would scream bloody murder if he were to disappear. So if Parnell were killed, the two women would have to be done away with as well, and that was out of the question. One of them was an aide to the president's top advisor.

"Let me see if I understand this," Charlie had said in his final debriefing interview with Marley. "I don't have to return to my army unit, because you're going to keep me assigned to you until I get released from active duty. That will be two years from now. In the meantime, you're going to hold me in some kind of reserve capacity where you can tap me if you want. But you don't want me to show up for work, and I'll continue to receive my paycheck."

"Correct," said Marley. "In addition, we've found a small hedge fund in New York that's willing to try you out as a co-manager for their portfolio."

"And what do you want in return?"

"Your absolute silence." He stopped talking for an entire minute and stared at Charlie. "We want you to destroy every document you gave to your girlfriend and anybody else. If those materials ever show up, we will cut off your balls." He scowled.

Charlie grinned. "Finally, we're on the same page. The last thing I want is anybody knowing what you guys got me into."

———

To celebrate his good fortune at getting out from under the agency's thumb, he took Isabel and Angelita to dinner just before they left Washington for New York. Isabel bought new outfits that would be appropriate for the historic Hay-Adams restaurant that Charlie chose. Seated by a window overlooking the Washington Monument, he smiled as he watched her beaming proudly at her daughter, Angelita, dressed up in white stockings and a red flannel dress. They were perfect for the Christmas season.

"And the best thing, Isabel," said Charlie, leaning across the table, "this gives us a great way to deal with those jewels we stuffed into those safe-deposit boxes down in Homestead."

"How so?"

"The free-wheeling nature of this hedge fund job gives me the perfect excuse to fly to Zurich now and then to scout out European investments. Each time we go, we'll take a package of jewels with us. We'll work out a deal with Meyer Lansky to give you a share of the jewels, and when we get to Zurich, we'll each have a secret Swiss bank account—one for your jewels and one for mine. For all practical purposes, the jewels will never have entered the U.S., so we won't get charged with smuggling or get taxed on them."

"This makes me nervous, Charlie. I'm in a very vulnerable position. If the government finds out about those jewels, it will throw a monkey wrench into my hopes for citizenship. If they deport me to Cuba, I'll be killed."

"They can't deport you, and they won't find out about the jewels as long as we don't try to sell them in the U.S. Once we get them to Switzerland it'll be as though they never existed."

"I need security, Charlie. I need stability. I need to know that my daughter is safe."

"What do you want me to do?"

"If you married me, I would be better off on all those counts."

It took a fair amount of talking, however, to persuade her that he needed to gain closure with Vanessa. She clearly didn't want him reconnecting with a former lover, especially one as beautiful as the woman in the photo Charlie showed her. Isabel had already been betrayed by one fiancé who wandered, and she didn't want it to happen a second time.

"I'm not going to betray you," he protested.

She rolled her eyes. "Men are putty in the hands of a beautiful woman."

"Nonsense. I'm not putty in your hands."

She gave a wry smile and put her hand on the back of his neck. "Thank you for calling me beautiful. It's nice when the statue doesn't realize it's being molded."

But Charlie had been too close to Vanessa for him to simply

disappear without touching base. He didn't relish telling her he had found another woman. Consequently, he was relieved to discover that she was just as eager to end the affair as he was.

"Charlie, you told me you were just going on an information-gathering junket. In fact, you agreed to kill someone. I can't live with that," Vanessa told him.

"But in the end, I decided not to do it."

She rolled her eyes. When she told him about being manhandled by Bishop, Charlie's shoulders sagged and his mouth dropped open. "I am so sorry, Vanessa." He apologized profusely for exposing her to Bishop's assault. "I don't know what to say. I never thought anything like that would happen. I am so sorry."

She set her hand on top of his as they sat across from each other at her kitchen table. "There isn't anything you can say, Charlie. I know you didn't intend it." She gave him a wan smile. "You're just trapped by your personality. We all are. But in your case, you're an operator. You think you can charm everyone. You thought you could finesse Bishop the way you finesse everything. In my case, I think I can ramrod anyone who does me bad."

Ramrod anyone who does her bad? Was she telling him that she was the one who had kicked in Bishop's face? She was strong enough and trained well enough to do it if she caught him by surprise. If she was the one who did in Bishop, why was she so upset that Charlie had agreed to do in Castro? However, he thought, it was better not to ask about that. Whatever she did or didn't do, she was the one who had to live with it. Just as he had to live with the knowledge that, at one point, he had intended to kill Castro. At heart, Charlie and Vanessa both recognized that they had grown too far apart and accumulated too much baggage to renew their old relationship.

———

IF SETTLING WITH VANESSA HAD been easier than anticipated, settling with Meyer Lansky was more difficult. Charlie contacted him as soon as they finished their CIA debriefing, and they agreed to meet at Wolfie's Delicatessen in Miami Beach's South Beach.

MEYER OBJECTED TO CUTTING ISABEL in on a share of the jewels. "I already upped your share from twenty percent to thirty, kid. And that's it. If you want to reward this young lady from your own share, that's your business." He lit a Tareyton cigarette.

"God, Meyer," said Charlie, waving the smoke away from his face. "Do you have to smoke that thing in here?"

"Yes," said Meyer, blowing a puff of smoke off to the side. He motioned for Charlie to walk alone with him to the edge of the water, where the roar of the waves would cover their voices.

Charlie wasn't sure how far he could push Meyer on the issue of giving Isabel a share of the jewels. Considering Meyer's background, maybe Charlie should count himself lucky that he was getting a share himself. But his face flushed with anger when he recalled that he and Isabel had risked their lives to get these jewels in the first place. Meyer owed her a share of them as much as he owed a share to Charlie.

They reached the edge of the beach where the soft sand turned hard from the tides rolling in and out. Meyer turned to look up at him. "You mean you gave up that beautiful blond bombshell for this skinny little Cuban?"

"That skinny little Cuban, as you call her, saved my life. And if it hadn't been for her, your jewels would still be sitting next to Dolf Luque's grave in Havana. She deserves something."

Meyer finally relented. "I'm going to do you a big favor, kid. Someday, maybe you can return it. We're going to give her five percent, half from you and half from me. Now tell me how we're going to make the exchange."

They asked for a private room at the Homestead State Bank. Meyer brought in a small scale they used to total up the weight of all the jewels. Satisfied that they added up to the thirty-seven pounds he had originally stashed away, they divided them up according the three-way split they'd negotiated. Giving a rare grin, Meyer extended his hand to Charlie and Isabel. "Thanks, kid. I never really thought I'd get these back. It's been a pleasure doing business with you."

He cocked his thumb and forefinger as though they were a pistol and touched his finger to Charlie's chest. "But don't forget that I gave a share to Isabel, and you owe me a favor."

———

CHARLIE'S COFFEE HAD GROWN COLD as he pondered these things. They had a lot to be thankful for this Thanksgiving. As each month passed, the danger diminished that Meyer Lansky would show up to call in the favor that Charlie owed him. Or that CIA operatives would come back and demand his services again. Or that the army would terminate his inactive reserve status and call him into active duty in Vietnam. Or that things would fall apart with Isabel. When she stirred, he got up to brew her café con leche. She was going to the doctor that day to find out if she was pregnant. He put his coffee cup in the sink and went into the shower.

———

BEING THE LAST DAY BEFORE Thanksgiving, the markets were subdued, and Charlie left work early. It was barely two o'clock when he emerged from the subway into the crisp air at Washington Square Park. The Empire State Building towered in the distance, with its spire shining gold and silver in the bright sun. He felt a warm glow as he walked to their apartment. Isabel was remarkably easy to live with. She added a feminine touch to their living space, a touch he'd never had before. And he liked the Cuban mementos she placed about the rooms and the Mariposa flower on the windowsill. Even her nylons hanging to dry over the shower rod were less of an annoyance than a sign of their shared intimacy. That morning he had been late for the office because he had gone back to bed for an extra fifteen minutes just to watch her go through the ritual of putting on her clothes.

He adopted Angelita so that she would have a father like the other kids. Totally unexpected was how much he enjoyed playing games with her. He took her on the subway to ice skate at Rockefeller Center and to enjoy other highlights of the city. They spoke both English and Spanish at home, and Charlie marveled at how seamlessly she switched between them. Maybe she thought every six-year-old in the world was bilingual. Or maybe she just thought it was all one language.

As he mounted the stairs to their apartment, Charlie carried a dozen roses. Just in case the pregnancy test was positive. And even more so if it was negative.

Under his arm was tucked the day's newspaper with a headline of more troops being sent to Vietnam. He pushed open the door to their apartment and thrust his right hand forward, so that the first thing she'd see would be the fistful of roses.

The End

Read more from J.J. Harrigan

https://books2read.com/rl/jjharrigan

Goodbye Bobby (2023)

"Classic historical fiction!"
—Timya Owens, President MN chapter Sisters in Crime

Goodbye Virtue (2023)

The Jeeptown Sock Hop (2012)

"Spellbinding!"
—Karen Wright, KMSU radio host

"A captivating story of America's past."
—Bonnie Jo Davis, Book Worm Reviews

The Patron Saint of Desperate Situations (2012)

"Exciting Debut!"
—*St. Paul Pioneer Press*

"Compelling."
—*Romantic Times*

ABOUT THE AUTHOR

JJ HARRIGAN WRITES HISTORICAL THRILLERS that stem from his experiences as a soldier stationed in Germany during the Cold War, a U. S. Foreign Service Officer in Latin America, and a Professor of Political Science. He graduated from Loyola University of Chicago and earned a Ph.D. at Georgetown University. Currently, he scribbles his tales of intrigue on the banks of the St. Croix River in Minnesota, where he lives happily with his wife Sandy.

WWW.JJHARRIGANBOOKS.COM

Printed in the USA
CPSIA information can be obtained
at www.ICGtesting.com
LVHW062130031023
760071LV00036B/742